ALSO BY MAGGIE O'FARRELL

After You'd Gone
My Lover's Lover
The Distance Between Us
The Vanishing Act of Esme Lennox
The Hand That First Held Mine

Instructions for
a Heatwave

Instructions for a Heatwave

Maggie O'Farrell

ALFRED A. KNOPF   New York   2013

THIS IS A BORZOI BOOK
PUBLISHED BY ALFRED A. KNOPF

Copyright © 2013 by Maggie O'Farrell

All rights reserved. Published in the United States by Alfred A. Knopf,
a division of Random House, Inc., New York. Originally published in Great
Britain by Tinder Press, an imprint of Headline Publishing Group, an
Hachette UK Company, London.

www.aaknopf.com

Knopf, Borzoi Books, and the colophon are registered trademarks
of Random House, Inc.

Library of Congress Cataloging-in-Publication Data
O'Farrell, Maggie, [date]
    Instructions for a heatwave / Maggie O'Farrell. — First edition.
        pages cm
ISBN 978-0-385-34940-6 (Hardcover)
1. Children of disappeared persons—Fiction. 2. London (England)—Fiction.
3. Domestic fiction. I. Title.
PR6065.F36I57 2013
823'.914—dc23   2013004580

Jacket photograph © Image Source / Getty Images
Jacket design by Kelly Blair

Manufactured in the United States of America
First United States Edition

*For S and I and J
and B, of course*

Thursday

15 July 1976

4) (i) . . . the only permitted use of water will be for:
   (a) Drinking, and or;
   (b) The washing of clothes or of the body, and or;
   (c) Both public and private toilets.

DROUGHT ACT 1976
An Act to respond to water shortages and droughts in
the United Kingdom

Highbury, London

The heat, the heat. It wakes Gretta just after dawn, propelling her from the bed and down the stairs. It inhabits the house like a guest who has outstayed his welcome: it lies along corridors, it circles around curtains, it lolls heavily on sofas and chairs. The air in the kitchen is like a solid entity filling the space, pushing Gretta down into the floor, against the side of the table.

Only she would choose to bake bread in such weather.

Consider her now, yanking open the oven and grimacing in its scorching blast as she pulls out the bread tin. She is in her nightdress, hair still wound onto curlers. She takes two steps backwards and tips the steaming loaf into the sink, the weight of it reminding her, as it always does, of a baby, a newborn, the packed, damp warmth of it.

She has made soda bread three times a week for her entire married life. She is not about to let a little thing like a heatwave get in the way of that. Of course, living in London, it is impossible to get buttermilk; she has to make do with a mixture of half milk and half yogurt. A woman at Mass told her it worked and it does, up to a point, but it is never quite the same.

At a clacking sound on the lino behind her, she says, "Is that you? Bread's ready."

"It's going to be—" he begins, then stops.

Gretta waits for a moment before turning around. Robert is standing between the sink and the table, his large hands upturned, as if he's holding a tea tray. He is staring at something. The tarnished chrome of the tap, perhaps, the runnels of the draining board, that rusting enamel pan. Everything around them is so familiar, it's impossible sometimes to tell what your eye has been trained upon, the way a person can no longer hear the individual notes of a known piece of music.

"It's going to be a what?" she demands. He doesn't reply. She moves towards him and places a palm on his shoulder. "You all right?" She has, of late, been finding herself reminded of his age, the sudden stoop of his back, the look of mild confusion on his face.

"What?" He swings his head around to look at her, as if startled by her touch. "Yes." He nods. "Of course. I was just saying it's going to be another hot one today."

He shuffles sideways, just as she'd known he would, towards the thermometer, which clings, by a spit-moistened sucker, to the outside of the window.

It is the third month of the drought. For ten days now the heat has passed 90°F. There has been no rain—not for days, not for weeks, not for months. No clouds pass, slow and stately as ships, over the roofs of these houses.

With a metallic click, like that of a hammer tapping a nail, a black spot lands on the window, as if pulled there by magnetic force. Robert, still peering at the thermometer, flinches. The insect has a striated underside, six legs splaying outwards. Another appears, at the other end of the window, then another, then another.

"Those buggers are back," he murmurs.

Gretta comes to see, jamming on her glasses. Together, they peer at them, transfixed.

Swarms of red-backed aphids have, in the past week, been passing over the city. They mass in trees, on car windscreens.

They catch in the hair of children coming home from school, they find their way into the mouths of those crazy enough to cycle in this heat, their feet adhere to the sun-creamed limbs of people lying in their back gardens.

The aphids fling themselves from the window, their feet detaching at the same moment, as if alerted by some secret signal, and they disappear into the azure sky.

Gretta and Robert straighten up, in unison, relieved.

"That's them gone," he says.

She sees him glance at the clock on the wall—a quarter to seven. At precisely this time, for more than thirty years, he would leave the house. He would take his coat off the peg by the door, pick up his bag, call goodbye to them all, shouting and squawking in the kitchen, and slam the door behind him. He always left at six forty-five, on the proverbial dot, no matter what was happening, whether Michael Francis was refusing to get out of bed, whether Aoife was kicking up a stink about Godknowswhat, whether Monica was trying to take over the cooking of the bacon. Not his department, all that, never was. Six forty-five, and he was out the door, gone.

He seems to feel a twitching in his limbs, she's noticed, a kind of vestigial urge to set off, to get going, to be out in the world. Any minute now, she knows, he'll be off to the newsagent's.

With a hand on her bad hip, she pushes the chair out from the table with her foot, and Robert says, "I'll just go round the corner and get the paper."

"Right you are," she says, without looking up. "See you in a bit."

Gretta sits herself down at the table. Robert has arranged everything she needs: a plate, a knife, a bowl with a spoon, a pat of butter, a jar of marmalade. It is in such small acts of kindness that people know they are loved. Which is, she reflects as she moves the sugar bowl to one side, surprisingly rare at their age. So many friends of hers feel overlooked or outgrown or unseen by their husbands, like furniture kept too long. But not her. Robert likes to know where she is at all times, he frets if she leaves the house without telling him, gets edgy if she slips away without him seeing, and starts ringing the children to question them on her whereabouts. It used to drive her crazy when they were first married—she used to long for a bit of invisibility, a bit of liberty—but she's used to it now.

Gretta saws a hunk from the end of the loaf and slathers it with butter. She gets a terrible weakness in her limbs if she doesn't eat regularly. She told a doctor, years ago, that she thought she had hypoglycemia, after reading about it in a Sunday newspaper. Which would have explained her need to eat quite so often, wouldn't it? But the doctor hadn't even looked up from his prescription pad. "No such luck, I'm afraid, Mrs. Riordan," he'd said, the cheeky so-and-so, and handed her a diet sheet.

The children all love this bread. She makes an extra loaf if she's going to visit any of them and takes it, wrapped in a tea towel. She's always done her best to keep Ireland alive in her London-born children. The girls both went to Irish-dancing classes. They had to catch the bus all the way to a place in Camden Town. Gretta used to take a cake tin of brack or gingerbread with her to pass around to the other mothers—exiled like her from Cork, from Dublin, from Donegal—and they would watch their daughters dip up and dip down, tap their feet in time to the fiddle. Monica, the teacher had said after only three lessons, had talent, had the potential to be a champion. She always knew, the teacher had said, she could always spot them. But Monica hadn't wanted to become a champion or to enter the competitions. I hate it, she'd whisper, I hate it when everyone looks at you, when the judges write things down. She'd always been so fearful, so cautious, so backwards in coming forwards. Was it Gretta's fault, or were children born like that? Hard to know. Either way, she'd had to allow Monica to give up the dancing, which was a crying shame.

Gretta had insisted on regular Mass and communion for each of them (although look how that had turned out). They'd gone to Ireland every year for the summer, first to her mother's and then to the cottage on Omey Island, even when they'd got older and started to moan about the journey. When Aoife was little, she'd loved the excitement of having to wait for the tide to draw back off the causeway, revealing the slick, glassy sand, before they could walk over. "It's only an island sometimes," Aoife had said once, when she was about six, "isn't that right, Mammy?" And Gretta had hugged her and told her how clever she was. She'd been a strange child, always coming out with things like that.

They were perfect, those summers, she thinks now, as she bites down into her second slice of bread. Monica and Michael Francis out roaming until all hours and, when Aoife came along, a baby in a crib to keep her company in the kitchen, before she went out to call the others in for their tea.

No, she couldn't have done any more. And yet Michael Francis had given his children the most English of English names. Not even an Irish middle name, she'd asked. She wouldn't allow herself to think about how they were growing up heathen. When she'd mentioned to her daughter-in-law that she knew of a lovely Irish-dance school in Camden, not far from them, her daughter-in-law had laughed. In her face. And said—what was it?—is that the one where you're not allowed to move your arms?

About Aoife, of course, the less said the better. She'd gone off to America. Never called. Never wrote. Living with somebody, Gretta suspects. Nobody has told her this; call it a mother's instinct. Leave her alone, Michael Francis always says, if Gretta starts to question him about Aoife. Because she knows Michael Francis will know, if anyone does. Always as thick as thieves, those two, despite the age gap.

The last they'd heard from Aoife was a postcard at Christmas. *A postcard.* A picture of the Empire State Building on it. For the love of God, she'd shouted, when Robert handed it to her, is she not even able to stretch to a Christmas card, now? As if, she'd continued to shout, I'd never given her a proper upbringing. She'd spent the better part of three weeks sewing a communion dress for that child and she'd looked like an angel. Everybody said so. Who'd have thought then, as she'd stood on the church steps in her white dress and white lace ankle socks, veil fluttering in the breeze, that she'd grow up so ungrateful, so thoughtless that she'd send a picture of a *building* to her mother to mark the Christ Child's birthday?

Gretta sniffs as she dips her knife into the red mouth of the jam pot. Aoife doesn't bear thinking about. The black sheep, her own sister had called her that time, and Gretta had flown off the handle and told her to mind her bloody tongue, but she has to concede that Bridie had a point.

She crosses herself, says a swift novena for her youngest child under her breath, under the ever-watchful eye of Our Lady, who looks down from the kitchen wall. She cuts another slice of bread, watching the steam vanish into the air. She will not think about Aoife now. There are plenty of good things to focus on instead. Monica might ring tonight—Gretta had told her she'd be near the phone from six. Michael Francis had as good as promised to bring the children over this weekend. She will not think about Aoife, she will not look at the photo of her in the communion outfit that sits on the mantelpiece, no, she will not.

After putting the bread back on the rack to air for Robert, Gretta eats a spoonful of jam, just to keep herself going, then another. She glances up at the clock. Quarter past already. Robert should be back by now. Maybe he bumped into someone and got talking. She wants to ask him will he drive her to the market this afternoon, after the crowds heading to the football stadium have dispersed? She needs a couple of things, some flour, a few eggs wouldn't go amiss. Where could they go to escape the heat? Maybe a cup of tea at that place with the good scones. They could walk down the street, arm in arm, take the air. Talk to a few people. It was important to keep him busy: ever since the retirement, he can become brooding and bored if confined to the house for too long. She likes to organize these outings for them.

Gretta goes out through the living room into the hall, opens the front door and walks out onto the path, sidestepping that rusting carcass of a bicycle Robert uses. She looks left, she looks right. She sees next door's cat arch its back, then walk in mincing, feline steps along the wall, towards the lilac bush, where it proceeds to scratch its claws. The road is empty. No one about. She sees a red car caught mid-maneuver, farther up the road. A magpie keens and moans overhead, wheeling sideways in the sky, wing pointing downwards. In the distance, a bus grinds up the hill, a child trundles on a scooter along the pavement, someone somewhere turns on a radio. Gretta puts her hands on her hips. She calls her husband's name, once, twice. The flank of the garden wall throws the sound back to her.

Stoke Newington, London

Michael has walked from Finsbury Park station. A mad decision in the heat, even at this time of day. But the roads had been choked when he'd emerged aboveground, the buses stranded in traffic, wheels motionless on the softening tarmac, so he'd set off along the pavement, between the houses that seemed to transpire heat from their very bricks, making the streets into sweltering runnels through which he must toil.

He pauses, panting and perspiring, in the shade of the trees that fringe Clissold Park. Removing his tie and freeing his shirt from his trousers, he surveys the damage wreaked by this never-ending heatwave: the park is no longer the undulating green lung he has always loved. He has been coming here since he was a child: his mother would pack a picnic—hard-boiled eggs, bluish under their crumbling shells, water that tasted of Tupperware, a wedge of tea cake each; they would all be handed a bag to carry off the bus, even Aoife. "No shirkers," his mother would say loudly, as they stood waiting for the door to open, making the rest of the bus look around. He can remember pushing Aoife in her striped buggy along the path by the railings, trying to get her off to sleep; he can remember his mother trying to coax Monica into that paddling pool. He recalls the park as a space of differing shades of green: the full emerald sweeps of grass, the splintering verdigris of the paddling pool, the lime-yellow of the light through the trees. But now the grass is a scorched ocher, the bare earth showing through, and the trees offer up limp leaves to the unmoving air, as if in reproach.

He draws in a breath through his nose and, realizing that the dry air burns his nostrils, takes a look at his watch. Just after five. He should get home.

It is the last day of term, the start of the long summer holidays. He has made it to the end of another school year. No more marking, no more classes, no more getting up and getting out in the mornings for six whole weeks. His relief is so enormous that it manifests itself physically, as a weightless, almost dizzy sensation at the back of his head; he has the sense he might stumble if he moves too quickly, so unburdened, so untethered does he feel.

He sets off in the most direct route, straight across the burnt-out grass, out into the shadeless open, where the light is level and merciless, past the shut café where he longed to eat as a child but never did. Daylight robbery, his mother called it, unwrapping sandwiches from their grease-proof shrouds.

Sweat breaks out in his hairline, along his spine, his feet move jerkily over the ground and he wonders, not for the first time, how others might see him. A father, returning from his place of work to his home, where his family and his dinner will be waiting. Or a man overheated and sweaty, late, carrying too many books, too many papers, in his briefcase. A person past youth, hair thinning just a little at the crown, wearing shoes that need resoling and socks that require a darn. A man tormented by this heatwave because how is one supposed to dress for work in temperatures such as this, in a shirt and a tie, for God's sake, in long trousers, and how is one meant to concentrate when the female inhabitants of the city walk about pavements and sit in offices in the briefest of shorts, their legs bare and brown and crossed against him, in narrow-strapped tops with their shoulders exposed, just the thinnest of fabrics separating their breasts from the unbearably hot air? A man hurrying home to a wife who will no longer look him in the eye, no longer seek his touch, a wife whose cool indifference has provoked in him such a slow-burning, low-level panic that he cannot sleep in his own bed, cannot sit easily in his own house.

The edge of the park is in sight now. He's almost there. One more stretch of grass in full sun, then a road, then around the corner, then it's his street. He can make out the roofs of his neighbors and, if he stretches on tiptoe, the slates of his house, the chimney pot, the skylight beneath which, he is sure, his wife will be sitting.

He swats a bead of moisture from his upper lip and switches his briefcase to the opposite hand. At the end of his street, there is a queue at the standpipe. Several of his neighbors, a lady from down the road and a few others he doesn't recognize, straggle across the pavement and onto the road, empty drums at their feet. Some of them chat to each other, one or two wave or nod to him as he passes. The thought that he ought to offer to help the lady passes through his mind; he ought to stop, fill her drum for her, carry it back to her house. It would be the right thing to do. She is his mother's age, perhaps older. He should stop, offer help. How will she manage otherwise? But his feet don't hesitate in their movement. He has to get home, he can't brook any further delay.

He unlatches his gate and swings it open, feeling as though it has been weeks since he last saw his home, feeling joy surge through him at the thought that he doesn't have to leave it for six weeks. He loves this place, this house. He loves the black-and-white-tiled front path, the orange-painted front door, with the lion-faced knocker and the blue glass insets. If he could, he would stretch himself skywards until he was big enough to embrace its red-gray bricks. The fact that he has bought it with his own money—or some of his own money, along with a large mortgage—never ceases to amaze him. That, and the fact it contains at this very moment the three people most precious to him in the world.

He unlocks the door, steps onto the mat, flings his bag to the floor and shouts, "Hello! I'm home!"

He is, for a moment, exactly the person he is meant to be: a man, returning from work, on the threshold of his home, about to greet his family. There is no difference, no schism, between the way the world might see him and the person he privately knows himself to be.

"Hello?" he calls again.

The house makes no answer. He shuts the door behind him and picks his way through the flotsam of bricks, dolls' clothes and plastic teacups on the hall floor.

In the living room, he comes upon his son, reclining on the sofa, one foot balanced on the magazine rack. He is dressed only in a pair of underpants and his eyes are fixed on the television screen, where a grinning blue square-shaped being perambulates across a yellow vista.

"Hello, Hughie," he says. "How was the last day of school?"

"Fine," Hughie says, without taking his thumb from his mouth. With his other hand, he twirls a strand of his hair. Michael Francis finds he is, as ever, pained and moved in equal parts by his son's resemblance to his wife. The same high brow, the milky skin, the snowstorm of freckles over the nose. Hughie has always been his mother's creature. All those ideas of sons loyal to their fathers, those invisible male links: it has never been like that for him and this boy. Hughie came out of the womb as Claire's defender, ally, henchman. As a toddler he would sit at her feet, like a dog. He would follow her about the house, head always cocked, alert to her whereabouts, her conversations, her passing moods. If he heard his father so much as say that he couldn't find a clean shirt or where was the shampoo, he would hurl himself at him, tiny fists flailing, so enraged was he by even the slightest implied criticism of his mother. Michael Francis has always hoped it might change, as the boy got older. But there's no sign of his favoritism ending, even though he's almost nine.

"Where's Vita?" he asks.

Hughie pops his thumb free of his mouth for long enough to say, "In the paddling pool."

He has to lick his lips before asking, "And where's Mummy?"

This time Hughie takes his eyes from the screen and looks at him. "In the attic," he says, very clearly, very precisely.

Father and son regard each other for a moment. Does Hughie, he wonders, have any idea that this is what he has been dreading since he left work, since he forced himself onto a crowded, sweltering tube train, since he made his way across this burning city? Does Hughie know that he has been hoping against hope that he might come back to find his wife in the kitchen, serving something fragrant and nutritious to his children, who would be dressed and clean and sitting at the table? How much does Hughie understand about what has been going on lately?

"The attic?" he repeats.

"The attic," Hughie affirms. "She said she had a lot to do and that we weren't to disturb her unless it was a matter of life and death."

"I see."

He moves through to the kitchen. The stove is empty, the table covered with an assortment of objects: a tub of what looks like shreds of newspaper in dried glue, several paintbrushes, which appear to be stuck to the table, a half-devoured packet of biscuits, the packaging ripped and torn, the leg of a doll, a cloth soaked with what is possibly coffee. The sink is piled with plates, teacups, beakers and another doll's leg. He can see, through the open back door, his daughter sitting in the empty paddling pool, a watering can in one hand and the legless doll in the other.

He now has two choices. He could go outside, pick up Vita, ask her about school, coax her inside, perhaps feed them both something from the freezer. Assuming there is anything in the freezer. Or he could go upstairs and find his wife.

He dithers for a moment, gazing at his daughter. He reaches down for a biscuit and crams one into his mouth, then a second, then a third, before realizing he is not enjoying their sandy sweetness. He swallows quickly, hurting his throat. Then he turns and goes up the stairs.

On the landing, he finds his way blocked by the aluminum ladder that leads to the attic. He himself had installed it when they first moved here, after Hughie was born. DIY is not his strong point but he had bought the ladder because he had always wanted a playroom in an attic when he had been a boy. A space under the eaves to which he could have escaped, a dark place smelling of mice and exposed wood; he imagines the cacophony of his family would have sounded distant, benign, from it; he could have pulled up the ladder after himself, sealing the entrance. He had wanted this for his son, this place of refuge. He had never anticipated it being commandeered—because this is how he sees it, a military move, a requisition—by his wife, of all people. No, the attic is not how he had envisaged it at all. Instead of a train set, a paper-strewn desk; instead of a den, perhaps made of cushions and old sheets, shelves of books. No model planes hang from the rafters, no collections of butterflies or shells or leaves or any of those things children covet, just paperbacks and notebooks and half-filled folders.

He grips the rungs of the ladder. His wife is there, just above his head; if he concentrated hard enough he could almost hear her breathing. He is so close to reaching her but something makes him stop, there on the landing, his fingers curled around aluminum, his face pressed to his knuckles.

What he finds hardest about family life is that, just when you think you have a handle on what's going on, everything changes.

It seems to him that, for as long as he can remember, he would come home to find his wife with at least one child attached to her body. When he returned from work, she'd be on the sofa, buried beneath the combined weight of their son and daughter, standing in the garden with Vita at her hip, sitting at the table with Hughie on her lap. In the morning, he would wake to find one or other of them entwined about her like ivy, whispering secrets in her ear with their hot, sleep-scented breath. If she walked into a room, she'd be carrying someone or there would be a small person attached to her hand or hem or sleeve. He never saw her outline. She had become like one of those matryoshka dolls with the long-lashed eyes and the swirl-painted hair, always containing smaller versions of herself.

That was the way things had been, the way life was in their house: Claire was two people or sometimes three. Presumably she had thought this, too, because in the last while, since Vita had turned four, he had been greeted by the unprecedented sight of her standing alone in the kitchen, one hand resting on the table, or sitting gazing out of the bay window into the street. He could suddenly see all of her, in her astonishing separateness, the children away, gone, living their children lives: upstairs, crashing about in their bedroom, giggling together under a blanket or out in the garden, scaling the walls or digging in the flower beds. You might have thought she'd be feeling relieved at this change, after a decade of intense child-rearing, a break in the clouds. But the look on her face, when he chanced upon her in these moments, was that of someone who'd lost their way, who'd been told to go somewhere but had taken the wrong turning, the look of someone who had been on the verge of doing something important but had forgotten what it was.

He had been thinking about a way to vocalize to her that he mourned its passing, too: the sense of the children's intense, zealous need of you, their overwhelming urge to be near you, to study you, to watch you as you peeled an orange, wrote a shopping list, tied your shoes, the feeling that you were their study in how to be human. He was thinking how he might say to her, Yes, it's gone but life holds other things, when everything changed again. When he got home, she was no longer in the kitchen or the bay window but elsewhere in the house, upstairs, out of sight. There was no dinner simmering on the stove, or roasting behind the oven door. He began to notice strange things lying around. An old exercise book with his wife's maiden name inscribed on the cover in careful cursive. A much-thumbed, soft-cornered copy of *Madame Bovary* in the original French, with Claire's grave, adolescent marginalia. A worn old pencil case in red leather, filled with freshly spiked pencils. These things he would pick up, weigh in his hand and put down again. Claire began to need him to babysit because she was suddenly going out in the evenings or at weekends. "You're around tonight, aren't you?" she would say, on her way through the door. There was a new look in her eye—one of trepidation mixed with a kind of spark. One night, finding her side of the bed empty, he wandered about the house, searching for her, calling her name into the dark; when she answered, her voice was muffled, disembodied. Several minutes passed before he worked out that she was up in the attic, that she had gone up there in the middle of the night, leaving their bed, pulling the ladder up after her. He had stood in the middle of the landing, hissing at her to let him come up—what, in God's name, was she doing up there? No, her voice had come down at him, nothing, no, you can't come up.

From ripping open an official-looking letter addressed to her, one evening when she was yet again mysteriously out, he learned that she was taking an Open University history degree. He flung the piece of paper down on the table between them when she came back. What on earth, he demanded, was this? Why was she doing this course?

"Because I want to," she'd said defiantly, twisting her bag strap in her hands.

"But why the Open University?" he'd said.

"Why not?" she'd said, twisting her bag tighter, her face pale and tense.

"Because you're far too good for them and you know it. You got three As at A level, Claire. The OU take anybody and their qualifications aren't worth the paper they're written on. Why didn't you tell me about this? We could have discussed it instead of—"

"Why didn't I tell you?" she'd interrupted him. "Maybe because I knew you'd react exactly like this."

Soon after this various new friends had appeared in the house, hot on the heels of the sharpened pencils and the Flaubert. They, too, were taking OU degrees and, Claire said, wasn't it great because most of them lived just around the corner? Claire would be able to get help with her essays from them, and Michael managed not to say, Why don't you ask me for help, I am a history teacher, after all. I have a history degree and some of a history PhD. All of a sudden, these people rarely seemed to be out of their house, with their course notes and essay sheets and files and their talk of personal expansion. They were nothing like Claire's other friends—women with young children and houses full of beakers and toys and finger paintings, befriended at the school gates or coffee mornings or Housewives' Register meetings. The Open University crowd left his house with an edgy, electrical charge hanging in the air. And he, Michael Francis Riordan, was not comfortable with it, not at all.

He takes a moment to collect himself before he climbs the ladder. He smooths his hair, he tucks his shirt back into his waistband.

His wife appears to him as he ascends into the roof space that he created, installing this ladder, hammering chipboard over the beams, clearing the skylight of dead leaves, from the feet up. Bare toes, narrow ankles, crossed calves, her rear, seated on a stool, her back curved over the trestle table, her thin white arms uncovered, her hand clutching a pen, her head turned away.

He stands before her, offering himself. "Hello," he says.

"Oh, Mike," she says, without turning around. "I thought I heard you."

She continues to write. He reflects, for a moment, on that "Mike." For years, his wife has mostly called him by his first and middle name, as he is known in his family, as he was called as a child. She picked up the habit from his parents and sisters—and their vast web of cousins, aunts and uncles. Colleagues call him Mike, friends, acquaintances, dentists—not his family, not his beloveds. But how to tell her this? How to say, Please call me by both my names, like you used to?

"What are you doing?" he asks instead.

"I'm"—she scribbles frantically—"just finishing an essay about . . ." She stops, crosses something out, then writes again. "What time is it?"

"Around five."

She lifts her head at this piece of information but doesn't turn around. "Working late, were you?" she murmurs.

The figure of Gina Mayhew seems to pass by them, across the attic, like a poltergeist. She throws a look at him from under that squarish brow of hers, then disappears down through the hatch. He swallows—or tries to. His throat is constricted and dry. When did he last drink anything? He can't remember. He is, he realizes, thirsty, horrendously, horribly, unbearably thirsty. Glasses of water, rows of standpipes, burnt yellow stretches of grass ripple through his mind.

"No," he gets out. "Last day of term stuff and . . . the tube. Delayed . . . you know . . . again."

"The tube?"

"Yes." He sets up a vigorous nodding, even though she's not looking at him, and asks in a rush, "So, what's your essay about?"

"The Industrial Revolution."

"Ah. Interesting. What aspect of it?" He steps forward to see over her shoulder.

"The Industrial Revolution and its effects on the middle classes," she says, turning to face him, putting an arm over her page, and he experiences a dissolving feeling in his abdomen. Part lust, part horror at her short hair. He still hasn't got used to it, still can't forgive her for it. He'd come home a few weeks ago and opened the front door, as yet innocent of what had occurred behind it that day, as yet full of trust that his wife was still the person she'd always been. The fan of hair he'd thought would still be there; he had no reason to believe otherwise. The hair that rested on her shoulders, the color of honey held up to the light, the hair that spread itself over her pillow and his, the hair he'd gather up in his hand like a silken rope, the hair he'd liked to form a tent around them in the dark as she rose and fell above him. The hair he'd noticed in the first term of his PhD, in a lecture about postwar Europe: the clean, smooth, sun-catching length of it. He'd never seen hair like it; certainly never felt hair like it. The women in his family were dark-haired, red-haired, curly-haired; they had unruly hair, kinked hair, thin hair, hair that required setting and lotions and pins and nets. Hair to be lamented, complained about, wept over. Not hair that was celebrated, like this, left to hang and sway in its full, uncomplicated, Anglo-Saxon glory. But as he'd stood there in the doorway of the upstairs bathroom, keys still in hand, he saw that the hair he loved and had always loved was gone. It was off, scissored, finished. It littered the lino in strange, mammalian drifts. And in place of his wife was a shorn-headed boy-child in a dress. "What do you think?" the changeling said, using his wife's voice. "Lovely and cool for the summer, isn't it?" And it laughed, with his wife's laugh, but then looked at itself in the mirror with a sudden, nervous twist of the head.

He gazes at her, sitting before him, and feels again this keen, irreversible loss and wants to ask her if she might consider growing it again, for him, and how long it might take and would it look the same?

"What kind of effects?" he asks, instead.

"You know," she says, moving her arm so that it covers the page. "Various ones."

He can see that the effect of the shorn hair is meant to be gamine, puckish, like that girl in the film about Paris. But it doesn't come off, with his wife's round face, her flat nose. She looks like a Victorian convalescent.

"Make sure you mention the mass migrations from countryside to town," he hears himself say, "the emergence of big cities, and—"

"Yes, yes, I know," she says, turning back to the desk, and is it his imagination or do her teeth sound gritted? Let me help you, he wants to say, let me try. But he doesn't know how to say this without sounding like what Aoife would call "a desperate eejit." He would just like there to be one thing they were united in, one part of their life in which they stood shoulder to shoulder, as they used to, before—

"And the railways," he hears himself say, and is it just him or is he employing the deep, authoritative voice he uses in the classroom—why is he doing that here, in the attic of his own house, to his own wife?—"the way they gave ease and speed of transportation, built by the Irish, of course, and—"

She scratches her head with a quick, irritated movement, goes to make a mark on the page in front of her but then pulls back the pen.

"Also, I'd recommend reading—"

"Hadn't you better answer him?" she interrupts.

"Answer who?"

"Hughie."

He tunes his hearing beyond the attic, beyond his wife, and becomes aware of his son's voice, calling, Daddy, Daddeeeeee, are you coming baaaaaaaaack?

. . .

When he'd first been taken to meet Claire's parents, the thing he'd been most struck by was how nice they all were to each other. How extraordinarily polite, considerate. The parents called each other "dearest." At dinner her mother asked him, if she could trouble him, would he mind awfully passing the butter? It had taken him a moment to decode the grammar of this sentence, to grope his way along its abstruse semantic loops. The father fetched a scarf (silk, with a pattern of brass padlocks) for the mother when she mentioned it was chilly. The brother talked voluntarily about the game of rugby he'd played that day at school. The parents asked Claire-Bear, as they called her, about her essays, her lectures, the dates of her exams. The food came in china serving dishes, each with its own lid; they helped each other to portions and then seconds.

It had amazed him. And made him want to laugh. There was no shouting, no swearing, no people flouncing off from the table, no silent brooding, no scramble for your fair share of potatoes. No spoons were thrown, no one picked up the carving knife, held it to their throat and cried, Will I kill myself here and now? He didn't think anyone in his family would be able to identify the vague area of his PhD, never mind get down the calendar and write the dates and details of his exams, never mind reel off a list of books that might be useful for him, never mind fetch those books from their library.

He found their inquiries as to what he was studying, how much teaching he did, whether he had enough time to devote he wanted to say. She wasn't meant to be the one I married. I was going to do my PhD, sleep with everyone I could lay my hands on, then go to America. This marriage and baby were not part of the plan.

"The wedding's in two weeks."

"Two weeks!" His mother started to cry.

"In Hampshire. You don't have to come if you don't want to."

"Oh, Michael Francis," his mother said again.

"Where in Hampshire?" his father asked.

"Is she Catholic?" Aoife said, swinging her bare foot, biting a crescent from her biscuit.

Their mother gasped. "Is she? Is she a Catholic?" She glanced across at the Sacred Heart that hung on the wall. "Please tell me she is."

He cleared his throat, shooting a furious look at Aoife. "She is not."

"What is she, then?"

"I . . . I don't know. C of E, I'd guess, but I don't think it's a very important part of—"

Their mother lurched from the table with a wail. Their father slapped his newspaper against his palm. Aoife said, apparently to no one, "He's gone and knocked up a Prod."

"Shut your bloody mouth, Aoife," he hissed.

"Mind your language," his father thundered.

"This will be the death of me," their mother cried from the bathroom, rattling the bottles of her tranquilizers. "You might as well just kill me now."

"Fine," Aoife murmured. "Who wants to go first?"

Hughie was born and the lives of Claire and Michael Francis were rerouted. Claire would have finished her history degree and taken up the kind of job girls like her did then after graduation: she might have worked on a magazine or perhaps as a solicitor's secretary. She would have shared a flat in London with a friend, a place full of clothes and makeup. They would have taken messages for each other, entertained their boyfriends with meals put together in the narrow kitchen. They would have washed their smalls in the sink and dried them over the gas fire. Then, after a few years, she would have married a solicitor or a businessman and they would have moved out to a house like her parents', in Hampshire or Surrey, and Claire would have had several well-groomed children and she would have told them stories about her bachelor-girl days in London.

Michael would have done his doctorate. He would have worked his way through the best-looking women in the city—and there seemed to be lots of them, all over the place, in London in the late 1960s—the women in black kohl and polo-necks, the ones in floaty dresses, the ones in impossibly short skirts and long boots, the ones with hats and sunglasses, the ones with chignons and tweed coats. He would have tried them all, one by one. And then he would have got a professorship in America. Berkeley, he'd been thinking, or NYU or Chicago or Williams. He'd had it all planned. He would have sailed away from this country and he would never have come back.

But, as it turned out, he had to abandon his PhD. It wasn't possible to support a wife and child on his grant. He got a job teaching history at a grammar school in the suburbs. He rented a flat off Holloway Road, near where he'd spent his childhood, and he and Claire took turns to heat baby bottles on the gas-ring. They went to Hampshire for the weekends and endlessly debated whether or not he should let his father-in-law lend them the money to buy "somewhere decent to live."

. . .

He circles a wooden spoon around the saucepan, then tips the spaghetti hoops onto two plates.

Sometimes, when he catches a distant expression on his

wife's face, he wonders if she is thinking about the house she might have had. In Sussex or Surrey, with a lawyer husband.

He is careful to keep the hoops clear of the toast on one plate—Hughie won't eat if one type of food has contact with another. "No touching!" he'll yell. Vita's he heaps on top of the buttered toast. She can and will eat anything.

He is just setting the plates in front of their respective chairs when he feels something butting his leg, something solid and warm. Vita. She has come in from the garden and is knocking her curly head into his thigh, like a small goat.

"Daddy," she croons. "Daddy, Daddy, Daddy."

He reaches down and lifts her into his arms. "Vita," he says. He is, again and for a moment, completely the person he is meant to be: a man, in his kitchen, lifting his daughter into the air. He puts down the wooden spoon. He puts down the pan. He wraps his arms around the child. He is filled with—what? Something more than love, more than affection. Something so keen and elemental it resembles animal instinct. For a moment, he thinks that the only way to express this feeling is through cannibalism. Yes, he wants to eat his daughter, starting at the creases in her neck, moving down to the smooth pearlescent skin of her arms.

She is arching back, wriggling her legs. Vita has always been an earthbound child; doesn't like to be held. Her favored form of affection is a hug around the legs. She hates to be off her feet. She's always had a solidity, a firmness to her body that Hughie never had. Hughie is a sprite, a light, reedy being, his too-long hair flying out behind him, diaphanous, an Ariel, a creature of the air, whereas Vita is more of a soil-dwelling animal. A badger, she reminds him of, perhaps, or a fox.

With a sigh, he puts her down, whereupon she proceeds to run around the kitchen table, shouting, inexplicably, "Happily ever after," over and over again, with a variety of emphases.

"Vita," he says, endeavoring to talk at a normal volume over the noise. "Vita, sit down. Vita?"

Hughie wanders in and slumps at his place at the table. He picks up a fork and toys with his spaghetti hoops, the orange sauce of which is cooling and congealing. He frowns, looping one, then two, then three hoops onto a tine of his fork and Michael Francis is torn between telling him that he's sorry it's spaghetti hoops again and telling him to eat up now.

Last time his mother visited—she comes every two weeks but only for a cup of tea, refusing to stay any longer because she doesn't want to "put Claire out"—she'd remarked at a dinner such as this that, for a man with a full-time teaching job, wasn't it surprising how much cooking he did? Claire had been in the living room but she'd heard. He knew she'd heard by the way she slapped down the book she'd been reading.

"Vita," he tries again.

Vita prances around the table, naked, dust-smudged, chanting, "Happily ever *after*. Happily ever af*ter*."

Hughie smacks a hand to his forehead and slams down his fork. "Shut up, Vita," he hisses.

"*You* shut up," Vita shouts back. "You *shut* up, you shut *up*, you—"

He seizes hold of his daughter as she dances past him and holds her above his head, kicking and yowling. He has, he knows, two choices at this point. He can go stern, tell her to behave, to sit down this instant. This has the attraction of venting some of the frustration that's been building in him all day long, but the danger is that it will backfire and that Vita will take things up a notch or two. Or he can joke them out of the standoff. He decides to opt for the latter. Quicker and less risky.

"Gobble, gobble," he says, pretending to eat Vita's stomach. "I'm a monster and I'm going to eat you up." He hoists her into a chair. "I'm so hungry that unless you eat your food I'm going to have to eat you. You're only safe if you're eating."

Vita laughs but—magically—stays on her chair. He holds his breath until he sees her pick up her fork.

"What kind of a monster, Daddy?"

"A big one."

"A hairy one?" she shrieks.

"Yes. Very hairy. Green hair all over." And because she's yet to take a bite, he takes the fork gently from her grasp and inserts some food into her mouth as she is saying, "Have you got big teeth?"

"Enormous. The biggest teeth you've ever seen."

"The shark," Hughie suddenly announces, "has several rows of—"

"And claws?" Vita says, spraying masticated pellets of spaghetti onto the table.

"I was speaking!" Hughie yells. "I was speaking! Daddy, she interrupted me."

"Vita, don't interrupt. Wait for a gap. Yes, I have claws. Go on, Hughie, what does a shark have?"

"It has several rows of teeth that—"

"Do you live in a cave?"

"She did it again!" Hughie is shaking with rage. "Daddy!"

Claire chooses this moment to enter the kitchen. She has changed, he notices, into a skirt and a rather thin blouse, knotted at the waist.

"Hello, darlings," she says. "Are you enjoying your tea?"

"You're going out?" he says.

Her eyes are roving over the surfaces, the shelves, the floor. "Has anyone seen my—"

"Mummy, Vita interrupted me twice," Hughie says, turning in his seat towards his mother.

Claire runs her hand along the cupboard top, stops, takes a step towards the back door, then stops again. "I'm sorry to hear that but you just interrupted me."

"Where are you going?"

"I didn't interrupt you."

"You did. Just now. You need to wait for a gap."

"You never told me you were going out."

She focuses on him briefly. "I did. We're watching an OU program together and then having supper back here afterwards. I told you yesterday, remember? Did you happen to see my . . ." She seems to give up on the idea of asking for his help. "Oh, never mind."

"Your what?"

"Nothing."

"No, tell me."

"Daddy." Vita lays a hand sticky with tomato sauce on his sleeve. "Do you have two eyes or lots of eyes?"

"Nothing," Claire says. "Doesn't matter." She picks up a cloth bag he's never seen before from the floor and he catches the briefest glimpse down the front of her blouse, the lace fringe of her bra, the twin mounds of her breasts. It occurs to him that others might do the same, at this study group or whatever she said it was. "I'm off." She kisses each of the children on the hair. "I'm saying night-night now, sweethearts, because I may not be back until after you're asleep—"

"What time are you coming back?" he asks.

"Two eyes, Daddy, or lots of eyes? Lots of eyes in funny places, like on your arms or on your ears?"

"Who's going to put me to bed?" Hughie says, in his neglected-orphan voice.

"Later." Claire waves a hand in the air. "Not sure."

"Or on your feet? Eyes on your feet would be useful, wouldn't they, because—"

"What about my bath? Who'll give me a bath?"

"Daddy, of course." Claire gives Hughie a quick squeeze. "But you can't have a bath anyway because of the water ban. Remember?"

"What time, roughly? You must know."

"I don't. I might stay on or—"

"Or on your hands. Then you could see the thing you want to pick up, you could see it as you pick it up, a small human to eat, maybe, or a—"

As Claire exits the door, Hughie is handing him a triangle of toast.

"'Bye, darlings," Claire calls from the hall.

"I can't eat this," Hughie is saying. "It's got sauce along the crust."

"Daddy, you're not *listening*. Where are your eyes?"

The phone starts to ring. Vita is talking louder and louder; Hughie is removing bits of food from his plate, saying he can't eat this either, or this, and Claire is shouting something from the hall.

"What?" he says, darting up, through the living room and to the hall, where his wife is poised on the doorstep. "I can't hear you."

She is framed in the doorway, the sunlight illuminating the stuff of her blouse, her hair aflame around her small, freckled face. His heart hurts with the sight of her. Stay, he wants to say, don't go. Stay with me.

"I said," she says, "that's probably your mother. She's been calling and calling all afternoon."

"Oh," he says.

"She's lost a key or something."

"Right."

Behind him, he hears the ringing telephone stop abruptly and Hughie say, "Hello?"

"Claire?"

"Yes?" She has one hand on the door, a foot out on the step.

"Don't go."

"What?"

"Please." He takes hold of her wrist, where the gathered bones of her hands meet with the long bones of her arm.

"Michael—"

"Just tonight. Just stay here tonight. Don't go to this thing. I'll tell you everything you need to know about the Industrial Revolution. Stay with us. Please."

"I can't."

"You can."

"I can't. I promised them—"

"Fuck them."

A mistake. Her face contorts in anger. She stares at him. Behind him, he hears Hughie telling his grandmother that Daddy can't come to the phone because he's shouting at Mummy on the doorstep. Claire looks at him as if she will speak but then she bows her head, she shifts her other foot out onto the path, she closes the door after her.

It takes him a moment to comprehend that she's gone. He stares at the door, the tarnished brass of the lock, the way the glass fits so neatly into the wood. Then he realizes Hughie is next to him.

"Daddy! Daddy!" he is shouting.

"What?" he says, looking down at him, this miniature version of his wife who has just left, has stepped out of the door, away from them all.

"Granny's on the phone. She says—"

He moves through to the sitting room and picks up the receiver. "Mum? Sorry I was—"

Disconcertingly, his mother is in the middle of a sentence, a paragraph or possibly something even longer. ". . . and I said to the man, Well, I don't need any pop today, you'll just have to come back on Thursday, and do you know what he said to me? He said—"

"Mum," he says again. "It's me."

"—not as if he had that much in his van anyway and—"

"Mum!"

There was a pause down the line. "Is that you, Michael Francis?"

"Yes."

"Oh. I thought I was talking to Vita."

"No. It was Hughie."

"Oh. Well. I was telling Claire this afternoon—and she sounded so busy, I can't tell you—that the problem is that he's got the key to the shed and—"

"Who?"

"And I told him that breakfast was ready but you know what he's like with the paper—"

"What paper?"

"The thing is that the freezer's in the shed, as you know."

He puts a hand to his brow. Conversations with his mother can be confusing meanders through a forest of meaning in which nobody has a name and characters drop in and out without warning. You needed to get a toehold, just a slight grasp on your orientation, ascertain the identity of one dramatis persona and then, with any luck, the rest would fall into place.

". . . she said she didn't have time today but—"

"Who? Who didn't have time?"

"I know she's always so busy. She's got a lot on."

This is a definite clue. There is only one person for whom his mother uses this phrase. "Monica? Do you mean Monica?"

"Yes." His mother sounds injured. "Of course. She doesn't have time today because of the cat and so I was wondering whether you—"

"Me?" He feels the floodgates of his temper open and it is a glorious relief, a wonderful, raging release. "Let me get this straight. You're asking me, who has a family and a full-time job, to come and help you with a lost shed key. You're not asking my sister, who has no children to look after and no job, because she's *got a lot on*?"

How he loathes that phrase. He and Aoife use it to each other sometimes, as a joke. But, really, their mother's partiality for her middle child, her endless sympathy with her, her ability to forgive Monica anything, isn't a joke. It's annoying. It's ridiculous. It's really time it stopped.

He hears his mother inhale sharply. There is a silence between them for a moment. Which way will she jump? Will she shout back? She can always give as good as she gets, they both know that. "Well," she says, in a quavery voice, and he sees that she's opted for hurt and just a tiny bit brave, "I just thought you might be able to help. I just thought I could ring you in my hour of n—"

"Mum—"

"I mean, he's been gone for eleven hours now so I'm just not sure what to do and—"

He frowns and holds the receiver closer to his ear. This is the other thing that can happen in conversations with his mother. She has an odd inability to sift important information from irrelevant information. Everything is crucial to her: misplaced shed keys and an absent husband take equal precedence.

"Dad's been gone for eleven hours?"

"—it's not as if he's gone off like this before and I wasn't sure who to turn to and Monica's so busy so I thought—"

"Wait, wait, did you tell Monica that Dad's disappeared?"

There is a pause. "Yes," his mother says uncertainly. "I'm sure I did."

"Or did you just tell her you don't know where the shed key is?"

"Michael Francis, I don't think you're listening to me. I do know where the shed key is. It's on your father's key ring but if he's gone, then so has the key and—"

"OK." He decides to take control of the situation. "This is what's going to happen. You're going to wait by the phone. I'm going to call Monica and speak to her and then I'll call you back, in ten minutes or so. OK?"

"All right, darling. I'll wait for you, then."

"Yes. You wait there."

Gloucestershire

For Monica, it began with the cat. For years afterwards, her father's disappearance would forever be associated with its death.

She didn't even like the cat—never had. Peter's daughters loved it, though, and had grown up with it. When the girls arrived on Friday evenings, after Peter had collected them from their mother's, they would streak up the path, through the front door and, without stopping to remove their coats, run about in a loud, shrieking clatter, searching for the animal. When they found it, curled on the sofa or stretched out by the range, they would hurl themselves upon it, burying their faces in its flank, crooning its name, playing with the soft triangles of its ears.

They conducted long conversations with it; they made it elaborate houses out of newspaper; they wanted it to sleep on their beds at night, and Peter allowed this. They carried it about like a furry handbag; they dressed it up in dolls' clothes and pushed it about the garden in an old, squeaking pram they extracted from the barn. Monica hadn't even known the pram was there (she avoided the barn, a dark, spidery place full of twisted, rusty shapes) but the girls had. She had watched through the kitchen window as they dragged it out through the barn door, as if they had done this many times. It gave her a peculiar, tense feeling, the notion that these two girls, practically strangers to her, knew her home better than she did.

She had remarked on this, airily, she thought, laughingly, when they were making biscuits together at the kitchen table (or was it that she was frantically cutting out biscuit dough with the cat shape she'd bought a few days previously, trying to ignore the fact that the girls sat with their arms crossed, glaring at her?). Monica hadn't been able to find a clean oven glove (because she had burned through yet another one on that blasted range) and the elder girl, Jessica, had slid from her chair, gone to a drawer in the dresser, pulled out a clean one and handed it to her without a word.

"You know your way around this place better than I do, don't you?" Monica had said, forcing a smile.

Jessica had fixed her with a long, steady look. "We've lived here all our lives," she'd said. "Florence was born right there"— she pointed to her left—"on the floor. Mummy swore *a lot*. Daddy was allowed to cut the cord."

Monica was frozen, a limp dough-cat spread out over her fingers, unable to look away from the floorboards by the window. She hadn't been able to tread on them since.

She tried with Peter's daughters. She tried very hard. The weekdays—which they spent with their mother—took on a distinct rhythm for her. Monday, the day of their departure, was consumed by shock, her head enveloped in a black cloud of panic and uselessness, Tuesday in recuperation, Wednesday in gloom and despair: Florence and Jessica hated her. They hated her, no matter what Peter said. She could see it in their eyes, in the way they wheeled away from her if she happened to come near, like startled horses. The whole situation was untenable, a disaster, she would never make an adequate stepmother, let alone a good one. Thursday, she woke early and gave herself a talking-to: she was good with children, she'd practically raised Aoife and she wasn't exactly what you'd call easy—how hard could it be to win over Peter's two? Friday was spent in elaborate preparation: Monica bought coloring books, paint boxes, French-knitting dolls, soft balls of yarn. She put a vase of flowers on each of their bedside tables. She laid out flower presses, nature books, comics, glue, modeling clay, bright embroidery threads on the coffee table: she could teach them to embroider, to sew! They would make Christmas presents together—glasses' cases, shoe shiners, pajama bags, monogrammed handkerchiefs. She pictured Peter finding the three of them huddled together on the sofa, sewing a surprise tobacco-tin cover for him. How happy it would make him, to know she had triumphed, she had won them over.

Then Friday evening rolled around and she'd be confronted by the sight of two children in those matching corduroy smocks from mail-order kits, the hems of which were always slightly uneven—how Monica longed to unpick the seams and resew them properly; it would be the work of minutes—streaming through the house, looking for the pet they loved.

Jenny, their mother, had been quick to ensure Peter took custody of the cat when they separated, insisting the creature remained in residence with him. And it didn't take Monica long to work out why. The animal simply had no sense of what it could and couldn't eat: it would consume bits of paper, elastic bands, lengths of string, the labels in clothing. She had never known anything like it. If foxes slit open the rubbish bags in the lane, the cat would snack on old bones, half-rotted fish heads, moldy crusts, chewed shards of yogurt pots, old shoelaces. And then it would come inside, yowling deafeningly at the back door until Monica gave in, and regurgitate the ill-thought contents of its stomach on the carpet, the newly polished floorboards, the kilim in the hall, the kitchen table.

As Monica had told Peter the other day, if she had to scrub cat vomit off the furniture one more time, she would scream.

Today was the day for its grooming—Thursday, the day she liked to clean the house, to erase all traces of the girls, to put things to rights, to remove all bits of leaves and grit from the cat's pelt. But the odd thing was that she couldn't find it. She called its name, at the bottom of the stairs, at the back door, at the mouth of the old rotting barn. She rattled the box of its rank-smelling food. She opened and shut the fridge door, with ostentatious volume. But nothing.

Monica clicked her tongue with irritation. She had on the apron she reserved specially for this task. And the rubber gloves. She had the metal-toothed cat comb all ready, soaking in Dettol. Where was the creature?

She called a few times more, then gave up, took off the special apron and gloves and began to attack the mantelpiece with a duster.

But later, as she was taking out the rubbish, a dark shape in the flower bed startled her. At first, she thought one of the children had dropped something, or someone in the lane had thrown something over their wall—a hat, a shoe, perhaps. She shaded her eyes against the sun and realized it was the cat, hunched oddly, awkwardly, at the base of the yellowing jasmine plant.

"There you are," said Monica, but her voice was faltering.

A filmy glaze over the cat's eyes, the chest expanding and contracting with a rapid, fevered in-out, its head bowed low. Monica bent her knees into a crouch and saw, on its hind leg, skin torn like fabric, a clotted mass of red, a patch of something white. She let out a small shriek and staggered back onto the path. She looked up and down the lane, as if seeking help, then ran into the house, hands working at the cloth of her apron.

The phone was ringing as she burst into the hall and she snatched up the receiver.

"Hello, Camberden three eight three—"

Her mother's voice was mid-sentence: ". . . and so I was wondering if you had any idea of where he might have gone because—"

"Mammy, I can't talk now. Oh, it's terrible and—"

"What's happened?" Her mother snapped into the situation instantly, scenting danger near her child. "What is it? Is it Peter?"

"No. The cat."

"What about the cat?"

"Its leg. It's all mangled and bleeding. It's sitting out there now, hunched up and strange and I don't know what to do."

"Ah, the poor thing. Hit by a car, maybe. Alive, is he?"

"Yes. It's breathing, anyway. I don't know what to do," Monica said again.

"Well, you'll need to bring him to the vet."

"The vet?"

"Yes. They'll be able to help him. Poor thing," Gretta said again. Her mother's soft heart, when it came to small mammals, preferably helpless ones, always took Monica by surprise.

"I can't."

"Why not?"

"I can't pick it up. Not like that."

"You'll have to, darling. Drape a towel round him, if you really can't touch him. Just put him in a cardboard box and take him along."

"A cardboard box?"

"Yes, pet. Do you have one?"

"Probably. I don't know."

"You'll be fine. Do you remember when Aoife found that kitten? And she—"

"Mammy, I can't talk now. I have to—"

"Before you go, I just need to ask you something. It's about the shed key. You see, your father—"

"I have to go! I'll ring you back." Monica put the phone down and pulled open the door to the cellar. She was going to rescue the cat, she was, nobody else: it was to be her triumph. She felt a righteous excitement flooding through her veins. She could tell the story to the girls at the weekend and they would listen gratefully and perhaps a little bit tearfully. They would see the cat; it would have a bandage on by then and would be sitting docilely by the range, and they would know that she, Monica, had saved it.

She scrambled down the cellar steps, into the damp dark. She was sure she had a cardboard box down there, left over from Christmas.

.   .   .

Monica couldn't understand what the vet was saying. He didn't seem to want to help her, not at all. She'd got herself and the cat there, in one piece, in this unbearable, white heat. She'd got it into a box, she'd got herself and the box to the bus stop; she'd sat on the bus, looking straight ahead, despite the fact that the cat had been making a nerve-jangling noise throughout. And now to be told something about spinal cords was too much.

"What?"

"We need to end his suffering." The vet was talking in a specially gentle voice that Monica did not like.

"End his . . . ?"

The vet hesitated, seemed to look at her carefully. "We need to put him down."

"Down?" Monica couldn't assemble the words in a comprehensible form. The vet was saying things about sleep and pain and letting go. It seemed to be even hotter in here than it was outside. Sweat was collecting in her hairline, across her upper lip, around the waistband of her dress. She was terrified that if she raised her arms the vet, a man of about her age, not unattractive, would see the dark patches spreading there. The cat was a pool of clumped fur on the table between them.

"The cat, Mrs. Proctor," the vet was saying, "is seriously injured and—"

Monica stopped dabbing at her forehead with a hankie, aghast. "You mean kill it? But you have to make it better, you have to . . . My stepdaughters, they'll . . . You have to fix this cat. Please."

"Um . . ." The vet floundered, diverted from his usual script. Then he rallied himself. "It's a very quick, very peaceful procedure," he said uncertainly. "Well. Some people like to stay with the animal while it happens."

Monica looked down at the cat, which was making a terrible scrabbling motion with its front paws, trying to crawl back inside the cardboard box. It had taken her a good ten minutes to get it into the box—it hadn't wanted to go in, not at all, had fought and struggled with desperate, froglike movements. And now, here, all it wanted was to get back inside. Did it somehow know? Did it realize they were discussing its imminent death? No, it seemed to be saying, not now, not yet, there are many more things I need to do. Monica thought suddenly of Aoife. How she'd cried and cried when that kitten died. Her knees raw above her school socks as she stood in the garden. The tiny form, wrapped up in an old towel, cradled in her arms. Their father digging a hole in the earth. Make it deep, now, Robert, won't you, their mother had whispered, then pressed Aoife to her pinny. It was the kitten's time, she'd said to her, that's what it was. But Aoife cried, couldn't stop. A sickly thing, the kitten had been, right from the start, but she had cried and cried.

Monica had her hands on the cat, in the fur of its shoulders. She could feel the raised beads of its spine, the triangles of its shoulder blades. Taken aback, as always, at how frail its bones felt. It seemed such a solid, large creature, this cat, but when you actually had it in your hands, it felt birdlike, insubstantial, hardly there at all. Surprisingly warm, too. It was purring now, rubbing its face into her fingers, in a way she'd never allowed before, and it was looking up at her and its expression was reassured, trusting. As long as you're here, it seemed to be saying, then everything is going to be all right. Monica couldn't look away, couldn't break the gaze between her and the cat, even though she was aware of the vet filling his syringe, sliding a treacherous length of silver into the cat's fur; even though she knew this, she kept looking at the cat, she kept talking to it. The cat purred, she ran her hands over the herringbone marks of its fur, and then it was as if the cat was struck by a preoccupying thought, as if it had just remembered something important, and Monica was wondering what it might be, what cats think about, when she realized its head was slack in her hands, its eyes were no longer looking at her, but past her, as if it could see something behind her, something coming towards her, something bad, something she didn't know about.

"Oh," she said, at the same time as the vet said: "That's it now."

The speed of it was horrifying. That slippage from life so easy. There one moment and not there the next. Monica had to fight the urge to look about her. Where, where had the cat gone? It must be here somewhere. It couldn't have just vanished like that.

Aoife, strangely, surfaced in her mind again. Grown up, now, no longer in school socks. In the hospital that time: Aoife leaning over the dish, before the nurse came to take it away.

Monica bowed her head, wanting to shake the cat, to rouse it back to life, desperate for it to stretch out its paws and claw at her sleeve. You'd have thought such a passing would involve a struggle, a fight, a battle between states. But perhaps not. Perhaps it was always such a drift, such a slide.

Terrible to think it could happen with such ease.

It was Aoife who had leaned over and looked in the dish. She, Monica, had said: Oh, don't, Aoife, it's bad luck. But Aoife hadn't listened, of course. She'd looked at it for a long time.

Monica kept her fingers under the cat's jaw, which was fragile as a wishbone; the other hand touched the fur behind the cat's ear, the very softest fur of all, she'd always thought, impossibly soft, like dandelion down.

How quickly it had happened, Aoife growing up. It seemed to Monica that one day Aoife was a child, with dragging shoe-laces and plaits that undid themselves, and the next, she was a woman with draped clothes and numerous necklaces, stand-ing beside Monica's hospital bed, not listening when she'd said: Aoife, don't look. Her hair slid over her face so Monica couldn't read her expression. A long time it was that she looked. And then she said, in a low sort of voice: It died before it could even live. And she, Monica, sitting up in the bed, had banged her fist on her knee and said, No, not at all. It had lived. She had felt it live, for all those weeks. Felt its presence running through her veins, felt its existence undeniably in the odd dizziness of the mornings, in the nausea induced by cigarettes and exhaust fumes and furniture polish. It had lived, she'd said to her sister. Aoife raised her head then and said, Of course it did, I'm sorry, Mon, I'm so sorry.

It would have been almost three, that child.

There was no use in thinking these things. Monica took her hands off the cat's body. She turned away. She blew her nose. She pulled her bag higher onto her shoulder. She thanked the vet. She paid at the reception desk. She took the cardboard box, which felt peculiarly light (was it the soul, she wondered, that carried all the weight?). She went out onto the pavement. She looked up and down the high street for a moment. She walked to the bus stop.

Back at the house, Monica went around opening the win-dows. Let some air in, for God's sake. But there seemed to be no air, inside or out. Heat seemed to reach in through the narrow gaps, like smoke under a door. Monica slammed the windows shut again, dabbed some cologne on her wrists, her temples, redid her hair. Gretta and Aoife had thick hair that grew in all directions but hers was gossamer-thin, straight as straight, once pale but now a kind of washed-out mouse. There was nothing to be done with it. Just have it set at the hairdresser's every week and use a net at night.

Monica strode across the landing and into the bathroom. She looked around her wildly, ripped some tissue paper off its roll, pressed it to her nose. Her throat was raw and sore—hay fever, maybe?—her eyes smarting. She flung the tissue paper down the loo and began to pull at the zip on her dress. She had to freshen herself for Peter, who would be home soon; it was important to keep your husband interested, everyone said that.

She was going to have a bath. Yes, she was.

She didn't care about the bloody water ban—she needed a bath, she had to have one. To hell with the government and their miserly quotas, to hell with everyone. She pushed in the plug and opened both taps. Water gushed forth. She was, for a moment, mesmerized by the sight of it, frothing, shivering, at the bottom of the bath. The zip was stuck halfway down; Monica swore and tugged at it and didn't even care when she heard the sharp sound of fabric tearing; she had to get out of this dress, she had to bathe, she had to be looking nice, seeming calm, for when she told Peter about the cat, for when she asked him to say that it was him who'd had it put down. She had to make him see that this was the only way, to tell the girls that it was him who had found the cat, that it was him there with it at the end. But would he lie to them for her? She had no idea.

The dress fell at last in a pool of heated cotton around her ankles. Monica upended the box of bath salts Peter's mother had given her for Christmas—and what kind of a present was that to give your daughter-in-law, anyway? Monica had said nothing when Jessica had let slip that Granny had given Jenny a cashmere scarf, but it had hurt. It had hurt a great deal.

Monica stepped into the illegal water. She'd got it just right. A lovely, reviving tepid. She slipped her body under the silken water, feeling the grit and rasp of undissolved crystals, not unpleasant, beneath her.

There had been no word from Aoife, again, at Christmas. Whereas she, Monica, had sent a card to her place of work. Some things needed to be observed, no matter what. Her mother had had a card, of sorts, from Aoife, she'd noticed. And Michael Francis, too. But she'd said nothing.

The bathtub was cast-iron, large enough to lie down in. She would have liked to put in a new suite but Peter, of course, wouldn't hear of it. That was what came of marrying an antiques dealer. Peter went on and on about—how did he put it?—the integrity of houses. It's an early-Victorian farmhouse, he would say, why confuse the place with horrible, modern tat? She would have liked to ask how a house could possibly be confused. And why couldn't she have a bathroom carpet? But she kept her counsel. She had a suspicion that his reluctance to change a single thing about the house had more to do with wanting it to be the same as when the children were living there all the time, in Jenny's era, to foster the illusion that nothing had changed. As Gretta always said: some things were better left alone.

So she had a bathroom with a flaking iron bathtub that stood on lion's feet. A toilet with a peeling wooden seat and a pull chain that constantly broke. Shelves that should have held bath foam and shampoo bottles but instead displayed some of Peter's collection of nineteenth-century medicine bottles. Their bed had a sagging feather mattress, which made her sneeze, and a rusting iron frame. She wasn't allowed a nice electric oven, like everyone else, but had to struggle away with the range that Peter had found on some wasteland, dragged home and done up, blackening it himself, and most of the floor, in the process. The thing ate wood like a great, fiery-mouthed monster and the effort involved in rustling up dinner when the girls were hungry was unbelievable. The hallway and driveway and barn and backyard were forever jammed with stacked chairs, tatty sofas, tabletops that Peter was "in the middle" of doing up for the shop. It was beyond Monica why anyone would want to buy this stuff. But buy it they did.

Monica sat up when she heard the phone ring. Could it be Jenny? No. Those weeping phone calls seemed to have stopped recently. Peter? Her mother again? She contemplated the bathmat, the distance to the towel. She wasn't ready to have the conversation about the cat yet. Her throat closed again at the thought of it, the drifting look in its eyes, that cardboard box waiting in the barn. What on earth was the matter with her?

It would have been three this coming autumn.

She sloshed back down into the water, closing her eyes as the phone continued to ring, only opening them again when the house was silent.

It had been an antique necklace that had started everything between her and Peter. She'd been temping for a few weeks at a school in Bermondsey, typing letters to parents about sports day, about uniform requirements, tallying up the registers, writing out the teachers' pay slips. Those first few months after Joe had left, after what had happened in the hospital, with the bills to pay and the rent mounting up and the flat so dreadful and empty and the whole thing with Aoife: Monica hated to think about that time. She had, that morning, put on the emerald necklace Joe's grandmother had given her when they'd got married. It wasn't something she wore often but Joe had taken her rings, the pendant he'd bought her for her twenty-first. To sell, she supposed. They had always been short of money.

So she had put on the emerald necklace, not something she'd ever particularly liked. Too ornate, too old-looking for her taste. But she'd thought it would go with the green belt on her skirt. She'd been on the bus taking her south of the river, standing up on the running board because those early-morning routes were always jam-packed, when a man had offered her his seat.

It always made her think of Aoife, whenever this happened. Because they'd been on the tube together once and a man, not old, middle-aged perhaps, had stood up for them and just at the moment where she'd been saying, Thank you so much, and moving forward, Aoife had caught her by the arm and said, No, thank you, to the man, it's not necessary.

Anyway, so the man had offered her his seat and she had accepted with a nod—shutting her mind to Aoife and her principles—and lowered herself onto the seat and, as she did so, the man had exclaimed, "What a beautiful necklace."

She had turned, surprised, ticket in hand. The man was leaning with one hand on the rail, examining her throat area, his eyes intent, his face absorbed. It seemed extraordinary to be looked at like that, with such attention, such concentration. So when the man had asked if she was fond of early-Edwardian filigree, she had breathed, "Oh, yes." And he had taken the seat next to her, when it became vacant, and talked about metalworking and artisans and Venetian influence, and she had looked up at him, eyes wide, and when he asked if he could touch the "piece," as he called it, she'd said, "Of course."

She should dig out that necklace, Monica thought, as she soaped her shoulders. The phone rang again, more briefly this time, and Monica turned on the tap to top up the water, looking down at her body. Not bad, she decided, for someone approaching her mid-thirties. She still had a waist, which was more than could be said for most women her age. She was still trim; she was careful about what she ate, these days. She kept celery on hand in the kitchen for those moments of hunger. There was the sense that everything was being pulled downwards a touch, as if her flesh had suddenly become aware of gravity. The last time she'd seen Aoife—how long ago was it now, three years, almost four?— she'd been struck by her youth. The flawless, taut skin of her face, the way the flesh clung to the bone, the smoothness of her throat, her chest, the supple flex of her arms. It had given Monica a shock; everyone said they looked alike but Monica had never seen it, not at all. As children, they couldn't have been more different, Aoife so dark and she, Monica, so fair. But she suddenly saw that, the older they got, the more similar they became, as if they were converging on a single destiny, a unified identity. Monica felt herself to be so clearly separate from Aoife, so different in every conceivable way, but looking at her that day, that day in the kitchen, she could see herself ten years previously.

When Peter had told her, the second time they'd met—he'd taken her to a pub in Holborn, a dark-walled place with the severed heads of deer mounted on the walls—that he had children, Monica had felt a jolt that wasn't entirely disagreeable. Of course, she'd put down her drink and gathered up her bag, saying that she was not the sort of girl who went out with married men. Because she wasn't, not at all. She was, she knew, the sort of girl who went out with a nice boy, then married him and lived above a shop with him and stayed married to him forever. That was who she was. The question, however, was what did that sort of girl do when this destiny, decreed from a very young age, went awry, went horribly, horribly wrong?

She didn't say this, though, to Peter, in the Holborn pub. She gathered up her bag and made to leave but he put his hand on her arm and said simply, "I understand." Just like that: I understand. Such a lovely thing to say and uttered with such profundity, looking deep into her eyes. She straightaway forgot why he'd said it and it became just a beautiful general statement. He understood. Everything. Every last thing about her. It was as if great soft blankets had been folded about her. He looked into her eyes and told her he understood.

She'd sat down again, of course, and listened to what he said about how he and Jenny weren't married and they didn't believe that people could own each other and that Peter had been feeling lately that perhaps he and Jenny had come to the end of their story, and Monica asked about his children. Peter's face had softened into an expression she hadn't seen before and he described to her his two daughters, Florence and Jessica, and how he had been making them a tree house in the oak in the meadow, and Monica's mind became filled with the idea of herself in a green place, grass beneath her feet, leaves above her head, a man at her side. In this image, she was loading a basket with cakes and squash and sandwiches so that two little girls high up in a tree could winch up the basket. The girls wore sandals and print smocks and had delighted, open faces, so much so that when Peter asked if she'd like to take a walk to the river so they could watch the sunset from Waterloo Bridge, she'd said: Yes. Yes, I would.

Monica scrubbed vigorously at her feet with a pumice stone. Aggravating how, the older you got, the harder your feet became. This heat was making the skin on her heels crack and blister, her shoes feel constantly tight. No, she wasn't doing too badly in the aging department yet. The few gray hairs she had, she was plucking out. When the time came, she would dye them away. She was still, more or less, the same dress size she'd been when she'd got married. The first time she'd got married, that was, aged eighteen. Which was not something most women could say. She would never say this to anyone, of course, but having a husband considerably older than you made you feel younger and look younger to others, by comparison. And having had no children, of course, was an advantage. In terms of keeping your figure and so forth. In those situations where women gathered in states of undress—in changing rooms, the few times in her life she'd ever been to a public swimming pool—Monica was seized with a horrified fascination at the devastation childbearing wreaked. The slack pleating of stomach flesh, the silvered scars that found their way over dimpled legs, the deflated sacs of breasts.

She shuddered as she rose out of the water, tossing back her wet-ended hair. No, the whole childbirth thing was not for her. She knew that. She'd always known that.

.   .   .

The summer Monica turned nine, something happened to her mother. Her mother had always been a large presence. She made noise when she moved, when she ate, when she breathed. She couldn't put on her shoes without holding a conversation with herself, with the air around her, with the chair she sat on, with the shoes themselves: "Get on there now, you two," she would address the brown leather lace-ups. "I don't want a moment's trouble out of you."

Her mother, you could say, made her presence known. Monica could tell when she returned home from school whether her mother was in or not just by the quality of the air, the thickness of the atmosphere. If she was out, the house had an odd, suspended feel to it. Like a stage set before the lights go up, before the actors emerge from the wings, the house felt to Monica unreal, as if the furniture and vases and plates and crockery were only props, as if the walls and doors were nothing more than painted scenery that could topple if leaned against.

But if Gretta was in, there was a sense of bustle, of urgency about things. The radio would be on or the record player would be churning out ballads by that tenor with the trembly voice. Monica might find her emptying a cupboard, jam jars, teacups, soup tureens, candle stumps strewn around the floor. Her mother might be cradling a tarnished silver spoon in her lap, muttering to herself or the spoon, and, on seeing her daughter, her face would break into a smile. "Come here now," she'd say, "till I tell you about the old woman who gave me this." Gretta might be energetically scissoring up one of her dresses to alter it for Monica. Or Monica might find her passionately engaged in one of her short-lived hobbies: crocheting milk-jug covers, varnishing plant pots, threading beads onto twine to make a "gorgeous" necklace, edging hankies with chains of daisies, pansies and forget-me-nots. These projects would be found, abandoned, half finished, a few weeks later, stuffed into a drawer. Gretta's hobbies burned brightly and for a short time. Years later, Monica's first husband, Joe, after watching Gretta balance her checkbook in about five minutes, would remark that maybe all her mother's craziness was caused by never finding an outlet for her intelligence. "I mean," he said, "she never even went to school, did she?"

But that summer, it seemed at first that Monica had lost her instinct when it came to her mother. She remembered very clearly the day she came through the front door, felt the flat, dampened air of the house and assumed her mother was out. Doing the altar flowers, perhaps, lighting a candle for somebody, visiting one of the neighbors down the street. Monica let her satchel slide to the floor, chewing the end of her plait, and walked into the sitting room, where she was confronted by the sight of her mother stretched out on the good sofa, in the middle of the day, asleep, with her hands crossed over her, her feet on the upholstery. Monica could not have been more astonished if she'd come in and found her serving tea and scones to the Pope himself.

She waited in the doorway a moment longer. She stared at her mother's sleeping form, as if to be sure that this was her mother, that she was really sleeping, that this wasn't one of her elaborate jokes, that she wasn't going to spring up in a moment, shouting, "Fooled you, didn't I?"

Her mother was asleep. At four o'clock in the afternoon. The paper was folded next to her. Her chest rose and fell and her mouth was slightly open, taking small sips of air. When Michael Francis crashed in through the back door a few minutes later, Monica was still standing there. She hushed her brother frantically and they both stood and stared at the unbelievable sight of their mother napping in the middle of the day.

"Is she dead?" Michael Francis whispered.

"'Course not," Monica snapped in fear. "She's breathing. Look."

"Will I go and fetch Mrs. Davis?"

They had been told to call on the next-door neighbor if there was ever an emergency. Monica considered this option, her head on one side. Although Michael Francis was ten months older than her, it was generally left to her to make all the decisions. They were in the same class at school; people took them for twins. He was older but she was more responsible. She and her brother had forged this arrangement between themselves and never questioned it.

"No." She shook her head. "Mammy wouldn't want us to."

"Who'll make our tea, then?"

Monica scratched her head. "I will."

Michael Francis stood at the sink to scrub the potatoes and Monica did her best to peel and slice them. Michael Francis fidgeted and fretted as he rubbed at the tight, muddied skins.

"What will we do if she doesn't wake up?" he said, his voice low and scared.

"She will," Monica said, pushing her hair out of her eyes.

"Will we make tea for her as well or just for us?"

"For her as well."

"What will we have with the potatoes?"

Monica had to think. "Fried eggs," she said decisively, because she knew they had eggs: she'd seen them that morning in the covered dish, and she knew how to make fried eggs. She was sure. She'd seen her mother do it often enough.

"Fried eggs," Michael Francis repeated to himself, under his breath, in a satisfied way. All was right in his world if he knew what he'd be having for tea. He set to scrubbing the potatoes with a renewed vigor but his elbow made contact with the waiting saucepan and it fell to the lino with a clang.

"Michael Francis!" Monica hissed.

"Sorry." His eyes, she knew, would be filling with tears. He had, their mother always said, a thin skin. You couldn't shout at him or he got too upset. Something like a dead bird or a pony with a limp could set him off. A sissy, their father called him sometimes and said that he needed toughening up. Monica had been obliged, several times, to give what their mother called a piece of her mind to some of the boys in their class; they could be very hard on Michael Francis, who was bookish and, although big for his age, useless at fighting. She sighed and gave him a nudge. "It's all right. I don't think Mammy—"

From the sitting room they heard a voice. A faint, soft voice. Nothing like their mother's booming tones. "Is that my darlings in there getting the tea on?"

They looked at each other. Michael Francis wiped his face on his jersey sleeve. Then they ran through to the sitting room. Their mother was still lying as she had been but her eyes were open and she was holding out her arms to them. "You're a pet and you're a pet," she said to them. "Fancy the two of you making the tea for me. I'd say you'll need ice cream after this. Will one of you run to the shop and get a block?"

Everything seemed back to normal. They finished making the tea; they ate it; they had their ice cream, cutting slices off the striped block, yellow-brown-pink; their father came back and had his tea. But the next day, after school, she was asleep again. At the weekend their father took them—alone—to the park so that their mother could "rest." Monica scuffed her toe against the ground as she sat on the swing. She eyed her father as he sat on the bench, hidden behind a screen of newspaper. She looked over at Michael Francis, who was flinging a ball into the air and catching it against his chest. She wanted to get up off the swing, cross the grass and say to her father, What's wrong with Mammy, what's happening? But her legs wouldn't carry her, she couldn't form the words, and even if she could, she wouldn't have been able to say them to her father, wouldn't have been able to listen to his answers.

It was her father who told them a few weeks later that their mother was "expecting." She and Michael Francis looked up at him from the rug in front of the fire grate. He seemed taller than ever, waiting there at the edge of the room, his hair standing upright from his head, like the flame on a match. Expecting. Her head was filled with a vision of a railway station, full of people looking down a track to see if their train was arriving yet. An animal, alert, eyes wide, on its hind legs. A person crouched next to a letter box, waiting for the post. Expecting.

"You'll need to help her a great deal in the next few months. Understand?"

They nodded from habit. They knew this was the correct response to being asked if they understood.

"She's not to lift a thing. Shopping bags. Buckets of water. Nothing. You must do all that for her. Understand?"

They nodded again, in unison.

"She's to rest every day and you mustn't disturb her."

"Yes, Daddy," Monica said.

She watched her mother every minute she was with her. She became scared to go to school, not wanting to leave her mother for a moment. If her mother lifted a plate, a cup of tea, her knitting, Monica shut her eyes. She would not see it occur. Something terrible could happen to her mother at any moment. She'd gathered this from eavesdropping on the hushed conversation her mother had with other women over the back wall, outside church. It was dangerous, she'd learned. After all those other times. The doctor had told her never again; it wasn't worth the risk.

Monica stopped sleeping. She lay awake, threading her fingers into the blanket edge, then out. In, then out, in, then out, until the blanket edge was rucked up around her knuckles. She listened for the sounds of her parents going to bed. She listened out for them scrubbing their teeth in the bathroom, for her mother to climb into bed, for her father to lock the front door. She lay awake after she heard her father start to snore, like an engine struggling uphill. She listened for whatever else she might hear: a late cyclist in the street, the milk van in the early gray dawn, a neighboring cat yowling at a back door. Whatever it was they were expecting, she wanted to be ready.

She found out what it was by listening in on a conversation between her mother and her aunt Bridie. They were visiting Bridie on a Saturday afternoon; Monica was meant to be minding her cousins in the back garden while her mother and Bridie caught up over a pot of tea. But the cousins were whiny and dull and she found it more interesting to sit beside the kitchen door, in the small space beneath the mangle, hidden from all eyes. Her mother and Bridie had had a long chat about one of their other siblings, who was, apparently, "in with a bad lot"; they discussed the shocking price of shoes for the children; there was a lot of sighing over something Monica's mother referred to as "one of Robert's black days"; Bridie told a long story involving a bus to Brighton—Monica wasn't concentrating at the beginning so couldn't ascertain the story's significance. Then Bridie said, in a cozy sort of voice, "Now, when's this baby due again?"

Monica picked at the green paint on Bridie's skirting-board. She pushed her fingers as far as they would go into the mangle's rollers until it began to hurt too much. And she listened, she stilled herself with the act of listening. She learned that her mother had lost babies, many babies. Monica imagined her mother carelessly dropping these infants from a shopping basket, or from her coat pocket, like stray pennies or a loose hairpin. There were murmurs about a baby buried somewhere, without a baptism, but Monica had been unable to hear whether it was a baby of her mother's or some other woman's.

She held her mother's hand very tightly on the way home. She examined her mother's familiar form carefully, right from her good Sunday-and-visiting shoes, all the way up to the hat on her head. Expecting.

.   .   .

Towel-wrapped, Monica padded carefully over the bare wooden boards into the bedroom. The number of times she'd spiked a splinter into the flesh of her feet, but if Peter even heard mention of the words "fitted carpet," he jammed his hands over his ears. So she had to put up with it.

Monica flicked through the hangers in the wardrobe (triple-doored, walnut-veneered, late-Victorian, procured from a probate sale in Gloucester). Dressing was a particular difficulty in this weather. What to wear that was decent yet cool enough? Monica considered a shirtwaister in a crimped fabric, a halter-necked top in orange seersucker, a striped all-in-one with a zip up the middle, before settling on a frilled dress in lawn cotton. One of Peter's favorites. He said it made her look like a milk-maid. Apparently this was a good thing. They had gone together to a boutique in Oxford to buy these clothes. Shopping with a man was not something Monica was used to. She had always gone with her mother or her sister; she wasn't one for shopping alone, found it hard to make up her mind, could never decide if something suited her or not. So she had taken Gretta or, in later years, Aoife, who, despite dressing like a tramp, was surprisingly good at knowing what looked right on people. Monica wasn't at all used to the idea of coming out through the curtained door to display yourself to a man waiting in a chair, to elicit his approval before you even knew yourself whether you liked it. Joe had hated shopping, would never have gone with her, even if she'd asked.

Monica pushed the tiny pearl buttons through the frills and into their holes. So many of them and all so small. She'd forgotten that. She faced herself in the dressing-table mirror (Art Deco, oak, with a rosewood inlay) and pushed her earrings into place (marcasite and ruby, flower design, 1930s). She hadn't wanted children. She'd known that. She'd told Joe so. Right from the start. But it seemed that he hadn't believed her, that he'd thought she'd come around, that she'd change her mind. She'd told Peter, too, and he had said, Fine, don't fancy doing it all again anyway. Peter came with a ready-made family, with spare children; she'd hoped she might slot into their lives almost as if they were her own. It had seemed perfect, really, when she'd thought about it: children without having to give birth to them.

She hadn't ever wanted children and yet she had. She had and she did.

She pulled the brush (enamel-backed, silver-handled, initialed *H*, another probate sale) through her hair, again and again. A hundred strokes a day, her mother had always decreed. Keeps it healthy.

Careful was the word she used. Monica was careful with herself. She had learned to blank out what she didn't like to see; there was a trick she had perfected, a slight narrowing of the eyes so that the lashes rendered the scene soft, furred at the edges, an ability to slide her pupils sideways should anything untoward come her way. She had a problem, she'd realized recently, with children of about three or four.

It wasn't a baby Monica wanted. It was a child. She had no desire for those cocooned beings in blankets, terrifying in their fragility, insistent in their demands, so new as to be still redolent of bodily fluids, of milk and blood, all the gore and effort and violence of birth. No. She couldn't have done it, couldn't have gone through what her mother had with Aoife.

Monica liked Michael Francis's youngest, Vita. Not the boy, who looked too much like his mother—that rather moony forehead. Vita was a real Riordan; Gretta was always saying how she was the spit of Aoife at the same age. "But mercifully without all the weirdness," Monica had once added, and her mother had laughed and said, "True enough." The last time Monica had seen her, Vita had taken her hand and shown her a doll's house. Tiny rooms, precisely arranged, books with real pages lined up on the shelves, a cook preparing a painted ham in the kitchen, a dog curled up on a minuscule hearth rug before a crackling polyethylene fire. Monica had thought then, as she pressed her eye to the window with its own flowered curtains, that she would have liked a little girl with a doll's house, a girl with hair slides and red T-bar shoes, like Vita's. Monica had seen a charming miniature sideboard in the window of a toy shop and had gone in and bought it and sent it to Vita and she'd received a crayoned card by return. Claire was good about that sort of thing; Monica appreciated a thank-you letter. Who wouldn't?

It did no good dwelling on these things. There would be no children. It had been her decision and it was the right one, ultimately. Monica was sure of that. Earrings in, hair done, lipstick applied, but not too much, as Peter didn't like the taste of it, Monica stood up from her dressing stool, ready to face the evening.

By the time Peter came in—in a pair of filthy overalls, reeking to high heaven of turpentine—she had the table laid with a white linen cloth, candles lit, the silver salver filled with shelled almonds, just as he liked.

"Darling," she murmured, as he came through the kitchen door and almost went to kiss him but remembered her frock in time, "what have you been doing?"

"I had a brilliant idea." Peter tossed a handful of nuts into his mouth. "Remember that pine table I told you I'd got hold of last week? Well, I suddenly thought in the night . . ." Peter continued to talk. Monica watched his mouth moving, eyed the oil stains on his overalls, wondered whether they'd got through to the clothes underneath, asked herself how soon she could request that he take off the overalls so that she could check, noticed his black-rimmed fingernails sifting through her nuts. He was still talking about how he and his helper had set about the table with some metal chains to give it "that worn-in patina" that people were starting to go crazy for. Monica thought that she had to say about the cat soon, otherwise it would seem strange. She had to tell him. She had to get it out.

"Peter," she interrupted.

". . . don't know why I'd never thought of it before. Buy new stuff or recent stuff and then just duff it up a bit. No one will know the difference. It's genius." He seized her around the waist, his overalls pressing up against her tiny pearl buttons, like rows of frozen tears. "Your husband is a genius."

"Darling—"

From the hall, the phone rang again. Peter released her and made as if to go and answer it.

"Leave it," she said, and she was, inexplicably and suddenly, crying, the tears coming from nowhere, spilling down her cheeks, dripping onto the high collar of her dress. "Peter," she sobbed. "Peter, listen—"

He was there right away, cupping her face in his palms. "What's the matter? What happened?"

The phone was still ringing. Who on earth was plaguing her like this? Why wouldn't they go away and why couldn't she stop crying today?

"What's the matter?" Peter said again.

Monica found she was about to say: Aoife came, Aoife saw. The words were ready in her mouth: It would have been almost three.

But she managed not to. She managed to stop them, to swallow them down, she managed to change them into: "The cat died." She got these words out instead; she managed to say them to her husband, to the father of the children who had loved the cat.

· · ·

The phone rang again while they were having dinner: a rather successful casserole Monica had made. She'd got a new recipe from a magazine, which said to add dried apricots. She didn't normally like sweet things in savory dishes but this had come off quite well.

Peter went to answer the phone. She poured herself a touch more wine, the red liquid glugging throatily from the bottle. She tore a crust off the bread and ate a mouthful of the soft innards. She had that washed, tremulous feeling you get after a bout of crying. Like a London street after the cleaners had been down it; dark, wetted, cleansed.

Suddenly Peter was back in the room, standing beside her chair. She turned in her seat to look up at him.

"Monica . . ." he began, laying a hand on her shoulder.

She didn't like that voice; she didn't like his grave face. "What?" she said, flinching away from his touch. "What is it?"

"It's your brother on the phone."

She continued to stare at her husband. "What's happened?"

"You'd better talk to him."

Monica sat for a moment, then darted out of her seat. Halfway across the room, she was aware of the floorboards rippling and undulating beneath her shoes, felt herself to be on the verge of collapse. She had suddenly realized why the day had been odd, why she'd been on the brink of tears, why the air around her had felt charged, frayed. She knew. She knew what Michael Francis was about to say. She knew what it was but she didn't want to hear it. Something had happened to Aoife. A car accident, a drowning, an overdose, a murder, a horrible illness. Her brother was ringing to tell her that their sister was dead.

She couldn't get her legs to work; she couldn't make it through the door. She wanted to stay here, with the wine and the casserole. She did not want to hear this.

It was a new sister for her, the nurse said, as she stood with Monica at the nursery window, where babies were laid out like buns in a baker's shop. A little baby girl. It was hard to tell because she was wrapped in so many blankets and swaddles and bits of cloth. She had a red face and tiny fists, squeezed shut. She was called Aoife. Aoife Magdalena Riordan. A long name for such a small person.

And then, it seemed to Monica, the baby opened her mouth and started to scream and that she did not stop screaming for a long time. She screamed to feed, she screamed while she was feeding, she screamed after she'd fed, so much so that she brought up all the milk she'd taken, in surprising yellow-white jets that hit the walls, the fabric of the sofa. She screamed if laid flat, even for a moment, on a bed or in the pram. She beat the air with those fists of hers, filled the room with sound; she clawed at Gretta's hair and neck, gripped by her own private agony, she wept tears that ran over her face and into the collars of her matinée jackets. Her legs would work up and down, as if she were a toy with a winding mechanism, her face would crumple in on itself and the room would fill with jagged sounds that could have cut you, if you'd stood too close. Gretta would sink her head into her hands and Monica would rise from her homework and take the baby, and together, she and Aoife would go on a grief-filled tour of the kitchen.

Her mother took the baby to the doctor, who glanced into the squalling pram and said, give her a bottle. So they trailed, Monica and Michael Francis and their mother and the pram, to the chemist and bought gleaming bottles with orange lids and a tin of powdered milk. But Aoife took one suck on the bottle and turned her head away and howled.

Monica stood in the hallway, which Jenny had painted a dark brown that resembled melting chocolate. She'd meant to get around to redecorating it—it made her feel queasy every time she passed through it. But she couldn't decide what color. Shell pink or cheerful orange? A dusky yellow? A springlike green?

She picked up the phone receiver and held it in her hand. Her brother, she knew, was going to tell her about their sister's death. He would give details, times, dates. And then what would she say? There would be arrangements to make. Aoife, she knew, was in New York. Their parents were in London. How to get them all in one place? And which place? Would they all go to New York? Or London? Or Ireland? Where would be the place for this?

She lifted the receiver to her ear and listened for a moment to the noise of her brother's house; a voyeur, she was, ear at a keyhole. A child was wailing in the background—a blaring, rising note. Another child's voice was clear over it, saying something about Mummy and a bedtime story. She could hear her brother saying, ". . . going to count to five and by the time I get to four, I want you down off that windowsill, do you hear me?"

"Michael Francis?" Monica said, sending her voice down the line to reach him, all the way in London. She didn't want to hear what he was about to say, she didn't want to accept the words, to take them from him and fold them into herself, where they would stay for the rest of her life.

"Jesus Christ, Monica," Michael Francis spat down the phone, and Monica instantly knew that no one was dead, that this was something else and the newness of the situation frightened her, "where in God's name have you been?"

"Here," said Monica, pulling herself upright. How dare he speak to her like that? "I've been here."

"I've been calling and calling. Why haven't you answered the phone?"

"I've been busy. As I am now. What do you want?"

"Dad's gone."

"What?"

"He's missing."

"Missing? He can't be missing. He's probably just . . ." Monica trailed off. That their father might do anything even remotely unexpected or unplanned was a ridiculous idea. He was a man who thought carefully about a trip to the supermarket, weighing up the pros and cons. "He can't be missing," she said again. "He'll just be . . ." She had to stop, to take a few breaths. Her mind, she found, was still running on the tracks of Aoife's demise and the problem of where they would hold her funeral. This thing—whatever it was—was so unlikely, so unaccountable that she couldn't divert herself towards considering it. "Has Mum looked . . . I don't know . . . around the house?"

"They've looked everywhere and—"

"Who's they?"

"The police," Michael Francis said impatiently, making it clear that she wasn't in on the seriousness of the situation, that she'd missed several stages in the drama. "Mum hasn't seen him since this morning and they—"

"This morning?" Monica demanded. "But that's ages!"

"I know that."

"But have they checked with—I don't know. Did he go out somewhere? Or—"

"Mon," he said, and his voice was gentler now. "He took money out of their account."

"Oh."

"He's not had an accident, as far as we know. He's . . . taken off."

"Well, where's he gone?"

"We don't know."

"What do the police say? What are they going to do?"

"They say they can't do anything."

"Why not?"

"They say it's not a disappearance. We think he's taken his passport, too. He went to the bank first thing but after that we don't know. He's just gone."

Monica gazed at a place where the chocolate-brown paint had chipped off the banisters, revealing layers of color underneath, like rings in a tree. A dull turquoise, a violent mauve, a creamy white. She thought for a moment of the other people who had stood there in the hallway, like she did, considering what color to paint it.

Michael Francis was talking again, about how she needed to come to London, to help their mother, how they had to contact Aoife but that he didn't have a number for her; he'd called the one she'd given him but the person who'd answered had said Aoife didn't work there anymore.

Typical Aoife, Monica thought immediately, to move jobs but not inform them. Then she felt a prickle of irritation to observe that her mind had, once again, been pulled back to her younger sister. What was it about today that was making Aoife so present, so dominant in her thoughts, as an adult, as a child, as a baby? The age gap between them meant that Monica had a clear view of Aoife at every stage of her life. And Aoife had howled, Monica remembered, as she stared at the chip in the paint, for years. Pretty much nonstop. They had got used to it in the end, to living their lives with the foreground noise of Aoife's rage. She had screamed in her high chair, in her buggy, in the car, on the bus, in her cot, in her baby carrier. If Monica had put her on reins to walk down the street, which she had done a great deal because Gretta had to have a break sometimes, just fifteen minutes or so, Aoife would cast herself facedown and kick the pavement in a frenzy of fury. If Monica didn't let her explore some steep stairs, she would bite and scratch and scream; if Monica did let her climb them, because she was tired of being bitten and scratched, and Aoife fell and banged her head, she screamed as well.

Sleep didn't seem to be something Aoife needed. She woke five times a night, well into her childhood, lacerating the dark with her sudden yells. Their mother would lurch, gray-faced, through the door to attempt to coax her back to sleep. Monica, who had the bed next to Aoife, tried to get there first, tried to make Aoife be quiet so their mother didn't hear her, so their mother could sleep, so their mother could get back to being the way she used to be, before all this: large and in love with life, always popping in and out of other people's houses or jamming on her hat to go and see the priest, not the ghostlike wisp of a woman who haunted the rooms of their house. But Aoife would not be comforted. There was always something, with her. She had nightmares about creatures under the bed, about things tapping at the window, about a black shape behind the bathroom door. If Monica took her across the landing and showed her that the black shape was nothing more than their father's dressing gown, hanging on a hook, Aoife would stop twiddling her hair for a moment, stare at the dressing gown and say, "But it wasn't that before. Not before."

Their father said Aoife was difficult; their mother said she was her cross to bear, her comeuppance for wanting one more; Bridie said that child needed the arse tanned off her; the doctor said, "Oh, you've got one of *those*," and gave Gretta a prescription for tranquilizers—her first.

After that their mother slept a lot and, sometimes, even when she was awake it was as if she was asleep, somewhere in her mind. Monica would often come home early from school, pleading a headache or an upset tummy, but really knowing that if she made it home before Aoife woke up from her afternoon nap, she could take her out of the cot and have her downstairs or out in the back garden and their mother wouldn't be woken by her squawks and yells. Sometimes Gretta would sleep on until the early evening. Monica would put Aoife in her playpen with a pan and a wooden spoon while she got the tea on. When her mother emerged, face crumpled and somehow vague, she would rest a hand on the top of Monica's head and say that she was an angel, a heaven-sent angel. And Monica would stand there, feeling the weight of her mother's hand, and what would wash through her was not so much pleasure at her mother's words but relief that she had got everyone through another day.

Aoife walked before she was one, taking everything off the kitchen shelves, dragging the ash out of the grate, pulling teacups down off tables. She talked in full sentences at a year and a half: "I don't want that red bowl, for some reason, I want the green one." By her second birthday, she could count to fifty, say the alphabet, recite a poem about a mouse. It seemed to Monica that her parents were relieved at this point. There was a reason why Aoife was the way she was: Aoife was gifted, Aoife was special, Aoife was a genius. "Of course," her mother could now say to people in shops, if Aoife was lying across the entranceway, kicking the door and screaming, "she's terribly bright."

But then, to their surprise, things didn't go so well for Aoife when it came to school. She came home each afternoon with a cross, set face, smudged with ink. If Gretta asked her whom she had played with at break time, Aoife scowled and said nothing. She would slide off her chair and disappear under the table. Monica happened to pass the infants' school on her way to a games lesson with her class and, scanning the groups and clusters of small children, caught sight of a familiar figure, socks fallen around her ankles, hair escaping from its plaits, standing alone in the shade of the plane tree, engaged in an animated conversation with herself.

Aoife had turned, almost overnight, from being "difficult" and "a genius" to "a worry." Her writing unfurled from her pencil tip in an incomprehensible, spidery scrawl. She used both hands indiscriminately; she seemed to have no concept that she ought to favor one over the other. She wrote her s's backwards, her t's upside down. The spaces between words were elided or appeared randomly, mid-syllable.

"Look, Aoife," their mother would say, "here's an A, a lovely tall A. Can you see it? An A for 'apple' and 'amen' and 'Aoife.'"

Aoife kicked her heels against the chair legs, squinted at the letter, then laid her head on her arm and shut her eyes.

"Can you see it?" Gretta persisted.

"Mmm," Aoife said, into her sleeve.

"Can you write one for me?"

"No."

"Why not?"

"Because it looks like the side of a house, a house that's been sliced in half so that all the roof is cut and open and all the people have fallen out and—"

"Let's move on to *B*." Gretta was being firm. The teacher had said that Aoife needed to be taken in hand, that she mustn't be indulged in her fancies. "Now, *B* is for—"

"'Bolster,'" Aoife said. "And 'buoyant' and 'bulbous' and 'bosom' and 'bottom.' Mrs. Saunders has the biggest bottom—"

"Aoife, we don't say things like that about—"

"—you've ever seen. It's so big it doesn't fit into the teacher's chair. She has to sit sort of—"

"Aoife—"

"—sideways to squeeze it in."

Michael Francis, across the table, doing his geometry homework, started to snicker. "She's right, you know," he said. "She does."

Gretta leapt up, swept the alphabet book to the floor. "I don't know why I bother," she shouted. "I'm trying to get you to better yourself but you don't care. You don't try. You have to try, Aoife. Anyone can do this—anyone! You just need to put a bit of effort in. I'd have killed for the education you're getting and you're just throwing it all away."

Mrs. Saunders said that Aoife's reading age was very low and that she couldn't even write her numbers properly, let alone add them up, and that, in short, her recommendation was that Aoife be kept back a year. Mrs. Saunders referred to Aoife throughout this talk as "Eva" and when Gretta corrected her, Mrs. Saunders replied that didn't Gretta think it would be better "for everyone" to use what she termed "the proper spelling" of the name? If only to give Eva a better chance of learning to write it? Monica, who was standing in the classroom with her mother, felt Gretta inhale, saw her pull herself up to her full height and place her knuckles on the teacher's desk and Monica closed her eyes.

Either way, Aoife/Eva repeated the year, then repeated it again. At the age of seven, she was still in the first year of infants' school, sitting with her knees jammed under a tiny desk at the back of the class, writing her letters the wrong way around and upside down, words that ran diagonally or backwards, unreadable numbers that streamed right to left, as if reflected in a mirror.

It was at this point that Monica started going out with Joe, or was spending her evenings studying her nursing books, so she slightly lost focus on "the Aoife problem," as the family termed it. It was as if the presence of Joe in her life gave her special absolution—for the first time—from looking after Aoife, from taking responsibility for her.

But there was one night when Aoife, still in the infants' class, was struggling through a first-stage reading book about a cat and a rat, Michael Francis spelling out the letters for her, when Joe leaned forward from his chair. "Why do you do that?" he said.

No answer.

"Aoife? Why do you do that thing?"

She looked up reluctantly, her face screwed up, her hand over one eye, and it was possible to see the cat and its exploits with the mat and the rat drain from her features. "What thing?"

"With your hand over your eye," Joe said, tapping his ash into the grate.

"It stops the letters leaping about the page," she said, replacing her hand and looking back down at her book.

Joe had been hugely amused by this reply and told it to several people that night at the pub. Monica had felt hot as he did so. She didn't want people to laugh at Aoife; she didn't want people to know she had a strange sister.

But then Joe asked Monica to marry him and it no longer mattered if Aoife mysteriously refused to learn to read. It didn't matter that Aoife still couldn't write or spell. It didn't matter that she, Monica, had to share a room with a child who woke her in the night by talking to herself or bawling through a nightmare. It no longer mattered that she hadn't done well in her first-year nursing exams or that her father rarely spoke or that her mother insisted on wearing a mackintosh repaired with staples. Nothing mattered anymore because she was getting out of that family and into her own. It didn't matter if she left nursing college because, really, what was the point in staying when soon she'd have a husband and a flat above a shop, a home all of her own?

"Well, don't ask me," Monica said to her brother, down the phone. "I've no idea how to get in touch with her."

New York

As Michael Francis is arguing with Monica, as Monica is putting down the phone and recrossing the hall and going back into the dining room, as she is allowing herself to collapse into Peter's outstretched arms, to submit herself to his particular smell—a fumy mix of paint stripper, oak dust and varnish—Aoife, 3,500 miles west, five hours behind in time, is laboring up the stairs in an apartment block in the Upper West Side. A bag is slung over her shoulder, a pair of unlaced boots are on her feet and they are beginning to bother her but she's gone too far now to stop.

The bag is heavy, the day is hot and gritty, and her feet slip and slide inside the boots, which are a size too big but she hadn't been able not to buy them. Russian Army boots, the man with the flea-market stall had told her as she pulled them on, sitting on the edge of the sidewalk, her feet in the gutter. Should see you through a couple of winters, he'd said. She had yanked and fiddled with the knotted laces, her toes spreading and stretching into the hardened leather innards. Funny, she always thought, how your feet spend so long in a space you never see. She has squinted into the dark, half-seen toe spaces of shoes but has never been able to equate those semicircular tunnels with the soft, humid places her feet know so intimately. They've probably trekked across the steppes, Gabe had said, lifting up her foot to examine the boot sole. Pretty small for a soldier, he said.

Michael Francis is trying to herd his children into their night-clothes; he is squeezing toothpaste onto their matching brushes. Gretta is opening a cupboard and discovering an old macramé kit holding a half-finished plant-pot-holder. Monica is accepting a brandy from Peter; she is tucking her feet under her on the sofa. And Aoife is pausing to catch her breath before the last flight of stairs.

On her feet are dead men's boots; in her bag are boxes and boxes of photographic film, a particular type that Evelyn needs, which takes well to the silver-bromide processing, that likes to soak up the white of Evelyn's blenched backgrounds, likes to take the imprint of every curve, every dip, every contour, every tensed muscle in the expressions of her subjects. It's sold in only one shop in Brooklyn so every couple of months Aoife is dispatched to stock up. She likes the ride over there, starting in the innards of Manhattan, then rising into the light, which crosshatches the passengers' faces with shade.

The sign next to where she stands, leaning on the handrail, would to anyone else say 6TH FLOOR, but Aoife turns her head away, avoiding its eye, as if it is a person who has committed some offense against her. Text to Aoife is slippery, dangerous. It cannot be trusted. One minute the sign might say 6TH FLOOR; the next, the letters will have shifted, with sickening ease, into GUT FLOUR or GIRTH LOOT or 9TH HOOR.

When she first came to New York, she knew no one. She arrived in a rush, like someone who trips as they enter a room. She had dismantled her life in London in a matter of days, giving away what she couldn't carry, leaving her bicycle on the pavement with a notice: FREE TO WHOEVER NEEDS IT. She knew someone who knew an American bloke who said his godfather ran a music club in somewhere called the Bowery. He'd give Aoife a job, he was sure of it. It was a tenuous lifeline, but she'd taken it.

When she first came to New York, she found herself always on the lookout for families. In the street, in cafés, in queues at the movies, under the leafy canopies of trees in Central Park. When she saw one, she would study them. She would walk behind them in shops, position herself near them on a bench and lean in to catch their conversations. She wasn't particular about ages: any family would do. She looked into prams and strollers, and felt a sort of satisfaction when she found an echo in the baby's face of the mother's unusually wide eyes or widow's peak. She watched a father and a teenaged daughter eat bagels together, outside a corner deli, both licking their bottom lips in exactly the same way, apparently unconscious of their mirroring. On her way to the subway every morning, she crossed paths with an elderly mother and daughter who wore the same color lipstick; they had the same fine, flyaway hair. The mother wore hers swept up into a chignon; the daughter had cut hers—defiantly, Aoife always thought—into a severe bob that didn't suit her. Aoife often got the urge to whisper, Just give in, grow it and put it in a chignon, it will look better.

When she first came to New York, she knew no one, she was on the lookout for families, and felt herself to be as broken as the city. She rented a one-room walk-up in which everything was something else: the tiny bathtub masquerading as a counter in the kitchen, the bed hiding upright in the wardrobe, like an assassin. Cockroaches and something she couldn't identify skedaddled up the walls and into cracks when she walked in. The man with a music club did give her a job: she had to take a rubber stamp, bang it on a purple-soaked ink pad and press it to the backs of punters' hands. Each gentle blow inked a bee on their skin, wings outstretched in flight, antennae raised, seeking something. Music-obsessed young New Yorkers would file past her, arms outstretched, waiting for the insignia, the impermanent tattoo that would permit them to exit the real world and enter the world beyond the thick curtain, a world of heavy, smoke-hung dark that reverberated with sound and thin beams of light. If it was a slow night, Aoife inked herself over and over again so that hundreds of bees swarmed over her skin, up her arms and into her sleeves. Later, when the club was full and the doors were closed, she went behind the bar to help serve the drinks, and there she would mix cocktails, slip straws into liquid, pack glasses with ice, yell, "What'll it be?" into people's ears over the music, her legs moving to the bass, her torso weaving side to side to the guitar riffs, her bee-patterned arms pumping counterwise to the melody. The music filled her skull; she thought of nothing the whole time she was in the club. She liked dancing to the bleached-hair woman with large eyes, who sang angrily with an impassive face, and the man who moved as if made of machinery, as if his joints were hinged with oil; she was less enamored of the ones who spat at the crowds or lashed the walls with their guitars, if only for the leaping, volatile crowd they brought with them.

She knew that none of this—the music, the apartment, the being there—would ever distract her from what had happened between her and Monica. It ran in her mind, on a constant loop. Aoife didn't think she would ever get over it, that what had occurred between them in the kitchen at Michael Francis's house would be carried within her forever, like a splinter she couldn't remove. She had tried to fix things, she really had. Months after that time in the kitchen, even though she still smarted with the things Monica had said, even though it had shifted something deep within her, when she had heard that Monica had moved house, she had caught a train to Gloucester, then a bus. She'd gone to the place Monica was living, a strange sort of farmhouse, like something a child would draw, like something on a postcard of England, down a long lane with overarching trees. She wanted to say, What's going on, why did Joe leave, why are we out of touch, what are you doing here? But that Peter bloke came to the door and said that Aoife wasn't welcome and that he'd thank her not to call again. Aoife had stood on the worn step of her sister's house and had had to hold on to the door handle, just to be sure, just to know that, yes, the door had indeed been shut in her face, that her sister was inside, that she had sent her husband, fiancé, whoever he was—Aoife had met him only once; she doubted Monica had met him many more times herself—to the door to tell her to go, to leave, to not come back. Was Monica watching from inside? Aoife had wondered later. Was she behind one of those net curtains, peeping out as she, Aoife, had stood on the doorstep, tears scoring her face. Aoife scrubbed them off, started back down the path, nearly tripping over a cat, and around the corner, on the lane, she had had to stop, to put her hand on a wall because she was shaking so much she couldn't walk.

By day, in New York, she straightened tubes of paint in an art-supplies store, sorted brushes by size, polished the glass display cabinets, working until her face appeared, and she was always surprised at how serious she looked.

Mainly, she lived. She got on with the small acts of life. She continued to ensure that—in the phrase she always used inside her own head—she got away with it. No one found her out. She got into bed each night and closed her eyes with relief that one more day had gone past in which no one had rumbled her.

She has, over the years, perfected a number of tried-and-tested methods to cover up her problems with the printed word. She says she is shortsighted or has forgotten her glasses or that her eyes are tired. In a restaurant or a diner, she will shut her menu—not too fast, never too fast—turn to whoever is with her and say, with a confidential half-smile, Why don't you order for me? She has an eye for the kind of person who is only too happy for a chance to show off the speed of their reading or the neatness of their handwriting or their flair for composition; she will seek them out to say, offhandedly, Could you fill in this form for me, my handwriting is illegible, you know, everyone says so. She has a casual way of passing a page or book to someone next to her and saying, Read that for me, would you, and then she listens so carefully, so concentratedly, and opens up that part of her mind that records things, like a stenographer, so that if any-one were to question her about the content of the text she could repeat it back to them flawlessly. On her first night behind the bar at the club, she asked the bartender to tell her which bottle was which and she recited the names to herself, like a novena, first forwards, then backwards, testing herself over and over again until she could find them in the dark: whiskey on the far left, then bourbon, gin next to it, then rum, then vodka. No one would ever know. This is what she aims for, what she strives for, every moment of her days: that no one will catch on. She appears to the world, she knows, as slightly odd but otherwise benign, a little watchful, perhaps, a little detached, but no one knows. No one realizes that when she tilts her head and says, Order for me, would you, or when she turns to the row of inverted spirit bottles, each with its convex Cyclops eye, her jaw is locked with the ten-sion and terror of being found out.

She cannot read. This is her own private truth. Because of it, she must lead a double life: the fact of it saturates every mol-ecule of her being, defines her to herself, always and forever, but nobody else knows. Not her friends, not her colleagues, not her family—certainly not her family. She has kept it from all of them, felt herself brimming with the secret of it her whole life.

She'd been in New York for six months, perhaps more, per-haps almost a year, she forgets these things, when she was shelv-ing sketchbooks in the art-supplies store, her mind blurred with tiredness, as she'd been working at the club until four a.m., and she saw Evelyn Nemetov through the window. She was look-ing up at the store sign, which, from where Aoife was standing, said: ꓘꓛATTA TꓤA or sometimes KCATTATRA or KCATARACT or RATATATTAT. Aoife recognized her straightaway: she'd been to an exhibition of hers, several times, in London. Evelyn Nemetov, on a sidewalk in New York, in a raincoat several sizes too large and a canvas hat pulled down low on her forehead, standing there, hands in her pockets, as if she was just another member of the human race. To Aoife, it was as if a Greek god had materialized right there on Fifty-second Street, had decided to pay a visit to the mortals of New York, to see how life was, before returning to her insubstantial, deified form. Aoife stood in the store, a stack of sketchbooks in her arms, and willed Evelyn Nemetov to come inside, to open the door and walk in. And, after a moment, she did. Not only that, she walked right up to Aoife and said she was looking for some tape, not just any kind of tape, the one that was adhesive on both sides. Did Aoife know what she meant? She couldn't find it anywhere. Double-sided sticky tape, Aoife said, speaking ordinary words to Evelyn Nemetov, as if she might understand. Yes, Evelyn Nemetov replied, do you have it? Yes, Aoife said. And she went to get it, and when she was ringing up the tape on the till she turned to Evelyn Nemetov and said, Do you need an assistant, I could be your assistant, please let me try, just give me a chance.

When she first came to New York, she knew no one, she was obsessed with studying families, she felt herself to be broken, like the city, but then she found the club and then she met Evelyn and everything was different.

.   .   .

Aoife reaches the top floor of the building and fishes in her pocket for the key. She pushes her way through the heavy door, easing the bag in after her.

She always gets the urge to shout at this point. That is what you do, isn't it, when you arrive in an apartment with someone else there, someone who is expecting you? She has to stop herself every time. Evelyn doesn't like shouting: it makes her jump and disturbs her concentration. This is not, after all, your average apartment.

Aoife advances over the floor in her too-big boots. She could walk through these rooms at midnight in a blackout, if she had to. She knows where everything is, where everything goes. If asked, she could find anything at all within two minutes. This is, after all, her job. But it gives her a strange, unfamiliar pleasure because she is not known for organization, for knowing-where-things-are. If her family were told that she was good at this, that she could do it, they would laugh and gape in disbelief. But they don't know and no one will ever tell them.

"Is that you?" she hears Evelyn murmur, from what sounds like the direction of the darkroom.

"Yeah," Aoife says.

"My God, I thought you'd been kidnapped. Eaten by wolves. Joined a cult or something."

"Nothing so exciting."

"You've been hours."

"Sorry," Aoife says, resting her palm on the darkroom door for a moment. "The subway, queues, you know. I'll put the film away."

Evelyn has lived in the apartment below for most of her life; she keeps this place as her workspace, her studio, her retreat. Aoife goes into the room they use for storage: what would once have been a bedroom is now filled with shelves, cabinets, cupboards. Pigeonholes stretch from floor to ceiling, along the windows, up and over the lintel. And every single one has a label: FILM B+W, reads one, FILM COL, reads another; FILTERS, LENS CAPS, SPARE STRAPS. Aoife doesn't even glance at these labels, tightly typed by some predecessor or other, because she memorized the contents when she first arrived. She drew a diagram of the pigeonholes when she got home, standing up beside the covered bathtub, drawing arrows and writing what she remembered in her own sometimes backwards, mostly left-handed scrawl. The result, incomprehensible to anyone else, she'd pinned to the shuddering skin of the refrigerator, until she had it committed to memory.

Along the other wall are cabinets containing Evelyn's archives—boxes and boxes of negatives and contact sheets, drawers filled with lists of whom she has photographed and where and how much she was paid and by whom. Files and files of contracts, tax returns, letters from fans and non-fans.

This whole side of the room, Aoife stays away from. Which is becoming a problem with every passing day. She has begun to dream about this side of the room; it has started to invade her nocturnal life. It pops into her head, unbidden, as she stamps bees on the skin of music-lovers, as she clunks whiskey sours down on the bar.

She has got away with things so far. But she knows, this side of the room knows, that it cannot be for long.

Other photographers' assistants she has talked to have said they never do anything other than filing or dealing with contracts or answering mail or raising invoices: they are, they grumble to Aoife, nothing more than an administrative assistant. That Evelyn takes Aoife out on shoots is incredible, they say; Aoife doesn't know how lucky she is.

Lucky is not how Aoife sees it. She feels herself to be cursed, like those people in folktales who are singled out for the random cruelty of some higher being, condemned forever to have a wing instead of an arm or to live underground or to take the form of a reptile. She cannot read. She cannot do that thing that other people find so artlessly easy: to see arrangements of inked shapes on a page and alchemize them into meaning. She can create letters, she can form them with the nib of a pen or the lead of a pencil, but she cannot get them to line up in the right order, in a sequence that anyone else could understand. She can hold words in her head—she hoards them there—she can spin sentences, paragraphs, whole books in her mind; she can stack up words inside herself but she cannot get these words down her arm, through her fingers and out onto a page. She doesn't know why this is. She suspects that, as a baby, she crossed paths with a sorcerer who was in a bad mood that day and, on seeing her, on passing her pram, decided to suck this magical ability from her, to leave her cast out, washed up on the shores of illiteracy and ignorance, cursed forever.

On her first day in the studio, Evelyn had handed her a contract and asked her to check it over, then fill it in. Aoife had taken it and laid it on the table and, when Evelyn left the room, Aoife had bent over it, one hand held over her left eye. There was a sudden, crushing weight on her chest and it was difficult to draw breath into her lungs. *Please,* her mind was saying, she wasn't sure to whom, *please, please.* Let me get through this, just this once. I'll do anything, anything at all. *Contract* she could recognize, right at the top of the page. That was good. Evelyn had said it was a contract. Or did it perhaps say *contact?* Was there an *r* there? Aoife pressed her left eye hard with the heel of her palm and scanned the now undulating string of letters that made up the words. Was there an *r* and, if so, where ought it to be? Before the *t* or after the *t* or next to the *c* and, if so, which *c?* Panic cramming her throat, she told herself to leave *contract* or *contact* or whatever the hell it said and look down the page, and when she did, she knew she was doomed. For the page on the table was crammed with text, impossibly small text, closely printed, words like lines of black ants crawling over the white. They clustered and rearranged themselves before her eyes, they dissolved themselves from their linear left-right structure and formed themselves into long, wavering columns, top to bottom; they swayed and flexed, like long grasses in a wind. She saw, for a moment, a *v* reaching up for an embrace with the empty arms of an *h;* she noticed an *a* in proximity to an *o,* which brought to mind the arrangement of her own name. She caught hold, briefly, of a collocation of letters that said, possibly, *fraught,* or maybe *taught,* but the next moment it was gone. She was fighting down tears, knowing that it was over, that this job, this chance she'd been given, was scuppered, like so many before it, and she was weighing up the pros and cons of just walking out when she heard Evelyn coming back along the corridor.

Aoife wasn't aware of the moment in which she made the decision. All she knew was that she was lifting the contract by its corner, up and away, with only the tips of her fingers, as if it radiated some kind of toxic material. She was sliding it into a blue folder and she was putting the blue folder into a box on top of a filing cabinet.

As she came into the room, Evelyn said, "All finished with the contract?"

And because Aoife wanted this job, she wanted it so badly, and why shouldn't she have a good job, an interesting job, like other people did, damn that sorcerer to hell and back, she turned around, she smiled her confidential half-smile, she folded her hands together and said, "Yes. All done."

In Evelyn's storeroom, she empties the boxes of film onto the table and starts to stack them in their respective places.

Since that day, over the many months she's worked for Evelyn, the blue folder in the box on top of the filing cabinet has swelled and grown. Every bit of paper she is handed, every letter she opens, every request or application or contract that comes through the door, she puts in there. Anything with numbers and dollar signs—checks and bills and invoices—she sends straight to the accountant so she knows at least that the money is going into and out of the business. But everything else gets put in the folder. To deal with later. When she can. As soon as she's worked out how to do it. And she will. It's just a matter of time. Any day now, she will get down the blue folder, which is bulging, sides straining, and deal with it. Somehow.

She slides box after box of film into the pigeonholes. "How's it looking?" she calls.

Evelyn appears in the doorway. A tall woman, she towers over the diminutive Aoife by at least a foot. Her mink-gray hair is pulled back from her face and held in what looks to Aoife like a bulldog clip; her shirt, which must be an old one of her husband's, has several clothes pegs hanging off its front. She has her long, sinewy arms crossed over herself. "I don't know," she mutters, in her sixty-a-day husk. "It's kind of grainy."

Aoife eyes her. "Grainy can be . . . good, though . . . can't it?" she says, with care. It is never entirely clear when Evelyn needs verbal reassurance or just mute understanding.

"Not grainy." Evelyn runs a hand along the shelf. She stops by a box of lightbulbs and frowns at it. "Murky."

"Murky?"

"Murky-grainy."

Aoife picks up the last box of film.

"Did you send off that magazine contract?" Evelyn says suddenly.

The sides of the box are slippery, textureless; it falls from Aoife's fingers as if drawn to the floor by a magnet. "I . . . um . . ." she gets out, as she fumbles on the tiles for the film. "I'm sure I . . ."

"Odd," murmurs Evelyn, at the window now. "They called to say they hadn't had it but—"

"You need to get ready," Aoife interrupts.

Evelyn turns. "I do?"

"Yeah. You have to be downtown in twenty minutes."

"Oh. I'm having lunch with . . . thingy, aren't I?"

"Thingy?" Aoife raises an eyebrow at her. Evelyn's terrible memory for names is a long-running joke between them.

"Dan? Bob? No . . . Paul," Evelyn says, fishing a half-smoked cigarette from the shirt pocket. "Paul . . . something. Ah!" she says, with a triumphant wave of her crumbling cigarette. "Allanson. Paul Allanson."

"Close," Aoife says, gesturing at the pegs on Evelyn's shirt. "Allan Paulson. Curator at MoMA." Evelyn comes forward and holds her arms up in the air, allowing Aoife to remove each peg with a snap. "Make sure he takes you somewhere nice."

"I'll bring you a doggie bag. I can never eat at these things."

"Thank you." Aoife extracts the bulldog clip from Evelyn's hair. "You want me to come in the cab with you?"

Evelyn shakes her head. "No. I'm not totally useless. You carry on with . . ." She nods towards the darkroom. "Don't forget to"—she waves her hand in a vague arch—"well, you know what to do. Maybe you should go to the store and pick up some things for the refrigerator. It looks horribly empty. Take some money."

"Don't worry." Aoife follows Evelyn to the door, where she hands her a jacket and then a satchel.

At the top of the stairs, Evelyn stops, puts her hand to her head. "Oh, my, I almost forgot. There are messages on the machine. That guy called again. Whatshisname. Kitchen man. He said something about being back in town. You know what? You should just go. Go home. Go and meet him. Everything here can wait until tomorrow." She sets off down the stairs, muttering to herself. "Can't believe I almost forgot to tell her, what kind of a person am I, forgetting that, almost forgetting, Jesus, am I getting so old I can't even remember basic . . ."

Aoife goes back into the apartment and stands on the landing of the studio, clasping and unclasping her hands, knuckles whitening through skin. She shuts her eyes for a moment or two, enough for the chambers of her heart to contract once and expand again, taking in the returning blood. A reprieve. For now. Got away with it one more time—and a phrase of her sister's pops up in her head: by the skin of her teeth.

Then the moment is broken. Aoife opens her eyes. She releases her hands and moves off, pulling open the darkroom door and letting it shut behind her. She disappears, like an actor into the wings, swallowed up by the gloom.

The answering machine glows with four messages. The first one is from a magazine editor, the next from the assistant of an actress Evelyn is due to shoot next month, and there's a long one from Evelyn's husband about the new coffee machine. Then another voice comes on the line: "Hey, Aoife, it's Gabe. I'm back in town, not sure for how long but I was wondering if you were free this afternoon. I know it's short notice but . . . anyway . . . I hope you can get away. You can call me on . . . Actually, that won't work. I'll call again in an hour or so. Bye."

Aoife raises the receiver, listens to the purr of the dial tone and replaces it, trying to ignore the pulse that is suddenly clicking, clicking in her neck. She flicks on the red bulb and goes over to the strips of film, hanging by their ends to a washing line. They jostle and shift, like animals sensing the approach of a predator. She picks up one by its edges and, finding it dry, holds it up to the light: tiny ghosts flare up within the frame, white mouths agape, pale hair on end, the skies behind them dark as Doomsday.

Taking the scissors from a hook on the wall—also installed by her, amazingly, since hammers and nails are not her natural tools—she begins to slice the developed films into strips of ten, counting as she goes.

It always reminds her, this counting, of helping her mother in the chapel before one of the big days, Easter or Christmas or Harvest Festival. Her mother at the altar, slotting lilies and roses into vases, tugging straight the cloths she had laundered and ironed, staying up the previous night, sweating and swearing over the starch and heat and tension of it all. It was Aoife's job to put a hymnbook on each seat, straightening any skewed hassocks as she went. And she liked to count as she did this. "Thirty-three, thirty-four," she whispered, under her breath, "thirty-five, thirty-six. I got to thirty-six, Mammy!" Her mother would reply, without turning around, "You're going great guns there, Aoife, aren't you? You keep it up now."

Aoife keeps it up with the film, just as she did with the Easter hymnbooks, methodically slicing through every tenth frame, stacking the shiny strips in slippery piles.

All this—this work, this apartment, this city, what she's wearing, what she does, who she is—is so removed from what she was brought up for, from what she was taught, from what she learned, that it makes her smile sometimes. The thought of Evelyn in her parents' house, at her convent school, is as incongruous as a flamingo in a field of cows.

Aoife left school without a single qualification. The nuns described her as "quite literally unteachable." She failed every exam she sat (apart from art, in which she scraped a pass). She hadn't written a word on any of the papers. In some, she didn't even bother to turn over the exam sheet, just filled the margins of her paper with doodles.

The local priest, having had his ear bent by Gretta, who was given to regular laments about poor Aoife and what was she to do with a girl like that, what would become of her, suggested that Aoife help out with the Sunday-school classes. They always needed people to read Bible stories to the children and help them draw pictures afterwards. Maybe in time, the priest suggested, Aoife could use this experience to become a teacher.

When Gretta had returned with this news, Aoife had sat in her room, in the dark, looking out of the window. The list of things she couldn't do seemed to her endless. She couldn't hit a ball or catch one, she couldn't spell, she couldn't play an instrument, she couldn't hold a tune, she didn't have the ability to blend in with other people, she always stuck out, was always mystifyingly noticeable, odd, different. She couldn't even read aloud a Bible story to children, and never would be able to.

Gretta was over the moon about the Sunday-school classes. Aoife overheard her telling someone on the phone that they had of course feared that Aoife would never amount to much but after this she might be able to hold down a respectable job.

Imagine, then, the uproar when Aoife announced one night over dinner—Monica and Joe were there but Michael Francis was not—that she wasn't going to help at Sunday-school classes, that she had been to see the priest that very day to say she wouldn't be doing it. She didn't want to be a teacher, she wasn't good with children; she could think of nothing worse.

It was one of the Riordan family's louder uproars. Gretta hurled a plate of spinach to the floor. She would later deny this and say it had slipped from her hand. Either way, spinach ended up on the carpet and there would be a green stain there for years, always referred to within the family as "the Sunday-school stain." Gretta said she would die of shame, that Aoife would be the death of her, that she didn't know what to do with her.

Not long after this, Aoife left. She simply walked out. It was so straightforward she didn't, afterwards, know why she hadn't done it before. "See yous," she said, giving a wave from the door, then stepping out into the light. And that was that, as far as Aoife and Gillerton Road went. They heard later she was living in a squat in Kentish Town. Michael Francis was dispatched to visit her and found her in the back room of a terraced house, cross-legged on a mattress, a half-strung necklace in her hands, a girl with a guitar next to her. The squat had mold on the walls, violent orange wallpaper, a bearded man digging up the back garden and a parrot sitting on top of the cooker. Aoife, Michael Francis revealed, under close questioning from Gretta, was fine. Fine, Gretta shrieked, fine? What was she eating? Who was she living with? Did she look ill, unhappy? Did she have a job? Did he talk to her about doing the Sunday-school classes? Was she decently dressed? Was she sharing the house with men? Men, Michael Francis shrugged, and women. Lots of them. Gretta couldn't bring herself to ask what she really wanted to know, which was, was Aoife sharing her bed with any of them? What else, she said, tell me more. Michael Francis said, after a pause, that he thought her hair was different. Different, Gretta demanded, different how? Longer—he gestured around his own head—with beads in.

The hair beads were the last straw. It was agreed after this, among the Riordans, that Aoife had Gone Off the Rails. Rumors passed from Gretta to Monica and back again about Aoife and drugs; Aoife and men; Aoife and the dole office. There was the time Monica claimed that a friend of a friend had seen Aoife on the canal bank in Camden, selling patchwork bags from a blanket. This was never confirmed or denied by Aoife herself. Someone told Michael Francis he'd seen her on top of a bus in the King's Road area with a man in purple flares. This piece of information he kept to himself. Aoife still turned up, from time to time, for Sunday lunch in Gillerton Road but she smiled enigmatically at Gretta's questions about jobs, lifestyle, clothing, and helped herself to more potatoes.

The truth was that she had given herself a time span of five years. She didn't know what she wanted so she set about sampling all the things she thought she might like. She began an evening class in pottery but left after a term. She helped a friend who ran a gardening firm (the bearded man Michael Francis had spied from the squat's back windows). She worked at the tearooms in the British Museum. She slept with some men, then some more, then with a couple of women. She tried grass, then acid, but decided, like sleeping with women, that, while pleasant, it wasn't for her. She knew what she was searching for: something to set a flame under her life, to heat it into activity, into transformation, into a momentum all of its own. But nothing had, so far. She had liked the pottery; she liked the mornings in the museum tearooms, before they got too busy, when it was just the academics, thinking their abstruse thoughts while chewing yesterday's scones; she hadn't liked the gardening—just outdoor housework, she thought—or the acid or the moldy walls of the squat. She found work as a set designer at the BBC and for a while she thought this might be what she'd been looking for. She could do it, she was good at it; she had the right kind of photographic memory, the right kind of devotion to detail. She could construct a set in her mind, then go out and reproduce it in a studio. But after she was briefed to create a Regency drawing room for the fifth time, she felt her attention begin to loosen and wander.

During her sixth Regency drawing room there had come the split—for this is how Aoife thinks of it, of the two of them cleaved apart, like a tree hit by lightning—with Monica, starting with the hospital, then Joe leaving like that and then Peter closing the door on her, so fast she'd had to shuffle backwards. The humiliation, the shock of it. The man almost a stranger, after all. Her sister somewhere in the house behind him; the knowing Monica was there. Going down the path, Aoife had been seized by an urge to throw back her head like a wolf and call her name—Monica, Monica—the way she used to when she was little and Monica was minding her, their mother out somewhere, and she couldn't find Monica, had lost her in the house. Aoife would stand in the hall and shout her name, terror building in her chest. Shapes were passing and passing outside the sunburst-patterned glass in the front door: what if one of them were to turn, come up the path and loom large and faceless through the striated pane? The space under the sofa was beginning to bother her, the way the stuffing hung down limp in places, like the bodies of rodents. And the hole in the skirting where the old boiler used to be—a horrible mouth into the dark, cluttered intestines of the house. She made it into the hall and no farther because she couldn't climb the stairs and run the risk that there would be no one upstairs and she'd be alone up there, the light switches too far up the wall to reach, the curtains not yet closed over the dark, and she shouted her sister's name, over and over. Monica would always come. Always. And she'd always be running. Running down the stairs to her. Running to catch her up in her arms, to hold her face against the soft wool of what she called her sweater set. I wasn't far away, she'd say, not far at all. And she'd make Aoife cinnamon toast to help her feel better.

On the path outside the farmhouse, Aoife had nearly tripped over a cat with a tufty black coat and she had wanted to call her sister like that, wanted her to come running and to say, not far at all. But instead she sidestepped the cat, even though it was coming at her with its tail held vertical and questioning, and made it away down the leaf-crammed lane.

In Evelyn's darkroom, Aoife flicks the switch on the developer and, in its cone of white light, arranges the films in strips of ten, lining up the frames the way Evelyn likes: each one trapping a moment in life, a glass placed over a bee.

She is just lining up the last one when the phone startles into life. She leaps across the room and lifts it to her ear. "Nemetov Studio, Aoife speaking."

"Hey."

She drops to the floor, almost with relief, pulling the phone into her lap. "You're back," she says.

"I am. I got in this morning. I took a train. Several trains, in fact. You wouldn't believe how long I've been traveling."

"You can tell me later."

"I can?" She hears the smile in his voice. "You can get away?"

"Sure. Evelyn's gone off for a lunch and I've been officially set free for the day."

"Your place? In half an hour? Forty minutes?"

"I'll see you then."

She shuffles the contact sheets into a rough heap, empties the developing trays and rinses them under the tap. When she emerges from the darkroom, she is surprised by the blaze of afternoon sun, taken aback not to find an answering dark in the apartment, as if she's lost track of the day, the season. Aoife darts about the apartment, in search of her scattered jacket, sunglasses, keys, bag. She makes her way downstairs, out of the building and down the steps into the subway.

The platform is crowded, the heat overwhelming, but the passing and passing of trains bring a sudden, relieving movement of air. Aoife takes her place among all the other people waiting. To her left two men are arguing in Italian, one smacking his forehead for emphasis; to her right is an elderly woman in a fox fur and lace gloves. For some reason, Aoife's mother surfaces in her mind. Gretta had told her once that her aunt had a fox fur and that she'd loved the way its mouth had a spring that would clip over its tail.

Aoife stands on the platform, subway breeze stirring the hem of her dress, thinking of her mother as a child, the head of a fox in her hands. Then her train arrives and she moves forward. In the crush to get through the doors, she allows the tendrils of the fox to brush against her arm.

When she emerges at Delancey Street, Aoife knows she ought to go to the store. She needs milk, she needs cereal, a loaf of bread: basic food items that most people have in their apartments. She hovers outside a store, she contemplates a display of oranges, she picks up a peach and stands there with it in her hand, feeling its solidity, its mouselike skin. A woman with a child balanced on her hip reaches across her for a bunch of bananas and says, as if to Aoife herself, You'll get what's coming to you. In the doorway an old man is laboriously counting coins from one hand to the other. Impatience seems to envelop Aoife like a cloak; she finds she cannot face going in, cannot face waiting in line to pay. She puts down the peach, carefully, so that it nestles among others of its kind. As she walks away, the child is refusing the proffered banana with a high-pitched wail.

She lets herself into her apartment with a feeling of such relief it's as if she hasn't seen it for weeks. She leans against the door to close it, lets her bag fall to the ground; she chucks her keys onto the board that covers the tub, straightens the sheets and starts to kick things under the bed—loose clothes, used mugs, odd shoes. She is just pushing a bundle of scattered clothes into the bottom of the closet when there is a knock at the door, and suddenly Gabe is there, and he is lifting her off her feet and his hair is shorter and his jacket is wet and he is saying something about what a shithole of a neighborhood this is and how can anyone in their right mind live here?

. . .

Aoife met Gabe on a shoot, three months previously. Evelyn was doing portraits of people in their workplaces. She'd done a tattooist, brandishing a needle in his parlor, a dog groomer beside her array of brushes, a costumer in a back room at the Met, her mouth bristling with pins. The last in the series was to be a chef famous for his temper, his exacting secrecy over recipes and the snaking queues of Manhattanites eager to get a table at his restaurant.

Evelyn wanted Arnault, the chef, leaning against a counter in his kitchen. She liked the kitchen, Aoife could tell, a place of steam and gleaming steel, the racks of knives, the stacks of plates, the burners roaring like dragons. Arnault, however, had other ideas. He wanted to be photographed in his tailored suit, among the mirrors, candles and gilt chairs of his restaurant.

Aoife had said nothing during the debate. She unpacked the bags. She opened the tripods. She set up the lights, taping the leads to the floor so that no one would trip. She loaded the cameras with film, set out an array of lenses she thought Evelyn might need. She unfolded the reflector, propped it against the wall. She did all of this in the kitchen: she knew Evelyn would get her way. And, sure enough, just as she was taking Polaroids from various angles, Arnault came back into the kitchen wearing his chef's whites. Aoife didn't meet his eye but busied herself laying out the drying snaps for Evelyn to see.

But Evelyn didn't look at them. She rarely did. She drifted into the room; she moved towards the window, then away from it. She stood for a moment, watching the junior chefs slicing and dicing vegetables into cubes and discs.

Then she moved quickly but imperceptibly, with a minimum of words. She got Arnault to sit on the gleaming chrome counter. He held a knife in each hand. His white top was half undone, his hair combed smooth under his pushed-back cap. Aoife looked through the lens as Evelyn directed her subject. His bearlike frame seemed diminished in the distorted, aquatic, convex world of the camera but Aoife could see that in the finished product he would appear huge, looming, dominating.

At this point, Evelyn appeared at her elbow. She had a peculiar way of moving so that you hardly noticed her. Evelyn looked at Arnault, or through him or around him, as he turned, ranting at one of his assistants about some past misdemeanor.

Aoife handed Evelyn a Polaroid. "I wasn't sure you'd want—"

"Lights," Evelyn filled in.

"So I didn't put them on. I could, if you wanted—"

"No. No need. I like the . . ." Evelyn trailed off, gesturing at something she believed Aoife could see. "But I'm not sure about the . . ."

They both considered Arnault, in profile, still ranting, their heads on one side.

"We could move him," Aoife suggested.

"Hmm." Evelyn turned and they both considered the empty space by the window. "But the sous chefs . . ."

"The sous . . . ?"

"Kitchen porters. Sous chefs. Whatever they are. I like them."

"Ah. Maybe behind him?"

"Yes. Two on . . ."

"Each side."

Aoife arranged them, getting them into frame. When she peered down the lens again, she smiled. The angle made the sous chefs appear small, slight pygmies behind their master.

Evelyn held out her hand for the Polaroid. She glanced at it, she pushed her hair back off her face, she stepped up to the camera, and Aoife found that she, as she always did at this point, exhaled, a long, outgoing breath and she waited for the reassuring *click-sclurr-click* of the camera's intricate inner machinery.

But there was just silence. Evelyn straightened up. She frowned. She said, "Oh."

Aoife darted forward. "What?" She glanced over the camera, she examined the light in the room. "What's the matter?" She looked back at Arnault and saw that something was wrong. What was it? Arnault was there, crouched threateningly on his counter, the sous chefs huddled behind him; the knives were flashing pleasingly in the sun. But something was missing. Then she saw that one of the sous chefs wasn't there. He'd gone. Instead of four, there were now three.

Aoife found him out the back, by the garbage cans, smoking a cigarette.

"Hi," Aoife began, resisting the urge to seize his sleeve and drag him back in. "When you've finished, do you think you could—"

"That's Evelyn Nemetov, isn't it?" he cut across her.

Aoife raised her eyebrows. "Yes."

"I thought so." He took a drag. "That's quite something, though I doubt he"—the sous chef tipped his head towards the kitchen—"has the faintest idea who she is."

"Right. Listen, I really need—"

"I saw her last show at MoMA. Incredible. Those shots of families living on the streets. Were you working with her then?"

"Um, yes." Aoife nodded her head and then shook it, confused about where the conversation was leading them. "I was. Do you think—"

"Must be amazing, assisting her."

"It is. So, it would be great if you could come back into the kitchen because—"

"I can't be in your photograph."

Aoife stared at him. He was about her age, perhaps a little older. He had the milk-pale skin of someone who spends too long indoors, a lanky frame, wild black hair that fought for release from its kitchen cap and eyes so dark they concealed their pupils. He stood with his arms folded, leaning against a garbage can, looking at her with a frown on his face.

"It'll be published, won't it? In a magazine, a newspaper. I'd love to be in it. But I can't."

Aoife shifted from one leg to the other. "I don't understand. What could possibly—"

He gave a short laugh and threw his cigarette butt to the ground. "You're English, aren't you?"

"No."

"You sound English."

"Well, I'm not."

"What are you, then?"

Aoife sighed. "Busy is what I am. Look, we need four people behind him. The shot won't work if there are three. I need you to come back into the—"

"How about"—Evelyn was suddenly there, stepping between them—"if you wore sunglasses? And we pulled your hat down low? Would that work?"

The man looked at her. He rubbed at his stubble with a palm. "For you, Evelyn Nemetov," he said solemnly, "I would do that."

Evelyn inclined her head. She fished in her pocket and brought out a pair of sunglasses, small blue discs suspended in wire frames. "You can wear mine." And she patted him on the arm as she gave them to him.

"I don't get it," Aoife burst out. "Why on earth . . ."

Evelyn looked from the sous chef to Aoife and back again, or at the stretch of air between them, as if finding some text there that was interesting to her. A shadow of a frown passed over her face and then was gone. "I believe our friend here to be a man of principle. Am I right?"

He put on the sunglasses and gave Evelyn a smile.

Evelyn turned to her. "He's a draft dodger, Aoife," she muttered. "Don't you ever read the papers?"

The shoot settled itself over the afternoon. Evelyn clicked, then looked, clicked, then looked. She shuffled her feet one way, she shuffled them the other. Aoife darted in and out of the set, changing lenses, replacing film, labeling the used reels and storing them in the bags. She'd be working late tomorrow, she knew, developing them. When Evelyn said, "That's it," Arnault leapt down from the counter, enveloped her in an enormous embrace and led her off for a glass of wine. Aoife began the long process of dismantling the tripods, packing away the cameras, taking down the lights. As she was placing the lenses back in their bags, someone came to stand next to her.

"We get left with all the good jobs, huh?"

Aoife squinted up at him. "Certainly do."

"I've got to peel and dice ten pounds of carrots first thing tomorrow."

"Lucky you."

"I hope you at least get paid well for this."

Aoife gave a short laugh. "I don't get paid at all."

He stared down at her, aghast. "You're kidding."

"Nope."

"She doesn't pay you? How come?"

She looked up. He was out of his chef's clothes, in a T-shirt that revealed long, pale, muscled arms. A FIRE EXIT sign behind his head seemed to be rearranging itself to warn her: FIRE SHIT or was it HIRE IT?

"Photographers' assistants don't get paid, generally. We do it for . . ."

"The glory?"

"I was going to say 'the experience.'"

"Hey, listen." He stretched out a leg and tapped the bag with his toe. "I'm sorry I called you English. Aoife," he seemed to consider the name, grinning. "I get it. That's Irish, isn't it?"

"Uh-huh. For Eve."

"How do you spell it?"

She chanted her answer: "A-O-I-F-E."

"Amazing. It's only got one consonant. It's like your parents dropped a pebble on a typewriter and just called you what came up on the page."

She zipped up a bag. "Are you always this polite?"

He grinned again. "How about we go for lunch?"

"Lunch?" she repeated, pointing out of the window at the darkening sky.

"A late lunch," he said. "Come on, you can teach me more Irish. I can teach you six ways to chop a carrot and the best ways to fake your identity. How can you resist?"

She shook her head. "I've got to go to work."

"Work?"

"Paid work. I do nights on the door at a place in the Bowery."

"Not that music club? Everyone keeps telling me I should go there. So maybe I will. I'll walk with you."

. . .

Aoife lies on her back, one arm behind her head. Gabe's head rests on her stomach; she feels the weight of it with every breath. He is trailing his fingers up and over her hip bone, across her abdomen. She touches the newly shorn hair at the nape of his neck. She has never known hair like it: thick, black, standing out in all directions. It is not so much hair as upholstery. Or foliage. She grasps a handful of it and pulls, hard.

"Where did you go?" she says.

"Um," he objects mildly, "that hurts?"

She doesn't let go.

"I had to leave, OK? A couple of guys I know got picked up. It just felt too . . . close."

She releases his hair. "But where did you go?"

"I told you. Chicago. I know some people there. I went to see them and to wait until things cooled down."

"And have they cooled down?"

He turns over so that he is facing her. He lays a hand in the dip between her breasts. "Some things clearly haven't."

Aoife pushes his hand away. "Gabe, I'm serious. Is it safe for you to be in New York?"

He flops to the bed and buries his head in the sheets. She suspects he is doing this so he doesn't have to meet her eye. "I'm sure it's fine. I don't want to hide out in Canada. I mean, I like Canada but, you know, New York is my town, it's my place and"— he takes her hand in his, still without looking at her—"there are people here I want to be with."

Aoife gazes up at a crack in the ceiling. She follows its path from the window frame to the light fitting. "But what about the amnesty-program thing? Evelyn says if you turned yourself in under that, you wouldn't go to prison. She knows someone whose son did it. He just has to do some kind of community work for—"

"For two years." Gabe sits up. "I know. But it's bullshit, Aoife, that program is bullshit. It's a *conditional* amnesty. That's not enough—for me or any of the other thousands of men waiting. I'm not submitting myself to some kind of admonishing, finger-wagging, punish-me-until-I-say-I'm-sorry crap. I haven't been putting my life on hold for almost six years to accept that kind of bargain. No. It's a full, unconditional amnesty or nothing."

"I just thought—"

"It will come, you know," Gabe interrupts her. "The unconditional amnesty. I know it will. It's just a matter of time now. They have to issue it. It's the only way. For the constitution to survive for the next decade or so . . ." Gabe continues to talk. Aoife creeps up from the bed; she pulls on her dress, she fills the kettle and lights the gas-ring. Gabe is ranting now about the minute differences between draft evasion and draft avoidance. She forgets, sometimes, that Gabe was about to start law school when his number came up. Deferments for graduates had just been abolished and he had chosen, he said, not to fight it—it would have been exercising privilege, using his education and background to get out of being drafted. No, he would tackle it like the "common man," he said. He would go into hiding. It was the only way he would be able to live with himself afterwards. Aoife wonders sometimes if he regrets this. She is sure Gabe could have talked his way out of being sent to Vietnam; Gabe could talk his way out of most things.

Aoife opens the cupboard where she keeps her food, finds some chopsticks and a box of half-burnt candles. She opens the other and finds a necklace she'd thought she'd lost and a heel of stale bread. She picks up the necklace in one hand, the bread in the other and contemplates both.

"Come back to bed," Gabe says, holding out his hand. "I'll shut up now, I promise."

Aoife smiles and proffers the necklace and the bread. "Hungry?"

He raises an eyebrow. "If that's what's on the lunch menu, then no. If we can go out for some of those noodles across the street, then yes. But, first, come here. I need to talk to you."

She continues to stand by the stove. "About what?"

"About whether you've thought about what I said."

Aoife's smile fades. Before Gabe went to Chicago, he'd asked her whether she thought they could get a place together. He had sat on the bed, buttoning his shirt, looking up at her, and his face had been full of such hope, such trust that she was a good person, that she was who he thought she was, that she was not the kind of person to hide things or lie about things, and she had found that she was divided, knowing perhaps for the first time that she loved him, she loved this man with his peculiar, shadowy life and his stubborn principles and shoes with mismatched laces, but also knowing that she couldn't share an apartment with him, ever, because how could she hide her difficulties from him if they lived in the same place? How could she keep it a secret if he was there all the time? He would see her struggling to decipher a bill. He would catch her asking a neighbor to tell her what the label on a can of food said. He would hear her saying, I've lost my glasses, and he would say, But you don't wear glasses, Aoife, you never have. It was impossible. She had to tell him no but she had to come up with a way that said no but also yes, and how was she to express that?

She is just moving towards him when she is interrupted by a noise. For a moment, she can't think what it is. A loud noise, one that makes her jump. Then she realizes it's the phone.

"Don't answer it," Gabe says immediately.

"I really should."

"Don't." He lunges for her but she sidesteps him. "It'll just be Evelyn, wanting to yak on about lighting. Or paper textures. Or whatever the fuck is on her crazy mind."

"Gabe, that's mean."

"I know. I am mean. Come here." He grabs the hem of her dress just as she picks up the phone.

"Hello?" she says.

The line crackles and roars with static. Someone is speaking, as if from the eye of a storm, their words occluded by an aural blizzard. Gabe is gathering more and more of her dress into his hands and she is still holding the bread and the necklace in her free hand.

"Hello? Who's there? I can't hear you." She shakes the receiver in frustration. "Hello? Gabe, get off," she hisses, dropping the heel of bread, which hits Gabe on the head with a thunk. He swears and she starts to laugh.

"... with the car . . ." she hears from down the phone.

"What? I can't hear you."

She is trying to wrest her dress out of Gabe's grasp and the line buzzes with incomprehensible speech, cross-sounding, insistent, an insect behind glass.

"Do you want to call back?" she says helplessly, into the noise. Gabe has his arms around her now and he is pressing the length of himself into her back. "Can you hear me?"

And suddenly, astonishingly, she can hear her brother's voice, here, in the apartment in New York, where her clothes lie abandoned on the floor, where there is no food, where she lives alone, where police cars idle at the curb all night long, where nobody comes except her lover, who is on the run from the law. Her brother's voice reaches out of the receiver and Aoife can hardly believe it and the sound of it brings tears smarting into her eyes and she is finding it hard to listen to what he's saying, so moved is she by the sheer sound of him.

"Michael Francis?" she says.

"You need to come home," her brother says.

Friday

16 July 1976

5) (ii) It will be deemed an offence to "steal" water . . . and
will be punishable by a fine of no more than "£1500"
and no less than "£500."
(iii) To "steal" water is defined as the taking of water from
someone or somewhere without their permission.

DROUGHT ACT 1976
*An Act to respond to water shortages and droughts in
the United Kingdom*

Home

Early morning in Gillerton Road. The loamy not-quite dark peculiar to big cities is only just giving in to light. The brick terraces are still in shadow, the sky is the color of old milk and the trees along the pavements have gathered up the remaining gloom into their branches. The previous day and the day yet to come hang in a balance, each waiting for the other to make a move.

Today, far away in the county of Dorset, a patch of peat soil that has been smoldering for days will break out in flames. The very ground will blaze and conflagrate. Near St. Ives, a woodland will be consumed by a wall of fire moving at forty miles per hour. But, as yet, no one knows this. The thermometers hang from windowsills, from garage walls, from shed roofs, hoarding the heat, waiting; the firefighters are asleep, faces pressed into pillows, fists closed around nothing but bedsheets.

Strange weather brings out strange behavior. As a Bunsen burner applied to a crucible will bring about an exchange of electrons, the division of some compounds and the unification of others, so a heatwave will act upon people. It lays them bare, it wears down their guard. They start behaving not unusually but unguardedly. They act not so much out of character but deep within it.

A woman at the top of Gillerton Road, a Brownie Guide leader, has started meeting the man who runs the newsagent's after he closes his shop. The girl next door, a talented student expected to excel in her A levels, has stopped attending school and is spending her days in Hyde Park, circling around and around the algae-riddled lake on a pedalo, lighting match after match, letting each one burn down to a blackened wisp. A man who lives opposite has bought himself an Italian scooter. He likes the way he can weave its sleek body in and out of the traffic, the way it sings as it accelerates past lumbering buses. He likes the way the hot air and exhaust fumes swoosh over his skin, through his hair. He likes the puttering growl of the engine and the dazzling gleam of the sun off the chrome. And, as most people on the street now know, Mr. Riordan at number fourteen has disappeared, just upped and left, and his family have no idea where he's gone or when he's coming back. If he's coming back.

A fox skitters out from behind a parked van, pauses in the middle of Gillerton Road, then disappears over a garden wall with a circular flourish of tail. An early tube train shudders beneath the paving stones; the reverberation is felt in the houses' brickwork, their window frames, the floorboards and plasterwork. A percussive, trembling hum travels along the street, passing from one end of the terrace to the other. But the houses are used to it and so are the occupants. Tumblers judder together on kitchen shelves, a carriage clock on a mantelpiece in number four makes a half-strike; an earring left on a bedside table across the street rolls to the floor. Farther down the row a woman turns over in bed; a baby wakes and finds itself inside the rib cage bars of its cot and wonders, What is this, and, Where is everyone, and calls out for someone to come, now, please.

Aoife Riordan, walking down the middle of the road, hears the child's cry. It makes her turn her head. Her gaze passes over the shut curtains, the limp-blossomed hydrangea bush in the front garden, the tricycle abandoned halfway up the path, but she doesn't see these things, doesn't register their existence. She is barely even aware of the child, still crying, or what made her look that way.

It is the most disconcerting sensation for Aoife, walking down this road. She is at once conscious of its utter familiarity—the way the sight of her own hand, the boned row of knuckles, the flat fingernails, are familiar—and its disquieting strangeness. It has the upsetting surreality of a dream, this walk down Gillerton Road at six a.m. in the middle of summer. What is she doing here? How did she come, in the space of a night, from the apartment in New York, where she and Gabe had been together for the first time in weeks, to this—a road she has walked down a thousand thousand times, to and from school, back from the corner shop carrying her mother's cigarettes and a pound of flour, from those awful dance lessons, from her chess club after school, from the tube station? She feels light-headed and small waves of nausea keep breaking over her. She has thought, in the last three years, that she might never come back, might never walk down Gillerton Road again. And yet here she is. Here is the row of trees, roots rupturing the paving slabs. Here are the tiled front paths. Here is the triangular-capped concrete wall that runs along the fronts of five houses. She knows without putting her hand on it the exact rasping, grainy texture of the concrete, how it would feel to try to sit on its unyielding, unfriendly ridge, the way the inevitable slide off it would catch and mark the fabric of your serge school skirt. The adult Aoife suddenly sees that its shape is specifically designed to stop people—children—sitting on it and she is filled with disgust for the people in these houses who would put up such a wall. What kind of human being denies a rest to a child coming home from school?

Aoife gives the wall a kick.

Then she continues down Gillerton Road. Another eleven houses and she'll be there.

She yanks her bag higher on her shoulder. It's Gabe's duffel bag; her only suitcase disintegrated ages ago. Its presence is oddly comforting to Aoife. There is something in its worn, scuffed folds that is undeniably him, contains his essence. She is glad to have it here with her; it could almost be, standing in this street, that she's slipped through a loophole in time and that he and New York don't exist. The duffel bag is proof. She didn't make him up.

She looks up into the branches of the trees. Silver birches. She'd never noticed that before: they are all silver birches along this street, trunks peeling and curling, heart-shaped leaves limp and yellow. Poor things. When did they last have a bit of water? Hard to tell.

Everything looks smaller. Shorter. The trees, the houses, the curbstones, the garden gates. As if the whole street has subsided a foot or so into the ground.

Aoife presses the toe of her sneaker into the soil around the tree. Nothing. Not even the slightest give. Just dry soil, the consistency of kiln-dried clay.

She should go. Silly to delay like this.

Another tube train passes beneath the road. Aoife stands still a moment longer, feeling its reverberations pass up into the soles of her feet, her shins, her thighbones, her pelvis and then her spine. London, the city, entering her, claiming her again.

She touches her hand to the silver-birch trunk: the crackle of bark against her palm. Then she walks on.

The house, when she comes to it, has a green front door. It gives Aoife a shock. It's always been red, ever since she can remember. A cheerful color, her mother always said, gives people a proper welcome. Her father would have painted it, standing out here in the clothes he kept specially for jobs like that—emulsion-pocked trousers, shirts with worn-out collars. When she was small, she would have been out there to help him, watching as he scorched off the old paint with a blowtorch that made the air around it shudder. Her father had never been one for chat—her mother had made up for that, of course, filling the airwaves in their house—but he would have let her help him tip the paint into the tray, would have stood by so she could watch the thick red ooze spread itself into all four corners, perhaps rested a hand on her shoulder for a moment.

She thinks of her father walking down this path, knowing he was leaving, knowing he was off and not telling any of them. Where are you? she says inside her head. Where did you go?

As she stands there on the pavement, the front door, newly green, with the brass number "14" slightly askew, opens. For a split second, Aoife thinks that her father is about to step out, to collect the milk from the step, that it's all been a mistake, that he's back, it was simply a misunderstanding.

But it's not her father. It's her mother, stepping over the threshold into the dawn-lit street, in slippers and a housecoat, easing the door closed behind her in a pantomime of consideration. Of course it's her mother—she's always had strange sleeping habits: those pills she constantly takes have wrecked her body clock. She looks older, Aoife thinks, with a slight shock. No, not older. More vulnerable, somehow. Her hands anxious as they clutch the rim of a dustbin. Her hair dyed a peculiar teak color, growing out. Can it only be three years?

"Mum," she says.

Gretta whirls around, her face full of fear. She says, incongruously, "What?"

"Mum," Aoife says again. "It's me."

"Aoife?"

It strikes Aoife in that moment that her mother is the only one who can properly pronounce her name. The only person in whose mouth it sounds as it should. Her accent—still unmistakably Galway, after all these years—strikes the first syllable with a sound that is halfway between *e* and *a,* and the second with a mysterious blend of *v* and *f*. She drives the name precisely between both "Ava" and "Eva" and "Eve," passing all three but never colliding with them. Aoife, she says, exactly, and like no one else.

"Yes," Aoife replies, and puts down the duffel bag.

There is a woman standing at the end of her path, speaking to Gretta in a voice she knows. She has a scarf bound around her head and a bag at her feet.

"Dear God," Gretta says, and she almost drops the rubbish she's holding. "Is that you?"

The air is still at this hour, already thick with rising heat. Gretta gropes her way through it, the air between them, and then she has the girl by the arm, by the neck, by everything. She is right there in her arms, her third child, her surprise, her baby, her heartache. All the space and distance that has been separating them is gone, has been collapsed down. This is Aoife and she is here. She is surprised by many things but especially by the height of her. Gretta has always had it that Aoife is the same size as her—small, petite, however you want to say it. But now she sees that Aoife is taller than her by a good few inches. How did that happen?

"What are you doing here?" Her voice comes out as chiding; she can't help it. "I was about to phone you. I know you're five hours ahead so I—"

"Behind."

"What?"

"Behind. New York's five hours behind, Mum. Not ahead."

"Well, anyway, I was going to tell you not to come. I don't like to put you to all that trouble. Michael Francis told me you were planning on coming and I said to him, Michael Francis, don't go bothering your sister with all this. She has her own life to lead and she won't be wanting to coming over here to—"

"Of course I'd come." Aoife pats her shoulder. "I did come. Here I am."

Her daughter is gazing at her and Gretta feels that she must look a sight, out here on the front path at this hour of the morning. She puts her hands to her hair and then her cheeks. "Here you are," she whispers, then bursts into tears.

.   .   .

Michael Francis realizes that a fraught scenario involving a colleague and a bicycle is in fact a dream only when he becomes aware that he is lying in an extremely narrow bed and that he can hear his sister Aoife talking.

He allows himself to roll onto his back—a bloody narrow bed this is, not made with men of six foot four in mind, not at all—and finds himself looking at a ceiling he knows by heart. The what-do-you-call-it, the slope thing that covers the right angle where the walls join with the ceiling—*coving*, is it?—in three tiers. As a boy, he used to long to invert the room so that he could walk in bare feet on that pristine white space, touch the light fitting, run his toe over the coving. Is the word *coving*? Monica's husband would know. He's a terrible one for the correct terms for things no one else cares about. What was the thing he was going on about the last time they saw him? The word for the gaps between the teeth in a comb. He's forgotten it now, of course, but at the time he wanted to say: Who cares? Who'd ever need a word like that?

His mind proceeds to display for him the realities of the day ahead, around and around, like horses on a carousel.

He's in the room that was his for the first eighteen years of his life, the small one squeezed between where his parents sleep and the back room, which Monica and Aoife used to share.

His father has disappeared.

He had a row with Claire late last night, one of those terrifying rows where suddenly an end you never thought would come rears up in front of you, like a cliff edge you weren't aware of. A row in which you can hear the roar of the sea below, the boom of waves against the rocks.

He doesn't have to go to work. Not today, not tomorrow, not for six whole luxurious weeks. He has a summer's respite from the job he loathes, the job he took because he had to, the job he thought would be temporary, the job of which his wife seems to have no appreciation whatsoever, no sense of the sacrifice he makes daily by performing it.

Aoife is here. She is back after three years.

She seems, he suddenly notices, to be speaking in a series of questions. He frowns, straining to hear what's being said down there.

"And what did he say?"

"There was no further mention of it?"

"How about the hospitals?"

"Well, did you ask him?"

"You're sure there's no sign of it?"

"Is there someone there we can speak to?"

"And there's nothing else you can think of?"

It strikes him as odd that he can't hear Gretta's side of the conversation. Their mother has always had what a neighbor once politely referred to as "a very clear speaking voice." His mother's voice has blighted his life from an early age. He was six, possibly seven, in the lead at a school sports day sack race when he heard Gretta relating that Michael Francis still wet the bed. Needless to say, he did not win that particular race. At his wedding he was aware, even as he said his vows, that his mother was telling one of Claire's aunts that she'd known he'd marry young because he had started "messing with himself" at twelve. Which was altogether very early for "that kind of thing," wasn't it?

Claire claimed that it wasn't as bad as he thought, that he was too sensitive about it. But his mother had always embarrassed him, always shown him up. He used to look at other mothers, on parents' night, on Sunday-school outings, at street parties, on the steps after Mass, and wonder why he couldn't have a mother like them. Slim, stylish, mostly silent. Why did his have to be so overweight, so eccentrically dressed, so loud, so uninhibited, so wild-haired, so keen to tell everyone her life story? He used to cringe at the sight of the tent-sized, flower-splotched frocks, run up in the evenings on the sewing machine, the way her feet bulged over the straps of her shoes, her offers, often to complete strangers, of a sandwich from a plastic container, a sausage roll or a rock cake. It used to affect him physically—a weak, hot feeling in his limbs, a gathering of something behind his forehead. He used to insist on sitting apart from her in buses and trains, at any public gathering, just in case anyone made a connection between her and him.

"There's nothing else gone?" Aoife is saying downstairs. "Would you like me to look?"

What has happened? he wonders, as he lies there. Could it be that the shock of his father leaving has affected their mother's vocal cords?

Then he feels ashamed of himself.

He heaves himself out of bed, makes his way downstairs. In the doorway, he sees the reason for his mother's apparent reticence. Gretta has her head in a cupboard.

She is given, biannually, perhaps less, to what she calls a "good old clear-out." These rare frenzies of housework are often precipitated by trouble of one kind or another. A spat with Bridie, the new priest giving her "a funny look," someone pushing in front of her in a queue, a doctor refusing to take one of her self-diagnoses seriously. For a day or two, she will stamp about the house, emptying shelves, pulling the contents out of wardrobes, yanking things out of drawers, sorting her stray ornaments and tablecloths and hoarded crap into heaps. A porcelain foal attached by a gold chain to its mother, missing only one leg, a snuffbox with a jeweled lid, a bone-china teacup with a pattern of a Chinese lady crossing a bridge, minus its handle. All these treasures, collected over a lifetime of haggling in every jumble sale, every church bazaar, every junk shop in the area, will be tossed into random piles, some to keep, some to mend, some to give away. Then she will lose interest in the project. Back it will all go. The mantelpiece will be restocked, the shelves reloaded, the cupboards restuffed. Ready for next time.

"Morning," he says. "Having a good old clear-out, are we?"

She rears back out of the cupboard and looks at him over the opened door, and her face is so confused, so childlike in its bewilderment, that his irritation shrivels instantly. He realizes that, just for a moment, she'd mistaken him for his father. Their voices are similar, have the same timbre. What a thing this is to happen at her age.

He crosses the room and gives her a hug. She protests, of course, but hugs him back. The coral ring tree she is holding gets spiked into his spine. And then someone else is in the room, darting out from the kitchen, someone with a mass of hair and a fierce grip on the back of his neck as she hugs him. He is saying her name, *Aoife,* but part of him refuses to believe it's her because she looks so different.

"Wait, let me see you." He pushes her to arm's length. "My God," is all he can say.

"What kind of a greeting is that?"

"You look . . ." He doesn't know how to finish his sentence, doesn't know what he wants to say. "Completely different" isn't right because she is still unmistakably her. But she's also unrecognizable. He might, he sees, have walked past her in the street. She has more hair, but that's not it. Her face is thinner, perhaps, but that's not it. She looks older, but that's not it. Her clothes are different: none of that homemade, hippie-looking stuff she used to wear, but narrow trousers with zips coiling around the ankles and a T-shirt with the sleeves rolled up.

He and his mother look her up and down.

"Look at her," he says.

"I know," says Gretta.

"What?" Aoife frowns and smiles at the same time.

"All grown up," Gretta says and dabs at her eyes with her sleeve.

"Oh, stop it, I've been grown up for years. You lot just never noticed." She turns on her heel and heads to the kitchen. "Who wants tea?"

Aoife holds the kettle under the tap but flinches when the jet of water shoots sideways, soaking her wrist. Something is not right. This house, which she has known all her life, is playing tricks on her. Doorways she has passed through ten thousand times seem suddenly narrower, catching her elbow on their sharp edges. Rugs she lay on as a baby, toddled over as a child, are conspiring to trip her, to catch in her shoes. Shelves are lower, able to land a blow on her temple. Light switches have moved from one side of a window to the other. Something is going on.

She dabs at her arm with a tea towel. The row of tea caddies over the oven is mesmeric in its familiarity. She hasn't thought about them once in all her years away and yet she knows their every detail. The slightly dented lid of the red one, the rust patch on the green. "Bewley's," they shout, in a thick, gold cursive script. Is it the jet lag, the being back, the absence of her father? She feels half crazed, isn't sure what she will do or say.

Gretta comes into the kitchen to find the kettle lying on its side on the draining board, minus its lid. The cups are apparently still in the press. Aoife is staring at the shelf, a tea towel wrapped around her arm.

She'll say nothing. Gretta seizes the kettle, fills it, places it on the hob. She reaches out and unwinds the cloth from Aoife's arm.

"You've moved the breakfast tin," Aoife says.

"What?"

"The breakfast blend." Aoife points at the tea shelf. "It always used to be to the right of the afternoon blend."

"Did it?"

"Yes."

"Oh. Well, move it back if you want."

Michael Francis follows them into the kitchen. He doesn't seem to want to leave Aoife for long, he realizes, as if he's afraid she'll fly out of an open window, like those children in *Peter Pan*.

"Would you like the loan of a hairbrush?" his mother is asking.

Aoife spins around. "What do you mean?"

"I just thought . . ." Gretta shrugs as she sits down at the kitchen table.

"You just thought what?"

"That you might need one."

"Are you saying there's something wrong with my hair?"

And they're off, he thinks. Why is it Aoife and Gretta can't spend more than twenty minutes in each other's company without falling into a conversation like this one? Gretta calmly handing out remarks like sweets, but with a subtle lacing of poison, and Aoife hurling them back at her. Aoife is now saying she never brushes her hair, never ever, and Gretta is saying she can well believe it and aren't there such things as hairdressers in New York? He wants to say, Aoife, let her off, just this once, think of what she's going through.

He strains his voice to speak over them: "So, listen, what's the plan for today?"

His mother and sister turn to look at him and he sees, in the widening of their remarkably similar eyes, that they are both afraid, that they are just killing time, filling in airspace, that their hairbrush wrangle is just their way of putting things off.

· · ·

Eighty miles or so northwest of the kitchen, Monica is lifting the nineteenth-century lace of the bathroom curtain and peering through the blurry glass into the garden. She thinks of how she once read somewhere that gradually, after years and years, panes of glass become thicker at the bottom, that glass, while appearing solid and dependable, is subject to a slow, invisible downward creep.

She puts her palm to the glass, as if she might feel a treacle-like dropping. But there's nothing. Just an inanimate cool.

Out in the garden, Peter is digging a hole near the apple trees. She'd whispered, "Make it deep," to him, before realizing that she'd heard those words before, in similar circumstances. Always strange, to catch yourself echoing your parents' words, to find experiences coming around again. The same, yet different. Two wailing children this time. Neither of them hers.

Peter's put on his work overalls for the job. Peter, her husband. She would never tell anyone this but she still finds it strange to call him that, even after three years. The word *husband* is, for her, irrevocably linked with another man. Will it always be like that? A woman in a shop recently asked her if that was her husband waiting outside and Monica had turned and was searching the window for Joe's face, Joe's figure, Joe's waiting pose—slouched, hands in pockets—before her eye lit upon Peter. It took her a moment to compose herself, to wave back. Stupid, really, because what on earth would Joe be doing in a village in Gloucestershire?

People told her, again and again, how lucky she was to be leaving London, to be moving to the country. Bit of fresh air, they said. Out of all this hustle and bustle, they said. She'd love it, they said.

The truth is, she doesn't. The truth is, the countryside scares her. The truth is, she hates this house, hates its uneven floorboards, its historical bloody integrity, its cast-iron range, its rickety doorways, its eternal signs of Jenny, the wronged martyr. She hates her weekends as a stepmother, hates the constant weekly reminder that she has failed, hates the way they twine themselves around their father, the way the three of them sit interlocked on the sofa to watch TV while she must take the chair opposite, all the while pretending she doesn't mind. She hates the garden, full of slugs and flies and wasps and parched flowers and apples that have fallen off the trees too soon and plants whose tendrils hook into her tights. She hates the dark that descends every night, the awful silence, fretted by the yaps and twitches and hootings of creatures out there, beyond the garden's fences. She hates the terrible green screen of trees that press close to the house, their leaves turning and trembling. She hates that there is nowhere to go, no café around the corner, no shops to wander among, to soak up an hour or two, that the bus passes the end of the lane only twice a day. She hates that she can't go anywhere except the twenty-five-minute walk through fields and over stiles to the village where Jenny lives, where she might bump into her, where people look at her, then away, where no one smiles at her, where the woman in the post office takes her money, then slams down the change on the counter, where she is made to feel like a bad person, an interloper, a husband-snatcher. Peter says it's all in her head, that they don't think like that around here, but she knows that they do. I'm not a husband-snatcher, she wanted to say the last time she was there. How can I be when they weren't even married? But she didn't. If she wants to go anywhere these days, she waits for the bus to Chipping Norton, where there is a row of nice shops and a tearoom, where no one knows her or, if they do, no one cares.

She misses London. She misses it the way she missed Joe. A strange, cramped pain that leaves her almost unable to speak. She has never lived anywhere else until now. She hadn't really known that people lived anywhere else, or would want to. There are days when she can hardly bear it, when she walks across the landing of the house, again and again, her arms crossed over her middle, her mind overfilled with images of descending an escalator into the Piccadilly Line on a wet, darkened evening, everyone's umbrellas slicked with rain, of the ten-minute walk between her old flat and her mother's house, of Highbury Fields on a misty day, of the view over the city from Primrose Hill. Homesick: she's found that it really does make you feel sick, ill, maddened by longing. But by evening, she is always ready, her grief behind her, hidden, like a deformity she must cover up. Hair up. Makeup on. Supper on the range. She will make this work; she will not go back; she will not let on to anyone; she will not show them that she's been beaten again. Monica, with her failed nursing degree, her childlessness, her husband who left her: she won't be that person. She will live here in this house with its shaky roof, its skirting-boards that scuttle at night, its moth-eaten furniture, its hostile neighbors. She will live here and she will say nothing.

. . .

Gretta is sitting at the table with her tea, and she is saying, in a barely audible voice, that she doesn't know where he could have gone, that she's been racking her brains, why would he do such a thing? What kind of a person just walks out on his wife on a summer morning and doesn't tell her where he's going? She's asked the neighbors and no one saw him, no one at all, which is decidedly odd, wouldn't they say?

To Aoife, this is a sight almost beyond bearing: her mother, seeming so small and shrunken there at the kitchen table, brought so low. How strange it is when she's always made such a fuss and a scene about minor things. Melodrama is her special-ity, like the time Aoife returned home from school to discover her mother had been to visit a funeral parlor after finding a lump in her throat. She knew she was dying, she knew this was it, she could feel it in her bones, and she wanted a "good send-off" at the "right sort" of funeral home, with plenty of early-afternoon slots, so that there was time for a Mass to be said beforehand and time for the wake back at the house afterwards. It was the least she could do for them all. Aoife requested to see the lump, examined the place beside her mother's collarbone and told her it was an insect bite. Nothing more. Odd, Aoife thinks, that the first time Gretta has a proper crisis to grapple with, she seems to shrink in the face of it, to abandon all of her usual tricks.

Michael Francis is thinking how Gretta has said these things to him, in these exact words, yesterday—"decidedly odd," "his wife on a summer morning," "racking her brains." Every time she speaks these lines, she gives the impression that she's never spoken them before, that the words are coming to her spontaneously, as if she's just thought of them. "Never in a million years expected this of him," she is saying, and there's another one. She's either a good actress or extremely forgetful. But what a strangely selective memory—to be able to remember the exact words but forget that you've said them before. If she says the thing about him being so much happier since he retired, he may have to throw something at the wall.

"The thing is," Gretta says, putting down her teacup and fixing her eyes on Aoife, "he's been so much happier since he retired."

Aoife isn't sure what to say to this because she has been away, she missed the whole retirement thing, but she opens her mouth, hoping that something apt will come out. Beside her, Michael Francis is shoving back his chair and leaving the room.

"Where are you going?" Gretta calls after him.

"For a slash."

"I wish he wouldn't say things like that," Gretta complains. "The whole world doesn't need to know."

"You did ask."

Gretta makes a small noise of disgust and gestures as if wafting away a bad smell. "Oh, you two."

"You two what?"

"It's always the same, isn't it?"

"What's always the same?"

"Always taking the other one's side. No matter if they're in the wrong."

"He isn't in the wrong! He's going for a slash. That's allowed, isn't it?"

Gretta shakes her head as if she's suddenly decided the quarrel is beneath her. "Always taking each other's side," she mutters to the air.

"Well, somebody has to," Aoife retorts.

"What is that supposed to mean?"

Michael Francis looks at a sliver of his face in the tiny, plastic-rimmed mirror over the toilet. His father stands here, on this very spot, every day to shave. He fills a bowl at the kitchen sink then carries it in here, to the toilet under the stairs. "Away from all the bother" is what he said when Michael Francis once asked him why he didn't use the bathroom upstairs. The shaving things are still there: his razor, his badger-bristle brush, his dish of shaving soap, worn hollow in the middle, a tan-colored stain on the cistern to mark where the enamel bowl stands.

He stares at this stain. Odd to find it here. He can see how the rim of the absent bowl would fit it exactly; it's like a ghost of the thing. Did his father shave on the morning he left or not? He touches his finger to the bristles of the brush. Was it used or did his father walk out with a day's growth on his face?

His mother's and sister's voices seesaw back and forth beyond the wall.

It occurs to him that his father must have taught him to shave, must have guided him through the ritual he performs every morning of his life, but Michael Francis has no memory of this. It would have been upstairs: there isn't enough room for both of them in here. Did his father stand behind him as he picked up the razor? Did he instruct him to dip it into the water, to stretch his skin tight? Did their faces appear in the mirror together as he took his first, rasping stroke? He grew tall, taller than his father at around the age of fourteen; Robert had told him once, in an unguarded moment, that Michael Francis got his height from his uncle, the one who had died in the Troubles. It was never mentioned again but afterwards Michael Francis always had the sense that his height made his father uncomfortable in ways he could never understand. But they must have stood upstairs, on a day in his early teens, together, at the washbasin. He strains for a recollection, an image, anything, but nothing comes. One day, he supposes, he will have to teach Hughie. What a thought.

So much happier since his retirement. Michael Francis lets out a bark of laughter but he hasn't taken into account the extreme smallness of the room because the sound hits the wall in front of him and bounces back to slap him in the face.

"All I'm saying," his mother shouts from the kitchen.

Robert had not been happier since his retirement; if you ask Michael Francis, he'd been engulfed with pointlessness. If you ask Michael Francis, Robert's retirement is the worst thing that has ever happened to him. His job had provided an unswervable routine for his life, a reason to rise from bed in the morning, a place to spend the day, tasks to fill his time, and then a place from which to return in the evening. Without it, he is like a boat untethered from its dock, drifting and bumping aimlessly about.

He has no real sense of how his father has been spending his days since he left the bank. A typical conversation between them lately might go like this:

"Hello, Dad, how are you?"

"Well. How are you?"

"What have you been up to?"

"Not much. Yourself?"

Michael Francis suspects that Robert has been reduced to trailing about in Gretta's wake, which, on reflection, his father probably doesn't mind too much. Robert has always adored Gretta, always deferred to her judgments, her whims (of which there are many), her wishes, much more so than Michael Francis's friends' fathers, who tend to take the more patriarchal line. He recalls, when they were children, his father being utterly focused on his mother. If she left the house, which she often did, being of a restless and sociable nature, to visit neighbors or to go to Mass or to collar the priest for a chat or just for a jaunt to the shops for a pint of milk, his father would pace the front room, saying, Where's your mother, where's she gone, did she say when she'd be back? His anxiety would transfer itself, like a virus, to Monica, who took to standing in the bay window, her hands clasped, watching for Gretta, who would always come back, often with her apron still on, rolling up the street and through the door, humming to herself and saying, What's everybody standing about for—are you all waiting for a bus?

As a child he often wondered how his father managed at work, without Gretta to speak for him, to make decisions for him, to rally him along. It was unimaginable, his father spending all those hours without the enlivening force of his mother. He must have been about nine or so when he slipped out of school one lunchtime and, without really deciding to go there, went to the bank where his father worked. He knew where it was because Gretta had taken them there in the summer holidays, for a visit. He and Monica had been allowed to see the vault where people's money was kept, to twirl around and around on a chair, to see the button under the counter that the tellers could press if a robber came. His father worked in a bank. He was the assistant manager. Michael Francis knew this. But he'd still been surprised by people queuing to speak to the people at the counter, by the secretaries clacking away on their typewriters, by the desk with his father's name on it.

So he went there himself, walking along Holloway Road. It was after Aoife had been born, so he must have been nine or ten. He went in through the bank doors, walked between the looped velvet ropes until he found the row of red chairs that he remembered from the summer and sat himself down on one. And when his father's door opened and his father said, "Come in," in he went. He sat down on the chair opposite his father's and he was tempted to swizzle around and around in it again, like he had last summer, but he couldn't because his father hadn't said, What in God's name are you doing here, which was what he'd expected him to say. His father hadn't said anything at all. He was reading something in a file, which he snapped shut so fast it made Michael Francis jump. "Let's see now," his father said, and crossed over to a filing cabinet and wrenched open a drawer. Michael Francis could hear his own heart going *dub-a-dub, dub-a-dub,* his father's back so close to him, his eyes directed down into the depths of the drawer, which contained sheaves and sheaves of paper. He hardly dared breathe and he tried to grab at the sensations to file them away to consider later: the delicious cold of the chair arms, the pencils with impeccable pink erasers at their tips, the proximity of his father, bent in concentration next to him.

Then his father turned and reared back, dropping the file to the floor, and he said, "It's *you,*" and his voice was thin with shock—Michael Francis has never forgotten the sound of those two words—and then suddenly it was all over and Michael Francis was being marched back to school by a secretary. When he got home that afternoon his Meccano was up in a high cupboard and wasn't coming down for a week.

He brushes the tips of the badger bristles against his own chin, watching himself in the sliver of mirror. His father minus his mother is an unsolvable equation. His silence is leavened by her loquaciousness, his order and impassivity the counterpoint to her chaos and drama. Robert unanimated by Gretta is something none of them has ever seen. Michael Francis has never been able to picture his father in the years before he found Gretta. How had he survived? How had he conducted his life without her? Michael Francis knows precisely three things about his father from that strange hinter-life before his marriage: that he was born in Ireland, that he had a brother who died, that during the war he was there when the British Army got stranded at Dunkirk. That is all. The latter Michael Francis discovered one night while doing his homework at the kitchen table, his textbooks open before him, his hand moving his pen across the page, when an arm shot suddenly over his shoulder and flicked his textbook shut. Don't let your father see that, his mother had said, darting a look over her shoulder at the door. He'd taken the book to his bedroom and looked at photographs of fishermen hauling soldiers out of the sea and into their boats, at the map showing the positions of the different troops, and how the Allies were surrounded, pushed back towards the water. He thought about what his mother had told him, that his father had been among the last men to be evacuated and that he'd thought he wouldn't make it, that he'd be left behind, the sea in front of him, the enemy behind him. Michael Francis thought about this story and then, because he was seventeen and about to sit his exams and after that go to university, he shut the book and didn't think about it again for a long while.

· · ·

From her hiding place in the house, Monica sees Peter bending to pick up the cat's body. The vet had wrapped it in a blanket, which was a considerate thing to do, Monica thought. No need for the children to see the—she has to force the word into her mind—*wound*. Peter has arranged it so that just the cat's face shows. Jenny is ushering the girls forward now. They cling to her dress, to her arms, to her hands. How strange it must feel to be attached like that, lassoed like that, by two small people, like Gulliver and the Lilliputians (how Aoife had loved that story).

Florence is throwing back her head and roaring, her face shiny and scarlet. Jenny is hugging her body to her and Monica sees that she is crying, too; she reaches forward her hand and strokes the cat's head, the pathway between its ears, where almost invisible stripes gather and seem to flow through the narrow gap. Monica finds that her fingers twitch involuntarily into the position she might use to do the same. She would like to feel that soft nap one last time. But, of course, she cannot. She cannot go down there. She squeezes the fingers in her opposite hand.

Peter had refused to say that he had put the cat down; he had refused to do that small thing for her. She had lain next to him in bed and pleaded and pleaded for him not to tell the girls that it had been her. But he'd said no, his back to her in the dark. He couldn't lie to them. It was out of the question.

Jessica hangs back, Monica notices, sobbing into her palms. Peter lowers the bundle—a pathetic-looking thing it is, like an armful of old rags—into the hole. He turns and embraces the children, too, and the four of them are bound together on the lawn, a complicated knot of people.

Monica can't watch any more. She can't. She'll find something to do, something useful, set herself a task, put herself to work. She should make a list of people to ring about her father, people to ask, places to search. She doesn't believe this disappearance stuff, not for a minute. Something must have happened. Her father wouldn't just walk out on them, on her. He would never do such a thing, not in a million years.

She won't go downstairs, she won't. She doesn't want to see the girls, doesn't want to feel the force of their anger. And she doesn't want any questions about her father from Jenny. She heard Peter telling her earlier. The cheek of it. She'll have words with him about that later. How dare he share details of her life, her private family life, with that woman? She'll stay out of the way. There's lots to do up here. Jenny won't come into the house anyway, Monica is sure. Why would she?

But, astonishingly, she does. Monica hears her voice spiraling up from the hallway, speaking to one of the children in soothing tones, asking them to please leave their sandals on. Monica stands there at the top of the stairs, frozen, one hand on the banister, unable to comprehend what is happening.

Jenny. In the house. For the first time since she left it. Peter had never told her this might happen.

She can hear her in the kitchen now. Opening and shutting a cupboard door. Because, of course, she will know where everything is kept, where everything is. Someone is running the tap. There is a clink of cups, a murmur of voices, still soothing, the noise of a child still crying. Jessica, is it, or Florence? She's heard that a mother can recognize her child's cry instantly; the same is obviously not true for stepmothers.

She's in the house.

Monica feels moisture express itself through every pore in her body. It's so goddamn hot up here, her blouse tight and wet under her arms. Her joints seem to ache with stillness but she's unable to move, unable to retreat back into the bedroom and unable to go down the stairs.

．　．　．

When Michael Francis returns, everyone has disappeared. The sight of an empty table, discarded teacups, a folded napkin greets him. He hears a footfall in the room above, unmistakably his mother's, that emphatic, lurching tread. The back door is open so he moves towards it and gets a view of Aoife from behind, on the back step, knees drawn up, a line of smoke rising straight up, like a signal, undisturbed by any movement of air.

He lowers himself to sit beside her. She doesn't say anything but moves the hand with the cigarette towards him. He shakes his head and she turns to look at him, one eyebrow raised.

"Given up," he says.

She raises both her eyebrows.

"Mostly." He plucks the cigarette from her fingers and takes a drag. "Don't tell Claire."

She makes a small, scornful noise that means, As if I would, and he feels a rush of how much he's missed her and how much he loves that she's the one person in his family who will always keep a secret, who will be true to her word, and how much of a relief it is to have her here, and he is about to say his wife's name, he is about to say, Claire, about to tell Aoife everything because he knows she would listen until he ran out of words, and then she'd ask a question that would provide him with more words and she'd stay silent until the end, her head on one side, and then she'd say something, something so—

"Is Monica coming?" Aoife asks.

He hands the cigarette back to her, and as she takes it he notices that her nails are bitten down to the quick and he's puzzled because he didn't know she bit her nails—wasn't that Monica?

"Later today, I think." He looks across at her. "She's got a lot on."

Aoife smiles, like he'd known she would.

"Something about burying a cat," he says.

"Monica has a cat?"

"Had. Peter's, I think."

"Oh." She tucks her feet underneath her, rests her chin on her knees. "Look at this place," she murmurs.

He surveys the back garden, a narrow block of land, fitted in between its neighbors, the faded, balding grass, the dried, bloom-less flowers, the etiolated plum tree.

"I know."

"I mean, I'd heard the drought was bad but I didn't realize it was this bad." She grinds her cigarette into the step. "It's so *hot*. And it's only . . . what time is it?"

He turns his watch towards him. "Eight-fifteen."

"Eight-fifteen," she repeats, looking up into the lapis sky. "Christ."

They sit for a while longer. A bee drones by, scribbling on the air near their heads before changing direction for the branches of the apple tree.

"So, what's your view?" She nods towards the house.

He draws a breath. The bee returns to them, then seems to change its mind, heading upwards along the brickwork of the house. "I don't know," he says. "I really don't know."

"It's not good."

"Not at all."

"Do you think he's . . . ?"

"What?"

"You know."

Their eyes meet for a moment, then veer away.

"Done away with himself? Is that what you think?"

"I don't know." Aoife fiddles with a silver chain around her wrist, letting the links fall through her fingers. "I don't know what I think. I never know what I think about him. He's an impossible person to . . ."

"Fathom."

"Exactly. Do you think he's gone off with someone?"

"A fancy woman?" he says, employing a favorite expression of their mother's. "I don't think so."

"Sure?"

"I don't see him doing that."

"Who'd have him?" Aoife murmurs, opening her pack of cigarettes, then closing it again. "Do you think she knows more than she's letting on?"

He turns to look at her. "What makes you say that?"

She shrugs. "You know what she's like."

"What do you mean?"

"You know." She shrugs again. "Sees what she wants to and—"

"Filters out the rest. Give us one of those," he says, and she hands him the pack. He puts a cigarette to his lips and is about to take the matches when they are interrupted by a shout from above their heads.

"What are you two whispering about down there?"

"Fuck." Michael Francis snatches the cigarette from his mouth. He shoves the pack out of sight, and the matches, and turns to look up.

"Jesus," Aoife whispers, "what are you? Twelve years old?"

"Shut up," he hisses.

"You shut up."

"No, you shut up."

Aoife leans against him and the press of his sister into his arm is remarkable—the only good thing about the day so far.

"What's so funny?" Gretta's head and shoulders demand.

"Nothing."

"I'm coming down," she announces.

Aoife turns back to the garden. She raises both arms above her head and, with her eyes closed, stretches her neck one way then another.

"What is that? Some kind of yoga shit?"

"So what if it is?" she returns, her eyes still closed. Then she opens them and looks at him. "How's Claire?"

"Fine." He brushes something off his trouser leg. "How's things in New York?"

"Fine."

Gretta appears in the dark oblong of the back door, holding something in her hands, a long flex trailing after her like a tail.

"Do either of you want a hair dryer that once went on fire?"

·   ·   ·

The Irish are good in a crisis, Michael Francis thinks, as he eases back the clingfilm on a tray of sandwiches his aunt Bridie has left in the kitchen. They know what to do, what traditions must be observed; they bring food, casseroles, pies, they dole out tea. They know how to discuss bad news: in murmurs, with shakes of the head, their accents wrapping themselves around the syllables of misfortune.

A slight mist has gathered on the underside of the clingfilm. The sandwiches are warm, their edges curling apart. But he's not complaining. He eats one, two, then three. The first is some kind of meat spread, the third has a disquieting fishy flavor. The fourth he takes to eliminate the aftertaste of its predecessor. But then he is seized by a frantic hunger. He cannot stop eating. He has never, it seems, encountered anything more appetizing than his aunt's warm meat-paste sandwiches.

Just when his mouth is as full as it can physically be, Aoife appears in the doorway. She has pinned back all that hair of hers. The sight of her neck, her jawbone exposed, touching in their fragility, takes him by surprise. She looks at him, looks at the ravaged plate of sandwiches beside him. She withdraws again without speaking.

The sitting room is full, suddenly, briefly, of cousins and relatives and people he recognizes but can't quite place. He doesn't want to speak with them, doesn't want to meet their gazes, to receive their commiserations. He feels at a disadvantage in the midst of his mother's crowd: they all know who he is, know more about him than he'd like, he suspects, but he can never remember who any of them are. Neighbors? People from the chapel? Possibly both. Word has spread and here they all are, to offer their ruminating, murmuring support. He wishes they'd all get lost, go back to their damn houses, leave them to get on with it. He wants to talk to Aoife, to his mother, wants to sort out this disaster. He doesn't know where he'd start but he knows that the first step is to get rid of these bloody people, that nothing can be done with a houseful of strangers cluttering up the chairs and needing hot drinks. How does his mother stand it?

He approaches the doorway and peers into the sitting room. Not as many as he'd thought. Bridie and her husband; one of Bridie's daughters with her baby on her knee. A few random old geezers, shaking their heads. How is it they all know to come at the same time? Is there an unwritten code that you visit the wife of a disappeared man at exactly ten-thirty in the morning?

Bridie goes from person to person, offering another plate of sandwiches—meat paste, he wonders, or something else?—a word here and a nod there, her expression pleasant yet solemn, as befits the occasion. Yes, he hears her murmur, it is a terrible business; no, she's not getting any sleep at all, poor thing, who would; no word at all, just upped and offed; the police have been no help; will you have another sandwich?

It would be hard to find a more different woman from Gretta, he thinks, as he watches Bridie exclaim how good it is to see Aoife, and how gorgeous she's looking. You'd never know they were sisters, at first sight. Bridie is small, like Gretta, but slight and more youthful, somehow, despite being three years older. "Trim" is the word, he thinks, well groomed. He bets Bridie watches what she eats; her hair has never been permitted to go gray but is, these days, the color of ripe wheat, and stiff, brushed up and away from the forehead. Her house is neat, with a few glass ornaments along the windowsills. Tea is served in cups with matching saucers. He remembers wishing he could live there instead of here.

He returns to the plate, just for a small top-up. One or two more should do the job, then he'll leave them alone. He tosses one into his mouth but somehow misses: the sandwich drops to the floor, glancing first off the toe of his shoe before disappearing somewhere near the bin.

It seems only fitting that this should happen; it seems entirely in keeping with his current situation in life—a man with a wife who seems to loathe him, a man whose family is fragmented, in crisis, a man beleaguered by heat, by drought, by water shortages, a man whose father has run off to Godknowswhere.

He lowers himself, sighing, to all fours and peers into the slice of gloom under the cupboard. He spies what is possibly a sausage, moldering, rigid with decay, the ring-pull of a can, a reel of cotton, what appears to be a desiccated baked bean. How can his parents live like this, in such squalor? It's a wonder neither of them has contracted dysentery. Cholera, even. He sees the pale side of the sandwich, and even though he has now lost his appetite, he reaches in and pulls it towards him. When it comes out into the light, something has adhered to its buttery opening. A scrap of paper. He separates the paper from the sandwich and holds it close to his face.

It is folded in the middle, its edges torn, and it still has a corner of envelope around it. Just visible is the edge of a stamp depicting the stretched strings of a harp. Michael extracts the paper and written on it are the words *and they say the end is coming* in blue ink, a fountain pen, an unfamiliar hand. He lets the sandwich fall into the bin, allows the lid to clang shut, and reads it again: *they say the end is—*

Someone touches him and he jumps.

"Now, Michael Francis, is there any news?" Bridie is next to him, a hand on his arm, in accordance with her decree that any serious questions must be addressed to the male of the household. Another thing that marks her out as different from Gretta.

"No," he says, and stuffs the slip of paper and the corner of the envelope into his pocket. He reaches blindly for a sandwich off the plate she's holding, cramming the whole crustless triangle into his mouth, discovering too late that it's egg, his least favorite filling.

"None at all?" Bridie leans forward, whispering.

"Nuh-uh," he gets out, around the odious mouthful.

"I always knew that good-for-nothing—" Bridie lets fly but is interrupted.

"An awful business," says an elderly man in possession of an astonishingly large pair of ears, who has appeared beside them, and Bridie leaps in with a Yes, isn't it, before they all hear the front door slam and footsteps in the hallway. The clip-clip of high heels and Michael Francis thinks, The end is coming, and also, How come Monica still has a key?

Aoife is rubbing her mother's back, saying, No, no, to a woman on the next chair, we haven't heard from him yet but we're hoping to, anytime now, when she realizes something.

Monica is here. Behind her, in the hallway. She can feel it: she's aware of her sister's presence near her, and Aoife's pulse is thick in her ears. She cannot turn around, she cannot, and then she does and her first thought, when she sees Monica standing there, is: oh, it's only you. It's only you after all.

A wave of affection rises in her—instinctive, reactive— and she feels her face break into a smile. She can see that her sister has taken care with her appearance. She has done her hair in a way Aoife hasn't seen before, longer, in loose curls, swept up off her neck, and although it doesn't quite suit her, doesn't quite come off, Aoife is imagining her sitting at her dressing table with her kirby-grips and hairbrush, her fingers anxious as they tease the hair into shape, and the idea of Monica doing this is oddly touching. It's only Monica, after all, is what Aoife thinks. Just Monica. The Monica she has known all her life, her sister, not the terrible specter of doom Aoife has built her up to be, all that time in New York. It's just Monica, and Aoife is rising from her seat, because that is what you do, isn't it, when you see your sister after a period of years? You embrace her, and whatever problems have arisen between you in that time can be wiped clean, you'll be able to start again, and Aoife is thinking that maybe she could forget what happened that time in Michael Francis's house, that maybe nothing needs to be said.

She has almost reached Monica when she realizes that her sister hasn't even looked at her. Isn't even looking at her. Monica's gaze slips past her and away, as if Aoife isn't there, as if Aoife is an inexplicable, person-shaped hole in the atmosphere. Aoife is an arm's length from her when Monica does a neat sidestep into the hall, saying something about hanging up her jacket because it's a pain to press and she doesn't want to be spending an evening slaving over the ironing-board in this heat.

Aoife stands facing the empty doorway. Her pulse is still thudding in her ear, spurring her on to something, giving her the means to act. But what, exactly, should she do? Her mother is beside her, a vacant smile on her face; the people in the room are getting to their feet, saying it is time they were off. Bridie is clearing plates suddenly. Gretta heads after Monica, saying, Will I find you a coat-hanger?

Aoife goes back to her chair, she sits down. She registers the urge to lay her head against the familiar knots and grain of the chair's arm. When did she last sleep? Not last night, on the plane, and hardly the night before. She feels as though she's made of nothing but paper: insubstantial, frail, infinitely tearable.

She looks down at the plate on the side table next to her, the hailstorm of crumbs around it, the oxbow-lake rings of tea, finding that jet lag gives her a feeling split exactly halfway between hunger and nausea. She registers an urge to account for everyone, to map out their whereabouts, to keep tabs on them. In case anyone else decides to disappear. She ticks them off in her head. Michael Francis still lurking in the kitchen; her mother and Monica in the hall. Gabe far away, across the Atlantic.

Michael comes into the living room. It is blissfully empty, everyone having left at the same time. There is obviously an unwritten code about what time you leave as well. Aoife is slumped in an armchair, brushing crumbs into two piles on the table next to her. One, she begins to sculpt into a long, snaking line. He hears Gretta coming back in from the hallway, the sound of her shoes scuffing over the lino.

"Hi, Mon," he says, and hears that his voice has come out slightly strangled.

Monica doesn't break off her conversation with Gretta but crosses the carpet towards him and presses her cheek to his, her fingers gripping his shoulders with ten neat dents. The figure in the armchair behind them doesn't move.

Monica and Gretta are talking about the bus, about how difficult Monica's journey has been, about whether there has been any news, any phone calls, about the water ban in Gloucestershire and how it's worse there than anywhere else (of course it would have to be, Michael thinks), about whether Monica would like tea, should Gretta make a fresh pot, is what's in the pot already too old, perhaps a fresh one would be best, Monica will make it, no, Gretta says she will, no, Monica insists, because Gretta looks dead on her feet, she should sit down, but tell her first which tea is it she wants. Michael takes a scone off the plate, because he doesn't know what else to do, and he is thinking that if one of them doesn't give in and go to the kitchen and put the kettle on he is going to lose his temper. If they don't stop this goddamn double act of talking about anything apart from the real and urgent issues of the day—namely, their father's disappearance and the fact that Aoife and Monica are pretending that the other isn't there—he may throw something at their heads, then leave and never come back. Feck the lot of them.

Aoife tries not to look at their feet, in front of her on the carpet. Michael Francis's bare, her mother's in slippers, Monica's in burgundy sandals, red patches blooming under the straps. She looks instead at her hands and sees that they are still covered with words, in fading black ink, letters flowing forwards and backwards.

Gabe came to the airport with her. They ate waffles at a stand in the departure lounge, or at least Gabe did; Aoife watched him, smoked a cigarette and fingered the softened edges of her passport.

"It's going to be OK," he said, taking her hand. "You know that, right? You'll find him. People can't just disappear."

Aoife tapped the ash off her cigarette and looked him straight in the eye. "Can't they?" she said.

He looked away. He wiped his mouth with a napkin. He seemed to glance around him, as he often did, as if to check they weren't being watched. "That's different," he murmured.

She cleared her throat, turned her hand inside his so that they were palm to palm. "Listen, Gabe . . ."

"Yeah?"

"I have a favor to ask."

There was a pause. "Oh," he nodded, "sure. What is it?"

She saw that he'd thought she was about to say something else, something about them moving in together. It would have been so appropriate, so expansive a gesture, to say yes, to agree to it here, at the airport, as they said goodbye. She found her-self, just for a moment, picturing the place where they would live together. It would have plants along the windowsills and photo-graphs tacked to the backs of doors, and they would eat off plates in bright, ceramic colors. There was no better time to say, Let's move in together, than now: she saw that but she tried to blot it from her mind, tried to press on.

"There's . . ." She attempted to think her way quickly around the various perils in her path, to weigh up the different risks she was incurring, while all around her people arrived and left, ate waffles, lifted suitcases, as if nothing unusual was happening at all. ". . . a file. At Evelyn's. A blue file. There are some things in it I should have . . . things I've got a bit behind with. I was wondering if . . . if you might go over there and get it. Maybe . . . you could take a look at it for me. Tell me what's in it."

He frowned. "You want me to go to Evelyn's and get a file for you?"

"It'll be OK. She won't mind. I'll ring and tell her you're com-ing. Here are the keys. Would you mind?"

"No. I can go tonight."

Aoife pressed his hand, relief surging through her. It might all be all right. She might be delivered, saved, once more. "Thank you. Thank you so much. I just don't want her to find it while I'm away and I couldn't . . . I didn't know what else to do. I . . . Thanks. You sure you don't mind?"

"Of course not. It's fine."

"Take this, too." She pushed the key to her apartment across the table but he shook his head.

"No, you keep it, it can be—"

She leaned forward, over the table between them, and dropped the key into the pocket of his shirt just as he finished his sentence:

"—a guarantee that you're coming back."

There was an awkward, silent moment, while he gazed at her, as if trying to memorize her features, and she bit her lip, gabbling that of course she was coming back, there was no question about it.

Gabe lowered his eyes, put his hand over the key, over his heart. "Thanks," he muttered. "Might come in handy." He glanced at his watch. "You should get going."

They walked to the departure lounge, she clasped her arms around him until the last second, until she walked through the door. She found she wanted to close her eyes, as if to hold in the sight of him, scared that, if she filled her eyes with too many other things, she might forget what he looked like, might lose something of him.

When she'd stepped through to the other side, she turned and found that he was watching her from behind a glass wall. She went right up to it and pressed her face to it, near to his, so near that her eyelashes fluttered on the cold screen between them. He breathed on the glass and a nimbus of condensation billowed between them, and suddenly a fingertip was etching lines, curves, shapes into the mist. Letters. She watched as Gabe wrote something on the glass, a final message. Four words. Or possibly three. It was hard to tell as the gaps between them seemed to compress and expand, like the air in an accordion. It began with TH, she could see that, which might mean THIS or THAT or THING or THE and it ended with the curved coat-hanger hook of a question mark. But what was the question, that was the question.

Aoife looked at the string of letters, which undulated and swayed, like bunting in wind, and felt tears gathering in her eyes, bitter and alkaline. She looked at Gabe. That old, familiar knocking had started up inside her head, that feeling of not being able to get quite enough breath into her body, as if somebody were grasping the top of her windpipe with a merciless, unremitting grip.

There was nothing else to do. She gave him her half-smile, head tilted, and a small shrug.

It was the wrong thing, she saw that straightaway. Gabe took a step back from the glass, where the letters were being eroded by transparency. His face was hurt, dismayed, and she had to resist the urge to bang her forehead into the glass, to shout, Please, it's not my fault. I just can't.

At the gate, which was filled with people crunching peanuts or napping or sifting through their bags, Aoife took a pen from her bag and crouched to write on her left hand, fast, before switching the pen over to write on her right. She wrote what she could remember of the words she had seen. She had the mad idea that she could show it to someone, ask someone on the flight perhaps. The TH, the long string of letters at the end, the ?, the word that might have been PART or was it APART? She wrote with concentrated urgency, as if the act would rewind the moment of him standing behind the glass, his face falling, as if inking these things on her skin might undo the whole thing.

They emerged from under her nib like the words of bad spells. Then she climbed the steps to her plane, carrying the words with her.

. . .

Gretta seizes her daughter's wrist. "What's that?"

All over Aoife's hand are words and letters, scrawled in black. Some are worn away and some are written backwards, Gretta notices, and a dart of exasperation arrows through her, seeking out its old pathway.

"Nothing." Aoife twists out of her grasp, sprawls back in her chair, looking for all the world like the sullen-faced teenager she once was. Gretta can't get her mind straight, can't order her thoughts. She can't be the person she needs to be, with her children all here for the first time in years. Robert gone. Aoife sitting with a face like that. And Monica over by the sideboard, doing that tossing thing with her head and fiddling with a basket of laundry. The pair of them not looking at each other. As if they were strangers. She can't for the life of her work out how this happened, and in her own family, too.

"We need," Monica says, apparently to the wall, "to all sit down and make a plan."

"You shouldn't be writing on your skin like that," Gretta says, but doesn't know why because what she really wants to say is, Whatever happened between you and your sister, no one had ever told her, do you need a nap; please don't look so pale and sad. "You'll give yourself the septicemia. A little boy I used to know—"

"Died of septicemia after writing on his skin," Aoife finishes. "I know. You've told me. A thousand times. But it's bullshit."

"Aoife, I will not have language in my house."

"A plan of action," Monica says.

Gretta is sick to her back teeth of this. Your father is gone, she wants to shout. Why are the pair of you behaving like this, pretending the other isn't there? Aren't there more important things for us all to be dealing with?

"Any language at all?" says Michael Francis then, over his shoulder. "There's nothing we can do. Just wait. That's what the police said."

"You can't get septicemia from ink. It's a ridiculous idea."

Aoife stands up, so abruptly that the chair leaps back, making a high-pitched squeal on the linoleum. Michael Francis, always the sensitive one, flinches and covers his ears.

"I don't agree." Monica cracks a pillowcase in the air. "Nothing we can do. What nonsense. There's plenty we can do. People we can call, leads to follow, things to investigate. I made a list this morning."

Aoife stands there. Gretta watches her, eyes narrowed. She glances down at her hands, at the unreadable words written there.

"I'm going out to make a phone call," she says, and flounces away, just like she used to when she was a child. Gretta is almost pleased to see it again, the Aoife flounce. Nice to know some things don't change.

"Use the phone in the hall," Gretta says. "That's what it's there for."

"I need to call New York. I'll use the phone box." Aoife gets as far as the door before she turns. "Will . . . the library be open?"

The three of them stare at her: Gretta, Michael Francis and Monica.

"The library? For the love of God," Gretta cries, "what are you wanting to go to the library for?"

"To find a book."

"Well, I didn't think you were after a pound of potatoes. What book?"

"Doesn't matter. Just a book."

"And who are you off to phone?"

Aoife's face is set in an expression they all know well: Don't mess with me, my mind is made up. "Doesn't matter," she says, again.

"Go on," Gretta says. "Tell us. Is there a fella in New York?" She winks at Michael Francis, who frowns back, the miserable so-and-so. "Are you off to phone him?"

Aoife doesn't answer, just glances unhappily towards the tablecloth that Monica is folding.

"Is that it?" Gretta persists. "Won't the man be sleeping at this hour?"

"No," Aoife mutters. "It'll be . . ." She glances at the clock over the window. "I don't know . . . eight in the morning."

"Well, won't he be off to work?"

"Nmm," she mumbles, making a show of searching her pockets, backing out through the sitting room now. Gretta gets up from the table and follows her.

"Does he have a job?" Gretta says.

"Mum," Michael Francis murmurs behind her, "if Aoife wants to make a phone call, then—"

"Or is he an *artist* as well?"

Aoife turns at the front door, pushes her hair out of her eyes—how Gretta is itching to give it a good going-over with a hairbrush—and snaps, "No. He's a lawyer, OK? Or soon will be." She yanks open the door, just like she used to. "Back soon." And slams it behind her. Just like she used to.

"Well," Monica says, lowering herself into the chair Aoife has just vacated, "I can see a few years in New York haven't improved a certain person's temper."

Michael Francis sighs and is about to speak but Gretta bustles back into the kitchen.

"Did you hear that?" she is saying. "A *lawyer.* She's keeping company with a lawyer."

"Really?" Michael Francis asks. "When did she tell you that?"

"Just now. At the door. Who'd have thought it?" Gretta seizes all the linen Monica has just folded and starts to stuff it haphazardly into a drawer. "Aoife and a lawyer." She stops stuffing and turns to them. "Do you think he's Catholic?"

. . .

Aoife stands on the pavement, just outside the gate, turning to look one way up the street and then the other, as if she's forgotten where she's going.

Oddly weighty the British money feels in her hand, her purse bursting open, holding too many currencies: dimes and two-pences, nickels and ten-pence pieces.

Monica, her own sister, sidestepped her, looked through her or past her, as if she weren't there. It was an act that denied everything, that said: we never shared a room, I never once took your hand to cross the road, it wasn't me who bound your head when you cut it open on a railing, you did not grow up wearing my cast-off clothes, you never spooned tea into my mouth as I lay ill with glandular fever, you did not sleep beside me in a matching bed for years, it was not me who showed you how to pluck your eyebrows or buckle your shoes or how to hand wash a sweater. The unreason of it, the pain of it, baffles Aoife. The recollection of Monica swerving away from her like that, after all this time, seems to throb and ache, like a newly inflicted bruise.

The whole thing, she thinks, as she sets off down the street, clutching her bulging purse, was caused by a horrible chain of coincidences. If she hadn't gone to Monica's that day. Why had she gone? What was it now? She'd been in the area and hadn't seen Monica for a while, not since the month before at Gillerton Road, when Joe had announced that Monica was pregnant. Aoife had looked over at Monica when he'd said it because Monica had always said she'd never have children. Never, never, she'd said. Monica had sat very upright on the sofa, her hand in Joe's, her face expressionless, as their parents went into an uproar of congratulations.

So Aoife had gone to the flat to see Monica but she'd found her sister white-faced, hunched over, her skirt heavy and dark. Aoife had run downstairs to the landlord to call an ambulance.

She'd gone with Monica to the hospital, she'd stood by the bed, she'd held her sister's shoulder when the pain got bad, she'd said, I'm so sorry, Mon, I'm so sorry, and she'd wiped away her sister's tears with her handkerchief, and when that was too wet, she'd used the end of her scarf. When Joe had arrived, sprinting down the ward, Aoife left and she'd sat on the bus, with London passing the windows, but all she could see was the brightness of it, the way it was the essence of life but also of death. Monica had said, Don't look, don't, it's bad luck. But how could Aoife not look? How could she let the nurse take it away, as if it were nothing, instead of a person who never quite was? Aoife thought that someone had to look at it and say, Yes, you were here, I saw you, you did exist. Just not for long.

When Aoife returned to the hospital the next day, these thoughts were still churning in her head and she wanted to tell Monica what it had looked like. The fragile curve of its back, the unbearable perfection of its clasped fingers. But the scene with which she was met was entirely different. Her mother was parked on the bed, handbag, scarf, gloves and various parcels strewn around her, in the middle of saying, ". . . nobody knows this but he wore it on a chain around his neck for the rest of his life, under his clothes."

Her father stood by the window, looking out, apparently transfixed by the rotating silver air vents of the hospital roof. Joe was in a chair next to the bed, leaning forward, his hand locked in Monica's.

Monica herself was reclining on several pillows. She was wearing a bed jacket with drooping satin bows and lace-edged sleeves. Her hair had been what she called "done"; Aoife wondered who had brought in her rollers and dryer. Somebody must have, she reflected, because hospitals don't keep those things on hand. Or maybe they do.

Gretta was feeding soup to Monica, spoonful by spoonful. "Good girl," she said between mouthfuls, before carrying on with her story. She didn't offer Aoife any kind of greeting but turned and exclaimed, "Look at your sister! Isn't she doing well?"

Her father said, to the window, "We're leaving in nine minutes."

Monica, waving away the spoon Gretta was proffering, winced slightly and lay back on her pillows. Gretta leaned forward and touched her fingers to her brow, asked Monica if she was in any pain and would she go and find a nurse?

Aoife remembers what happened next so clearly it is as if she watches it on some small interior screen. She looked away from her mother and sister, forever excluded from their tight pairing, and her eye fell on Monica's coat, draped over a chair. It was Monica's smart coat, her Sunday coat, navy, with an Astrakhan trim and frogged loops over the buttons. She herself had lifted it from the peg in the hall as the ambulance men carried Monica down the stairs. It had been in her mind that Monica might be cold, might need it. Joe was stroking Monica's hand, Gretta was licking the back of the spoon, Robert was still looking out of the window and Aoife was thinking: Astrakhan . . . hadn't someone once told her it was made from the skins of lambs, aborted before their time? The pockets of the coat, she noticed, were also trimmed with squiggling, intricate, impossibly soft knots.

Aoife looked from the coat to Monica, reclining palely on her pillows, and back again. Her parents were starting to collect their belongings, their bags, their containers of food.

There is a kind of invisible osmosis that occurs between people who have shared a room. If you sleep near someone, night in, night out, breathing each other's air, it is as if your dreams, your unconscious lives become entangled, the circuits of your minds running close to each other, exchanging information without speech.

Aoife looked at her sister, she looked at the coat and suddenly she knew. There wasn't a shadow of doubt in her mind. She couldn't believe she hadn't realized yesterday, but then everything

had been such a shock and a panic that she hadn't been thinking straight. The clarity of it clanged through her: this had been
no miscarriage, no accident. Aoife saw this. Her mind unfolded
the information and laid it out for her. Monica had done this to
herself.

Goodbyes were being said—nine minutes had evidently
elapsed. Monica was embraced several times, there was a small
drama when Gretta couldn't find her scarf. It was located, under
the bed, put in place.

Aoife continued to stand beside the door and the knowledge
seemed to congest her chest, like asthma. As Gretta leaned in to
clasp Monica in her arms for the final time, Monica glanced over
her mother's shoulder at Aoife.

Aoife held her gaze. The sisters regarded each other for a
long moment, then Monica pressed her teeth into her lip. Color
sprang in patches to her cheeks, and as Joe rose from his seat to
see Gretta and Robert out of the hospital, Monica put out a hand
to stop him. "Don't go," she said. "Stay with me." Joe was patting
her hand and saying he wouldn't be a minute but Monica held on.
"Don't," she said. "I want you to stay."

"But Aoife's here," Joe was saying gently, peeling her fingers
off his sleeve. "You'll be fine."

And suddenly they were alone.

What to say? Aoife wondered. Who would speak first? What
was the protocol in such situations? Part of her wanted to say,
It's not my business, it's your life, your choice, the secret is safe
with me. The other part wanted to say, Mon, how could you, why
would you, what about Joe?

Monica wasn't going to speak, Aoife saw that. Her gaze had
skittered away, towards the ceiling, her chin had risen slightly,
her lips pressed together. It was an expression so familiar to
Aoife—one not so much of defiance but of valiance. Monica was,
Aoife knew, at that moment rallying her resources, mustering

her powers. Monica shook back her hair, brushed an imaginary piece of lint off her sleeve, her gaze directed out of the window. Aoife turned, pushed her way through the door and walked fast down the corridor. She had the sense of being pursued by a pack of animals snapping and baying at her heels. If she walked fast enough, far enough, she might get away from them, might stop them latching their jaws into her flesh.

Aoife turns left at the end of Gillerton Road. She shields her eyes as she checks the traffic, surprised momentarily by a car zooming in on her from the right. Outside the phone box, she pauses, as if to catch her breath, but it's just to wipe the line of sweat from her hairline, from her upper lip.

Gabe's voice, when he comes to the phone, is measured and distant. So disconcerting is the effect that Aoife finds herself saying, "So, how are you?" into the receiver for the second time.

"Fine," he says. "Good."

Aoife tunes her hearing to this new way of speaking, its odd deliberation, its tonelessness. It's the kind of voice you'd use for a friend you didn't particularly like or someone you didn't know very well and had no inclination to know better. Is it because he's at work? It's the early-morning shift at the restaurant, always the most relaxed because Arnault doesn't arrive until later. But is someone listening to them? Perhaps that's it.

Her hand tightens around the black phone receiver. She knows it's not that. She's called him plenty of times at work and he's never sounded like this before. The string of letters written in steam seems to unfurl again before her: THIS, was it, then something, then PART, then something else? What did it say? she wants to ask. Please just tell me. PART what?

"Any news on your dad?" he asks.

"Not yet. So . . . I was wondering . . . did you get a chance to . . ." She winces at herself for asking but she has to know. ". . . go over to Evelyn's?"

She hears Gabe draw a breath. "I did," he says, in his new voice.

"And . . . did you find the file?"

"I did," he says again, and Aoife waits for him to say something else, pressing the phone against her ear. "Jesus, Aoife," he says, and she feels as though he's carried the phone somewhere more private as there is a lull in the air around him. "There were things in there going back a year. Letters and contracts and really important stuff."

"Yes," she says weakly. "Yes, I know, I—"

"I just don't get why you would . . . I mean, does Evelyn have any idea that you've . . ." He sighs. "I don't get it."

She presses her fingertips into the sharp indent of the money slot until they turn white with the pressure.

"I don't know how you could do that to her. After everything she's done for you. There were uncashed checks in there, adding up to thousands of dollars. What were you thinking?"

"I . . . The checks usually go to the accountant but maybe a few slipped through . . . I just . . ."

"I know she's difficult sometimes and I know she works you hard but to just chuck all that stuff in a box and forget about it is, well, it's wrong, Aoife."

"I know," she gets out. "I just—"

He cuts her off. "Listen, I've got to go. Call me if you get any news of your dad, OK?"

Aoife bursts out of the phone box. The heat in there, inside all that glass, is unbelievable. Unbearable. She leans against the door for a moment, gulping for air. But the air outside isn't much cooler and seems to burn a path down into the branched pathways of her lungs. The metal of the phone box is searing through to her skin, she realizes, and jumps away from it. Is there no escape? she thinks. Is there nowhere away from this heat?

The file is with Gabe. This problem has been scratching away at her, like a burr in her clothing and now she knows the magnitude of it. Invoices going back over a year. Thousands of dollars in uncashed checks. What will Evelyn say? Aoife tries to picture the scene: Evelyn will be horrified, baffled, even angry. What she needed, she'd told Aoife when she'd started work, was someone to deal with all the stuff, all the distracting babble of life, so that she, Evelyn, could concentrate on the photographs. And had Aoife done that? No, she had not. She will lose her job. She knows this. Perhaps she has always known it, from the moment she put that contract into the blue file. The only job she has ever liked. And what about Gabe himself and his flat voice, him saying things like, How could you, Aoife?

She glances up at the sky and immediately has to shade her eyes. The sun has peaked above the roofs and trees. It must be midday, or thereabouts. The scene in front of her—cars, buses, shop fronts, a young woman with a pram—shimmers and refracts. The light of the sun seems to have infiltrated everything, boring into her retinas from shopwindows, from car bumpers, from the wheels of that pram.

The idea of someone else withdrawing from her makes her feel unbalanced, panicked. Soon, she thinks, you'll have no one left.

She watches a bus from Islington take the curve in the road, the standing passengers flung sideways, then back.

There had been no answer at Evelyn's, as she'd suspected. Even if Evelyn was there, she rarely picked up the phone. So Aoife had had to speak into the answering machine: she had to tell Evelyn that she had a meeting at eleven, a magazine editor was coming to the studio, not to forget to send off the prints to MoMA. It had cost her almost all of her change to say this, the machine gobbling coins at an alarming rate. She'd have to get more from somewhere. One of these shops, maybe. Couldn't ask them at home. It would provoke too many questions, and how could she answer them, how could she ever tell them when they knew nothing about Evelyn, nothing about Gabe or anything at all? There was too much to explain; she wouldn't know at what point she should start. No, best all around if she just went into a shop and exchanged a note for some ten-pence pieces. Her mother would only worry and lament and dramatize.

She'd been seized by the odd urge, in the phone box there, after calling New York, to phone her father. To dial a number and hear his voice coming out of the tiny holes in the receiver. When had she last spoken to him? Months ago. She phones her parents occasionally from New York, but they tend to view long-distance calls as an indulgence verging on illegal. They treat them as a form of telegram, exchanging the barest essential information before hanging up. They talk over each other, in their haste, both shouting into the receiver, their questions merging and competing, so that she can't hear either of them. Is she getting enough to eat? Is she going to Mass? Does she have a warm coat to wear?

She crosses the road. Black rivulets of melted tar are oozing out of crevices in its surface. She sidesteps these, thinking of that child's game of avoiding cracks in the pavement. If you tread in a nick. She remembers being horrified by the rhyme. Ridiculous, really, when the worst threat is that a spider may come to your funeral.

Her mind snags on the word *funeral*. She passes a hand over her brow, as if trying to erase something from sight, but still her mind persists, offering her images of a coffin, her father laid out inside a folded blue satin lining, her mother twisting a rosary into his stiffened fingers. What other explanation can there be?

She stops outside the library. She isn't sure why she's come: she'd asked about it only to deflect their interest in the phone box. Oddly, she used to spend a lot of time here when she was young. She'd loved its atmosphere of strict, dusty hush, the spines and spines of books. She'd loved to trail her hand down the shelves, as if hoping that, by her touching them, the books might yield their secrets to her. It had never worked, obviously.

OPENING HOURS, the sign on the door probably says and, to get rid of the idea of her father in a coffin, she permits these strings of letters to gain entry to the part of her mind that she strives always to suppress. Immediately, just as she knew it would, it does its usual thing of shuffling and reshuffling the letters, like a hand of cards. "Opening" dissolves into "pen," "gin," "open," of course, "gone," "peg," "gin," "pin," "nine," "nope," "pine." "Hours" tries to make itself start with "hr" and then "sh" and then the "ou" comes rearing out from the middle of the word and—

She cuts herself off. Enough. Needs to be firm with all that because it's the kind of thing her mind can run and run with and there's too much to be done today for all that distracting babble.

A week or so after the incident at the hospital, there had been a family gathering at Michael Francis's house. What had it been for? One of the children's birthdays? Aoife is presented with a definite memory of Hughie's face, startled and awed, behind a flaring seam of candles.

Hughie's birthday. Monica had avoided Aoife's eye the whole time, over the opening of the presents, during the singing of "Happy Birthday," during the endless rounds of tea. She was good at it, this very private kind of cold-shouldering, so that only the recipient and no one else noticed. Aoife couldn't stop herself looking at her sister, though; her eyes were drawn to her the whole time, as if to check that, yes, Monica was still pretending she wasn't there.

After an hour or so, Aoife had had enough. How could Monica treat her like this, as if she were the one who was lying and concealing and pretending? She had done nothing wrong and Monica had nothing to fear from her. She wasn't going to tell anyone; Monica would know that. What people did with their lives was their own affair: Aoife firmly believed this. But something needed to be said between them; that much was clear. So when Monica went into the kitchen to fill the kettle yet again,

Aoife slipped away, out of the sitting room and into the kitchen. She came up behind her sister, standing at the sink, right behind her, so there was no way out.

"Listen," she said, to the back of Monica's head, "I want to say that I don't—"

Monica had turned with a flash. "I often wonder," she began, in a strangely chatty tone, as if they'd been in the middle of a conversation all these weeks, those spots of color again high in her cheeks, "if you had any idea what having you did to Mammy."

Of all the things Aoife expected Monica to say, that wasn't it. Some part of her recognized that Monica was doing what she always did when confronted: directing the focus away from herself, shifting the blame to her opponent. It was a Monica-strategy as familiar to Aoife as her sister's name but she still took a step back, still felt for the table behind her, spreading her fingers against its cool grain.

"What do you mean?" Aoife said, even though she didn't want to know, she had no inclination whatsoever to hear what Monica had to say about that. She didn't want to hear any of it, any of the horrible, terrible things Monica proceeded to lay out for her, in a whisper, as they stood there in the kitchen: it was her fault Gretta took all those tranquilizers, all her fault, it had started with her birth—did Aoife know that she was a nightmare baby who never stopped crying, an absolute nightmare, that she had destroyed their mother, she had; it was she who had driven Gretta to the very brink, brought her to her knees. *To her knees*: Monica kept saying this. And Aoife didn't want to believe any of it—maybe she didn't believe any of it, maybe it was all just lies, it was because Monica was cornered, lashing out.

"Ask him," Monica said, gesturing at their brother, who had walked into the room, "if you don't believe me."

They turned to Michael Francis, who was still smiling at something somebody had said to him in the other room and

Aoife's heart lifted to see him because he was her defender, her pillar of truth and fairness, always had been. If he was here, everything would be all right. He would tell Monica to shut up, that she was talking nonsense. She knew he would.

"Ask me what?" he'd said jovially, putting an arm around Monica.

Monica tilted her head up towards him, her eyes bright with anger, with triumph. "Isn't it true that Aoife was a nightmare baby and it's because of her that Mammy takes all those pills?"

His face slid from his birthday-party smile into an expression of horror. His arm fell, slack, from Monica's shoulders.

"Why would you say that?" he said quietly. "What a thing to tell her."

There was no denial, no refutation. Aoife stood with the corner of the table pressing into her legs and let this fact wash through her: Michael Francis hadn't said, That's not true; he'd said, Why would you say that. And there was, she realized as she stood there, something about it all that made peculiar sense, as if she had been handed the final piece of a jigsaw she'd spent years puzzling over. Monica's words fitted into a space inside her with sickening, exacting precision.

So she left without saying goodbye to anyone. She walked through the sitting room, where Hughie was bouncing up and down on the sofa, his face smeared with chocolate icing, where her father sat, holding on to the tail of Hughie's shirt, so the child didn't pitch off the sofa, where Claire was stacking cake plates, one on top of the other, where her mother was slicing herself another wedge of cake and saying something about the birthday boy, but Aoife couldn't look at her, not at all.

Joe was the only one who raised his head as she moved through them all. In Michael Francis's hallway, she stopped, like a toy whose batteries had run down. She stared at the coats and bags on the hooks behind the front door: a tweed coat with unraveling leather buttons, a mackintosh with a buckled belt, a navy donkey jacket with glove-stuffed pockets, an impossibly small duffel coat with a tartan-lined hood, a snaking raspberry-wool scarf. She stared and stared at them, mesmerized, trying to work out which was hers and where her coat was, and when somebody touched her elbow, she jumped as if hit with a cattle prod.

Joe was standing next to her, putting a cigarette into his mouth. "Where are you going?" he said.

Aoife snatched up her coat from where it had fallen on the floor. "Nowhere," she said, stuffing her arms into the sleeves.

He struck his lighter and lifted the flame to the end of his cigarette, all without taking his eyes off her face. "What's going on, Aoife?" he said, and the lit end of his cigarette wobbled dangerously.

"Nothing," she said, putting her head down to button her coat. "I don't know what you mean. Nothing's going on."

"Between you and your sister." He followed her through the door and down the path. "Aoife? I asked you a question."

"I have to go," she said, and clanged the gate shut behind her, walking as fast as she was able to without breaking into a run. At the end of the road, she turned. Joe was still standing on Michael Francis's path, cigarette smoke unfurling behind him, watching her.

Aoife hesitates at the bottom of the library steps but then, with a surge of decisiveness, because she's here, because she might as well, she goes up them, slinging her bag higher on her shoulder, through the double doors, and is enveloped in the merciful cool of the library.

·　·　·

Minutes later, she is followed by her brother and sister.

Monica stops in the vestibule. The gloom is a relief after the glare of the street and she would like to take a moment to rest her eyes. Michael Francis, not paying attention as usual, barrels into the back of her, pushing her forwards so that she catches her elbow on a leaflet stand.

"Oh," he says mildly, "sorry."

Monica doesn't answer, just rubs her elbow without looking at her brother. "I don't think it's significant," she says, in a low voice. One should always whisper in libraries: she knows that.

"God, this place hasn't changed much, has it?" Michael Francis is looking at the curving dark-wood staircase that goes up to the children's library, the strange metal cagelike structure that contains a lift they were never allowed to use. His voice is louder than she is comfortable with. For all his education, he hasn't learned the whispering rule. "Why not?" he says finally, leaning closer to look into the cage lift-shaft thing.

"Why not what?"

"Why don't you think it's significant?"

"It's just a bit of paper," she says, looking down again at the scrap Michael Francis had shown to her as they walked here. "Torn from somewhere. A letter. There's no reason for it to mean anything."

"But Mum said she didn't recognize the handwriting. Didn't know where it was from. And look at what it says. It's so . . . apocalyptic."

Monica feeds the syllables of this word through her mind, once and then twice.

Her brother glances at her. "Doom-laden," he says quickly. "You know, as in—"

"I know what apoc—what it means, thank you very much."

"Fine. I was just—"

"What are we doing here anyway?"

"We're here to find Aoife." He moves towards the doors into the main library and peers through the glass. "I thought we should talk about things. Without Mum hearing."

Monica frowns. "Why?"

"Because we need some kind of a plan. You said so yourself."

"I meant why can't Mum hear?"

"Because she's . . ." Michael Francis trails away, still peering through into the library, where people are moving, slow as fish in a pond.

Monica sighs, dabs at her forehead with her hankie. "Aoife's probably not even here anyway."

"She said she was coming."

"But that doesn't mean she did. You know Aoife."

"Well, you're wrong," Michael Francis says, tapping the door. "Here she is now."

Monica steps up to the glass. For a moment, she can view the woman crossing the room beyond the door as a stranger might. Aoife is attractive, Monica sees, as if for the first time, her narrow, zipped trousers, the color of hyacinths, fitted snug around her hips, the hectically patterned top loose about her clavicle. Hair pulled up and carelessly secured at the back of her head. Who would have thought she'd turn out like that, when she'd been such an odd-looking, graceless child, her face always so screwed up and cross, forever stumbling over her own feet? Monica remembers being made to accompany Aoife here, to this library, after school. "Walk her along, would you?" Gretta would beg Monica. "I just need a bit of peace." Because Aoife was a terrible one for questions. Why does the Earth only go one way around the sun? Does it ever go backwards? What's behind the sky? How do you know? Who says so? What's the biggest city in the world? What's the smallest? Gretta used to say it gave her brain-ache, ten minutes in the company of Aoife. She had liked the library, though, despite having refused to learn to read for years. It used to make her go quiet and still. She treated books as the basis for her own imaginings. She would glide along the aisles, up and down the stacks: "Here's one I haven't read," she'd whisper to herself, and tilt it out of its place on the shelf. Then she would take it to a chair, sit down and turn the pages, looking through the pictures, muttering her own made-up version of the story. Monica would wait for her on the chairs, saying, "Hurry up, Aoife, let's go home."

Monica watches now as grown-up Aoife makes her way through the shelves, her top thing billowing and then deflating with the forward momentum of each step. Not something Monica would ever wear but she can see the appeal of it on Aoife. Aoife is holding a big, thick book in her hands, the size of an encyclopedia. And, as Monica and Michael Francis watch, Aoife does something truly shocking. Monica wouldn't have believed it, unless she'd seen it with her own eyes. Aoife, quite clearly, slides the book into her bag. *American Photography,* Monica reads, as it disappears into the canvas. She has put the book, this *American Photography,* into her bag. Without taking it to the desk. Without a backward glance. She zips the bag shut and keeps walking towards them, her head down.

"Did she just . . . ?"

"Yes," Monica breathes.

Aoife appears through the doors. On seeing her brother and sister standing in the lobby, she stops in her tracks. "What are you two doing here?" she has the gall to say.

"Looking for you," Michael Francis says.

"Did you just steal that book?" Monica raps out, and realizes those are the first words she has spoken to her sister in three years. "You take it right back in there this minute."

Aoife snorts, turns on her heel and walks out of the library.

"I can't believe she did that," Michael Francis says, his arms hanging loosely at his sides.

"I can."

Monica goes after her. Outside, they pursue her along the pavement. Michael Francis is the first to catch up with her and he says, "You can't steal from a library, Aoife."

Aoife, marching along, says, "It's not stealing."

Monica says, "It certainly looked like stealing."

Michael Francis says, "Monica's right, Aoife."

Aoife says, "Relax. I'm only borrowing it. I don't have a library card. I'll bring it back tomorrow."

Michael Francis says, "What do you want it for anyway?"

Monica says, "Of all the selfish, thoughtless—" She doesn't finish because Aoife suddenly grips her arm.

"Oh, God," she says, "isn't that Joe?"

It is Joe. Walking along Blackstock Road, his hand deep in the jeans pocket of a woman next to him. The woman is pushing a pram; his head is bent towards her to catch something she is saying and he is smiling and he looks carefree and untroubled, as if he had never cried and cried in a first-floor flat very near here, the noise of it terrifying and animal-like, head held in his hands as if it hurt him more than anything else ever had, as if he'd never pushed his face up close to that of a woman and said, You disgust me, you're inhuman, you make me sick, as if he'd never stood opposite that same woman in a church and vowed before God that he would love and honor her for better and for worse, as if he'd never held her hand as they stood in the cone of light from a streetlamp and said she was everything to him, he couldn't live without her. Here he was, living without her, walking along in the sunshine with that same hand tucked into the back pocket of a different woman's trousers. Here he was, still with that old checked shirt but with a new wife, who seemed to have a pram, inside which, Monica supposed, there must be a baby.

Michael Francis is thinking, Oh, shit. Aoife is thinking that it's the same woman she saw earlier, with the pram, and wasn't she a few years above her at school? Belinda something. Greenwell, was it? And Monica is thinking almost nothing at all. Her mind is a sheer drop of panic, of noiseless incomprehension. She cannot see how this has happened, how this is allowed to happen. She wants to say to someone or something: No, you can't do this, not now, not after everything, please, no.

Aoife takes charge. She steps back, opens the door of the nearest shop, pushes Monica through it and shuts it. Suddenly, all three of them are standing in the window of a florist, looking out. Always, afterwards, the scent of compost, mixed with jasmine blossom, will bring to Monica's mind the recollection of watching her first husband walking within a foot of her, unaware that she's there, his arm wrapped around another woman's shoulders, the blanketed chrysalis form inside a navy pram borne along the pavement before them, like a prize. Monica cringes behind a spray of carnations, unable to look away, until the window is blank again, until the three of them have gone.

"Well." Michael Francis exhales sharply. "That was a near miss."

"I didn't know he'd got married again," Aoife murmured, standing on tiptoe to catch a last glance.

Monica closes her eyes. She pulls her elbow away from Aoife because her sister is still gripping it, as if she's afraid Monica might stumble, as if she's forgotten everything that happened.

"Didn't you?" Monica snaps. "I always thought you and he were *so close*."

. . .

Gretta is walking through her house. She ought to be clearing up. Those plates, the teacups, the serviettes and crumbs—all over the sitting room. She should be collecting them and piling them into the sink. She needs to tidy the cushions, draw the curtains in the front room, keep the sun off the three-piece suite. She saved the dishwater from breakfast for the dishes: she's no water-waster, never will be.

She ought to be doing all these things. But for now she is moving about her house, passing through the doorways, rooms and corridors, running her hand along the varnished top of the banister, placing her palms on the back of the chairs, feeling the brush of the curtains, touching the raised, dry edges of the wallpaper.

It's not often the house is empty like this. Ever since Robert retired, she rarely gets the place to herself: he's always there, shaking his newspaper from the armchair or trailing her from room to room. It's this kind of emptiness she likes—signs of people around, their discarded possessions left as a reassurance of their return. Monica's jacket on a hanger, Michael Francis's car key on the hall table, that scarf of Aoife's draped over a peg.

Being alone is not something she's used to, growing up in a farmhouse with six siblings, parents, grandparents, an aunt and uncle or two all under the same roof. She doesn't think she ever knew that house empty.

This house has gone through phases, of course, Gretta thinks as she goes into the upstairs back room—the girls' room, as she still thinks of it. She straightens the eiderdown on Aoife's bed, plumps up the pillow on Monica's. Will Monica be staying here tonight? Hard to say, harder even to ask, as Monica never gives a straight answer to anything. She'll think of a way to put it to her later. When would have been the last time they slept together in here? The night before Monica's wedding, she supposes, Aoife only eight at the time, the age Hughie is now. She wonders, for the first time, whether Aoife found it hard to sleep in here alone after that, whether she missed her sister at night.

If Gretta closes her eyes, she can picture the room as it was in those days, the walls around Monica's bed covered with pictures of film stars, of wedding dresses, those around Aoife's decorated with her illegible lists, her drawings of wolves and foxes and staircases that went off into thin air.

The house is full of ghosts for Gretta. If she looks quickly into the garden, she is sure she can see the rib cage of the old wooden climbing frame that Michael Francis fell off of, breaking his front tooth. She could go downstairs now and see the pegs in the hall full of school satchels, gym bags, Michael Francis's rugby kit. She could turn a corner and find her son lying on his stomach on the landing, reading a comic, or baby Aoife hauling herself up the stairs, determined to join her siblings, or Monica learning to make scrambled eggs for the first time. The air, for Gretta, still rings with their cries, their squabbles, their triumphs, their small griefs. She cannot believe that time of life is over. For her, it all happened and is still happening and will happen forever. The very bricks, mortar and plaster of this house are saturated with the lives of her three children. She cannot believe they have gone. And that they are back.

As for Robert, Gretta cannot begin to think. His absence is beyond understanding. She is so used to him being here, being around, that she can't quite accept he has disappeared. She finds herself almost on the verge of speaking to him: this morning, she got two teacups down from the shelf. They have been together for so many years that they are no longer like two people but one strange four-legged creature. For her, so much of their marriage is about talk: she likes to talk, he likes to listen. Without him, she has no one to whom she can address her remarks, her observations, her running commentary about life in general. Her mind, these past days, has been filling up with things like, I saw the oddest-looking baby in the butcher's today, did you see there's a new ticket man at the tube station, do you remember that hairdresser's Bridie went to. Her temples ache with all that is unspoken, unlistened to.

In the bedroom, she stands in front of the chair at his side of the bed. A tweed jacket, far too hot for this weather, hangs off its back. She fingers the collar, warm in the sun, then runs her fingers down its slippery lining into the pocket. A couple of coins, a paper clip, the stub of a tube ticket. Nothing more. The kind of things anyone might find in their husband's pocket.

Stand in his shoes, the policeman had said to her, and then ask yourself, Where would he go? You need to think yourself into his head. The man had tapped his crown, as if to demonstrate where a head could be found. But the truth is that, although she has lived alongside him for thirty-odd years, although they spend every waking moment of their lives together, these days, Gretta can no more put herself in Robert's shoes than in those of the Queen of England. Despite his reliance on her, his enduring attachment to her, she still has no idea what goes on behind those glasses, what thoughts simmer beneath that thick, whitening hair.

When she'd first met him, she'd told the other girls at work that he was the quiet type, serious, didn't say much. Those are the ones you need to watch, a girl from Kerry had said. Gretta had laughed but she'd been sure, she'd been confident that he'd become less quiet as things went on because that was what happened. People got used to each other, people got less shy, more forthcoming; people came out of their shells.

She was working, along with all the other girls at the hostel, at a teahouse in Islington, the Angel Café Restaurant, which was an altogether lovely name. She'd seen the advertisement as she knelt in the farmhouse kitchen, stuffing newspaper into wet boots. "The Angel Café Restaurant, London, requires staff. Accommodation provided, wage and board. Apply by letter." She'd read it aloud in the kitchen to her mother. Listen to this, Mammy. The Angel Café Restaurant. As if, she'd said, the celestial beings were coming down from on high for a cup of tea. Her mother had said nothing, just hauled the door of the range shut with a clunk and wiped her hands on her apron. She hadn't wanted Gretta to go. But gone she had, telling her mother she'd be away only a few months, just until she had a bit put by, just until Christmas, just until Easter or perhaps the summer. But then, on one of her evenings off, she'd gone to the pictures with another girl and the man in front of them in the queue had turned around and lifted his hat and said, was her accent Irish? And she'd said, Who wants to know? He'd said that his mother was from Ireland, that he had been born there but came to England when he was just a little boy, he had changed his name from Ronan to Robert to fit in, and she'd said, fancy that.

He worked as a cashier in a bank, he told her the second time she saw him, he'd always been good with figures. He came to the Angel Café and waited until her shift finished, downing cup after cup of tea, watching her as she wove her way among the tables, holding her tray up high.

He had just come back from the war. He was older than others she'd stepped out with and had the black Irish looks she'd always admired, his hair parted in a straight line. He had a graveness to him, not like the boys she'd gone out with before, always shouting and larking and playing practical jokes. She liked the way his smile took a long time to arrive and just as long to leave.

He took her to Islington Green, where they sat under a tree for a time, before making their way down to the canal. He seemed to know and appreciate that she would have no problem with a long walk like that. She asked him where he'd been stationed in the war—that was always a conversation-starter in those days—but instead of a few lively stories about France, he had looked at the ground and said nothing at all. She'd had to jump in to fill the gap, telling him about the farm, her brothers and sisters and what they were doing now, scattered all over the world. He'd listened carefully, and at the end of the evening, he could recite the names and middle names of her six siblings, in order of birth. His party trick, he'd called it. Then he'd escorted her back to the hostel, all without laying a finger on her. She'd been sure that he'd have a go at the canal and had been ready for him, her rebuttal a practiced art by now, but he hadn't even tried, just touched the small of her back as they scaled the steps to the street.

He came again the next day and the day after that. He seemed to have decided that she was for him; she liked his certainty over this, his conviction. The subject of his war experiences came up only once more in the entire stretch of their marriage. They were walking along Rosebery Avenue, arm in arm, when they passed a newspaper seller and Gretta stopped to get one because she liked to know what was happening in the world. Robert took it and went to reach into his pocket for the change but then he stopped. Gretta looked at him; she looked at the newspaper in his hand. She saw the terrible stillness of his face. She saw the two men dressed in British infantry uniforms pass them by, oblivious, smoking, chatting as they went. She went into her purse to give the newspaper seller his money; she took Robert by the arm; she steered him to a café nearby, where she ordered him a cup of tea and eased the newspaper from his grasp. She knew that this was not a time for her to talk, to fill the gaps of silence with stories, so she waited, stirring sugar into his tea, her hand over his and, after a while, some words came for him and he told her things he said he'd never told anyone before. About the wait on the ruined docks at Dunkirk, the way German planes had flown over them, dropping leaflets that said they were done for, surrounded, as good as dead. That he was on the last boat that left—the very last—and until he'd felt himself hoicked out of the sea and onto the wet planking, he'd believed he wouldn't make it, that he'd be left behind, abandoned, stranded, having to find his own way home. Gretta sat and listened, and when he said that he never wanted to speak of it again, she'd said: Of course, we don't have to.

The "gentleman," the other girls called him: Here comes Gretta's gentleman, they'd sing to each other behind the Lyons' counter when they saw him come in the door, his black coat immaculate, his shoes polished, a spray of flowers in his hand. When he asked her to marry him, on the top floor of a bus heading along Pentonville Road, she had to hold his hand, her eyes closed, without saying anything, because she didn't want the moment to be over and gone.

Gretta slides the paper clip and the coins back inside the jacket pocket. She lowers herself to sit on the bed, his side of the bed, and looks out at the street, at the sky, at the ladybirds crawling on the windowpane.

She remembers, after they announced their engagement, being struck by how solitary he was. No parents, no siblings, no cousins or friends: there seemed to be no one for him to tell about their marriage. It was a shock to her because she was the sort who gathered people around her, wherever she was. How was it possible for someone like him to get so far in life and yet be so utterly alone? There had been a brother, he'd told her once, but he'd passed away, and just from the way he said it, Gretta could tell that he'd been mixed up in the Troubles and met his end there. Robert never spoke of the brother again and Gretta never asked him. That was the way of it.

How beautiful Monica had looked the day she'd married Joe. The way she'd come down the stairs, cautious in those ivory satin heels, her dress hitched up around her, as if she were an angel sitting on a cloud. Robert had cried when he saw her, cried and cried. He'd had to clutch the banister; she'd had to go and fetch an extra hankie. She'd hustled him into the downstairs' toilet and shut the door, the two of them in that tiny space, her in her new suit with the matching hat. What is it, she'd said to him, taking his hand, what ails you, her pulse tearing, tearing at her neck. Robert, you can tell me, she'd said, you know you can. She'd waited a good five minutes in there, him sitting on the toilet seat, her standing over him, and when it became clear he wasn't going to say anything, she'd said, Pull yourself together now, because the house was full of people, because they had to get to the church sooner or later. But he couldn't stop and Gretta had felt she was looking into a fissure that had opened, a fissure that was deep, dark and unnavigable, Monica out there in the hallway, all ready to go, her flowers in her hand, Aoife wriggling in her frock, saying, What's wrong with Daddy?

· · ·

Michael Francis had said at the gate that he needed to pop to the newsagent's to buy a paper. But the truth was that he had needed a moment away from them all.

Aoife and Monica had gone into the house together, without looking at each other, and he had hurried off down the road, hardly aware of where he was going but feeling an immense surge of relief that 14 Gillerton Road was behind him and he was moving away from it.

In the newsagent's, he stares at the paper rack, at the rows of chocolate bars, at the jars of sweets lined up on the shelves. It enters his mind to buy a treat for Hughie and Vita. Because he is going back there tonight to see them. He hesitates for a moment in front of the jars because Claire has an only-on-Saturdays rule with sweets. Dare he violate it?

Bugger it, he thinks, and asks for a quarter-pound of sherbet lemons, Hughie's favorite, and some pear drops for Vita. Bear drops, she used to call them when she was small, and the recollection of this makes him smile as he searches his pockets for change.

Outside, he dithers for a moment about where to go now, the paper under his arm, his pockets weighed down with sweets for the kids. He slips a pear drop into his mouth, the surface gritty, cratered against his tongue.

He is opposite a bus stop that would take him to Stoke Newington. He could wait there, get on a bus, go to the house, see Claire. But how can he, when he has to get back to Gillerton Road? And how can he, when his wife cannot seem to bear the sight of him?

He feels it again, that precipice, the proximity of the possible end, as he stands outside the newsagent's. He is aware, again, of the presence of Gina Mayhew sliding by him, like someone in a hurry to get past.

Joe had walked past them on the pavement as the three of them stood there. A new wife, a baby, a whole other life. It seemed the very essence of strangeness to see Joe like that when he had been a part of their lives for so long. He'd been coming to their house for years, taking Monica out when they were all teenagers. Michael used to be proud sometimes, when he was out, to see Joe, who was a couple of years older than him, with a cigarette in his mouth, with his lunch box under his arm, because Joe was working, he was an apprentice, he wasn't at school anymore, and he'd nod at him and say, All right, Michael Francis. His voice was always more London, more glottally stopped, than when he was in the house. Michael had loved it when he did that, especially if any of the boys from school were near. For him to know someone like Joe: there was nothing as good as that when you were fifteen and bullied a little bit at school for getting good marks. And then Joe had married his sister; Michael Francis had had his first ever drink at their wedding; Aoife had been a flower girl, admittedly not a very good one because she'd talked to herself all the way through the ceremony and lost the flowers. Joe had been with them every Christmas, every Sunday for dinner. He used to play Happy Families with Aoife, teasing her by not saying "please," then letting her win. He used to help Gretta shell the peas she grew in the flower beds, setting a sieve between his knees on the back step and saying, Now, give us a handful there, Mrs. R. It was unaccountable that he had slipped out of the fabric of their lives, unbelievable that he was now walking about the city with another woman, another family.

Was it possible, he wonders, as he retraces his steps back to Gillerton Road, that this could happen to him and Claire? That they might be parted, torn asunder, separated, divorced? That he would go and live—where? Some flat. See the kids at week-ends, come back alone every night, cooking meals for one, he and Claire speaking strainedly on the phone to make arrangements, times, places.

It was unthinkable. It must never happen.

And yet he doesn't know where to go from here. The argument had been one from which there seemed no way back.

"You're back," was what she'd said, in a tone of surprise, as if she'd received news that he was taking a round-the-world cruise. He'd gone back home from dealing with his mother, from talking to the police, from tracking down Monica and Aoife. He'd gone home to pick up his night things because he knew he should stay over with his mother, keep her company until his sisters got there. He'd gone back to his house and it was late and he had imagined that he might sit for a moment with Claire, with a beer perhaps, on the sofa, her hand in his. They used to do this early in their marriage, before they had a television, in the two-roomed flat off the Holloway Road, Hughie a wrapped bundle in the carry-cot in the corner and him and Claire just sitting together, contemplating the shape of their new lives. One of the things that had surprised him about Claire when they first lived in that flat was her stillness, her quietude. He was used to a house in which people clattered from room to room, shouted down staircases, banged open doors to yell, What time do you call this, where people threw themselves into chairs, slammed down teacups, used more words than perhaps they needed to. Moving in with Claire back then was like stepping from an overcrowded train into a stirring, cool mountain air.

So, he had arrived back at his house, wanting to feel again that touch and brush and curled warmth of her fingers: was that so much to ask? It was late and the children were in bed and his mother had cried and cried and he wanted to sit on his sofa, with his wife, for a few minutes, just like they used to. But Claire was in the kitchen, snipping herbs into a bubbling saucepan. She had an apron on over what he recognized as her best dress, a paisley number he'd always liked, with a fitted bodice. Her lips were stained dark with lipstick and bangles clattered up and down her wrist as she stirred her concoction: it was releasing heavy clouds of beef and wine and garlic into the air. For a heartbreaking moment, he thought she'd done this for him, that she had prepared a dinner for him, that she'd put on her paisley frock for him, and the lipstick and the bangles.

"That smells good," he'd said.

Claire had looked up and he'd seen it, the fleeting expression of dismay, before she'd said it: *You're back.*

They had spoken on the phone earlier; he'd wanted to keep her in the loop with what was happening and he'd also wanted to hear her voice, to reassure himself that he had a life outside the family he'd been born into, that the family he'd created for himself was still there, still available. She had been solicitous, concerned about his father, asking lots of questions and listening to his answers and saying, I'm so sorry, Mike. She even said "your poor mother," which was not a sentiment she often expressed.

But now everything was different. She did not seem like the person he'd spoken to on the phone, the person who'd said, Let me know if you hear anything, who'd said "your poor mother." This person was all dressed up, the table behind her laid with silver and folded cloth napkins, this person was saying things like she hadn't realized he'd be back tonight, she was so sorry, and was he intending to stay because her study group were coming round for a discussion over supper?

"Now?" he'd said, slumping sideways in the doorway, knowing that the frame would catch him, would offer him the bodily support he needed. "At this hour?"

Claire licked her lips quickly, brushed the hair off her face. "I'm really sorry, Mike. It never crossed my mind you'd be back.

If I'd known . . . You see, everyone thought there was more space here and I said you'd be out so everyone thought—"

"Everyone thought, everyone thought, is that all you can fucking say?" he had yelled suddenly, because he'd spent hours holding his mother's hand while she wept, because his father was gone, which was unbelievable and beyond strange. Because all he'd wanted was to come and sit with Claire on his sofa, in his front room, and he was being told that was impossible, that at any minute people were about to sit themselves down and discuss the First World War, as in some fevered nightmare where the pupils he most dreaded would invade his house and sit around the breakfast table, staring at him, telling him that school had been moved here for the foreseeable future.

"Oh, that's right," Claire had shouted back, and he was shocked because Claire never shouted, it wasn't in her, didn't come with her DNA. "Abuse me with—with phallocentric language."

He laughed, a loud explosion from somewhere deep in his chest. "Who are you parroting when you say things like that? What's happened to you? Why are you even doing this course? I mean, you're intelligent, you're educated, you—"

"Only partially!"

"What's that supposed to mean?"

"You know."

"No, I don't. Please tell me."

"My degree," she said, and tears sprang into her eyes. She dashed them away angrily. "I never did my degree. And why was that? Whose fault was it?"

He was tempted to shout: Ours. It was both of us. We were both there. But he suddenly saw himself from the perspective of her new, about-to-arrive friends: Claire's awful, shouty husband—look at the way he yells at her, tells her she can't have us here. He couldn't bring himself to discuss that night now, with all those places laid and ready at the dinner table.

"Claire." He tried to take his wife's hand—he had the urge to shake it, to try to rouse her in some way, to try to make her see that what was happening here should not be happening, to try to bring her back, "I'm sorry, I shouldn't have shouted. It's just been a terrible day and this . . . supper party. What about the children? Won't they be woken up by all this noise?"

At the word "children," she raised her head and looked at him. Claire loved her children; he was constantly amazed by how much. Constantly aghast at the sight of her getting out of bed at three a.m. to fetch Vita a drink, at her giving Hughie all her lunch, if he wanted it, at the selflessness and sacrifice of it all, at the effort she put into a nativity-play costume, at the patience, the sweet, angelic patience of her, when Vita was raging about having her hair brushed or wanting those socks, not these socks, or just needing her, Claire, to sit by her for hours on end, reading book after book after book. She was a marvel to him and he wondered if there was some way he could communicate this to her, via the touch of their skin.

But she said, "The children will be fine. If they wake up, they wake up. It's good for them to meet new people. It's good for them to have a mother who is fulfilled, who is stretched. They're too cocooned as things are, don't you think?"

Cocooned, he wanted to say, cocooned? But I want them to be cocooned. I want them to be sheltered, safe, insulated, protected, now and forever. If it were up to him, he would sew his children into eiderdowns so they could never hurt themselves, he would never let them leave the house; he would stop them going to school, even, to avoid the slightest possibility that someone might say something unkind to either of them. Cocooned didn't even begin to cover what he wanted for them.

"Anyway, it's not as if," she said, pulling her hand from his, "they've always been your first priority, is it?"

And there she was again, Gina Mayhew, among them. Claire put down her spoon and rubbed at her neck, as if she, too, were aware of Gina gliding into the room, taking up a place at the dinner table, crossing her legs and looking up at him with the preoccupied gaze that he'd noticed that first day in the staff room, as if she were absorbed by something no one else could see or understand, as if she held some fascinating secret that no one else could even guess at.

He wanted to say, But I never meant it to happen. He wanted to turn to his wife and say, I didn't mean it and I'm sorry. But could he put his hand on his heart and say that this was entirely true?

. . .

Gretta is in the bedroom, pulling things off the top of a wardrobe, when she hears Monica coming up the stairs. She can tell, in the careful hesitancy of each step, that it's Monica in her strappy sandals. Then she hears Aoife, who's been in the bedroom, burst out onto the landing to accost her. Gretta frowns. She'd been hoping that Aoife was having a nap.

"What did you mean," she hears Aoife demand, "when you said that thing about Joe—and me?"

A pause. Gretta can imagine Monica doing her cool, interrogative eyebrow-arching thing.

"What thing?"

"That Joe and I were 'so close.' What did you mean?"

"Well, you were, weren't you?"

Another pause. Gretta wants to get down off the stool she's standing on and tiptoe to the door, but she's afraid she'll give herself away, that whatever is taking place on the landing might be interrupted, diverted. She stays exactly where she is, stock-still, her hand on a hatbox that contains, she thinks, old shoes of the children's. She'd thought perhaps Claire might want them for her two. Might be something in there that fits Hughie. Big feet, that boy has, just like his dad.

"Monica, are you saying you think . . . something . . . happened . . . between me and Joe?"

"Didn't it?"

"Jesus, Monica. Of course not. What do you take me for? You're out of your mind if you think—"

"I don't mean," Monica says, tightly, "that kind of thing. I mean . . ." She trails into silence.

"What?" Aoife demands. Always demanding, that one, from the minute she was born. Never taking no for an answer. Couldn't be more different from her sister, who was a clamshell, just like her dad.

What Monica says next she says so quietly that Gretta isn't sure she heard her right. It sounds like, "That you told him."

Aoife doesn't say, Told him what. She doesn't say anything at all. Gretta leans forward on her perch, she lets go of the shoe hatbox to be sure of this. And the fact that Aoife doesn't say, Told him what, sinks down through Gretta like a stone dropped into a pond because something she has always half suspected comes into sudden focus. As if a lens has been twisted on a blurred scene, Gretta suddenly sees everything clearly. She runs her hand down the wood of the wardrobe; she removes a stray mothball from its top.

"I didn't tell him," Aoife says in an unsteady voice. "Of course I didn't. Why would I?"

"Well, somebody did."

"It wasn't me."

Silence, thick as fog, rolls in from the landing. Gretta feels that she could put out her hand and touch its cold form.

"So, that's why he left," Aoife whispers. "Because he found out. And you thought I'd—"

"He left because you told him," Monica spits out and Gretta wants to go to her daughter, to touch her on the shoulder and say, It wasn't her—it wasn't your sister, believe me, Aoife wouldn't do that.

"Monica, I did not tell him," Aoife says. "I swear."

Gretta hears Monica turn, go back down the stairs. She hears Aoife stand awhile longer on the landing. Then she moves into the bathroom; Gretta hears her rattling about in there, sipping water from the tap, though, God knows, Gretta has told her to use the mug a thousand times, then rip toilet paper from the roll, muttering to herself inaudibly. Strange she hasn't lost that habit, even in adulthood. Then Aoife returns to her room, banging the door. Gretta hears the squeal of bedsprings as Aoife hurls herself to the bed and the sounds make her smile, despite herself.

She gets down, then, from the stool. She sits on Robert's chair, the tweed jacket behind her, the stiffened collar pressing an *n* shape into her back. She registers an urge, at first dull, then sharp and jagged, to see her husband, to share this with him, perhaps not in words, but just to sit by him and know that he was feeling what she was feeling: their girls, their beloved offspring, in terrible disarray and nothing to be done.

She sits there and feels her aloneness and the lack of him, and she looks out at the plane trees, their yellow crinkled-up leaves, motionless in the still, heavy air. Her hands are folded on her chest, her ankles crossed. So, she makes herself think, to block out the awfulness of his baffling absence, there we have it. Monica in the kitchen, clattering about with dishes. Aoife in the bedroom. Michael Francis keeping his head down somewhere, no doubt.

The dry leaves of the trees outside the window could be a photograph, she thinks, the way they are so still.

Aoife came three weeks early. Gretta was walking back from the corner shop with Michael Francis and Monica when her waters broke. She wasn't put out. It was early February. She had on a thick coat, a pair of woolen stockings: they would soak up the worst of it.

She held out the shopping bag. "Here," she said to Michael Francis, who was walking ahead of her, as he always did. "Carry this, would you?"

He pretended not to hear, just kept going.

Monica materialized at her side, hair neatly plaited, her parting like a line of chalk bisecting her head. "I'll take it, Mammy."

Gretta patted her on the shoulder. "Don't you worry, it's too heavy for you, darling."

Monica looked at her. Gretta could feel the beam of that look, as if it burned her skin. She'd never been able to hide anything from Monica, anything at all. It was useless to try. Even before Monica could talk, Gretta had been aware that this child knew everything about her, and vice versa. She'd got used to the invisible telegraph wire that ran between them: all day long messages passed along it, without anyone else knowing.

"Don't worry," she repeated to her daughter.

Monica pulled the shopping bag out of Gretta's hands. She walked ahead and gave it to her brother, ten months older but a foot taller, then returned to Gretta's side. She took her hand. "Are you all right, Mammy?" she asked, her face white with anxiety, tipped up to look at her.

"I'm fine, pet." Gretta spoke through a surge of pain, managing to keep her voice even. "I'm fine."

At the house, Monica made Gretta a cup of tea (Gretta did not say that the thought of it, at this precise moment, made her want to be sick). She sent Michael Francis next door, where they had a phone, to get the neighbor to call their father: they had had the number written on a pad in the kitchen for weeks.

Gretta was gripping the back of a chair—because the pains were coming fast now, with barely a gap in between; it had never been as fast as this before, not any of the times she'd been through it—when the neighbor appeared through the living-room door. She had four children, three lodgers, a husband killed in the war, and had lived in Gillerton Road all her life. She and Gretta looked at each other for a long moment and Gretta was aware, as ever, of Monica intercepting that look, drawing it to herself, attempting to read what wasn't being said.

"I'll be back," was all the neighbor said.

Gretta wanted to let go of the chair but found she couldn't. Her arms were numb, prickling with pins and needles. "Won't be long now," she tried to say, noticing that her voice was coming out a little slurred. "Are you looking forward to meeting your—"

"Daddy wasn't there," Michael Francis was saying, from what seemed to be a great distance across the room.

"What?" Monica said.

Quiet, Gretta wanted to say. Be quiet, can't you see I'm trying to concentrate.

"He wasn't there. We phoned but he wasn't there."

"Well, where is he?" Monica said.

"Don't know. They said they didn't know where he was."

"Are you sure . . ." Gretta said, taking great care with each word, ". . . you dialed the right number?"

Her children looked at her. Her children. From across the room, their faces oval in the weak February light. The order of what happened next is a little jumbled for Gretta. She remembers the neighbor back in the room, saying the ambulance was coming, it would be here any minute, and she, Gretta, saying she wasn't getting in any ambulance because she had to wait for her husband. Michael Francis and Monica, she thought, had been sent to the neighbor's house, with promises of eating bread and jam with the neighbor's children. This baby isn't going to wait, the neighbor said, and reached for the vase on the mantelpiece just in time for Gretta to throw up into it.

Then she was somehow on the floor and the neighbor was there, gripping her hand and saying, Bear down now, Mrs. Riordan, and all Gretta could think was that the neighbor had covered the carpet in sheets from the airing cupboard and they were the wrong sheets, the good sheets. Gretta wanted to say, There are other sheets, old ones, and I keep them in the shed, but no words would come out because her teeth were clamped together. Bear down, the neighbor kept saying, it'll soon be over, and Gretta wanted to say, Shut up, shut your face, and where's my bloody husband, but waves kept overtaking her, cresting over her head. Suddenly, ambulance men were there, large and uniformed, striding into the room, and Gretta found the strength to rise to her feet and say, can I go to hospital now?

But the men—no more than boys, really—were taking her by the elbow and saying, No, there's no time, you're not going anywhere, lie back now, missis.

"Can't," she got out, "I can't, I—" She broke off because she was suddenly aware that there was someone else in the room with them. She peered around and caught a glimpse of thin legs with gray kneesocks. Gretta bellowed: Get her out of here, get her out. Monica, she said, get yourself next door, get in there now. But Monica did not move. Get her out, she screamed, for the love of God, she's ten years old. But the people in the room weren't listening, they were saying there was no time, that it was happening now, that she must push and push and push; someone was moving her back to the sofa and where in God's name was Robert or Ronan or whatever he was called, Where the feck is my husband, she heard herself shout, even though she knew Monica was there; she couldn't see her but she always knew because of that invisible wire. Right at the last moment, just before the baby came slithering out into the ambulance man's waiting hands, the neighbor seemed to snap into her senses and seized Monica by the shoulders and jostled her out of the room.

Gretta always knew everything about Monica; she always had, from the moment she first saw her. It was never this way with her other two, just Monica. And she knew, when she came around from the trance of birth, in the trundling ambulance, alone but for a howling baby, that Monica, while perhaps not having seen it all, had seen too much, far too much, that what she had witnessed she would never forget.

.   .   .

Monica pushes her fingers into the telephone's coils, winding them around and around the tight spirals.

The phone in Gloucestershire rings for a long time. She is about to hang up, thinking that Peter must have taken the girls on an outing somewhere, swimming, perhaps, or to a friend's house, when a voice answers, high with importance: "Hello, Camberden three eight three four."

Monica is so taken aback to hear one of the girls reciting her own phone number so fluently that, for a moment, she is speechless. Then she collects herself. "Jessica, sweetheart," she says, "is that you?"

There is a pause. Monica and the child listen to each other breathing.

"Jessica?" Monica repeats. "Is that you? Or Florence? Is it Florence?"

"Who is this?" The child's voice is clear and haughty.

"It's Monica, darling. Are you having a lovely weekend? Is Daddy—"

The voice cuts in: "Who?"

Monica lets out a little trill of laughter, trying to extract her fingers from the telephone coils but the longest finger, next to the index—whatever is it called? Does it even have a name?— remains stubbornly stuck. "It's me, Monica, your . . . daddy's . . . well . . ."

"Who?" the child says again.

Monica inhales, she presses her fingernails into her palms. "Would you please go and get Daddy and tell him I would like to speak to him?"

There is another pause. Then she hears the unmistakable noise of the receiver being slammed down.

Monica stands there for a moment, unable to believe what has happened. She thinks about calling back, demanding that Peter be put on the phone, but she hasn't the stomach for it, cannot listen to one more syllable spoken by that reedy, insolent voice.

She would bet anything it was Jessica. The little one, Florence, wouldn't have the nerve to do it. But Jessica: she's capable of anything.

Well, Monica thinks, as she pushes her way into the front sitting room, that little madam needn't think she's going to get away with it. Monica is going to tell Peter exactly what happened the very next time she speaks to him. And what will Peter do? Monica knows: absolutely nothing. He'll sigh and shift in his overalls and mutter about how hard it is on them, how she's just expressing her discontent, he's sorry, Monica mustn't worry, they'll come around.

She grips the back of the armchair that belongs to Robert and no one else. If she or Michael Francis or Aoife had done what Jessica just had, there would have been trouble. A slap on the bottom, early to bed and the prospect of a talking-to from their father when he got home.

Not that this had ever applied to her much. She was the good one, the well-behaved one, the responsible one. Still is. But she remembers Aoife and, occasionally, Michael Francis being punished with this formula: slap + bed + talk from their father. She remembers the heavy thudding of her father's feet on the stair carpet, still in his good work shoes, before eating his tea, and even though she wasn't the one waiting under the counterpane, it would scare her.

Monica moves from the armchair to stand in front of her father's rolltop desk. She runs a speculative finger along its top; she rests a hand on its side. Then, casting a quick look over her shoulder at the empty front room, Monica inserts her fingertips into the lid. She tugs. Nothing. Locked.

Monica is unperturbed. She goes to the bay window and, stepping onto a tapestried (by her) stool, reaches up to the pelmet and delves about up there.

She had caught her father doing this once; she must have been twelve or thirteen at the time and it must have been Christmas because she distinctly remembers her father having to lean over the Christmas tree to reach. As he stepped down, he saw her, standing in the doorway. There was a moment in which she caught her breath, staring at him, the key in his hand. She knew immediately what it was for: they were all fascinated by their father's desk, a wooden box with a brass lock and rows of drawers that crouched in the corner of the front room. He would take to it on a Sunday afternoon, sit there facing its depths, folding and unfolding bits of paper, writing with his fountain pen, ripping the tops off envelopes. But she needn't have worried. He had, after a moment, smiled, tapped his finger to his nose.

"Our little secret," he'd said. "Agreed?"

"Agreed." She'd nodded and moved forward to stand beside him as he sat down on the chair and opened the desk. She'd always loved the way the lid rolled back into nothing, the slats of wood sliding away, like a wave off sand. She'd loved the desk's cubbyholes and tiny drawers and little nooks more than anything, though, stuffed with bits of paper and bottles of ink and the wire loops of paper clips. There were photos in there, too, she knew. Pictures of Mammy as a young woman, with her hair all dark and her waist tiny, her hands hidden inside gloves. Pictures of people she didn't know, standing stiffly in the sunshine in gardens far away.

"Can I fill your fountain pen for you, Daddy?" she asked.

Her father looked up from the papers in front of him. "You can."

He got out for her the bottle of blue-black ink. QUINK, the lid said. QUINK, the curled letters on the glass read. Monica knew how to unscrew the barrel of the pen, how to dip just the silver nib and no more into the liquid, then squeeze until you saw the bubbles stop. Then that delicious feeling of the ink drawing up into the pen, that tiny noise of suction. She could hear Michael Francis clumping about upstairs; she could hear the rising screech of Aoife, in the kitchen, *Nonononono I do it myself*! But here she was, standing nicely, filling a pen with ink for her father, here she was, wiping the nib clean on her hankie for him and screwing on the lid. There was no act more right, more satisfying, than handing it back to him, saying, "Here you are, Daddy," and then the reward of his hand on her shoulder, him saying, "Perfect, darling."

Monica's fingers encounter something hard and cold and she snatches the key off the pelmet, which is furred with dust that showers her as she leaps back off the stool. She swipes at her dress, cursing her mother's haphazard housework.

Checking the room again, she steps up to the desk and inserts the key into the lock. She feels not a single qualm about doing this. It is her right. It is the only thing to do.

Her father has left. She still cannot accept this fact, still cannot believe it. He has walked out without so much as a thought for her, left behind to deal with all this, to calm a hysterical Gretta, to face a deluge of siblings and relatives. He must have known that she, Monica, would be left to bear the brunt of the trouble, and had he cared? No, he had not. He had gone and walked out without a backward glance. How could he have expected her to drop everything and come home to sort this out? It was the height of selfishness, the very essence of disregard.

Monica pushes back the rolltop with a sharp shove. It rushes into itself with a shocked rattle. She runs her hand over the embossed-leather surface; she sets the ink blotter straight; she touches the lid of the fountain pen, lying in its holder.

She has always known she is the favorite. It is, she tells herself, just the way things are. Nothing was ever said, of course, because that was not their way. But she knows it to be true, in both thought and deed. Everyone knows. Can she help it if they loved her more, if they took more pleasure in her company, if they found the path of her life to be the most compatible with their own? Their constant approval: she has never courted it, never asked for it. She cannot help it; it's forever been entirely out of her hands. She has always been aware that despite her parents' emphasis on study, on working hard at school, on getting good marks, on being top of the class, that she—not Michael Francis—is the one whose choices they applauded. She found herself a husband, she got married, she settled down and moved into a flat just around the corner. Nothing the others could ever do would make them as happy as that. Nothing would validate more the people they were, the choices they themselves had made, than their prettiest daughter getting married in a big white dress to a local boy from a good Irish family. Nothing. Not even her subsequent divorce—which caused seismic shock waves for her parents—was enough to topple her from prime position. If anything, they cleaved even more closely to her. Michael Francis could get himself three PhDs and it would never measure up. Aoife, of course, didn't enter into this, the way she was: she'd gone out of her way to make herself the least favorite. But Michael Francis—Monica often wondered if it bothered him. If that was why he had worked so hard, pushed himself to do so well at school. Only to mess it all up with a stupid mistake and end up just like her, married and living around the corner.

Monica smooths her hair, readjusts a pin at the nape of her neck and sets to work. She will start with the cubbyholes; she will work left to right. There will be something in here, she is sure, some clue, something that everyone else would overlook. She knows her father better than any of them and she knows that a man who has spent his life working in a bank is sure to account for everything. He will have left a trace, a mark, a record, even if perhaps he didn't intend to.

.　.　.

Aoife sits cross-legged on the bed, the American photography book open on her lap. She turns its pages, a few this way, a few that, blows smoke out of the window, then turns a few more. She hadn't known what she wanted when she went into the library and had almost headed towards the children's section, the blazingly familiar shelves with picture books, the inaccurately rendered murals of cartoon characters wobbling across the walls. But then she'd caught sight of a shelf she'd never seen before, with long-spined books all in a row. And there this book had been, squeezed between others on quilting techniques and cake decorating.

It's all here, right from William Henry Fox Talbot and his salt prints. Evelyn is the second last and, Aoife notices, one of the few women.

There are six of her photographs, not perhaps her most famous, all from before Aoife's time. One had been in the exhibition she saw, all those years ago, in London, when she walked among the images, aged eighteen or nineteen or whatever she was, utterly unaware that one day she would be developing film for the woman, laying out contact sheets, setting up her lights. Odd that your life can contain such significant trip wires to your future and, even while you wander through them, you have no idea.

Seeing Evelyn's work here, now, reproduced in a book, which she can look at sitting on her old bed, in her old room, is strangely reassuring. Aoife lays her hand on a double-page spread, one of a man with a startling birthmark covering half of his face, holding up a dead-eyed fish, another of a woman sitting in a slip on a bashed-up car, a railway track stretching out behind her. She puts her hand on these pictures and knows she isn't stuck. She has a life elsewhere. She isn't still living here, with no hope or brightness before her. She made it out.

She is just turning back to the photographer who precedes Evelyn when the door opens and her brother slopes into the room.

He doesn't look at her. He doesn't speak. He lowers himself, joint by joint, to the rug and lies there facedown.

Aoife flips a page over, realizes that she hates this photographer's work, that she met the man once and he was an arrogant pig. She eyes the long form of her brother. "You OK?" she says.

"Mmmnnng," Michael Francis says, or thereabouts.

His face is pressed to the rag rug in what was once his sisters' bedroom. It is, he suddenly sees, the best place in the world to be. The floorboards warm under his torso, his legs resting gently apart, his eyes closed, his cheek against the interesting terrain of the knotted fabric. Didn't Monica and his mother make this rug one winter? A flash memory of the kitchen table covered with shreds of fabric, his mother reaching across it, breaks the surface of his mind but then blurs and disappears. Maybe it happened; maybe it didn't.

"Do you think I can lie here forever?" he says, his voice pleasantly muffled by the rug.

He hears his sister turn a page in her book—the thin rattle of paper, then her hands smoothing the surface. "You could," she says, in her don't-you-dare-disturb-my-reading voice, "theoretically. But you'd die of dehydration in a day or two. Maybe less in this heat."

He moves up a hand to cover his eyes. He can hear someone— Monica?—moving about in the room below. A car grinds past outside. Aoife turns a page, then another. Someone, downstairs, clatters the teapot against the side of the sink.

"I did something," he says.

His eyes are still shut and Aoife is behind him but he is aware of her raising her head. She puts her book aside, on the bed next to her, as he knew she would. He hears the springs of the bed complain at this shift in weight.

"Is this to do with Dad?"

"No."

"OK. A good something or a bad something?"

"Bad."

There is a pause. Someone in a garden a few doors down is calling out a long imperative about a sun lounger, a hat and something else he can't make out.

"A job something? A marriage something?"

"Marriage."

"Ah."

It is a sound so full of wisdom, so empty of judgment that he cannot help but tell her everything—or as close to everything as he can manage. He cannot, for example, tell her that the first time he saw Gina Mayhew it was as if he recognized her, as if he'd been waiting for her to come. There you are, he almost said. What kept you? Or that he had never believed in the concept of love at first sight. Or that she wasn't what you might think of as attractive, or his type, or someone who might derail a marriage or the thoughts of the head of history, husband, father, family man. She was tall, with limbs that she didn't seem entirely in control of and white, freckled skin. She reminded him most of a giraffe. Her sleeves stopped short of her wrist bones. Her feet were big, long and thin, and she shod them in the kind of buckled sandals a child might wear. She wore divided skirts, cardigans that looked as though she'd knitted them herself, an Alice band that held back her bluntly cut hair. The kind of outfits that he knew would draw unkindness from her pupils. He couldn't tell Aoife that the first time he'd gone to find her in her science lab— on some pretext or other, because really he'd just wanted to see her on her own, he'd wanted to look at her, that was all, away from the smoke-hung boredom of the staff room—he'd found her wearing a lab coat too short for her, stepping out from behind a blackboard on which was displayed the carbon cycle. On seeing him, she blushed and his thought was: the blush cycle. He almost said this out loud. Blood flooding the surface of her face and neck, and his, too, as if in answer.

Instead, he tells Aoife the bare bones of the story. That he fell for a colleague and she fell for him. That they ate lunch together behind the fume cupboard. That they sometimes took the tube together in the evening, as far as Tottenham Court Road, where she switched lines. That Claire had found out. That Gina had returned to Australia. That, as revenge, Claire is doing an Open University degree and attends lectures and tutorials and fills up their house with new friends.

He doesn't tell his sister that he sometimes goes and stands beside the fume cupboard, even now, a year and a half on. Or that he once took the lab coat that was hanging by a peg and weighed it in his hand. Or that the sight of another teacher casually using the Ayers Rock mug she'd left behind so enraged him that he removed it from the staff room. It still sits in his desk drawer. He doesn't tell her these things because he doesn't want her to know; he doesn't tell her because he knows that Aoife is able to fill in such details for herself.

When he stops talking, it feels as though he's been speaking for an age, that it's impossible to remember a time when he wasn't moving his mouth and producing sounds. Behind him, Aoife is smoking and it occurs to him that this might bring Gretta vengefully up the stairs: she has not allowed smoking in the house ever since she herself gave up.

He listens to his sister suck on a cigarette; he watches smoke drift into the room. He clears his throat. "Say something."

"Like what?"

"Anything."

"OK. What happened when Claire found out?"

"It was . . ." He turns his face into the tufts of the rag rug, breathes in the silt of it, the microscopic layers of dust and debris from his sisters' early lives; he is imagining wisps of baby hair, lint from childhood sweaters, particles of teenaged skin, nail clippings, cuticle shreds, the peeled-away bits of split ends. ". . . awful. Just awful. The worst thing ever."

.   .   .

If it hadn't been for the school trip, everything would have been all right. He would have been able to keep things under control, keep his life ticking over. But a few days before the annual A-level visit to the trenches of the Somme, the head had called him into his office.

The teacher who usually accompanied the trip—a chain-smoking elderly woman who'd taught geography apparently since the glaciers withdrew from Britain—had had to go into hospital for "tests." Here the head blustered and fiddled with a paperweight, so Michael guessed it was probably some gynecological issue, something that involved bleeding and probing and surgery in unthinkable places. But all was well, the head had assured him, because he had had the bright idea of asking that new biology teacher to accompany Michael Francis on the trip. Probably never even seen France, the head said, be good for her. Aussies liked to travel, didn't they?

They took the ferry. Only three of the pupils were sick, which was an improvement on last year. On the bus, he and Gina Mayhew sat separately. She had her head turned to look out of the window the entire way. She kept her bag—a shiny red leather box with a looping strap—perched on her knee, like a small dog. They were, he thought, courteous with each other and no more. "Scrupulous" was the word. They were scrupulous with and around each other. They made minimal eye contact; they spoke to each other only when necessary and only in front of the children; she addressed him as Mr. Riordan; she checked on the girls at lights-out time and he checked on the boys. Nobody would know anything was amiss.

It was, he saw after the first day, going to be fine. They were professional, they were a team, they were two teachers supervising a school trip. Nothing more. Whatever this was, it was nothing. Everything was going to be OK.

They saw the trenches; they saw the fields, they walked through the graveyards, and he had to send only one child back to the minibus. He distributed worksheets; he handed out pencils; he gave a talk (brief) about trench warfare; he pointed out the gradient, how the Germans were on higher ground; he showed them a stretch of ground on which fifty-seven thousand men fell in one day.

"Write that down," he said. "Fifty-seven thousand men, most of them—"

"Not much older than you," Gina burst out.

He looked down from his vantage point of a reconstructed ladder leading into no-man's-land. Gina sat at the end of the line, a yellow cagoule over a pair of shorts with lions embroidered around the hem, her hair in a swinging ponytail. She had a pair of bird-watching binoculars around her neck. He hadn't realized that she was even listening. He'd assumed she was there in body but that her mind was wandering over—what? He imagined the deserts of Australia, stained red in the sun; the byways and paths of the human circulatory system; those diagrams of worms mating; sewing patterns for divided skirts. Who knew where she went inside her head while he was giving the same old spiel about conscription and bully beef that he'd been giving for the past ten years?

As their gazes locked, she blushed. That same bright stain traveling up her neck, into her cheeks. He forced himself to look away, to look back to his notes, to find where he was in his lesson.

"Mmm," he said, playing for time. "Now. Weaponry. Who can tell me about that?"

That night, he was several fathoms deep in sleep when it came to him that someone was knocking on the door of his single-bunked room at the youth hostel. He stumbled from the bed and opened the door and there was Gina Mayhew, in a pair of flowered cotton pajamas, short, her bare legs gleaming in the strip lighting.

"Oh," he said. "Gina, I don't think—"

But she was off down the corridor. "You'd better come," she said, over her shoulder.

The pupils had, perhaps inevitably, got hold of some alcohol and there had been a party in the girls' room. He and Gina stood in the doorway and he took a quick inventory. Five were drunk, one seriously, four were semi-naked, two were in a clinch, three were vomiting or looked as though they were about to. For the next half hour, he and Gina worked steadily, upbraiding, cleaning, separating, segregating, confiscating. Gina dressed the girls—he carefully averted his eyes from this—and got them into bed. He marshaled the boys back to their dormitory and shut the door. Then he went back.

Gina was standing in the corridor, her arms full of confiscated bottles of vodka.

"All fine?" he said, keeping his sight lines vague and above all shifting: the walls, the floor, the door handles. He did not need another view of those shortie pajamas, those pale, freckled legs.

"Yeah," she whispered. "They're all in bed."

"Great. Well," he lifted his arms and dropped them back to his sides a couple of times, as if embarking on a doomed attempt at flight, "I guess we should—"

"Do you ever . . ." she began, tilting her head back, as if studying the ceiling.

He looked at her, and it struck him in this moment that he hardly ever looked at her. He couldn't. If he did, he lost track of how long it was appropriate to look at a woman. Better not to risk it at all. He saw the long, stretched tendons of her neck, the vertical groove above her lip, the pale russet of her lashes.

". . . think that you're in the wrong job?"

All the time, he wanted to say, every minute of every day. I should be taking seminars at Berkeley, at Williams, at NYU, not mopping up after drunk teenagers in a French youth hostel.

"Is that what you think?" he said instead. "Don't. You mustn't. I've seen you with the kids. You're great. You're more than great."

"I'm not."

"You are. You'll be fine, you'll see. The first year is always the hardest. After that, it becomes second nature." He put up his hand, and before he knew what he was doing, he was patting her on the shoulder.

It was a mistake. Tears brimmed in her eyes and she couldn't wipe them away because her hands were filled with bottles.

"Sorry," she said.

"It's OK, it's—"

"They . . ." More tears brimmed and slipped down her cheeks. ". . . they put a frog in my bed."

He let his hand fall back to his side. "What?"

"And I hate frogs, I really do. I'm fine with most animals but frogs . . . live ones . . . there's something about them. I can't touch them, I can't pick them up, I just can't, and I—"

Her voice was getting louder and louder so he took her by the arm, opened the door of her room and steered her inside.

Everything was fine, he was telling himself, in a very clear voice. He was helping her. Just as he helped Vita or Hughie at nighttime, if they had a bad dream. He would remove the frog, he would say good night, he would leave. Simple. Everything was fine. He was saying this to himself as he pulled back the sheets of her bed, as he absolutely did not inhale the smell of them, as he stood there in her room, with her behind him. The frog was an arrow-shaped blot on the mattress, legs folded under itself. Gina was there, in a pair of short pajamas; he was in her room. But he was doing nothing wrong. He was helping her with a school prank.

He put both hands over the frog and it leapt inside his palms, much as a human heart might if lifted from the body.

"The window," he said.

Gina sprang towards it and opened the catch. It swung open and he leaned out into the night. In the moment before he released the animal, he was struck by the strangeness, the otherness of the outside—that place out there, devoid of light but pulsing with crickets and birds and invisible creatures. It seemed to him that he had spent weeks, years, perhaps, in the closed environment of the youth hostel, with its glaring lights, wood-lined walls, spidery shower stalls, echoing dining hall, narrow bunks, shouting children. But this place, this velvet dark and star-pierced sky, was right here, just outside its walls, and how beautiful it was, how soft the air, how utterly mesmerizing its secret noises.

He opened his hands and the frog fell into the undergrowth with a cushioned thud. He heard it rustle, right itself, then spring away. He took one more breath of the night, one last look, then withdrew.

It seemed as if something of the night had entered the room. Gina was still standing there, in her pajamas, in the gloom, but she had a bottle in her hand, filled with a silver liquid.

"Don't look," she said, with a small laugh, and she held the bottle to her mouth and tipped it up. He saw her throat constrict once, twice.

She coughed, smiled, wiped her mouth with the back of her hand. "I needed that," she said. "Sorry."

"Don't be," he said, and reached out.

Did she deliberately misunderstand him? He was reaching for the vodka, of course, not her. He suddenly wanted the fierce, hot path of it down his own throat. He was not reaching for her; it was the bottle he wanted.

Either way, she gave him her hand.

And it seemed to him, as he felt the hand of Gina Mayhew in his, a surprisingly small hand, smaller than—he permitted this thought but no more—Claire's, that he was reaching through a space that was as vast and limitless as the universe, and that space was stacked with assumptions that he held about himself. Himself as a family man, as a father, as a husband, as a teacher, who never, unlike some colleagues he could mention, eyed the long legs of sixth-form girls in hot exam halls, never responded to the smitten gazes of certain students, never indulged in those staff-room confidences and allegiances and dalliances, a man who had never looked at another woman since his marriage, a man who had wed the girl he knocked up at university at the start of his PhD, who had given up his dreams of being an academic, of escaping to America, of leaving everything behind, a man who did his share of all the washing and lifting and coaxing and feeding and tidying of family life, a man who very frequently drove his mother to Mass, a man who sent birthday cards and purchased presents and carved the turkey at Christmas. He was a good man. He knew that to be true. But still he reached through it all, all that goodness and duty and assiduousness and care, until he got to something else on the other side.

When he woke, it was just after dawn. The window was still open and the outside was nothing again—gray-lit, damp, birds squawking, insects clouding the air. He stumbled from the narrow bunk, unwinding himself from the sheet. His mind was sprinting ahead of the situation in which he had found himself. He had to get out of there, down the corridor, to his own room, without anyone seeing him. What had he done, what had he done, what, in God's name, had he done? He snatched up his clothes from the floor. It would be OK, he told himself, as he forced one leg then the other into his discarded pajamas, which seemed suddenly to be invested with so much static that they would not admit a human limb; it would be OK. He knew that to panic meant to die; he had learned that in Scouts. Keep calm, keep a clear head, above all don't panic. It would be fine, he would deal with this, he would get himself out of here and everything would be OK. Claire would not find out, he would not tell her, he would never tell her; it was just the once, it would never happen again. Claire would never know and nothing would change; he would talk to Gina and she would understand. She knew he was married, after all. She'd known that from the start—she'd known it last night when she'd slid herself beneath him in the bed, when she'd lifted her pajama top over her head. Claire would never know what had happened here. It was a moment of madness but it was over.

He turned the door handle; he poked out his head. Nothing. No one. The corridor was empty. This seemed to him an extraordinary piece of luck, a sign, if you like, that from now on everything would go his way. He would return home; he would put this behind him; he would be a model husband, a perfect father, from now on. Claire would never know.

Impossible, though, to legislate for chance. Who could have predicted that, at the moment he was lifting the frog from Gina Mayhew's sheets, Hughie, on his way to the toilet in the dark, would trip over a truck left on the landing (and hadn't Claire warned them, again and again, not to leave toys lying around at the top of the stairs?) and fall against the banisters and need to be taken to hospital in the middle of the night for eight stitches across his brow? Who would have thought that Claire would ever have cause to use the emergency telephone number he'd been leaving stuck to the fridge for the nine years he'd been coming on this trip? And who could guess what went through Claire's mind as she stood in Casualty, with two wailing children, in the middle of the night, listening to a cross-sounding French youth-hostel worker telling her that her husband was not in his room, that they didn't know where he was and did she want them to try a different room?

. . .

He rolls over onto his back and looks at Aoife. She is sitting with her legs drawn up, her back to the wall. "Don't hate me," he says.

"Of course I don't hate you."

"I hate me."

"Well, I don't see how that's going to help." She twists a hank of her hair around and around her index finger. "If you look at it one way, you could say it was all the frog's fault."

"That's not funny."

"OK."

"It wasn't the bloody frog's fault."

"All right. Sorry. Bad joke."

"Very bad joke. It was my fault. Mine and mine alone."

"Well, whatsherface—Gina—was there as well, wasn't she?"

"Yes . . . but . . ."

"But what?"

"It was all my fault."

His sister rolls her eyes. "I don't think you can appropriate all the . . ." She shakes her head, as if trying to order her thoughts. "So how long did it go on?"

"Well, she joined the school at the start of the year, in September, and I spoke to her for the first time in, well, probably October, or was it November? And then I remember at the Christmas concert, which would have been December. Mid- to late December—"

Aoife cuts across him with a sigh. "How long was the actual affair?"

"I was trying to tell you. She joined the school in September and at Christmas there was a concert at which all the teachers had to—"

"Are you being deliberately annoying?"

"What do you mean?"

"Why are you droning on about Christmas concerts? Just tell me how long you and she were fucking."

He sits up, outraged. "I really don't think you need to use that—"

"What?"

He lies down again. "It was just the once."

"Just the once?"

"Yes."

"And you got caught?"

"Yes."

"That was bad luck."

"That's not the point, Aoife. The point is I did a terrible thing. If you're married you don't just go around sleeping with colleagues. You're supposed to—"

"Do you still see her?"

He sighs. He covers his face with his hands. "She left. The following week. Went back to Australia."

"Hmm." She grinds out her cigarette and flicks the butt out of the window. "You want to know what I think? I think it's not as bad as you think it is. Of all the shitty things people do to each other, all the awful, dire, cruel things that happen in a marriage, this isn't one of them. You shouldn't have slept with her, sure, but it was only the once. You didn't repeat your mistake. And you didn't leave. You didn't abandon your kids. Claire should be glad that she's got a good one, she should realize—"

"Well, she's not. And she's right. You shouldn't go around sleeping with other people when you're—"

"Jesus, Michael Francis, you're only human. It happens. People fall for other people. So you got a crush on someone. You had a one-night stand. We've all been there. But you realized you'd made a huge mistake. You put Claire first, you put the kids first."

"No, I didn't," he moans, his face in his hands. "Not at all."

"Oh, spare us the drama and the guilt. You did. You had a crush, you slipped up, you dealt with it, you got out. End of story."

"It wasn't a crush," he mutters.

"Whatever you want to call it."

"I loved her."

"No, you didn't."

"I did."

"You didn't."

"I did."

"Didn't."

"Did."

"You can't tell until you've slept with someone at least three times."

He pulls his hands away from his face. "Who says?"

"Me."

"That's shit."

She leans forward on the bed. "Michael Francis, how many people have you slept with?"

"None of your business."

"Two. Right? Maybe three, at a push?"

"I'm not telling," he says, but starts to laugh.

"Well, then. You're going to have to take my word for it. Sex is the great decider. The only decider. And you can never tell on the first time—that's just the equivalent of a throat-clearing."

"How many people have you slept with?"

"I'm not telling you."

"Go on."

"No."

"Please?"

"No. You'd be shocked. You're a different generation from me, remember."

"Give us a hint. Is it more than five?"

"Oh, God."

"More? More than ten?"

"Enough. I'm not playing this game. Tell me about Claire's new friends."

"More than twenty?"

.   .   .

Monica hovers on the landing; she turns her foot one way, then the other, observing how the instep of her shoe has acquired a scuff. She'll have to deal with that today; always better to treat scuffs as soon as they happen. But will her mother have burgundy polish? She doubts it very much.

Beyond the door, in the room that was once hers, then hers and Aoife's, then just Aoife's, she can hear her brother and sister talking. More than ten, Michael Francis is demanding, more than twenty, and there is the sound of Aoife laughing, and she wants to say: How can you be laughing at a time like this? And also: More than twenty what? Tell me the joke.

Monica feels herself to be once more on the verge of tears. She tips her head back to stop them coming and finds herself looking up at the light fitting. An inverted bowl of swirled glass. Venetian, her mother said it was, but Monica found this hard to believe. It dates from the time their mother had a thing for the junk shops of Holloway Road. One of Gretta's longer obsessions. Every week she'd come back with something—a picture made entirely of shells, an ashtray in the shape of the Isle of Man, an elephant's-foot umbrella stand. *Gorgeous,* she'd call her purchases, *an absolute bargain.* How those shopkeepers must have rubbed their hands when they saw her coming. Her mother believed anything they told her, caught in the grip of an urge to buy, thinking she could transform her life, her home, with just one more purchase, just one more thing.

She has had just about enough of this day, Monica decides. It's been a horrible day, the worst day, and its events turn and twist inside her, like a meal she can't digest: the burying of the cat, the journey here on, first, a bus, then a sweltering train, seeing Joe, of all people, and the baby, and the phone call to Gloucestershire and the search of her father's desk, and then there was Aoife saying, It wasn't me, I didn't tell him. She wishes it were over. She wishes it had never happened. She wishes she could walk out of this house and never come back.

It can't be more than thirty, Michael Francis is saying, beyond the door, you're joking me, and Aoife is still laughing and saying, I'm not discussing this.

Monica steps up to the door and pushes it open. The laughter and talk stop, swallowed by silence, just as she had known they would. It is, she reflects, as she surveys her siblings, the downside of being the favorite. You are regarded as one of them, a spy from the parents' camp; when they are together, you are tolerated but never included.

How to play it? Monica considers her options as she stands there. Michael Francis is sitting up, combing back his hair with his fingers, a chastened look on his face. He knows he shouldn't have been chatting and laughing on a day like this. Aoife, however, shoots her a baleful look, extracts a cigarette from a pack at her side and places a book on her lap. The stolen library book, Monica sees.

Should she attempt to join in, to ask them, More than thirty what? Or should she produce the check stubs, shame them into focusing on the problem in hand?

The latter comes to the fore, without her even having decided upon it.

"What," she demands grandly, "are you two doing up here? I've been working away downstairs, going through Dad's things. You might think about helping, rather than just sitting about chatting, rather than just leaving it all to me, as usual."

She continues to talk. Michael Francis stands, as if ready to help in whatever way she suggests; it's always been the easiest thing in the world to make him feel guilty. Fish in a barrel. Aoife, though, rolls her eyes and slumps back against the wall. How can it be, Monica finds herself thinking, that she didn't tell Joe? The fact of Aoife telling him has sat for so long inside her head, has eaten away at her thoughts for years now. Her sister destroyed her marriage: this has been Monica's internal drama, her defining injury. How can it be that she didn't? And if she didn't, then how did he find out? Did a nurse tell him, at the hospital? Or did he just work it out for himself?

Then there was that time in Michael Francis's kitchen. She doesn't like to think about that, can't think about it, can't even recall it clearly. It came in the midst of such a confusing, ruptured time. Did she really say those things to her sister? Did she really let them out into the space between them? She can't have done. And yet she has the distinct feeling that she did. She had told Aoife about what had happened to Gretta after she was born. How can that be?

The sensation of wanting to speak to Aoife surges up in Monica—what exactly she might say is unclear—but there it is, the urge, unfamiliar, unaccountable, to express something, to communicate something to her sister.

Instead, she finds she is saying, "Have you seen these?" to Michael Francis and pressing the check stubs into his hands.

Her brother has to grab at them so as not to drop them. "No," he says. "What are they?"

Monica is glaring at him. "Check stubs," she enunciates.

"Well, I can see that, but what—"

"He"—Monica steps with a flourish towards the window and affects to be looking out at the garden, before turning around again—"makes a monthly payment of twenty pounds to someone he marks down as 'Assumpta.'"

Her brother and her sister stare at her, eyes wide. She feels triumphant but isn't sure why.

"It goes back"—she seizes a check stub at random from Michael Francis's cupped hands—"as far as I can find. Every month, on the first, he makes out a check for 'Assumpta.' Look."

She brandishes an entry, first at Michael Francis, then at Aoife. "Twenty pounds, first of the month."

"Christ," Michael Francis murmurs. He sits down on the bed opposite Aoife. He places the check stubs in a little pile next to him and starts flicking through them.

"Do we know anyone called Assumpta?" Monica asks.

"I don't think so," Michael Francis says. "Doesn't ring any bells with me—although wasn't there a cousin of Mum's?"

"Assumpta," Aoife mutters in the background. "Sounds like a nun, if you ask me."

They ignore her.

"Who?" Monica demands.

"You remember. In that farmhouse up a valley somewhere in Galway. Full of dogs and rotting machinery. Dogs everywhere."

"I remember," Monica says.

"I don't," Aoife says.

"Wasn't she Assumpta?"

"Assumpta? Assumpta," Monica intones to herself. "Was she Assumpta?" She closes her eyes, pictures the kitchen of the cousin, the dogs thrashing about their legs, dogs careening up and down the stairs, in and out of the doorways, on and off the furniture. "No, she was Ailish. And, anyway, she was about a hundred then—she can't even still be alive."

"Fucking hell," Michael Francis, still flicking through the stubs, says, first quietly, then more loudly: "Fucking hell! There are loads of them—"

"I know."

"Every month. Do you think this means—"

From the room below, Gretta can be heard to shout, like the ghost in *Hamlet,* "MICHAEL FRANCIS, I WILL NOT HAVE LANGUAGE IN THIS HOUSE!"

"Well, what else could it mean?" Monica says.

"You think he's gone off with this Assumpta, whoever she is?" Aoife says. "Would he do that?"

"DO YOU HEAR ME?" Gretta booms.

"I don't know," he says. "But it doesn't look good, does it? YES,.WE HEAR YOU."

The three of them take a breath, look around at each other.

"We're going to have to tell her, aren't we?" Aoife says.

"Not yet," Monica says quickly.

"Let's wait," Michael Francis says, "until—"

"Until we have more evidence."

"How are we going to get that?" Aoife asks.

Monica smooths her skirt over her knees. "The same way I got these." She points at the stubs. "We're going to search the house," she says, in her best bossiest sibling voice. She fishes a piece of paper out of her pocket. "I've made this list."

"What list?"

Monica, as he'd expected, ignores his interjection. "Now. I've already been through the desk. I was going to do the wardrobe next. Michael Francis, perhaps you could take the attic and Aoife can do the metal shelves in the shed."

He scratches at his day-old stubble. A treat he always allows himself at the start of the summer holidays: not having to shave. "In what sense 'take the attic'?"

"It'll be tricky," Monica continues, "without Mum seeing. But I'm sure you'll manage."

"I don't know," he says. "What exactly are we looking for?"

"Everything. Anything," Monica says, walking over to the cupboard and pulling it open. "Anything at all." She extracts a cardboard box from a shelf and lifts out of it a wooden chicken, then a Christmas bauble and an owl made from a pine-cone.

Michael looks on. He glances at his watch. Aoife gets off the bed and leaves the room. Outside, on the landing, she listens, while biting at a ragged edge to her fingernail. Stupid idea, she thinks. The stupidest idea she's ever heard. What the hell good is that going to do? And: Monica needn't think that everything is just going to be all right now. And: my God, how monumentally tired I am.

She takes a few steps and finds herself in the doorway of her parents' room. There is a bed, she thinks. How good it would be to be horizontal on it. She lays herself down on it sideways so that her head juts towards the bay windows. Just for a moment. She might sleep. Just for a moment. She inhales the smell of her parents: talcum powder, cough drops, naphthalene, hair oil, shoe leather. She stares at the faded lilac candlewick tufts of their bedspread, enormous, geographic at this proximity, shifting in and out of focus.

. . .

Aoife wakes, confused by the lacy curtains, the electric light spilling in from a door in the wrong place. She jerks up, onto her elbows, and is astonished to find herself in her parents' bedroom, in Gillerton Road.

She feels indescribably terrible. Parched, sickened, light-headed, hot, unbearably so. She kicks her legs, struggling out of whatever she is wrapped in—some kind of itchy covering.

Someone has been in here, while she slept, and tucked a blanket around her. A woolen blanket. Who in their right mind would put a woolen blanket on someone in the middle of a heatwave?

As if in answer to this question, the porcine stutter of her mother's snoring comes through the wall.

Aoife kicks crossly at the blanket until it lies like a shed skin on the carpet. She finds herself riding waves of nausea, as if the bed is coasting up and down on the sea, up and down, up and down. There is a moment in which she is gripped by the certainty that she is about to throw up, right there, and she is assessing the etiquette of vomiting on your parents' bed. But the moment passes. She lowers her head to the bed again, to the disturbingly familiar lilac candlewick, which, she finds, summons many

Christmas-stocking openings, her disemboweling the lumpy sock on this bed—a net bag of chocolate coins, a yo-yo, a peg doll, an orange in the toe—her father feigning sleep, her mother saying, Ooh, and, Ah, and, Now, look at that.

She has no idea what time it is. From the silvering light beyond the net curtains and the nervy arpeggios of the birds outside, it must be dawn, but Aoife refuses to believe it. It's as though she's slept for only ten minutes. She cannot possibly have slept through the evening and some of the night as well.

The split green hands of her father's alarm clock tell her it's twenty past four. Twenty past eleven in New York, where it's still yesterday. Will Gabe be awake?

Aoife drags herself upright. Another moment of near-vomiting presents itself but, again, it passes. She looks under where she was lying for her shoes. She kicks the blanket aside to see if they are there. She lifts the Christmas-morning bedspread, she crawls around the perimeter of the bed, she looks under both her parents' bedside tables. Nothing. Aoife sits down on the bed, pressing her hands into her skull. Not being able to find her shoes suddenly seems like the worst thing that's ever happened to her. Where, in God's name, can they be? They are quite ordinary sandals of red leather but their very absence has imbued them with talismanic value.

She knows, of course, what will have happened. She can see it, as if she'd been awake during its execution. Her mother coming in here with that goddamn blanket will have seen them, picked them up and decided to tidy them away somewhere. It's a habit of hers that drives Aoife to the very brink of insanity: the overzealous tidying. Anything left lying around in Gretta's presence can be tidied away at any moment. Leave your keys out at your peril. Never put down your purse. Don't for a moment think that the cardigan left draped over your chair for convenience will be there when you get back.

Suddenly, magically, she spies them. Pushed almost entirely out of sight under her father's chest of drawers. Aoife leaps from the bed, grabs at them and straps them on quickly, as if fearing they might be dragged from her grasp at any moment.

She ventures out onto the landing. Her mother's snores sound from behind Michael Francis's door. She must have gone to sleep in there. Does that, Aoife wonders, mean that Monica is asleep in their room? She steps nearer the door, presses her ear to its grain. Is she in there? Aoife would like her book, she would like to lay her hands again on Evelyn's work. But she can't risk waking her. Monica has never been one who takes kindly to being woken up.

Aoife makes her way slowly down the stairs. She isn't sure what to do. It's just before dawn. Everyone is asleep. Her book is locked in with her sister. She feels peculiarly awake, as if her body has woken her to say, Time you were at work, off you go to the club.

In the front room she is confronted by the shocking sight of her father's desk, its lid gaping open, its contents scattered all over the floor. She's never seen it open before, let alone disemboweled like this. Did Monica leave it like that? she wonders. And what did Gretta say when she saw it? That would have been an interesting conversation to witness, although, thinking about it, Gretta probably said nothing at all to Monica. Probably said: Whatever you think is best, darling, yes, throw your father's things around, I'll clear up after you, don't you worry.

Aoife sits down heavily in her father's desk chair and pushes her hair out of her eyes. It's so hot. How can it be this hot? It seems hotter down here than upstairs, which can't be right because everyone knows that heat rises.

She eyes things strewn around the desk: sheets of paper, old passports with their corners clipped, receipts, letters. The sight of an insignia on one bit of paper makes Aoife shudder but she isn't sure why. She snatches it up and realizes it's the school crest. *Our duty to God,* the swirling script underneath it reads; she knows this because they were reminded of it, daily, in those interminable assemblies. She glances down it and sees line upon line of typescript before she tosses it away from her.

She is contemplating making coffee or maybe tidying this stuff up or perhaps going out into the garden when she puts her head down on her father's desk. The leather is warm under her cheek, smooth, the smell of polish, paper, ink soothing. She eyes the room, tilted sideways, and thinks she's never seen it from this angle before, which is odd, and then the next thing she is thinking is how loud her mother's voice is, talking like that behind her.

Aoife sits up, lifting her head from the desk, and finds that the room is filled with plinths of light, placed lengthways along the carpet. Is it possible that she fell asleep again?

"You don't say . . ." her mother is saying. "Well now . . . and what did he say to . . . never . . ."

Gretta is talking to Ireland: Aoife can tell by the extra lean in her voice, the slightly more sibillant *s*, the softer *t*. It'll be one of her many relatives; they always seem to call at strange hours. A phone call at six in the morning is nothing to them.

Aoife staggers upright, across the room and into the kitchen, where she looks about her. What to eat? There is a box of cereal standing on the table, her mother's bowl, with a spoon disappearing into milk. The loaf of bread on the counter looks dry, concave across its incision. Aoife leans into the sink and, turning on the tap, drinks from its flow. She is just sitting down at the table with an apple from the fruit bowl when she realizes her mother is standing in the doorway of the kitchen, hands in her dressing-gown pockets.

"What?" Aoife says.

Gretta looks at her, unfocused.

"What's the matter?"

Aoife gets up, goes to her mother, takes her hands in hers and steers her to a chair. "Who was that on the phone?"

"Mary," Gretta whispers.

Mary. A friend, a neighbor, a relative, Our Lady?

"Dermot's wife," Gretta whispers again.

Aoife, still none the wiser, says, "Ah."

Gretta covers her face with her hands. "Get me my pills, would you, Aoife? I've a terrible head on me."

Aoife goes to her mother's pharmacopoeia, kept in a kitchen cupboard. There are about twenty-five bottles, all of differing sizes. Aoife picks up two at random, glares at the labels, puts them down, picks up two more. "Jesus, Mum, what are all these for?"

"Never you mind. Just give us the . . . the pink ones."

"Seriously, what are they? You shouldn't be taking all these. Who prescribes them?"

"*Aoife.*" Gretta is holding a hand to her head. "Just give them to me."

Aoife is getting all the bottles out of the cupboard and lining them up. "Does the doctor know you've got all these? Mum, you've enough Valium here to fell a horse and you really shouldn't—"

"Monica says—"

"Oh, Monica says." Aoife slams a bottle of something beginning with *P* onto the counter. "Monica would benefit from a bit of Valium herself," she mutters. "Give us all a break."

Gretta barges across the kitchen, snatches up a bottle, tips two into her palm and swallows them dry. She turns to Aoife. "They," she says, "have seen him."

Aoife turns away from the bottles towards her mother. "Seen who?"

"Your father."

Aoife examines her mother. Gretta looks odd, her eyes wild, her skin white as parchment. "Who's seen him?" she asks warily, thinking, Please don't say anything like *the little folk* or *the spirits.* Gretta could sometimes go off on superstitious rambles and it could be hard to bring her back.

Gretta sighs. "Didn't I just say? Dermot and Mary."

Aoife is about to snap, Who the hell are Dermot and Mary, but stops herself. "Where?"

Gretta glares at her, as if Aoife is being particularly stupid. "On the Roundstone road."

"What's the Roundstone road?"

"What's the Roundstone— Are you out of your mind?"

"No," Aoife shouts. She has had enough. "I'm very much in my mind. Now will you stop talking in bloody riddles and tell me what's happened?"

"Roundstone," Gretta shouts back, "is a place in Connemara, which you would know if you'd ever listened to a word I said, if you behaved as if you were part of this family, instead of going off and—"

"And what?" Aoife demands. "What were you going to say?"

"Ach." Gretta waves a hand at her. She opens the back door and disappears out of it.

Aoife stands in the kitchen, eyes shut, fists balled. She registers a desire to see Gabe, to stand with him. She would give almost anything, she thinks, to be able to lay her hand on his shoulder at this precise moment, to have him here in this kitchen with her, his face clear of judgment.

After a moment, she goes out of the door, down the steps and towards her mother. Gretta is sniffing into a hankie by the dried-up laburnum. She can tell, as she gets nearer, that their mutual anger has blown away, like clouds off a landscape. She puts her arms around her mother and says, "Tell me."

. . .

Aoife rings Michael Francis's bell again, then lifts the knocker. It's just before eight. She has walked from Gillerton Road, all the way to Stoke Newington. She has seen postmen, bin lorries, milk vans. She has seen empty buses plowing along empty roads.

She has seen the sun insinuate itself into the lightening sky, the streets rise into illumination. Not such an anti-social hour to come calling. And don't people with children always get up early?

Before she can let the lion-faced knocker fall, the door is wrenched open and there is Monica, a dressing gown held closed at her throat.

Aoife is so astonished she almost steps back to look up at the house. She is sure, so sure, that she's walked to her brother's house. But perhaps she didn't. Perhaps Monica moved here and no one told her.

"It's you," she says instead.

"Yes, it's me."

"What are you doing here?"

"I might ask you the same question." Monica sighs. "Do you know what time it is?"

"Just before eight."

Monica thrusts her arm out of her dressing-gown sleeve. "Seven," she says. "Quarter to seven."

"Oh." Aoife looks down at her own watch, which says, unmistakably, eight. "Maybe I didn't . . . set it right."

Monica swivels on her bare foot and disappears into Michael Francis's house. After a moment, Aoife follows.

Monica is in the kitchen, snapping the lid down on the kettle. "Where's Mum?" she says, without turning around.

Aoife slides into a seat at her brother's table, moving aside a cricket bat, a cat collar, a comic and a doll's teacup. "Asleep," Aoife answers, employing the same clipped tone as her sister. Two can play at that game, she thinks. And: You damn well owe me an apology, several, in fact, and I'm not going to let you forget it. In irritation, she snatches up a small, unidentifiable piece of orange plastic and turns it in her hand.

Michael Francis slumps into the kitchen, wearing a T-shirt and a pair of underpants. "Jesus," he says, yawning in Aoife's direction, "was that you ringing the bell?"

Aoife nods. "Sorry."

"What time do you call this?"

"My watch was wrong."

Monica lifts the kettle from the hob. "She'd set it wrong," she says.

In her sister's tone, Aoife hears it all, the entire script of her upbringing: Aoife the dunce, Aoife the idiot, Aoife the girl who can't tell left from right, who can't read or write, who can't manage a knife and fork together, who can't tie her own shoelaces.

"It was a mistake!" she shrieks, gripping the orange-plastic thing (she thinks it may be part of a larger toy or some kind of vehicle). "I'd just got off a transatlantic flight! I set my watch wrong. That's all. It doesn't make me an idiot. I've apologized. What else do you want me to do?"

Her brother and sister are staring at her, as if they know they have seen her somewhere before but can't quite place her. They turn away from her in unison, Monica to the kettle, Michael Francis to get down some mugs, leaving her alone with her ire.

Aoife has to resist the urge to grind her teeth, to throw something at the wall. Why is it that twenty-four hours in the company of your family is capable of reducing you to a teenager? Is this retrogression cumulative? Will she continue to lose a decade a day?

"Look," she says, trying to level her voice, "I wanted to tell you both. Someone's seen Dad. In Ireland."

"Someone?" Monica says, turning around. "Who?"

"Mary. And Declan. Whoever the hell they are."

"Mary and Declan?" Michael Francis tries out the names as he sits at the table, a cereal box tucked under one arm.

"Mary's married to *Dermot*," Monica says, "not Declan. He's Mum's cousin on her father's side. Lives out beyond Derrylea."

Aoife and Michael Francis look at each other.

"Anyway," Aoife says, breaking eye contact with her brother, "they phoned this morning at some ungodly hour to say that someone had seen Dad near a place called Roundstone. He was coming out of a convent, of all bloody things. The last place you'd think to look. It was some cousin of a cousin and apparently Dad stopped and had a chat, then went on his way."

"That makes no sense." Monica's face is unreadable, fierce. "None at all," she says, and her hand darts to her neckline. "What would he be doing there? And at a convent? And why would he go without telling any of us?"

"Where's Mum?" Michael Francis asks.

"She's"—Aoife waves a hand in the air—"at home. She had one of her turns. She went all weird, anyway. Took some pill or other, then went and shut herself in the bedroom and wouldn't come out. By the way, have either of you seen the number of pills she's got?"

They ignore her. "Did she say anything else?" Monica demands. "Anything at all?"

Aoife wrinkles her forehead, trying to remember. She had helped her mother into the house and up the stairs; at the bedroom door, Gretta had shaken her off and disappeared into the room alone. She'd said she needed a lie-down, but Aoife could hear her moving about in there.

"No," Aoife says, "but something's up. She knows something but isn't letting on. She had a whole bad-head drama—"

"Ah," says Michael Francis, "the eternal smoke screen."

"Not at all!" says Monica, putting down her teacup. "What a thing to say. She has high blood pressure, you know that, and to suggest that she's faking her bad heads is just—"

"Do either of you know who Frankie is?" Aoife says, over Monica. "She said, 'Why didn't I think of Frankie?' but then wouldn't tell me any more, so I was wondering—"

"Frankie," her brother says, "was Dad's brother."

Aoife looks at him. She looks at her sister. She looks back at her brother. "What?" she says.

"His brother."

"He doesn't have a brother."

"Yes, he does. Or did, rather. He died. In the Troubles. Years ago, before we were born. You knew that, didn't you?"

Aoife cannot speak. She has to hold in her breath, not let any of it escape. She feels herself filling with rage, from the bottom up. Rage, not at her father for disappearing, for walking out of their lives without a backward glance, for leaving their mother in the lurch, for apparently having had a brother. It is rage at her siblings. At all of them. For keeping this from her. Their father had a brother? The idea is outlandish, unheard-of, ridiculous. But why has no one ever told her? Why has she, yet again, been left out?

Her siblings are looking at her with that mixture of superiority and pity. She is again a pygmy, a Lilliputian in the shadow of their implacable knowledge. She is again five, asking her mother one night how the kittens got in the cat's tummy and wondering, in the blistering gale of their laughter, what Monica and Michael Francis found so funny and why she couldn't join in. She can recall asking them whether it was morning or afternoon and whether she'd had lunch yet and the look they gave her was the same as this one: a pitying glance, cast down from a Mount Olympus of experience. She has no chance of ever catching up; even to try would be futile.

"You knew that," Monica says, sliding into the seat next to Michael Francis.

"I didn't."

"You must have done." Monica slips a diet sweetener into her tea.

"You must have done," Michael Francis echoes, but he's looking doubtful now. "She didn't know." He's speaking to Monica again. "How can she not have known?"

They turn to look at her with curiosity, and Aoife feels their gazes start to prickle her skin, as if she is near something to which she is allergic, like pollen or wool. Monica is murmuring how it wasn't ever talked about, hardly ever mentioned, maybe Aoife just missed it, maybe it had ceased to be something spoken about by the time she had come along, hadn't he died years ago—

A child appears in the doorway and they all fall silent. She is naked, apart from a pair of rainbow Wellies, worn, Aoife notices, on the wrong feet. She holds, by its tail, a one-eyed tiger. "Who are you?" she says, pointing at Aoife.

"Aoife Magdalena Riordan," Aoife says, pointing back. "Who are you?"

"Vita Clarissa Riordan."

They regard each other for a moment. The tiger does a slow, aerial turn, his single eye trained on the floor.

"Why have we got the same name?" Vita says.

"Because we're related. I'm your daddy's sister."

Vita frowns. "That's Daddy's sister." She stabs a finger in Monica's direction.

"I'm the other one."

Vita sidles across the kitchen and comes to stand at the table's edge. She places the tiger squarely in front of her so that it is looking straight at Aoife.

"What happened to your tiger's eye?"

"Pulled it off."

"Oh."

"With my teeth."

"How come?"

"Did not like it, not one little bit."

"Fair enough."

Vita puts her head on one side. "What is it like off the rails?"

Aoife leans forward. "What was that?"

"Granny says—"

Michael Francis looks up from his cereal. "Vita—"

"Granny says what?"

"Granny says you've gone off the rails."

"Does she now? That's very interesting. What else does Granny say about me?"

"She says you've thrown it all away, that you had chances she never—"

"Vita," Michael Francis says. "That's enough."

"Shall I tell you something, Vita?"

"What?"

"You know what it's like off the rails? It's great. It's grand. It's—"

"Aoife," Michael Francis says. "That's enough." He puts his hands over his eyes. "Jesus Christ," he says, through his fingers.

Vita and Aoife look at him.

"Jesus Christ!" Vita moans with glee, covering her own eyes.

"Don't let Granny hear you say that," Aoife says.

Monica says, "Michael Francis, do you still have that bit of paper?"

Aoife says, "What bit of paper?"

Michael Francis says, "Yes," and digs in his pocket.

Aoife says, "What bit of paper? Why haven't you told me about a bit of paper? Why am I the last to know?"

Michael Francis hands it to her, saying, *". . . and they say the end is coming."*

Aoife says, "Why didn't you tell me?"

Vita, laying a hand on Aoife's arm, says, "He didn't tell me either."

. . .

Aoife and Michael Francis argue for a long time over whether they should bring Gretta here or whether they should all go over to Gillerton Road. Michael Francis keeps saying that they have to confront Gretta, that they need a family conference. He uses that phrase over and over again: a family conference. Maybe, Monica thinks, it's something he got from school. If they all go over to

Gillerton Road, how should they travel? Tube or bus or car? If they do go over there, should they all go? Is there enough room in the car? Is it wise to wake Gretta or should they let her sleep? Maybe they should leave it until after lunch.

Monica stands in her brother's back garden. She can hear them batting the subject back and forth, with occasional interjections from Claire and Vita. She stands with her toes curled into the lip of a crevasse that has opened up across the lawn, a fork of dark lightning through the yellowed grass.

"We've lost seven cars down there," says a voice to her right.

She turns to see her nephew. He is wearing a pair of pajama bottoms, his hair sleep-rumpled, his chest bare, his rib cage delicate, branchlike under his thin white skin. He eats from a bowl of cornflakes with a motion as regular as the ticking of a clock.

"I put one down," he continues, through a mouthful of cornflakes, "by mistake, but Vita drove six down there *deliberately*."

"Oh," she says. "I'm sorry to hear that."

He crouches to look into the crevasse, putting down the cereal bowl. "Six," he murmurs again. "Mummy said if she did it again she'd lose her sweets on Saturday. Do you think we'll get them back?"

"The sweets?"

"No, the cars."

Monica looks down into the jagged black tear. "I don't know," she says carefully. "Maybe it's—"

"I'd say not. Vita said she pushed them down there to see if the devils would drive them out."

Monica considers this sentence. She takes each idea separately: pushing cars into a crack in the earth, the devils, the driving out again. No, she concludes, it makes no sense at all.

Hughie seems to glean this because he looks up at her. She is struck by the perfection of his skin, its flawless translucence, the meander of veins beneath its surface.

"Granny says that devils live there, inside the earth," he explains, "so Vita thought that if she put the cars down there, the devils might find them and drive them out. Vita said she wanted to see them."

Monica blinks away an image of tiny red creatures boiling up out of the crack like ants.

"Do you believe it?" Hughie asks.

"Do I believe what?"

"That devils live down there."

"I . . ."

"I don't," he says helpfully.

"Neither do I. And I'm not sure that they'd know how to drive."

He lifts his head and gives her a smile of such charm and trust and brilliance that she feels tears start into her eyes.

"Is Grandpa going to come back?" he says.

"I don't know," Monica says, "but I'll tell you something: if they don't stop arguing about who's going where, I'm going to scream."

Hughie looks impressed and a little bit scared, and Monica goes into the house to find that Claire—who's recently had a most unfortunate haircut that Monica is hoping she got her money back on—is leaving to fetch Gretta.

It has been decided that Claire appearing on her doorstep will wrong-foot Gretta into compliance. Any of them, and she would throw herself back on her old tricks for avoiding things she doesn't want to do: the pills, the headaches, the shrieking. But Gretta will be so disconcerted by her well-spoken English daughter-in-law arriving, alone, to take her to a family conference that she will be hoodwinked into agreeing.

They gather on the pavement outside Michael Francis's house to wave Claire off.

"Don't tell her it's a family conference," Michael Francis says to his wife, through the car window.

"I won't," Claire says.

"Don't even say the words 'family conference,'" says Monica.

"I won't."

"Say 'cup of tea,'" Aoife advises. "Tell her you've come to bring her over for a cup of tea."

Claire nods. "I will."

"Cup of tea," Michael Francis agrees. "Good thinking."

"Bye-bye, Mummy!" Vita calls, dancing up and down on the pavement, caught up in the drama of the situation.

As Claire drives off, Hughie runs down the pavement along-side the car in his bare feet, waving and calling, with Michael Francis shouting after him about putting on some shoes, for God's sake.

By the time Gretta steps through the door, everyone is dressed, more or less. Vita is naked in the back garden and Hughie is inside a tepee, so Monica can't see if he's clothed or not. Monica, her brother and sister are in the sitting room, which has, like Claire's hair, taken a distinct turn for the worse, with the furniture pushed back, the mantelpiece bare and the cushions piled up in a corner.

When Gretta arrives, there is a great deal of bustle: the children surge in from the garden and fling themselves at her; Monica is surprised by the avidity of their affection. Vita holds on to the stuff of Gretta's dress, incanting, "Granny, Granny," and Hughie dances around her, shouting something about marbles.

Monica conducts a careful examination of her mother as she talks to the children. She hasn't, Monica noticed, glanced their way since coming through the door. Which is more than signifi-cant. Gretta looks determined, steely, Monica decides. *Prepared* might be the word. Her hair, for once released from its eternal curlers, has been brushed out and up. A line of firmly applied lipstick across her mouth. She has on her good dress and her proper shoes.

The shoes are the giveaway. Gretta would do anything to avoid wearing shoes, especially in this heat. She has always suffered from swollen ankles, bunions, fallen arches, corns, heel pain, toe pain—her feet, she is fond of saying, are the bane of her life. She spends her time shuffling about in fabric slippers or soft mules and will put on shoes only for special occasions. The fact that she has forced her feet into these leather sandals tells Monica one thing: Gretta is more than ready and they have a battle on their hands.

For a good five minutes, Gretta talks. She gives them a long description of the spuds she'd been peeling and the various people who've called and the heat and the general uselessness of the London Metropolitan Police Force. She still doesn't meet the eyes of any of her offspring.

It would be Aoife, of course, who cuts across her.

"Mammy," she says, interrupting a litany about who slept where and for how long, "do you have any idea why Dad might have gone to Round . . . Round-whatsitsname?"

"Roundstone?" Gretta gives them a strangely wild smile and dabs at her neck with a hankie. "I haven't the foggiest."

Monica leans forward in her chair to catch every nuance of her mother's tone. Gretta is a hopeless liar: Monica can catch her out every time.

"No idea at all?" Aoife persists.

"If it was even him at all this cousin saw," Gretta says, replacing the hankie in her handbag and shutting it with a resonant click. "It might well not have been. You know, I was thinking I'd manage chips for lunch. I've no appetite, none at all, but I might get down a few chips. Egg and chips. It was always your favorite, Aoife."

The mere sound of the word "chips" makes a kind of fury balloon in Monica's esophagus. How can their mother be talking about food, here and now? She battles it down again.

"I'd understood," Monica says, with control, "that Dermot had said it was definitely him."

Gretta's shoulders give a small shrug. She opens her bag, takes a look inside, then shuts it again. "I don't know," she says. Her face is the obstinate mask of a child caught out in a falsehood or exaggeration. "It was Mary, anyway."

"Mammy, does the name Assumpta mean anything to you?"

Gretta's face brightens, as it always does when she talks about anything to do with Connemara. "Assumpta is the name of . . ." Her face falls as she cuts herself off. She gives them a narrow look. "Why do you ask?"

Monica grips the arms of the chair. "The name of what?"

"Is it too much trouble to ask for a glass of water?" Gretta twists her neck around and calls through to the kitchen. "The heat of this place, Michael Francis, it's worse than our house. What have you got in the walls? Sheep's wool?"

"What were you going to say," Aoife asks, "about Assumpta? That it's the name of what?"

"It's the name of—" she begins then cuts herself off again. Her hand flies to the collar of her dress, to her hair, to the arm of her glasses. "It's the name of the convent outside Roundstone, all right? The Servite Convent of St. Assumpta."

"The one Dad was seen going into?"

Gretta shrugs again, fiddling with a loose thread on the hem of her dress.

"Mum, did you know," Aoife says, "that Dad sends money to something he marks as 'Assumpta' every month? It must be that convent."

Gretta continues to wind the thread around and around her finger.

"Did you know that?"

"I did not," Gretta snaps, "and I'd like to know how you know that. Sniffing around the house, going through private papers. I always brought you up to respect private property, not to poke your nose into other people's business. I don't see why anything should have changed."

Monica waits. This is always her policy when her mother is hiding something, hedging something, obviously lying.

Her mother heaves herself about in her chair, snapping open the bag once more. "Rifling around in people's possessions," she mutters, pulling out one bottle of pills, then another. "Never seen the like." She leans her head back on the chair, in a show of weakness. "My head," she moans.

Monica still waits. She can feel Aoife and Michael Francis begin to crack, to look at her and then their mother, wondering where to go next, but she, Monica, knows. She's in complete control. She can read her mother's mind, as if Gretta were a comic-book character with her thoughts appearing as words in the air beside her. Her mother shoots her a quick glance from under her lids. Monica crosses her arms, but says nothing.

"I don't know why he's there!" Gretta shouts abruptly, opening her eyes, struggling with the cap on a bottle of pills. "You have to believe me. Could I have a glass of water, to take my pills? Would that be too much to ask?"

Monica waits a moment longer. Then she uncrosses her arms. "I believe you when you say you don't know," she says, "but I think you might have an idea. And I'd like to know what that idea is."

. . .

Gretta gazes at the bottle in her hand, as if wondering how it got there.

She will not tell them, these children of hers. It is too long a story and happened so long ago, and there's no use in raking up these old things and they wouldn't understand. There is no need for them to know. She only has the story herself because of a strange accident, one of those odd coincidences that can happen with the long arm of the Catholic Church.

The priest had had a cup of tea in one hand and a sandwich in the other and he'd looked at her and said he'd known two Riordan brothers in Liverpool and could they be any relation to Gretta?

They will never understand that, these children of hers, the stretch and influence and all-seeing eye of the Church. Not one of them still attends, not Michael Francis, not even Monica, although there probably isn't a Catholic church out where she lives, in the deep heart of English England. There are Catholic churches in New York, of course, she knows that, but she would bet her last penny Aoife's never darkened the door of a single one of them.

It's enough to break a mother's heart.

If they went to Mass, she might tell them. She says this to herself. If even one of them went, just every now and again, she might see her way to telling them. But, as it is, she can't.

If she hadn't said her surname to the priest, if she'd kept it to herself, it would never have come out, she would never have known, she could have carried on as normal.

She surveys her children opposite her: Monica sitting, arms crossed, so composed, so neat, on the edge of the sofa; Michael Francis next to her, slumped against the cushions, looking as though he'd rather be anywhere else than here; and then Aoife at the end, sitting all tight in a ball, screwed up with crossness and tension. She wants the story, she wants the solution, she *wants to know*. Always has, always will.

Claire is in the room now, handing her a slippery glass of water—she might have thought to wipe it before serving it, but no—and she is whispering to Michael Francis. Gretta hears her say, How can Robert be at a convent, surely men wouldn't be allowed? Michael Francis is whispering back that a Servite convent is one that serves, a working convent, not a closed one. And that, right there, Gretta thinks, is what comes of marrying a Protestant. They have no proper idea of how things work.

Gretta herself only knows by accident. She never sought out the story. She had gone with her sister-in-law to Galway for the day, to hear a priest visiting from Boston. Quite a day they had made of it, catching the bus from Clifden with ten or twelve others early in the morning to make it in time for the special Mass the priest was giving. Aoife was only a baby, so Gretta had taken her along; her mother had stayed behind to mind Michael Francis and Monica. On the bus, when Aoife cried, there were plenty of hands to take her and pass her around, plenty of laps to be bounced and dandled on as the country slid past the windows.

After the Mass, there was tea and small sandwiches, and at one point Gretta found herself being introduced to the visiting priest. Father Flaherty was his name, a Wexford man, by the sound of it, and he laid his fingertips briefly on Aoife's head and Gretta sent up a short prayer of thanks that, for once, Aoife was sleeping quietly. On hearing her name and that she lived over in England, Father Flaherty had looked at her and said he'd known a family of Riordans during his time in Liverpool. Two brothers. Perhaps they were relations of Gretta's.

Her sister-in-law and everyone who knew her was across the room and Gretta stood before the priest in a group of women she didn't know, and there was something in his face that made her say, "No."

A tragic story, the priest said, shaking his head, a lesson to us all in the importance of brotherly love. Gretta's tongue was stuck fast to the roof of her mouth and Aoife felt like a lead weight in her arms and she knew she was going to hear a story about her husband, about the father of her children; she was going to hear the story he himself would never tell her.

She stood there and she thought about her house in London, her lovely little house, and she thought about her children: Michael Francis, the clever one; Monica, the pretty one; and Aoife, the baby. She thought about her garden, with the nasturtiums in pots by the back door and the peas climbing bamboo canes with their hooking green tendrils. She had the passing sensation of wanting to gather it all to her, as if somebody or something were threatening to take it away.

And while she was thinking this, the priest was plowing on with his story about two brothers called Robert and Francis, but everyone called him Frankie, and how they were terribly close, and the hard life they had had after their father died and their mother brought them to England so that she could work as a cook to keep them.

They will never understand that either, these London-born children of hers: how hard it was then, how there was no work in Ireland, nothing to be done, how the mail boats were full of desperate people, coming over to England to earn a crust. These children of hers think they had it bad, people calling them names at school, telling those wearisome jokes in front of them, certain neighborhood kids who said their parents didn't want them to play with dirty Catholics. But they have no inkling what it was like to be Irish in England then, a long time ago, how much you were hated and derided and disrespected. How her brothers had had to go off to hiring fairs in their teens, how her sisters had gone into service in big London houses and never come back. How people spat at you on buses if they heard your accent or turned you out of a café or asked you to move along if you tried to get a bit of rest on a park bench or put up notices in their windows saying NO IRISH. These children of hers have no idea how lucky they are.

Even now—especially now, with all this trouble happening all over the country—the English don't like them. They never will. There are certain shops she won't go into, certain places where she hears a whisper behind her back or someone giving her a disgusted face. She was waiting to pay for a pat of butter at a local shop recently, a place she'd been going to for years, when the shopkeeper slammed something down on the counter before her and told her to get out, he didn't want her sort around here. She was so astonished that for a moment all she could do was stare at him, thinking that in a moment he'd realize he'd made a mistake, mixed her up with someone else, that he would surely apologize and smile. But then she'd looked down at the counter and seen that his fist was resting on a newspaper and on the newspaper was a headline about an IRA bomb. She should have drawn herself up, should have said, My family are decent people, not murderers. But she didn't. She left the butter and backed away. Robert says time in England does that to you. Knocks the fight out of you. Better to keep your head down.

Anyway, so, the priest continued his tale about these Riordan boys, how the elder one, Frankie, always looked out for his younger brother, who was really called Ronan but who had changed his name to Robert, was a quiet, bookish sort of boy, not like Frankie at all, who was a big fellow and liked everyone to know it. How a girl had come to Liverpool, and because she was from the same part of Sligo as the Riordan family and known to their relatives, they'd had her over for tea on her day off.

She was a strange girl from the start, the priest said. Although she was young—couldn't have been more than seventeen or eighteen—she had this mane of silvery-white hair, down past her waist. A tiny, slight thing she was, like a nightingale or a mouse.

Gretta stood and absorbed this description. She built a picture in her mind. She considered it from all angles. She knew straightaway that this image of a girl with silvery hair spread about her shoulders, like a bridal veil, she imagined it, would haunt her for the rest of her life, would live alongside her, like a house ghost.

The priest took another biscuit and said that the Riordan brothers both fell for her in a big way. Both of them. They would go over to the house where she worked, the two of them, hang around the back door to talk to the girl with the silvery hair.

"We could all see trouble brewing," the priest said, with a wry smile. "Their mother came to find me and said what was she to do? Frankie took the girl flowers he'd lifted from the public park. Ronan, or Robert, as he called himself, gave the girl his clothing coupons, his sugar ration. What, their poor mother asked, should she do?"

In the end, things resolved themselves. Robert and his mother came in one day to say that Robert and the girl, Sarah was her name, were to be married. The girl had chosen the more reliable, less wild brother and that was that.

"I married them myself," the priest said, and was it Gretta's imagination or did he look straight at her as he said this? "A beautiful wedding, a baking hot day in the middle of summer. A fine-looking couple they were."

Sometime on the day after the wedding—and, of course, the party back at the Riordans' house was still going on—it became clear that no one could find Sarah. Guests started looking in and out of the rooms and, as word spread, out in the backyard and the street. It was high summer, the middle of a heatwave; no one could sleep for the heat. Soon everyone at the party turned away from the celebration and the music and the drinks, asking, Where's Sarah? Until someone asked, Where's Frankie?

"You can see where this is going, can't you?" the priest said.

Frankie and Sarah had run off. To Dublin, some said, or back to Sligo, said others. Either way, they had disappeared, together, still in their wedding clothes. Some said that Sarah was with child and it wasn't clear by which brother, but no one knew for sure.

"A terrible business," the priest said, chewing his sandwich.

Gretta thought this was the end and she was telling herself to move off, to go, to walk out of there and not come back. But the priest was telling another woman about how Robert had tried and tried to find them. How he went to Dublin and searched the whole city, he went to Sligo but no one had seen them. He wanted the girl back, despite everything. The priest had never seen a worse case of a broken heart.

Not long after, Robert was called up and went off to Europe to fight; the mother was killed when their house was hit by a bomb. Several years after the war, Frankie resurfaced, in Ulster, in prison.

"Prison?" Gretta repeated, because Robert had told her that his brother, Frankie, was dead, killed in the Troubles.

"It was a contentious case and caused a furor at the time. He was convicted for shooting a police officer during the Northern Campaign but another man later claimed he had been the one who did it, that Frankie had had nothing to do with it. Only God knows. Frankie was released, I believe, after many years but, of course, his health was broken. The girl, Sarah, was long gone by this point, to America, some said. And the most touching part of the story, which I heard years later from another priest, is that after Frankie came out of prison, even though they have never spoken to this day, Robert or Ronan makes sure that Frankie is looked after. He arranged for him to be cared for, and if that isn't the very essence of . . . Ah, hello." The priest turned away to greet someone and began a conversation about a particular building in Boston and Gretta was left standing there, until she had the presence of mind to move away, out of the room and onto the pavement outside, where she held Aoife in the darkening air, as swallows flitted around in great wheeling, invisible tracks.

They would never understand, these children of hers. Never.

· · ·

Monica waits. Aoife waits. Michael Francis waits and Claire, who has come to stand beside them, waits.

"It all happened a long time ago," Gretta bursts out, then swallows one of her pills. "I don't even know the details myself."

"Just tell us what you do know," Aoife says.

"The thing is . . ." Gretta says, dabbing again at her brow, "it's not my story to tell. It's your father's and he . . . he didn't even . . . Well. It doesn't seem right for me to be telling it here."

"I think the time for what's right has passed," Aoife says, sitting forward. "Dad's gone. Let's just hear the story and get on with deciding what to do next."

"I can't just . . . The thing is . . ." Gretta screws up her face, as if considering where to start or perhaps which version to tell. ". . . the thing is, there was bad blood between your father and his brother."

Monica puts her head on one side. "Why?"

"I don't know!" Gretta snaps, then looks away. "It was all before my time. But it was a tragedy. A shocking tragedy."

Aoife pounces: "What kind of tragedy? What happened?"

"It was . . . I can't say . . . It was all during the war. A political disagreement. Your father was fighting for the British and then Frankie got mixed up in the Troubles and . . ." Gretta trails into silence, looking frightened.

"And what?"

"There was . . . other trouble."

"What kind of trouble?"

"There was a woman and . . . well, she ran off with Frankie in the end." Gretta is sweating, beads of moisture running down the sides of her face. "And now his health is broken so . . . so let that be a lesson to you." Gretta waves a hand in the air, as if that is the end of the matter.

"A lesson?" Aoife says.

"I thought Frankie was dead," Michael Francis says, at the same time.

"You automatically become an invalid if you fall out with your siblings?" Aoife continues.

"Yes," Gretta says, with emphasis. "No. That's not what I meant."

"You definitely told us he was dead," Michael Francis insists. "You told us that many times."

"I thought he was dead! Your father told me he was dead but then . . . then I found out he wasn't."

"Frankie's alive?" says Michael Francis. "I can't believe this. How long have you known that? And why didn't you tell us? We've got an uncle and we've never even met him. That's really . . . peculiar. Why wouldn't you just tell us? And what has all this got to do with Dad disappearing now?"

"Quiet, Michael Francis," Monica hisses. "Just let her talk."

"Don't tell me to be quiet," he retorts.

"I will tell you, if I want."

"You will not. This is my house and—"

"Don't you two start," Gretta cries. "That's the last thing we need. When I think about you as children, the lovely times we had, I can't believe what's happened to you all. I can't believe that you've just—"

"I think it's underhand," Michael Francis says. "It's deceitful. It's downright strange not to have told us Frankie was still alive. I mean, I know he was mixed up in things over there but he's still family—he's Dad's brother, for Chrissake. Haven't we got a right to know—"

"We don't know if he was mixed up in things," Gretta cries, sitting upright, ever keen to dispel bad rumors about the Irish in general. "There are those who say Frankie's conviction was a miscarriage of justice. A case of mistaken identity. And I've always thought that—"

"The woman," Aoife says suddenly, "who ran off with Frankie. What about her?"

Gretta's head snaps towards her. "What do you mean?" she raps out.

"I mean, what happened with her? What's the story there? Is that why they fell out? Because she left Dad for Frankie?"

"What?" Gretta says. Then she says, "No." Then she amends this to, "I don't know."

Aoife frowns. "Was it quite a serious . . . I mean, were she and Dad engaged or something, beforehand?"

Gretta keeps her face absolutely motionless.

"Mum? Was Dad engaged to this woman before she ran off with Frankie?"

Gretta holds herself very still, as if the slightest movement might give something away.

"They were married," breathes Monica.

Gretta closes her eyes.

"So, did they . . . divorce?" Aoife asks, pronouncing the final word in a whisper, because that is how you always had to say it in Gretta's presence, as if it were the name of some fatal illness that might be contagious if spoken into the air, especially since it had happened to her own daughter.

"I . . . I can't say."

Aoife leans forward. "You can't say?"

"No."

"Why not?"

"Because . . . because it's not something I've talked . . . to him about."

"You've never talked to him about it?"

"No."

"Never? Not once?" Aoife is pushing too far too fast, Monica can see. She's in danger of tipping Gretta over into a place where tempers flare, a place where anger will contain and protect her. She motions at Aoife to stop, to ease up, but Aoife ignores her. "You're telling me you never talked to Dad about his previous marriage? You didn't ask any questions at all when he told you? You weren't curious in any way about it?"

Gretta fiddles again with her collar. She stares at the wall, at the mirror, her mouth set in a straight line. Monica can sense the storm coming and she has to head it off: if Gretta and Aoife get going, all will be lost.

"He wouldn't have told her—can't you see that?" she says to her sister, and Aoife looks at her with an appalled face. "He wouldn't have told you, would he, Mammy? He wouldn't have talked about it at all."

Gretta flaps the hankie at them. Tears spring from her eyes and course down her cheeks and Monica relaxes slightly. Tears, she can cope with. "No, pet," Gretta sobs. "No, he wouldn't. I asked and asked but he wouldn't tell me anything."

"So how did you find all this out?"

"A priest told me. Years later."

Monica comes across the room and puts her arms around her mother. "Come on, it's OK. Don't cry. It'll be OK." She says this over and over, almost as if she is trying to make herself believe it.

"Where, where, where has he gone?" her mother sobs.

"We know where he is, remember? He's in Connemara, at this St. Assumpta place."

"You think Frankie's there?" Gretta whispers. "You think that's it? Your dad sent all that money so that he'd be taken care of by the nuns?"

"It's possible, I suppose. But we'll find out."

Gretta starts to wail through her tears, not all of it coherent, "What else could I have done? I was so young and alone and away from home. I would never have done it but he said there was nothing he could do."

Monica looks at her siblings over the noise and they look back at her: Michael Francis horrified, ill at ease, desperate for this to be over, Aoife with her eyes narrowed.

"What do you mean?" Aoife demands. "He said there was nothing he could do? About what?"

"The . . . the . . . marriage."

Monica scans her mind for what her mother might be talking about and, catching sight of the rosary beads in the open mouth of Gretta's handbag, she hazards a guess: "Do you mean that he divorced this other woman? You mean it's a sin, remarrying after a divorce? Mammy, everyone gets divorced, these days. I know you find it hard that I . . . I mean, I know you were upset when I got divorced but it's not like that anymore. You mustn't think like that."

"No," Gretta sobs on. "No, you don't understand."

Monica holds the hot bulk of her mother to her side. She feels overcome, swamped by this: she would like nothing more than to be transported to the back of Peter's workshop. There is a chaise longue under a skylight, which, if reclined upon, gives a view of nothing but clouds and empty sky and the swaying tops of trees. She would give almost anything to be there now, instead of in a hot room full of people to whom she's related.

"Mum," Aoife is asking, in the hot room, far away from a chaise longue underneath a skylight, "are you and Dad actually married?"

Monica gasps. She turns on her, as if to strike her, as if to give this sister of hers what she deserves, as if to tell her she can't waltz back into this family she so easily abandoned and expect to cast judgments and ask such terrible questions. Monica goes to put her hands over her mother's ears: her instinct is to shield her mother from the person who is saying these terrible things.

But Gretta is strangely still. Her face is turned away. And Monica knows that downwards curve of the mouth, the slightly lowered lids. It's the face her mother wears when she's heard bad language, when she's confronted about some ill-thought purchase, when she has been asked to account for the whereabouts of one of her feckless relatives. The face she wears when called upon to reinvent, to edit, to retell a conversation or an encounter or an event from her past.

Aoife stands up from the sofa. She bends to pick up the glass of water and takes a swig. She rubs a hand over her face. "Wow," she says.

Sunday

〰〰〰   *18 July 1976*

〰〰〰

9) The Secretary of State for Home Affairs will be afforded the
   right to request the support of Her Majesty's Armed Forces
   in helping civilian authorities. Civilian authorities are hereby
   defined as including firemen, medical personnel and police
   officers.

DROUGHT ACT 1976
*An Act to respond to water shortages and droughts in
the United Kingdom*

Ireland

The engines surge into a guttural snarl and an answering vibration is felt throughout the endoskeleton of the ferry. Rivets strain, staircases rattle, doors hum inside their frames, glasses drying on the racks behind the bar tremble together. A dog in the lounge feels it through its paws and crawls under a chair to whimper consolingly to itself.

Michael Francis, in the throes of a debate with Vita about why cheese should not be inserted in your ears, lifts his head to say, we're off. Aoife, having a cigarette on deck, feels it and leans over the railing to see the massive churning of the waters from the rudders and she, too, feels a thrill of excitement. Gretta, rustling through boxes of sausage rolls and griddle cakes and chicken legs, straightens and looks speculatively at the darkening sky through the window. And Monica, who is somewhere in the hinterland between feigning sleep and actually being asleep, her head leaning back against the prickling fabric of the seat, opens her eyes a crack, contemplates the portion of her family opposite her and closes them again.

The night ferry to Cork. The Riordans have done this many times, in their many incarnations: first Gretta, alone, pregnant, then alone with baby Michael Francis, then Gretta with toddler Michael Francis and baby Monica, then Gretta with two children, then finally with Aoife in a carry-cot and the other two running up and down the aisles all night. Gretta went every summer for a month, to visit her mother; Robert joined them for the final week. He always hated leaving the bank, he said, but Gretta thinks it was because he felt uncomfortable in Ireland— belonging yet not belonging, Irish by name and birth but English by upbringing, embarrassed by his confused accent, his soft Irish consonants mixed up with elongated Liverpudlian vowels. They had one last summer at the farmhouse after Aoife was born. Her mother was able to strap Aoife to her back, as she had done with all the other children, to wade into the lough to fetch the eggs from the henhouse, built on a tiny island to keep it safe from foxes. Gretta can see it as if it happened yesterday: her mother with her skirts held clear of the water, Aoife's blue bonnet bobbing above the woolen blanket, the hens chit-chitting and hustling at her approach, her white feet dipping in and out of the lough's brackish waters.

Gretta extracts a sausage roll from its plastic container and chews it. Something to line her stomach. She offers the box to Michael Francis, who takes two, to Claire, who shakes her head.

Gretta's mother passed away four months after that, dropping dead outside the farmhouse door. She didn't suffer, the cousin told her when he telephoned. A clot on the brain. Gretta has pictured this clot, many times, a dark, ferric gathering of blood like a snarl in a skein of yarn, inching its way around her mother's skull, until the moment she reached the step of the farmhouse. Was she going in or coming out? Gretta has wondered. Was she looking up at the sky, her fists on her hips? Was she off to fetch the eggs? The cousin couldn't tell her. Just that she was found on the step by the man who collected the milk.

Then, of course, the farm had gone to Gretta's eldest brother and he had sold it before heading off to Australia. Gretta will never forgive him for that. Never, ever. After that, they visited less, until the old uncle who had lived alone on the island left his cottage to Gretta. As a young girl, she used to walk out across the strand, once or twice a week, sometimes more, if it was cold, with eggs for him, milk, bread and cake. She never forgot, not even when a storm whipped in off the Atlantic. She didn't like to think of him out there, alone in his cottage. There she is now, he would say, when he saw her, putting down his spade. Which was almost all he ever said to her. She would hand over the basket, he would pat her once on the shoulder. She would sit with him, tidy his kitchen, straighten his books and papers, make him a cup of tea, a fried egg. Tide's turning, he would say, after a while, and she would know it was time to go.

When she got the letter from the solicitor in Clifden, she could not have been more surprised. Why had the uncle chosen her, over all her brothers and sisters, over her cousins and her cousins' cousins? It had caused some bad feeling, especially among those who still lived in Galway. But Gretta didn't care. The uncle had given her his house on Omey Island—he had picked her. They could go to Ireland again, whenever they liked. Gretta rented out the cottage for most of the year, making a tidy sum, too, but she always kept August free. August was for them, for the Riordans, for her and her brood, and no one else. Aoife was three, Monica thirteen, Michael Francis fourteen when they had their first month on the island; Gretta would come out of the cottage door at the end of the day and call for them and they would return to her, down the bluff, back from fishing in the lough or collecting shells on the beach or talking to the tethered donkey up the road. Monica only came a couple more times because after that she started walking out with Joe and didn't want to leave him. But Aoife came with her for years, just the two of them, in the cottage together. They were always more harmonious there than in London, not fighting so much.

Gretta sits up now and swivels her head around, surreptitiously levering sausage meat out of her molars with a fingertip.

Where has Aoife gone? She went outside for a smoke ages ago, just as they left Swansea. She should be back by now.

"Where's your sister?" She nudges Monica, who is pretending to be asleep. She is, Gretta knows, not speaking to her but Gretta has decided to act as though she hasn't realized. It usually works with Monica.

"No idea," Monica returns, too fast for someone who was really asleep, and Gretta nods with satisfaction. She knew she wasn't really sleeping.

Monica rearranges the cardigan she has folded under her head and steals a glance at Gretta. Since their screaming match in Michael Francis's house, they have not communicated. Monica still seethes and smarts with it; she will not speak to her mother, she will not, not until she gets an apology or an explanation. The hypocrisy of her, the web of lies she has spun. When she thinks of the time her mother found out she had slept with Joe before the wedding—calling her all those terrible names, telling her she would burn in Hell. She'd been so terrified, so sorry, when all the time her mother, her own mother, was living in extended mortal sin. It turns Monica's mind inside out with disbelief.

But her mother is doing that thing she does when she knows she has annoyed someone: acting all blithe and innocent, pretending not to notice the frost in the atmosphere. She does it every time, and if Monica were to say, Why aren't we speaking, Gretta would turn to her with wide, injured eyes and say, But I would never not speak to you, never, ever. She is fanning herself with a ferry timetable, her polyester dress with its patterns of ferns tight and damp across her back, and she is humming. Monica knows that the humming signifies Gretta mending her mood, much as a roofer might repair a faulty roof. Gretta hums and smooths things over in her head: the ex-offender brother-in-law, gone; the absconding husband, gone; the jaw-dropping fact of her unmarried state, gone. Everything lovely and normal again.

Gretta's head is swiveling about. Monica knows that look, too, that expectant, gimlet gaze. Gretta is looking around for someone to engage in conversation. It makes Monica want to commit violence. How dare her mother be looking around for companions with whom to chat instead of doing what she should be doing, which is getting down on her knees and begging their forgiveness for lying to them their entire lives?

Spotting an elderly couple across the aisle, Gretta hails them with a booming, "Hot enough for you?" The couple raise their heads, like startled sheep, but Gretta is in. She shunts herself along a couple of seats. "Are you on holiday?" she asks. Within seconds, Monica knows, Gretta will have extracted a complete family history from the couple and a comprehensive travel itinerary and will be well on the way to returning the favor.

. . .

It's midnight or thereabouts; Aoife can't be sure. B-deck lounge is ablaze with light, and on every available surface people are sleeping. The corridors and aisles are filled with people stretched out under blankets and sleeping bags. Bodies are curled up in doorways, on tables, on windowsills. Over by the shuttered-up cafeteria, someone at floor level is emitting a throaty, drawn-out snore. The engines grind on and the boat rises and falls, rises and falls. Aoife, lying over two seats, tries not to see the tilting of the floor, the swinging of the overhead lamps, the way the door flings itself open, then pulls itself shut. She tries to think of other things, of the river delta of cracks on her apartment ceiling, of film-developing times, the way Gabe pushes his glasses back up his nose with the second joint of his index finger, the correct procedure with an enlarger and a filter. She tries to tell herself that the passage of the ship is moving her west, closer to Gabe and New York and her real life: it won't be long now until she can go back, until she can try to fix things with him. But the waves keep coming; the boat rolls on; that man keeps snoring; the grille over the cafeteria rattles in its frame.

Aoife sits suddenly. She stands. She steps over the limbs and bags of her family. Gretta murmurs something but doesn't fully wake.

Aoife makes it through the lounge into the corridor. Her mind is focused, her vision clear: she concentrates on this one task. She releases the handle to the toilets, she steps up and over the high metal threshold. She has her sights set on one of the cubicles and would have made it, were it not for the stench of vomit that hits her in the face like a fine mist. She is very clear in her movements. She knows she doesn't have long. She won't make the cubicle, she sees this, so takes a detour for the sink. She is just in time. She holds back her hair, she shuts her eyes, she braces herself. She is bent double by the force of it. She retches into the sink, once, twice and a painful third. She has never, she is thinking, been so sick before. She has never felt so terrible in her life. Her throat is rasped and sore, her stomach clenched like a fist, and those jittering flashes of light that have haunted her all her life are puncturing her vision again. She may never make Ireland: she may expire here, in these puke-washed toilets, and never see dry land. She turns the tap on before opening her eyes. She rinses her mouth, she sluices water over her face, she reaches for the roller towel, sees its grimy, gray, limp length, changes her mind, ducks into the cubicle for some toilet roll, presses it to her face and, as she does so, she is thinking about the oscillating pinprick lights, those familiar, minuscule, airborne ghosts. How they mean a migraine might arrive, like a train at a station, one of those grinding, three-day fogs that can descend upon her. How they flicker and flutter like fireflies. How they come if she's had too much coffee, or looks into bright light, or at the start of her period. How the last time she had them was on a cold day in April when New York was assailed by wind, blowing off the Hudson, whirling paper and trash up off the sidewalk, driving smuts into her eyes, her hair, the seams of her clothes. How she cannot, at this moment, recall having had a period since then.

Aoife stands for a moment in the toilet, with the loo paper pressed over her face. Then she slowly peels it off. She regards herself in the mirror. Her face has a waxen, yellowish look, her eyes are sunken, wide and disbelieving. It is as if it was another person who stepped in here a minute ago. This person, in the mirror, this Aoife, is someone else entirely.

She lurches along the corridor, gripping first the left-hand rail and then, as the prow of the boat dips, the right. She forces open the salt-spattered door and steps out onto the deck.

If there is a heatwave, this particular stretch of the Irish Sea is unaware of it. The wind immediately seizes her hair, her clothes and tries to tear them from her. She bends her head into the force and makes it to the barrier, where she clings on. She can see the rusted side of the vessel, dropping down to the boiling, iron-black waters. Great furls of spume fan out from the boat's path. Yards out to sea, they are flattened, obliterated, then claimed by the waves. Sea spray or rain, she can't tell which, is being hurled at her in great gouts. She is filled with an urge to shout something, anything, into this wind, into the sea, just to feel the feebleness of her voice, its ineffectuality against these Zeus-like, clashing elements.

"Christ!" she bawls. "Shit!"

She can't hear herself. She only knows that she is making the sound because her brain and tongue and mouth are forming the words. She clings to the cold railing with both hands; she lays her head on them, feeling the humming vibration of the boat, the surging of the sea.

The first time she and Gabe slept together was—when? She opens her eyes briefly, sees her wet fingers, patches of rust, thick white paint, the consistency of hardened toffee. Her mind is free-wheeling, unable to gain purchase, but she finds the answer, she knows it.

April. The morning before she left for Connecticut.

Her travel alarm clock had shrilled out at six a.m., hoicking her from a dream about cycling through Clissold Park to a room that seemed suddenly changed overnight. She was always alone in that room but not that morning. She flailed at the alarm clock and knocked it to the floor. It closed in on itself, its ringing muted, obliging, apologetic.

Next to her Gabe grunted, rolled over and clamped her into a one-armed embrace. "You'd better," he mumbled into her hair, "have a watertight excuse for waking me up this early."

"Hmm," she managed, pushing her hair out of her eyes. She did not share Gabe's talent for morning eloquence. She put one foot out of the bed. She put out the other and stood up. She fished around on the floor for something—anything—to put on, finding a pair of trousers, hers, Gabe's sweatshirt and some socks that neither fitted nor matched.

By the time Gabe emerged from the sheets, she was properly dressed, hair tied back, finishing her coffee and putting on lipstick.

"How can you do that without a mirror?" Gabe said, from the doorway, watching her as she shut her lipstick with a click. They grinned at each other, then looked away. He reached across the table for her coffee cup and took a swig.

"Jesus," he said, wincing. "Has anyone ever told you you make terrible coffee?"

She stood. "No. Other people who have stolen my coffee have been very complimentary."

He followed her to the sink and put his arms around her from behind. "Well, then, they're idiots with no taste buds." He lifted her hair and started kissing her neck. "Where are you going, anyway? It's practically the middle of the night."

Rinsing out her breakfast bowl under the tap, she said, "I'm going to a nudist colony."

Gabe was momentarily stalled in his exploration of her neckline. "Now, if anyone else said that to me, I'd assume they were joking. But you're not, are you?"

"Nope. Evelyn's doing some portraits."

"I'd kind of guessed that. I didn't think you'd become a nudist or anything." His hands parted her blouse from her waistband. "Although, if you had, I'd be all for it."

"Gabe, I have to go."

"I know." But his hands were latched onto her breasts and he had wedged her against the sink.

"I really have to go." She twisted around within the circle of his arms and faced him. "I'll be back in three days."

"Three days? That long?"

"I can't come back to bed now, Gabe. I honestly can't."

Gabe swept the crockery and cutlery from the counter into the sink. "Who said anything about the bed?"

She nearly missed the train to Connecticut. She reapplied her lipstick as she sat opposite Evelyn in the carriage. They went to the nudist colony. They spent their time photographing naked people sitting on deck chairs, standing at a barbecue, playing Ping-Pong. When she got back, she went to the restaurant to find him, and when he'd caught sight of her, through the steam and chaos of the kitchen, his face had shown mostly relief.

On the ferry to Ireland, Aoife peers out into the furious black night. How, in God's name, had this happened? The first time was the night before she left for Connecticut and there had been numerous times in between but they had used something, she knows they did, every time. Her last period was when? A couple of weeks before Connecticut. Three months, maybe. Could it be that long, could it—

"Are you about to throw up or have you just done so?" Michael Francis, who has appeared from nowhere, asks.

Aoife rears her head, like a frightened horse. Her face is wet, rain-lashed, her hair wild. She stares at him as if she doesn't recognize him.

"You OK?" he says, patting his pockets. "I have a mint here somewhere, if you want it."

She shakes her head. "No, thanks."

"I always thought you were the one with the iron stomach," he says, putting an arm about her shoulders. "Maybe you lost it out there in New York."

"Maybe I did," she says, looking out to sea, still gripping the rail.

"Come on," he says. "Enough with the King Lear-ing. Let's go inside."

She shakes her head again. "I'm going to stay out here."

"Really? It's bloody cold."

"I know. I'm enjoying the novelty."

"OK. Suit yourself. I'll see you later."

Michael Francis staggers back across the slippery deck, forces open the door and steps inside. He gives her a wave from behind it. She removes one of her hands from the railing to wave back. She watches the lit windows of the lounge until she sees him reappear, sees him lope across the room, then wedge himself next to Claire and Hughie, sees him accept the sleeping form of Vita, laying her gently across his lap.

He'd come out to find her. The thought makes her almost smile.

The ferry rises and falls, with an inexorable rhythm, bearing her onwards. Aoife keeps holding on to the railing with both hands. If she stays like this, she tells herself, everything will be OK.

She doesn't understand. This thought sits, heavy as wet cloth, in her head. She doesn't understand at all. She's careful about this kind of thing, a lot more careful than other people. In some areas of life she knows she is a little lax, a little complacent, but not with contraception, partly because she knows what a useless parent she'd make. What kind of a mother would she be if she couldn't even read a bedtime story? How the hell did this happen? And how can she have been so stupid as not to notice? She tries for a moment to picture it, the being clinging to her insides, the way that silent-movie actor grips the clock's hands as he dangles above traffic, but she cannot. She cannot, she cannot, she cannot account for this. She cannot even begin to think what Gabe will say. She cannot do this.

. . .

By a concentrated feat of human origami, they have managed to fit into Michael Francis's car, Michael Francis driving, Gretta next to him, Monica, Claire and Aoife on the backseat, taking it in turn to have Vita on their knees, and Hughie in the boot, rolling around on top of the bags.

For the first leg of the journey, coming off the ferry and negotiating their way from the docks, through Cork and onto the road north, Aoife sat in the middle, wedged between Claire and Monica. But just outside the city she'd had to get out to throw up into a patch of dock leaves, then again two miles farther on, after they had been up and over a humpbacked bridge. After that, she had been stationed by the door, with the window rolled right down and the breeze blowing over her. Hughie complained about the wind, said it made his hair feel funny, but Gretta told him, from the front seat, to stop his complaining.

Only Monica noticed the way Claire twisted her head at this, the way she cast an unreadable glance at her son.

After that, for a while, everyone was quiet.

Michael Francis is keeping his thoughts very practical: after Limerick, they head straight up towards Galway, then towards the coast. He is aware of his wife, sitting at his back, with her arms around their daughter. He is not thinking about her, he is not thinking about the fact that she came, that she gave up going to a tutorial to accompany him to Ireland, he is not thinking about that, and what it might mean for them, not at all. He is also not thinking about his father and his marrying an Irish girl from Sligo and his brother running off with his bride the day after the wedding and the possibility that there might be another Riordan half sibling out there.

Aoife is letting the air blast into her face and, with her eyes shut, is inking a diagram in her head of their positions in the car, with unbroken lines for those who are communicating and dotted lines for those who aren't. Those in the second category: her and Monica, Monica and Gretta, Michael Francis and Claire, Hughie and Vita (after a brief spat over a packet of Refreshers). She is also picturing her father searching the streets of Dublin for his bride and his brother. Which of them had he wanted to find, most of all? She tries to inhabit this scene: her father asking at boardinghouses, at the docks. The unbearable familiarity of the face you were searching for. Did Frankie look like him? She can feel the flare and crackle of his anger, his heartbreak. How would it feel if your own brother betrayed you like that, stole away the girl you loved? Monica's thoughts run along one track: she hates this car, she hates this trip, she hates this whole family; she wishes she had never come: she wishes she had not worn her plaid dress, as the car is so cramped that it will look crushed when they finally get out, if they ever get out.

Claire is looking, every now and again, at the back of her husband's head, at the glimpses of his hands on the wheel, at the section of his brow, just visible in the angled rearview mirror, watching the back of the seat strain as he shifts his weight. She is feeling the strange dichotomy of a long marriage, when a person can seem at once toweringly familiar and curiously alien. She is feeling the hot, dense weight of Vita, the small rounded heels pressing into her thigh. She turns her head and Hughie instantly raises his eyes, alert; he looks to her still for explanation, for signs, for clues on how to behave, how to react, what to expect from the world. She smiles her most reassuring smile and he lies back among the luggage, satisfied.

And Gretta? Gretta is thinking about serendipity, all the coincidences of the world: how your husband can go off, disappear, you can search all over for him, call the police, rake through his possessions, but really all you need is a call on the telephone from a cousin remarking how someone had told someone that they had seen Robert walking along the driveway of the convent up the road, and wasn't that a strange thing?

Gretta smiles to herself. She'd told them all, these children of hers, who think they're so clever with their calls to the police and their insistence on searching the house, that things would work out. And work out they have. The day before, they'd stood on the pavement outside Michael Francis's house, Monica shouting those awful things at her, Aoife telling Monica to shut her face, Michael Francis trying to keep the peace, as ever, saying they knew where Dad was now, let's concentrate on that. Gretta and Monica had got back to the house in a terrible, frayed tangle. And then what had happened? They had packed for Ireland.

Gretta moves her handbag from her knee to the floor of the car, then back. She'd always known it would come good, that they'd find him. And here they all are, off the night ferry, going up to Connemara.

Past Limerick, Aoife says, "Stop, please." Michael Francis swerves to the side of the road and she bursts out of the car.

"Aunt Evie is sick *a lot*," Hughie observes, with interest, from the boot.

"Don't watch, sweetheart, it's not polite," Claire murmurs. "Look away."

"She is," Monica says.

"It's *Aoife*, Hughie, not *Evie*," Michael Francis says. "*Ee-fah*."

"Eefie," Hughie repeats obediently. He pushes his cheeks up, so that his eyes are obscured, then down, so that his lids are stretched wide. It makes Monica feel quite peculiar. "I'm surprised she's got anything left inside her," he says.

"Maybe she'll sick up her own stomach," Vita, whom they'd assumed to be asleep, pipes up.

Hughie laughs, delighted by this notion. "Maybe she will. And it will spill out all over the road and Daddy will have to pick it up and push it back inside and—"

Gretta releases the catch from the door and steps onto the grass verge. A swallow arrows above her, its wing flashing blue-black as it turns back on itself. She goes up to her daughter, who is still bent over, hands on knees, gulping mouthfuls of air. Gretta gathers the hair hanging in her daughter's face and holds it back.

"Thanks," Aoife gets out, and retches again.

Gretta pats her back, which feels clammy through the thin stuff of her blouse. Aoife straightens, eyes closed; Gretta hands her a tissue. She surveys her younger daughter; she sees the grayish pallor of her cheeks; she sees the tremble of her fingers. She hands her another tissue. "Is there something you need to tell me, Aoife?"

Aoife's eyes snap open; mother and daughter look at each other for a moment. Gretta feels, just for a moment, the presence of those babies, those people who never breathed air, five of them there were, her not-quite-children. They stretch between her and Aoife, now and forever, like a row of paper dolls. The swallow dives near them again, throat red, like a warning.

"No," Aoife says.

Gretta takes a step closer. "Please tell me you haven't got yourself in trouble."

Aoife, despite herself, despite everything, starts to laugh.

"What's so funny? I don't see anything funny about this."

Aoife balls up the tissue and shoves it into her pocket. "It's 1976, Mum."

"What's that got to do with anything?"

"You don't say 'in trouble' anymore."

"I'll say whatever I like. So you are? You admit it?"

"I admit nothing. It's none of your business."

"Oh, God." Gretta holds a hand to her forehead. "You're a young girl, unmarried—"

"You're one to talk," Aoife says, and Gretta draws back, as if Aoife has struck her.

In the car, Monica leans over Claire to get a better view. "What are they talking about?"

"I don't know," says Claire, who has caught some of the conversation and who had, anyway, come to her own conclusions about Aoife's peaky appearance and odd appetite.

"Yes, what are they talking about?" Michael Francis says from the front seat. He leans on the horn, briefly, irritably, shouting, come on, but he hasn't reckoned for the effect this will have on his children. It is instant: they hurl themselves in one movement into the front of the car and into his lap, shouting, can I do that, can I, can I, it's my turn, no, it's my turn, no it's mine.

"Stop it," he shouts, in between flailing limbs and the sounding of the horn. "Get back to your seats, I mean it, both of you, stop this minute." Hughie's hand catches him on the temple, an elbow—Vita's, he thinks—is driven into his throat and then a knee is ground, with sickening accuracy, into his groin. The horn drowns his screamed expletive; petals of pain open and blossom in his lower body, fireworks spray across his brain. He is immobilized by agony, by a seat belt, by the weight of his offspring.

"Move over." Claire is there, opening the door beside him, removing the children from his lap, one by one. "I'll drive."

. . .

By lunchtime, they have reached the Twelve Bens, great gray mountains that rear up from the line of trees, their elephant-hide sides replicated in the lough water. Even Vita is awed into silence by their shadowed presence. Before they reach the village of Roundstone, Gretta directs Claire to the right, then down a track.

"Drop me here," she says, as the car rumbles to a place where two tracks cross, under a cluster of oak trees.

"What?" Monica says, jerking forward. "Here? Why here? We can't leave you here."

"The convent's just up there." Gretta gestures with a hankie. She is rummaging in her bag. She extracts one bottle, seemingly at random, knocks back a pill, then finds another and tosses two into her mouth. She crunches them between her teeth and pulls a face. "I'm going alone."

Monica remonstrates, objects, argues; Michael Francis tries to say that he thinks they should all stick together; Claire gives Hughie and Vita a biscuit; Aoife steps out of the car.

"Where are you going?" Michael Francis says, just as Hughie asks hopefully, "Is she going to be sick again?"

"Just a wee," she says, over her shoulder, and disappears into the undergrowth.

Gretta stands firm. She gathers her bag, her headscarf, her pills, her hankie; she steps from the car and she sets off down the track. "Come back in two hours," she says. She pauses briefly to watch Aoife emerge from behind a tree, zipping up her trousers. They look at each other, then Gretta walks on, without speaking, disappearing up the track.

Aoife gets back into the car.

Vita leans forward from her perch on Claire's knee and looks closely at her aunt, this fascinating, vomiting person, who has appeared from nowhere, in a top printed with flamingos. Vita is overcome by an urge to lick Aoife's bare arm. She wants to taste that tanned skin, feel those tiny hairs under her tongue; she has an idea it would be smooth as honey and that the freckles might have a peppery tang. She stretches out quickly, before anyone can stop her, and runs her tongue up her aunt's arm, near the elbow.

Aoife swivels her gaze to meet her eye. "Did you just lick me?"

"No," Vita says, still with the tip of her tongue out. "Are you feeling better?"

"I am." She looks at the child for a moment longer, then whispers, "You know what I think we should do while Granny's away?"

Vita, quick to catch the confidential tone, whispers back, "What?"

"Go for a swim."

They park the car at Mannin Bay. As soon as they open the doors, the children are off, greyhounds from traps, haring about in circles and zigzags. Hughie whirls a plume of seaweed above his head and Vita heads in a straight line for the sea, tiny wavelets that turn and crisscross each other on the silver sand.

Monica sits down on a rock, dress tucked beneath her. She sifts handfuls of the beach—broken pieces of whitened coral, smoothed and jointed like the bones of tiny creatures. Touching it gives her a sensation akin to a bell sounding in a belfry, so deep is the familiarity of it. All her childhood summers seem to be distilled into this particular moment, into this particular act, with her fingers digging deeper into the sand, all those days of running on the beach in a swimming costume and an Aran sweater, Michael Francis always ahead of her, his pink feet sugared with sand, all those rides on the back of her grandmother's donkey, all those trudges through the rain that was only gentle water falling from the sky, warmish and clean, not like the rain in London. The digging for peat with her uncle and her mother, the slicing heft of the spade's drop, the twisting out the water from washed sheets, hens peck-pecking around their legs.

She looks up and sees silhouettes of people, her people, glowing black against the bright sea, her brother and his wife near the shore and Aoife, like a sprite, pulling off her clothes, the children screaming at the sight.

She looks down. Minuscule fibulas and tibias of coral caught in the creases at her fingers' base. It is at this scale Monica remembers Ireland best: the minutiae of this bay, the feel of this strange coral sand, the layers of color in the sea, the green, the turquoise, the deep blue, the great swags of bladder wrack that lie on rocks like fat seals.

Aoife is in the water now; Monica can hear her shout. Vita is going in after her, single-mindedly crashing through the waves. Two of a kind, Monica thinks. Does Claire realize there'll be trouble ahead with that one? Michael Francis is dashing after his daughter before a wave knocks her over. He is lifting her kicking, shrieking form high in the air, swinging her up, and when she comes down onto the sand, she is laughing again, her anger left up in the sky somewhere. Monica thinks she can see it dissipate into the blue beyond.

Hughie sets to work excavating a hole, working his hands like a dog, sand spraying up behind him in an arch. Vita watches for a second, maybe two, then copies him. Michael Francis turns and is surprised to find his wife standing by him. He puts his arms around her, closing the gap between them. It is an act of pure instinct, done without thought, and as he feels her body come into line with his—so familiar is that feeling, so exactly right—he wonders if she will pull away, whether she will accept it, and he wonders, too, why they haven't stood like this for so long, too long. When was the last time and how can they not have stood like this? Why don't they do it all the time?

She doesn't pull away. She goes so far as to put her arms around him. He feels them fasten and lock at his waist and he closes his eyes with the perfection of it all. He feels, he realizes, jealous of himself, as if he is looking back at the scene from a distance.

"Thank you for coming," he says to her.

"Don't be silly," she says, her head tucked under his chin. "Of course I'd come."

When he'd got back from taking his mother and Monica home yesterday, he'd had Aoife with him. Monica and Gretta had returned to Gillerton Road in a bad state, the two of them screeching and weeping at each other, Monica beside herself with fury. Monica, their mother's favorite, their mother's pet, their mother's confidante. How could you, she kept sobbing, how could you lie to me like that, how could you pretend to be married when all the time . . . And Gretta weeping noisily, I'm sorry, darling, I'm so sorry, I wasn't lying, I just, I didn't mean to, I just.

When he'd moved into the hall, ready to leave and go back to his own house to pack, Monica was ranting about the time Gretta had made her go to confession because she'd slept with Joe before their wedding and Gretta had said that she'd paved her way to Hell. He'd turned to call goodbye and found Aoife next to him, arms folded.

"Where are you going?" he'd said.

"Wherever you're going," she said. "There's no way I'm staying here with them."

So it was him and Aoife who had walked back through his front door, to find Hughie and Vita sitting side by side on the stairs, both with a kind of wide-eyed look on their faces. There was a noise of chatting from the sitting room, and cackling and a kind of sliding zither music that he'd never heard before in his house.

"What's going on?" he'd said to his children.

Hughie looked from him to Aoife to the shut sitting-room door. "A past-papers study group," he'd said, pronouncing the words with a care that broke Michael Francis's heart. He could feel it breaking right there and then as he stood in his hallway, with his children before him on the stairs, breaking and falling in pieces down through his body.

Claire appeared in the doorway, quickly shutting the door behind her.

"Oh," she said, "it's you. I didn't know if you'd be back or—"

"Of course I'd be back," he said. "Why wouldn't I be? Why are you talking to me as if I don't live here anymore?"

Claire held the door shut behind her, the handle between her palms. She looked flushed, disheveled, her hair standing on end, the way she often did after drinking red wine. "I'm not. It's just that—"

At that moment, a woman Michael Francis didn't recognize burst through the door. She had her graying hair in bunches, like Vita sometimes did, and she was wearing a long, loose, wrap-around skirt.

"Welcome!" she said, throwing her arms into the air.

"Welcome?" Michael Francis said, but the irony was lost on the woman, who was seizing Aoife by the arm.

"Have you come to join us?" she said to Aoife, her eyes alight with evangelical zeal, and Michael Francis didn't have much to be glad about at that moment—nothing at all, in fact—but he was glad that, of all his family, it was Aoife who was with him. Not Monica, not Gretta. Aoife was the only one who could have coped with this.

"You'll find us a very friendly crowd," the woman is saying to Aoife. "I'm Angela and this is Claire. It's her house and—"

Unperturbed, Aoife stepped away from the woman with bunches and onto the bottom step. "Why don't you," she said, taking Vita and Hughie by the hand, "show me your bedroom? I haven't seen it yet. Come on, let's go upstairs."

The woman returned to the sitting room and he was left in the hallway with his wife. He sat down on the bottom step. He leaned his head against the newel post and was surprised to find a modicum of comfort in the smooth, varnished wood pressing into his temple. He looked not into his wife's face, but at her feet, her bare feet. She'd always had particularly beautiful feet: slender, high-arched, with curving, pale nails. Not like his—hairy, wide as plates, the toes all broken and crooked from his days playing rugby. He would, he decided, keep things brief. He outlined in three sentences what he was going to do, keeping his eyes only on her feet, on the pearly tips of her nails, on the web of blue veins at the instep: he told her the whole family was going to Ireland, tonight, on the night ferry and they were leaving in half an hour.

"And," he said, "I'm taking the children. You can do whatever you want. I don't—"

"I'll get ready," the owner of the feet said. "I'm coming, too."

On Mannin Bay, Hughie is jumping in and out of his hole; Vita is kicking at the shallow water, sending it up into the air, where rainbows flash in and out of the spray.

"Listen," he says to Claire, who is still pressed to his side.

"Mike," she says, "I need to say something to you."

He pulls away. "Oh, God, no."

"What?"

"Please no." He puts his hands over his ears. He cannot bear this, he cannot, he doesn't want to hear it. He is filled with an urge to run, run up the beach, leap into his car and drive away, anything to avoid hearing his wife say what she is about to say.

"What do you mean? What do you think I'm going to say?"

"I . . . I don't . . ." He slumps down onto the sand. "Just don't say it."

"Say what?"

"It."

"What's 'it'?"

"That you've"—he circles his hand in the air—"slept with someone else. Don't say it. Not now. I can't take it."

Aoife, buoyed to a horizontal position in the sea, the sky above her, the seabed below her, feels her kicking feet hit solid sand. She stands up to the disconcerting discovery that she's in shallow water: she's up to her knees, the sea pouring off her, not far out, as she'd thought. She hoicks up her wet knickers and starts to wade out of the waves, her breath coming in sharp jags, her hair plastered to her back and shoulders. She passes Michael Francis, who is sitting on the sand, his head bowed, Claire standing over him, and the children, who are bailing water out of a rapidly refilling hole.

"You've got your work cut out there," she says, as she passes, and they look up at her, their faces distant, transposed, and she realizes she is calling to them across an invisible galaxy, that they are currently inhabiting not Mannin Bay but the realm of their game.

She collects her clothes from the ground, shakes the grit out of them, picks off a few strands of seaweed. Monica is sitting not far off, her knees together, skirt spread about her, as if, Aoife thinks, she is readying herself for a portrait. Aoife rolls her eyes to herself, strips off her sodden bra and pulls her blouse over her head.

"How was the water?" Monica's voice reaches her through the air between them. The beach and sea shimmer and refract in the heat; seaweed dries to rocks; sand cracks and powders in the sun.

Aoife looks up. Her sister has her hands clasped tight on her lap, her sunglasses obscuring most of her face. "Fine," Aoife says.

Monica waits for a moment, then nods. She clearly cannot think of anything else to say.

"Are you going in?" Aoife asks.

"Me?" Monica sits straight with the shock of this idea. "Oh, no. I can't swim."

Aoife, caught in the act of pulling on her trousers, stops. "You can't swim? Really?"

Monica shakes her head. "No."

"Is that true?"

"Yes."

"Really true?"

Monica bristles at this questioning. "Yes," she repeats with emphasis. "Ask Michael Francis, if you don't believe me."

Aoife comes closer. She sits down on a patch of sand, near but not too near her sister. "How come?"

"I don't know." Monica's voice is just at her shoulder, coming at her from behind. "I just never learned. I never . . . I could never get in the water. It terrified me. The depth of it."

"Weren't you made to go to those swimming lessons at the pool? Those sadistic teachers who stood on the sides and jabbed you with rods if you did it wrong?"

"I went once. But I hated it."

"Now, why would that be?"

Monica doesn't reply so Aoife turns to look at her. Her sister's face is uncertain, perplexed, as if unsure whether Aoife is making fun of her.

"Mon, I'm joking. Sadistic teachers? Rods? It's called sarcasm. Of course you hated it. Everyone hated it."

"Oh, I see." Monica nods, smooths her dress, a tailored checked number that looks—to Aoife—unbearably hot and restrictive. "Well, swimming isn't really very me."

"Right."

They sit on the beach, together but not quite. Aoife stretches out her legs, runs her toes through the sand in geometric arcs. She is looking at them one way, then the other, squinting to plot their imaginary remaining curves, when Monica speaks again.

"What do you reckon?" She indicates the figures of Michael Francis and Claire, who are down by the shoreline, Claire gesturing with expansive pushes of her hands, Michael Francis still slumped on the sand. "Do you think they'll stay together?"

Aoife twists a strand of her damp, salty hair. "I don't know."

. . .

By the time Gretta reaches the door of the convent, she is hot, out of breath and furious. She hadn't known the driveway would be that long, hadn't reckoned for the terrible stony terrain of it, how she'd have to watch each step if she didn't want to turn her ankle, her with her bad knee.

She is perspiring, panting and all of a sudden livid with her husband as she yanks the bell. How dare he? How dare he come here and tell no one and make her trek all the way out here, with all the kids and the grandchildren in tow? What, in God's name, did he—

The door opens and the figure of a nun appears and, at the sight of her, Gretta's outrage deflates, as if pricked by a pin.

"Hello, Sister." Gretta makes a humble beginning; she has to stop herself genuflecting. "I'm so sorry to bother you but I wonder if you can help me. I'm looking for my—" Gretta comes to a sinkhole. She finds she cannot say the word "husband," not to this lady, not to her face, lined yet serene, framed in white, beautiful gray eyes she has, her fair eyebrows raised in inquiry. "Well, my . . . He's here, you see, Robert . . . Ronan . . . Mr. Riordan, visiting . . . someone. Frankie, um, Francis, Francis . . ." Gretta cannot recall the surname—whatever was it now?—and then she remembers. "Francis Riordan."

The nun inclines her head. "Come in," she says. "I'll take you down."

She steps backwards, and Gretta follows her into a large vestibule, thickly carpeted. Her shoes sink into its mosslike texture. She follows the nun across the hallway, down some stairs, along a corridor. She is, she realizes, terrified, more terrified than she's ever been in her life. The hunt for Robert/Ronan has been all very well, thus far: the children arriving, the visitors, the detective trail, then the phone call to say where he was. But suddenly it strikes Gretta, as she walks, like a penitent, behind the nun, that Robert may not want to be found. He may not want to be brought back. He may have left with the thought that he would not be returning. He may, in leaving that day, have made the choice to discard the family and enter back into his past. Why had this not occurred to her before? What, in God's name, is she doing here?

They pass a huge wooden crucifix, a painting of the Holy Father, a tapestry of a religious scene, rendered in wools of orange and purple—Gretta hasn't a chance to identify it, something with a lumpish hill in the background and a tangerine-haired Jesus holding up His arms to Heaven. They pass into a narrower, darker corridor with a flagged floor. *Click, clack,* go Gretta's shoes on the stone, *click-a-clack.* She feels pain thumping its way into her head. She wants to reach into her bag to find her pills but she daren't in front of the nun.

"Have you come far?" the nun says, over her shoulder.

"Not too far, Sister." Gretta is having to almost gallop to keep up with her—long legs she must have under that habit. "Well, London, actually. But, you see, I'm from here. I grew up near Claddaghduff, so it doesn't feel far. If you see what I mean."

The nun says nothing to this.

"How long," Gretta ventures, and her heart is leaping, leaping because this is the only bit of the story she hasn't had, "has Francis been with you?"

The nun turns her head as they descend a smaller, narrower staircase. "Mr. Riordan has been with us a long time. Fifteen years or so, I believe."

Gretta puts on a last spurt of speed so that she comes level with the nun and they are walking down the steps side by side.

"His health has not been good, as perhaps you know. But he has kept the garden for us and worked on building maintenance, to the best of his abilities. We've always found him to be a peaceable addition to our little community. But, now, of course," the nun adds, "his time with us is coming to an end." She stops outside a door. "Here you are," she says, indicating with a hand. "You may go in."

"Is . . ." Gretta swabs at her neck with her hankie, adjusts her bag on her arm. "Is he in there?"

The nun inclines her head. "You can go in," she says again.

"Could I trouble you, Sister, for a glass of water? I'm so sorry. It's just I've had a long and thirsty walk and I've a pill I should take. Will I come with you to get it? Maybe that's easier. I wouldn't want to make you walk all the way back and—"

"Wait here," the nun says. "I'll be back shortly."

Gretta is left in the corridor, the door before her. She looks one way: a staircase. She looks the other: an uncomfortable-looking chair with clawed feet. Why hadn't she considered, in all the bustle of getting ready for this trip, then the ferry and the drive, that Robert may not want her here? He may not want to come back to London and Gillerton Road. Faced with this door, she sees suddenly that she has made a mistake, a terrible error. In that room is Robert and he is with the brother he told her was dead, the brother he has no idea she's known about for years, the brother he hid from her and all of them, the brother who ran away with his bride, the brother who spent most of his life in prison for a murder he may or may not have committed. Robert had his reasons for keeping all this from her, and now what has she done but ride roughshod over all those reasons and turn up here, unannounced. What is she doing? She must have been mad. Never chase a man, her mother had told her. No good will come of it. Why, why hadn't she listened to her mother? Why did she ever go to London in the first place? She could have been married to a nice Galway farmer by now instead of this, a humiliated woman without even a—

Somewhere nearby she hears the susurration of footfalls, many footfalls, people walking in unison, the clink of something like keys or cutlery, and the fear of being found standing here like a spare part propels her forward, through the door and into the room.

It is very bright after the dim corridor. For a moment, she has to shade her eyes with her hand until her vision adjusts, and when it does, she can make out a small room with a high ceiling, trees beyond the window, a bed, a chair.

The chair is empty. The bed is not.

Striped blankets, metal frame, the sheets disarrayed, rumpled, untucked at the sides. The person in the bed is long, Gretta allows herself to think, and thin. She hadn't expected that, when Robert is such a solid man, on the small side. These feet reach right down to the bottom of the bed, even with the knees turned slightly sideways. Rows of bottles on the bedside table, a silver kidney dish, an oxygen tank with its clear tube snaking towards the person's face.

Gretta sets to. She pulls the blankets straight, she smooths the sheet, raising its edge so that the corners can be tucked in, neat and folded like an envelope; she lifts each arm, with care, so that the bedclothes lie straight and uncreased, so that the person will be comfortable, because a creased bedsheet can feel like a knife-edge to the skin of a sick person, Gretta knows that.

She could have been a nurse. She'd have made a good nurse. She'd have done it, if only she'd had the chance.

The arms are as light and dry as branches. Gretta eases the person forward and plumps the pillows. The smell that comes off him Gretta knows from somewhere—sweetish, cloying, fusty—but she can't for the moment recall where. She lays the man back down, straighter than he was.

"There now," Gretta says.

She sits in the chair. Where is Robert? He must have been here, in this very chair, but where has he gone? She shifts herself against the unyielding seat, picturing her husband sitting here, as she is, seeing the things that she sees: that hole in the blanket, the upturned carcasses of wasps along the windowsill, the clock on the wall that hangs at a slight tilt. Is it her imagination or does the chair still feel warm? Odd to think that he might have been here just a moment ago. She straightens the bottles on the table; she flicks a stray feather to the floor; she refills the water glass, she holds it near the man's face.

"Will you take a drink?" Gretta asks.

She angles the straw towards the man's lips. Frankie's lips. Cracked and dry, they are, poor thing. She allows her gaze to edge over his face, a little at a time; she makes herself take in, feature by feature, the man who has existed at the edges of their lives for so long. A large scar, white and livid, runs like a seam through the skin of his brow, disappearing into his hair. It is a shock to her how much like Robert he looks: the same jut of the brow, the same thick, white hair, the same determined clench to the jaw. Stupid of her, really, not to have expected that. It is as if her husband is lying there in the bed or that Gretta is being offered a vision of the future. She shudders.

"You must be thirsty," Gretta says. "Just a drop now."

The lips open, the straw is admitted. Gretta watches the liquid travel the length of the straw, drawn upwards; Frankie swallows, once, twice, and it seems to take an enormous effort, like someone moving a heavy piece of furniture. Gretta puts down the glass.

Frankie. She lets the name roll, like a marble, around her head. Frankie. This is Francis. Francis Riordan. Caught by the British Army near the body of a police officer, the priest had said that time. How long would you get for that in prison and what would they do to you there? She glances at the scar on his forehead, then away.

Where, in God's name, is Robert? Gretta thinks, with a surge of irritation. He should be here: Frankie does not have long, anyone can see that, and how terrible, how deeply sad, that a person should come to the end of his life and have no one—no one but a brother he hasn't seen for thirty years. How is it possible, when there are so many people in the world, for a life to be so shockingly solitary?

She reaches out and eases the brittle white hair away from the brow. She tucks the sheet more comfortably under his chin. She takes Frankie's fingers in her own, gathering them up like twigs.

And because she is imagining another woman taking these fingers and holding them and running out after her own wedding, and how could a man do that to his brother, it just beggars belief, and she would like to cancel these thoughts from her mind because the man is dying, after all, and this is a time for forgiveness, for putting all that to rest, she decides to speak but doesn't know what else to say, what is there to say, really, in this situation, she says, "Hail Mary, full of grace." The familiar words fall from her mouth, into the still of the room, and just to make the shape of them is a comfort, to hear their rhythm: "The Lord is with thee. Blessed art thou amongst women."

She remembers her mother teaching her to refer to women as "ladies"; it was polite, she told her. Mind the lady now, she would say, if they were on a crowded pavement. Or: Give the money to the lady, if they were paying in a shop. Gretta had asked her, if saying "ladies" was polite, why wasn't it "Blessed art thou amongst ladies"?

She had sent her mother that photo of her and Robert, and her mother had framed it and put it on her windowsill, the one that had a view over the lough where the hens were. A lovely picture it was: they had gone to a photographer's studio on the Essex Road. Gretta had borrowed the suit from a girl she worked with—a beautiful lilac tweed it was, a color that has always flattered her. She'd pinned a lily to the collar, bought new gloves. She was slim then, still with a tiny waist, and her hand in its new kid glove had looked like another lily, resting on Robert's arm. Him in his suit, his hair parted so nicely. Who was to say it wasn't a wedding photo? She'd never said it was; she'd written to her mother to say that she and Robert were wed and here was a photo.

"Mother of God," she continues to murmur, with Frankie's hand in hers, "pray for us sinners."

Did she really say they were wed? Or did she just send the photograph? She can't have said that to her mother; she can't have lied to her mother. She would never have done that.

It was like one of those holes in the road in London. They dig them up and it all looks so shocking, those gashes in the tarmac, the rubble and the scar, the bare earth and mud so near to the surface of the city. Then they fill them in, cover them up and it looks new and incongruous, the fill-in tarmac black and glistening and domed against the old, gritty road. But then, after a while, it becomes bedded down, dusty, indistinguishable, so that you can no longer tell the old tarmac from the new, you'd never know that anything had been amiss there at all.

He'd asked her to marry him; he'd proposed on the top deck of a bus going down Rosebery Avenue. He'd got down on one knee and she was so surprised she'd thought for a moment that he was looking for something he'd lost. A cuff link or a penny, perhaps. There was no ring; they had no money but no one had any money then, with the war only just over. So they were engaged. Or were they? They were. But then he'd said they couldn't marry, not exactly, not yet: there was something he needed to sort out first. Was that it? Gretta finds it hard to recall. He'd said they were as good as married: was that it? Did he ask her to marry him or did he just say that they couldn't marry yet but they would later, as soon as was possible, and she'd thought it was something to do with what had happened to him in the war, all those terrible things he'd seen, which was why she didn't press him too much, because he hated to talk about that. He'd put down a payment on a house, he said, a lovely house with a garden out the back. They moved in. He gave her a wedding ring: You'll need this, he said. Gretta remembers that, him saying, You'll need this, and she was pleased. Or was she? Was she pleased with the wedding ring or did she cry in the kitchen of their lovely new house, holding it between thumb and finger? Was that her or someone else? The thing was, she was so frightened because she was already pregnant and she didn't know what else to do: she couldn't go home in that state, she couldn't tell her mother, the shame of it would have killed her, so she had to stay with this man, she had to slip the ring on—it caught on her knuckle and, for a moment, she'd thought it wasn't going to fit, but then it did and there it was. She said she wanted to go for a photograph and he said yes, which she took as a good sign. And the photograph when it came back was beautiful. She ordered three copies. She sent one to her mother, she kept one for herself and she gave one to Robert, saying he could send it to his family, whom she knew lived in Sligo. With the photograph on the mantelpiece and the ring on her finger, everything felt better. She introduced herself as Mrs. Riordan, said, Yes, I'm expecting, in February, yes, it's my first, no, I don't mind which, just as long as it's got all its fingers and toes. She even got up the nerve to go to Mass, where she said to the priest that they'd married in Liverpool. Did she really say that? Can she have said that to a priest? She told herself that it didn't matter, they were as good as married, it didn't matter that she'd found the third copy of the photograph stuffed into a drawer, instead of sent to Sligo; she was here and he was here and that was what was important. When Michael Francis was born, he was the most beautiful baby Gretta had ever seen, fine and healthy, and so good, never cried at all, would sit for hours on a blanket on the kitchen floor. She pushed him about Highbury, showing him off in the squeaking pram in the spring sunshine, and somehow it was never mentioned and soon she was expecting again, and Robert got a job at a bigger bank and he was busy and happier, and life seemed good, too good to be true, almost.

"Hail Mary, full of grace," Gretta says, coming back to the beginning of the looping, endless cycle of words, still clasping the hand of her husband's brother, "the Lord is with thee."

. . .

Claire stands over him. Again, he is presented with a view of her feet, fringed now with tidemarks of sand.

"Of course I haven't slept with someone else," she is saying, somewhere above him. "What a ridiculous idea. Who on earth would I sleep with?"

"I don't know. Someone on your course or—"

"Someone on my course?" Claire's feet turn, walk away, then stop. "You thought I'd slept with someone on my course? But . . . they're my friends, Michael. They're the most interesting friends I've had since I went to—" She stops, takes a few more stiff steps away from him, then turns. "I don't know what to say to you." Her voice is no longer angry, just puzzled.

"I'm sorry," he mutters. "I'm sorry. I just barely know where you are half the time. You're always out and you never tell me anything. I just thought you might want to . . . I don't know . . ."

"Want to what?" Claire says, standing over him again.

He says nothing; his heart is banging on the door of his rib cage, desperate for exit.

"Want to what, Mike?"

He can't look up: he doesn't want to see the ghost of Gina Mayhew, which he is sure will be there on the beach with them. He doesn't want to see it—not here, not now.

"Retaliate," he manages to say.

She is there, he is sure of it, between them on the beach, in her divided skirts and those cumbersome buckled sandals.

Claire is strangely still above him. It is, he realizes, the first time they have directly referred to Gina since that time he got back from France, when, after they had put the kids to bed, she had turned to him in the kitchen and said, Where were you when I phoned? The most awful of awful times, which went on from that question of hers, all evening and into the night and into the next day. When dawn came, they were still sitting at the kitchen table, him with his head in his hands, much as he is now, unable to look at her face.

"You know what I was going to say?" Claire says and, again, her voice isn't angry, but quiet, measured. "I was going to say that maybe you should go."

He looks up. "Go where?"

She looks back at him. She holds his gaze. The wind channels through and around their two figures. The cries of their children spin out across the beach. And he realizes that it isn't Gina Mayhew on the beach with them, it is the end, their end, standing there with them, like a third person.

"You mean . . ." He cannot finish his sentence. He cannot believe this has happened, that this has come about. The end has been reached; he has thought about it and dreaded it for so long and now he is meeting it here, on Mannin Bay. It seems peculiarly familiar, as if he has met it before, as if all the things they are saying have been said before. "You mean leave?"

"We can be civilized about it," she says. "Can't we? We can manage that. You can see them whenever you want. It's just that I'm so tired. I'm so tired of trying to keep you. I'm tired of trying to guess what kind of person it is that you want. I'm tired of always feeling in the wrong, that I should be constantly apologizing for you having to give up your PhD, for you having to become a teacher. We live in the house with you but you're not really there. You're off living your imaginary life as an American professor. Don't tell me you aren't because I know you are. So I want you to know that you can go. Wherever you want. You can leave. Vita's at school now. I'm going to get this degree. Then I'll get a job. You don't have to stay." She opens her hands as if releasing a small animal.

"Do you want me to go?"

Claire doesn't say anything, she doesn't nod or even acknowledge that he has spoken. Instead, she turns her face to the sea, to the wind, letting the breeze whip back her shorn hair.

Farther up the beach, Monica stands. She consults her watch, she looks out at the sea.

"We should get going," she says.

"Why?"

Aoife lies on the sand, curled up, her eyes shut.

"Mum said to pick her up in two hours. It's almost two hours now."

"It can't be."

"And the tide is starting to come in."

"So?"

"So we want to get over to the island before the tide comes up again."

Aoife sits up and eyes the sea. It looks just as it always has: green, foaming, restlessly rising up and falling down. "How can you tell it's coming in?"

Michael Francis stands. He feels, all of a sudden, completely awake, as if he is rising up out of his sleepless night on the ferry, kicking that fatigue aside. Claire's words seem to circle him, cloud the air around him, like flies.

"Claire," he says, "look—"

At that moment, Vita comes hurtling up to them. She flings herself at both of her parents at once, crushing them into a sandy embrace. In the knot of limbs and hair and joints and skin, he feels Claire's fingers slipping from his own. He is about to reach out for them, to snatch them back, but he hears his name being called. He turns and sees his sisters waving at him, then pointing back towards the car.

. . .

At the crossroads where they dropped Gretta, they have an argument. Aoife is all for driving up to the convent; Monica says they should wait, as arranged. Michael Francis appears to favor both opinions, depending on who is speaking. Claire keeps quiet.

They are still arguing, Aoife opening the car door, saying she'll walk up, then, when Gretta appears around the bend.

They fall silent, watching as she approaches, with her signature gait, lurching and uneven ever since that knee operation, her handbag gripped in one hand.

"Is Dad with her?" Aoife whispers.

"Doesn't look like it," Michael Francis says.

Gretta yanks open the passenger door and climbs in, with a great heave and exhalation and a rustling rearrangement of clothing.

"I'm dead," she announces.

There is a pause.

"You don't look dead," Aoife says.

"Don't be so bold, Aoife," Gretta snaps. "You've no idea what I've just been through. Not the faintest idea. I'm dead on my feet. The heat! Unbearable. Never seen the like. The sister said she'd get me a glass of water but she didn't come back. I swear if I don't get a cup of tea in the next half hour I will simply expire."

From the backseat, Claire proffers a flask. "There's still some juice in here, I think, Gretta."

"Ah, no." She waves it away, eyes shut. "I wouldn't take it from the children."

"They're fine. You have it."

"I couldn't."

"Go on. It's OK."

"I couldn't take it from them."

Michael Francis takes the flask, opens it, pours out a cup of juice and hands it to his mother. "Here," he says. "Drink it."

"I couldn't," Gretta says, gulping it down. "I really couldn't." She hands back the cup, rests her head back and shuts her eyes again.

Aoife leans through the gap in the seats. "So what happened?" Gretta doesn't answer.

"Did you see Dad? Where is he?" Aoife touches her mother on the shoulder. "Mum? What did you find out?"

"Can a body get no rest at all?" Gretta snaps. "The day I've had."

"Don't be ridiculous. We just want to know a few things, like did you see Dad, where is he, what's happening with Frankie, and—"

"The thing is," Monica says, in a mild voice, as if drawing their attention to something interesting seen from the window, a water tower, perhaps, or a particularly memorable tree, "that we have to get our skates on if we're to get over the causeway before the tide comes in."

It is exactly the right thing to say. Aoife marvels at the effect. Gretta's eyes jerk open and she sits up. How does Monica do it? She's like a sort of external heart valve for Gretta, responding immediately and precisely to every mood, every demand Gretta could ever make.

"The tide's coming in?" Gretta is suddenly wide awake, looking around at them all.

"Well," Monica says, still casual, still detached, "it's on the turn."

"Then we have to go!" She taps the dashboard with a flat hand, in the manner of a driving instructor with a particularly sluggish pupil. "Come on!"

Michael Francis puts his hand on the ignition key. "Is Dad . . . coming . . . or . . . ?" He stops carefully, not looking at his mother.

She busies herself with readjusting her shoes. "Not here," she says crisply. "The sister said he comes and goes. They never know where he is."

. . .

As the car rounds the last bend at Claddaghduff, they see it—a low-lying, sea-fringed stretch of land.

"Oh!" Gretta exclaims, her hands leaping to her chest. "Look at it now."

The strand out is a gleaming white path through the waves, which foam and turn on either side.

Hughie had said on the boat that he didn't remember the island, not one bit. His father said, But you must, you must remember; his mother said, Well, you were only five when we last went. But as the car slides down the concrete ramp and the tires begin to hiss over the sand, he realizes he does remember. He remembers this, exactly: the shock of driving on a beach, the soft expressive feel of wheels over sand, the rows of waves sliding past. He pictures suddenly an overgrown garden lined with a stone wall, a cracked path, an outhouse filled with gray-backed beetles, a bed next to a white-painted wall, a window looking out over grass and sea. He wants to say, I remember, I remember now, but he doesn't. He keeps the words in his head, shut inside. He crouches nearer to the suitcases, he watches as the island approaches them, its green shape the back of a sleeping sea monster, his father steering the wheel.

There is a flurry of activity when they get to the cottage. Gretta treads from room to room, extolling its merits, lamenting the appearance of certain cracks/marks/carpet stains/squashed insects. She embarks with zeal on a clean of the kitchen, removing all the plates and pans from the cupboards, but loses focus halfway through and goes into the garden, where she starts pulling up weeds, in the sudden grip of a low mood, saying to anyone who passes that she doesn't think Robert will come, that he doesn't want her anymore. Monica fiddles with the boiler switches, then pushes the carpet sweeper around, a handkerchief over her face. Michael Francis carries in boxes and suitcases from the car. Hughie and Vita careen through the front door and out of the back, around and around. Aoife builds a fire in the grate. Claire puts sheets on the beds.

Gretta gives up on the weeding and the lamenting and takes the children down to the beach, telling them they need to find a mermaid's purse before the day is out. Monica sits on the front step, looking out to sea. Michael Francis chops firewood, finding calm in the regular fall of the ax. Aoife, seized by a sudden hunger, starts frying eggs and bacon, and Claire, smelling the food, comes in to lay the table. She says nothing when Aoife starts eating standing at the stove, cramming eggs and bread into her mouth, as if possessed. She says nothing at all, just passes her a fork and a plate.

When dinner is finished and the oblongs of light in the cottage windows are indigo-blue, the children are put to bed, their hair stiff with seawater, and Michael Francis comes into the room where his mother, his sisters and his wife are sitting, a fire whispering from the grate.

"Come on," he says, taking Claire by the hand, "let's go for a walk."

She rises, without a word, putting down her book, and follows him out of the cottage.

After a moment, Monica and Aoife exchange a look, Monica with her eyebrows raised.

"I don't know what you two are smirking at," says Gretta, without looking up from her knitting, "but at least he knows how to fix a problem, that boy. Always has done, always will."

Aoife pulls a face, exasperated as ever by her mother's roving favoritism. She gets up, goes to one window, then another. She pokes the fire, picks up Claire's book, turns over a page, then puts it down. She has the strange sensation that her body has too much blood in it: she can feel it pumping and pumping around her body, uncomfortably persistent. She needs to decide what to do and when; she needs to get out; she needs to call Gabe or maybe she doesn't, maybe that's the last thing she should do; she needs to think, for God's sake, but how can she do that in this tiny cottage, with her family there, all ready to suck her thoughts out of the air?

"What time is it?" Aoife says and, without waiting for an answer, "Where's the nearest telephone?"

"Claddaghduff," Gretta says, "but you can't go now."

"Why not?"

"The tide's up."

"Shit," says Aoife, which makes Gretta drop a stitch.

"Aoife Magdalena," she says, "will you mind your mouth?"

Aoife goes to the door, looks out, confirms that her mother is right, then slams it shut and comes back, flinging herself down into a chair. In a moment, she is out of it again, rifling about in the log basket.

"For the love of God, will you stop it, Aoife?" Gretta says, counting off stitches.

"Stop what?"

"Crashing about like a bull in a china shop."

"I'm not."

"You are. Find something to do and—"

"—do it." Monica finishes the mantra for her.

Aoife sits back on her heels and regards her mother and sister with naked hostility. She doesn't know what it is about evenings with her family that make her like this—unbearably restless, that cooped-up, pent-up feeling, the sensation that she must escape, no matter what.

"OK," she says, getting up from the floor. "I'm going out."

She marches across the room and out of the door, and banging it after her.

Gretta sighs, switching her empty knitting needle from one hand to the other. "That girl," she says, to the air.

Monica turns a page of her magazine but doesn't answer. Gretta eyes her middle child over the top of her glasses. Back straight as a schoolmarm's, face set into a holier-than-thou expression, ankles crossed. Good legs her daughters have; she's always thought so. They got that from her, although neither of them has ever acknowledged it.

"The children have gone off easily, at least," Gretta says, needles clicking against each other, wool looping around, almost independently of her hands. "Must have been tired, poor mites."

Still no answer. Monica lifts her chin slightly.

"Should be another lovely day tomorrow. The sky was pink over the sea tonight. Did you see it?"

Gretta knits on, wool slipping into stitches, stitches becoming rows, rows forming the sleeve of what will be, soon, a cardigan. A lovely lilac wool blend, it is, fully washable. She'd intended it for Monica's Christmas present but she might change her mind if Madam doesn't start being a bit pleasanter.

"We'll go back to the convent tomorrow, I think," she says, and is aware of a prickle of interest from the person across the room. "You might think of coming, too."

Still nothing.

"I'll take you with me tomorrow. Just you. The others would be too much."

With a flourish of her index finger, Monica turns another page.

"That Frankie is in a bad way, poor soul. Had a stroke, by the looks of things. He doesn't have long. A matter of days, I'd say. He has that smell off him, you know, that smell of death. Same as my father when he was failing."

She looks up. Monica is staring at her but drops her eyes as soon as Gretta's meet hers.

"And my father? How about him?"

The sound of Monica's voice makes Gretta's heart leap—in relief and also triumph. She knew she could get her to talk to her again! She knew it!

To mask her glee, Gretta puts her head on one side, she drops her eyes, she lowers her tone. "Not there, pet. The sister said he comes in, visits Frankie, then goes off again. I . . . I just don't know what to think. What to do."

Monica is silent again. Gretta can't risk looking up at her now, so she continues in the same aggrieved voice: "The sister I spoke to seemed to think he'd be there again tomorrow, in the morning or the afternoon." Gretta frowns, trying to remember which it was or what exactly the nun had said. "One of the two, anyway. We could—"

Monica puts down her magazine with a slap. "You needn't think I've forgiven you!"

Gretta, hopeful and encouraged by this outburst, lets her knitting fall. "I don't think that," she says, keeping her head low, her hands meekly in her lap. She reminds herself of a painting she's seen—can't remember which one, though. Is it that grim-faced woman in profile by that Scottish painter? Perhaps. She could look it up when she gets home; the thought gives her a small thrill. How she loves those encyclopedias she got on a discount from that shop. Only a little water damage at some of the corners. Volumes A to M got the worst of it; N to Z, you'd hardly know at all, really, unless you were looking closely and who—

"I can't ever forgive you." Monica clasps and unclasps her hands, just as she did when she was a small girl and she'd realized she'd forgotten to do some chore Gretta had asked of her.

Had she been too hard on her as a girl? Was that why she'd grown up so fearful, somehow, so reluctant to make her way in the world? Was it Gretta's fault? She couldn't have done anything differently with Monica: they were so close, close as close, as she often put it to Bridie, who was, Gretta was sure, more than a little jealous, herself having only boys.

"I know, pet. I'm sorry. I'm sorry I let you down. It was . . . I don't know . . . all so long ago and after the war and all . . . they were strange times and—"

"I don't care how strange they were, you shouldn't have lied. You shouldn't have pretended."

"I know that." Gretta bows her head even deeper. "I'm sorry."

"What would the priest say?"

Fear jags deep into Gretta's heart, banishing all thoughts of encyclopedias, all reflections on upbringing. "Oh, now, don't say that, don't—"

"What would he say if I were to go in there and tell him you and Dad aren't married, that he is in fact still married to someone else, that you had all of us out of wedlock, that—"

"You won't do that, will you, please don't now, promise me you won't or I'll—"

"Of course I won't." Monica sighs, as if irritated by the very idea that she might. She sits back in her chair, arms folded, looking away. "What are we going to do about Daddy?"

Gretta is heartened by the "we" in that sentence. She raises her head. "We're here now," she says, "and he's here, we know that. I left a message at the convent, saying where we were. So we'll wait. See if he comes. We'll have to go and see Frankie anyway, a desperate state he's in, you wouldn't believe it, and he's family, after all, so—"

"That's it?" Monica demands. "We just wait?"

"There's nothing else to do," Gretta says.

Monica crosses her legs. She swings a foot up and down. As restless as Aoife, sometimes, Gretta thinks. Then Monica gets out of the chair and goes over to the window.

"We could at least give these curtains a wash," she says, reaching up. "Don't you think?"

Gretta is on her feet in seconds. "We could. I wouldn't like to say when those old things last saw a bit of soap."

.   .   .

Aoife treads up and over the spine of the island, along the track, over a wall and up the sandy slope of the bluff. To the right of her, she's aware of some shapes—vaguely human—flitting about, at the edge of the island. She keeps her head averted. Whatever Michael Francis and Claire are getting up to out there in the dark, she doesn't want to know.

The air is still about her, soft, the night gilded by a white glow from a near-spherical moon, puncturing the prickling sky over the mainland. It delineates the contours of the island for her, picks out the turf beneath her feet, the gray shapes of the dry-stone walls. At the highest point of the hill, she turns 360 degrees. She can hear the sea all around her. They are cut off from land, encircled by sea, for the moment a true island.

Ahead of her, she knows, is an overhang, then a drop and then a steep slope of sand. She has held the topography of this place in her head, she realizes, learned from her many summers wandering about here. It has been tucked somewhere into her consciousness since she was last here—ten years ago now, or thereabouts. But just walking on this terrain, just standing here at the highest point, with the island flowing away from her in all directions, brings it out, unfolds it like a paper map.

The lough is just below her; she sees its black mass, pooled in a hollow, as an absence of light, the only one under this bright moon. She feels her way over the edge of the drop, allowing herself the observation that she is being careful, she is not jumping or hurling herself off onto the sandy slope, as she might have done otherwise. She steps down the slope, aware of sand invading her shoes, again witnessing herself taking care.

She feels the lough before she sees it. A damp, spongy give under her feet, spiked marsh plants needling her trouser hems. At its edge, she discards her shoes, rolls up her trousers. The water is a shock, a delicious, skin-shrinking cold. Her feet find their way forward over the gritted, stony lake bed.

She stands up to her knees in the water. The sky above her is a blue-black, a purple-black, the hue of the ripest blackberries, backlit by silver, a color she has never seen anywhere else, not in the private gloom of Evelyn's darkroom, not in all those thousands of photographic negatives she has pored over.

Aoife puts her hand to her middle. How strange it is to feel so alone and yet know that you are not. There is a second heart inside her, beating away. She applies a light pressure to her abdomen. Quickening: isn't that the word? The best word of all to describe what is going on in there, in some hidden fold of her body, in some pressed corner of her being. She has given up, of late, trying to understand why things happen. There is no use in that line of thought, no use at all. What will happen will happen and there is often no reason at all. But this—this is something else. For it to arrive, to begin, to quicken now, when so many people in her life seem to be pulling away from her. How can it be?

As this thought threads its final syllables through her mind, there is, just to her right, a heave in the water of the lough. The surface parts, she sees the motion of a muscled back, a flash of sleek hide. She takes a step back, missing her footing as she stubs her toe on a sharp point of rock. She makes a small cry of pain. The lough seems to be waiting, flat again, its surface still as a mirror. Aoife looks left, then right, searching for a ripple, a line of bubbles, anything. What was that animal and where did it go?

A movement, a plash—where? She turns her head, alert for motion, and she is trying to push from her mind all her mother's tales of selkies, of watery spirits, of sailors lured to their deaths by apparitions on nights such as these. She wonders if she were to shout, to cry out, would anyone hear her? Would Michael Francis come running? He would. But would he be in time?

Then she sees it, not three feet in front of her. Its head rising from the water, looking straight at her. A blunt forehead, wetted fur, whiskers spread into the air, a pair of wide, dark eyes. A dog, she tells herself. It's just a dog, from one of the farms, having a swim. But its ears are too small for a dog, the muzzle too short.

Aoife and the creature regard each other. It's like an otter but big, like a seal but furred. Then it brings up a clawed paw and sweeps at its face, once, twice, the length of its nose and over its brow. There is a feeling behind Aoife's eyes as if she is about to sneeze, a gathering, a buzzing, like the sensation she gets if she looks too long at a page of text and doesn't work hard at keeping her mind in gear, a feeling that what she is looking at is slipping and sliding, might morph into anything if she isn't careful.

"Gabe?" she says.

Even as she speaks the word, she is aware of the ridiculousness of what she is saying. She knows this creature, whatever it is, isn't Gabe. She isn't crazy. Gabe is over the sea, that sea to her right, all the way over, in New York. And yet, there is something in that creature's gaze, something in that gesture of its forepaw.

She says it again, whispered this time: "Gabe?"

With a wheeling motion, the animal turns and disappears, diving down into the lough.

Aoife runs. She runs without thinking about where she is going and why, without picking up her shoes. She runs barefoot back up the dune, over the top, back down the grassed side. She vaults the wall, she passes two black cutout silhouettes on the track. Aoife, her brother's voice calls after her, come back, but she doesn't, she doesn't come back, and when she gets to the other side of the island, she is unsurprised to find that the waters have parted, that there is a narrow strip of gleaming sand, fretted by tides, leading to the mainland.

She takes this path, she runs along it. She sprints the length of the causeway, seawater reaching and reaching for her ankles. She runs all the way to Claddaghduff and, when she gets there, she sees the telephone box, lit up like a landing strip, and she goes inside.

She dials the number for her apartment; she isn't expecting him to be there; she just wants to call, to hear the phone and know that it's ringing there, on the wall next to her bed. It's seven in the evening in New York. Gabe will be at the restaurant, stacking plates, skinning vegetables, sluicing down surfaces. But, amazingly, she hears a pickup on the line, she hears the intake of his breath, the minute parting of his lips.

"Gabe?" she says.

"Yes."

"It's me."

"Aoife," he says, elongating the sound of her name. "How are you?" Is that her imagination, her wishful thinking, or is his voice a little bit less brusque?

"I'm in Ireland."

"Ireland?"

"Yeah. We came to Ireland, me and my family—all my family, even my niece and nephew."

"What's the news on your dad?"

"We've found him. Sort of. Well, we know where he is. We just haven't seen him yet."

"He's in Ireland?"

"Yeah."

"He just took off for Ireland?"

"It's a long story. I'll tell you another time. How come you're not at the restaurant?" There is a pause. She listens to him sigh. "Are you OK? Did something happen?"

"It's nothing," he says.

She grips the phone tighter. "Tell me."

"There was just someone looking for me."

"At the restaurant?"

"Yeah."

"Shit."

"It was probably nothing but Arnault said I should stay away for a few days."

"I'm so sorry, Gabe."

"It's OK. It just means I'll have to find another job. Which is a shame because I kind of liked Arnault's."

"You'll find something else."

"I guess."

Another pause. She hears him shift about, as if he's walking across the room or perhaps sitting down on the bed.

"I've been keeping myself busy, though," he says, after a moment.

"Oh?"

"I sorted out that file for you."

She snaps upright. "You did?"

"Yeah. I didn't have anything better to do and it kind of took my mind off things."

"You've done it all? The whole thing?"

"I've put the contracts in envelopes and I clipped all the checks together. You can pay them in when you get back. Or"— she can hear him plotting his way carefully around the fact that he thinks she might not come back—"I can take them along, if you tell me where Evelyn banks, or give me the name of the accountant, or—"

"Thank you, Gabe," she bursts out. "Thank you so much, I really, really—"

He cuts her off. "Don't worry about it. I couldn't just, you know, leave it like that. And, like I said, I had nothing better to do today."

Aoife flattens her hands against the glass of the phone box

and leans her head into it. The file has been sorted. She cannot believe it. The problem that has weighed on her for a year is gone. Just like that.

"Aoife," he says suddenly, "I know this isn't really the time, but I just want you to know that I'm not going to be bothering you anymore. About the apartment and stuff. It's OK. I get it."

"You get what?"

"I get it. The whole thing. I realized at the airport."

"You realized what?"

"That you don't want to move in with me—you don't really even want to be with me."

"But—"

"It's all right. Let's not get into it now. I'll be out of here by the time you get back."

"Gabe." She shakes her head in panic. "No, you've got it all wrong. Completely wrong. I do want to be with you, I want that very much, more than anything, and I would love to move in with you but the thing is . . ." She gets that old, familiar feeling of not being able to draw enough breath down into her lungs. ". . . at the airport . . . I couldn't . . . see . . . what you'd written . . . I had difficulty . . ." She tries and fails to produce her usual, casual, self-deprecating laugh. "Maybe I need glasses or something . . ."

There is a silence on the line, a great ocean of silence that rolls and surges and heaves between them.

"Glasses," he repeats flatly.

"I want to be with you," she says again. "Please believe me. The thing is . . ." She screws up her face so that the lights of Claddaghduff blur and distort before her. It is taking considerable physical effort for her even to contemplate saying this. She is raising herself onto her toes, she is tensing her shoulders, as if readying herself for a blow. "The thing is . . . I have a problem . . . I have a problem with reading."

For a moment, she cannot believe what she has said. It seems astonishing for those words to be out in the air. They fly around in the hot, narrow space of the phone box, circling her head. She wants to ease open the door a crack, to let them out, like bees from a hive, into the outside world. *I have a problem with reading.* Then she is worried that she might have to say them again because time is ticking on, her change is being swallowed by the phone, and Gabe hasn't replied. Is it possible that he didn't hear her?

"Huh," Gabe says eventually. "A problem with reading. Right. OK . . . You know something?" Each of his words comes out as if he is enunciating with care. "My grandfather had this strange trouble with the written word."

Aoife breathes in and breathes out. She cannot believe what he is saying. She cannot believe that he said "written" in front of "word." She loves him for that; she loves him for that distinction because, of course, there are so many forms of words, so many guises, and it is only the goddamn written kind that won't work for her, that trips her up, that makes a mess and a tangle, like string, inside her head. All the others, she can do.

"Really?" Aoife gets out.

"Yeah. He went his whole life pretending everything was fine. He had this stock of excuses to get him through. He used to say he could only read in Russian. Or that he'd lost his glasses. Or that he had a headache and would I read the paper aloud to him? But it wasn't true. We all knew he just couldn't read."

In Gabe's tone of studied casualness, in what he is saying, Aoife is suddenly aware of a buoyant, lifting sensation, as if flexed, feathered wings have unfolded from the muscle and bone of her back.

"When are you coming back?" Gabe says, after a while. "I miss you. We all miss you—me, the rats, the cockroaches, those spooky things that scratch from inside the walls at night."

"Soon," Aoife says, as she looks out to Omey Island. "I'm coming back very soon."

"Do you promise?"

"I promise," she says, the words spreading in steam across the glass. "But you know what?"

"What?"

"I think we should come here for a while."

"Here?"

"Where I am right now, Omey Island. I wish you could see it. It's so beautiful. My family has a house here. We can live in it, you and me, and we can just sit things out."

She hears him swallow, shift his fingers on the receiver. "Uh, maybe. Would I like it there? I mean, I'm guessing it's kind of different from Manhattan."

She laughs. "It couldn't be more different from Manhattan, I can tell you that. It's an island but that's about the only similarity."

"Aoife—"

"Just think about it."

"OK," he says. "Bring me back a photo and I'll think about it."

.   .   .

Monica leans on a stone wall and waits. It is past midnight, close to one o'clock. A moon hangs above the island, so impossibly round and bright that it looks like a fake moon, a Hollywood moon, one made from paper and trickery and electric lights.

She feels sleep approach her, again and again, like a draft from under a door. Her eyelids droop, her head starts to fall, but she jerks herself awake.

When Aoife didn't come back after dark, not after Michael Francis and Claire came in, Gretta was up and down from her chair, to the window and back, wringing her hands, saying, Where's she gone, did she fall in the sea, do you think, why is it people keep disappearing? Monica had sent her to bed, saying she would go out, she'd find her. Everyone was tired from last night on the ferry. You'd have thought Aoife wanted her sleep, too, what with all the jet lag, but then Aoife had never been much of a one for sleep.

Monica went out into the dark. She walked to the north of the island, around to the westerly tip, back to the south. Calling and calling Aoife's name, searching everywhere she could think of. It reminded her of those times Aoife sleepwalked as a child. They would come in waves, Aoife's nighttime wanderings. Weeks could go past without a single incident but then Monica would wake and the bed next to hers would be empty, sheets pulled back, and she'd know that Aoife had been propelled to her feet by some unknown urge. Monica used to search the house—the bathroom, the stairs, the living room, the kitchen. She had found her, crouched by the dying fire once. Sometimes she'd be sitting on Michael Francis's bed. Another time, she found her out in the back garden, trying and trying to open the shed door, her eyes half open and dazed, in the grip of some somnolent drama. Their father had screwed bolts into the doors, high up so that Aoife couldn't reach them, to keep her from wandering into the street.

So here was Monica again, out in the night, searching for the wandering Aoife, ready to lead her gently back to bed.

She saw her from up on the sandy bluff: a tiny figure walking back along the causeway, which shone slick in the moonlight. Monica picked her way down—she has her Wellingtons on, under her nightdress—and is waiting here, at the wall.

As Aoife reaches the rise of the track, Monica calls her name. "Aoife!"

The figure of her sister jumps, puts a hand to her heart. "Who's there?" she says, and Monica is surprised by the fear in her voice.

"It's me."

"Oh. You scared the shit out of me. What are you doing here?"

"Waiting for you. Where've you been?"

"Out," Aoife replies, without stopping, moving past her along the track.

"Out where?"

She flings her arm behind her, towards Claddaghduff. "There."

The dark is soft around them but she can see that Aoife's face is set, her mouth the slightly downturned line that Monica remembers so well from her childhood. Monica scales the wall, carefully, inexpertly, her Wellies catching on the stone edges, and runs to catch up with Aoife. "Were you phoning your boyfriend?"

Aoife makes a noise that means neither yes nor no and, without intending to, Monica stops. She says, "Aoife, listen."

Aoife stops, too, a few steps farther on, her back towards her.

Monica has surprised herself. She doesn't know what she wants to say, doesn't know what she wants Aoife to listen to.

"I . . ." she begins. ". . . about Joe . . ." She comes to a halt. "I was just so . . . Everything was in such a . . . after what happened, you know . . ." She takes a breath, then manages to say, "After what I did . . . I . . . well . . ."

"Just say it," Aoife says, still with her back turned.

"Say what?"

Aoife sighs. "For fuck's sake."

Monica flinches at the phrase. An ugly thing to say, a horrible thing. Joe had said it to her when—

"It's a word that everybody knows," Aoife says. "Except you, it would seem. It begins with *s*."

There is a pause. They listen to the high chirrup of a bird, the tussling flap of the breeze catching in Monica's hem, the distant pulse of the waves.

"I'm sorry," Monica says, on the track over Omey Island, to her sister's rigid back.

"For what?"

"For everything. For thinking you would ever have told Joe. Of course you never would have done that. I don't know why I forgot that about you. And . . ." Monica pauses, tugs at the cuffs of her nightdress. ". . . I said some terrible things to you, that day in the kitchen. Awful things. I've regretted them ever since."

"Have you?"

"Yes. I should never have lashed out at you like that and I shouldn't have said them and they're not true and—"

"Ah, now I know you're lying."

"What do you mean?"

"Well, they are true, aren't they, those things you said about Mum and me as a baby? I know they are."

"Well." Monica opens her hands and shuts them again. "I should never have said them, either way. The last three years have been horrible without you." Monica sighs, and as she does so she realizes that this is true and that she isn't going back to Gloucestershire: all that is over for her. She will not return to the farmhouse, she will not live there again. Jenny and the children will come back to live at the house that was never, after all, hers. She regards this notion with an odd calm. It is a fact, stolid and uncomplicated by indecision: she is not going back there. "Horrible," she says again.

Aoife turns now, to face her. "Really?"

"I . . . I don't seem to make the right decisions when you're not around," Monica says. "Like the dress I wore for my wedding. I bought it the week before, in a panic. I knew the skirt was too short and it made my knees look awful and it just didn't suit me. The woman in the shop told me it looked lovely and so did Mum, and I wanted to believe them. But when I saw the photos, I kept thinking, If Aoife had been around, she would have said, Don't wear that, not that, it looks terrible. You would have sorted it out."

"I would."

"It was a bad dress."

"Oh, yeah?"

"Turquoise watered silk, netted skirt, puffed sleeves."

They are walking now, together, back to the cottage, their steps in rhythm. Monica had forgotten that she and Aoife could do this, could walk in perfect unison; she's never found this exact, metronomic motion with anyone else. It must come from all those years of walking together, to school and back, to the shops and back, to the bus stop, the tube, the library.

"It sounds vile."

"It was."

Aoife stops at the cottage gate. "So you got married dressed as Little Bo Peep?"

Monica laughs. She wants to say to Aoife: That's it, I'm not going back to him, it's over. She knows Aoife will understand, won't ask too much. But there will be time for that later. "I did."

"Without me."

"Without you."

"Ah well." Aoife shrugs. "We all make mistakes."

Monica sighs. She puts a hand out and touches Aoife's arm and Aoife doesn't pull away. "We do," she says. "We do. And speaking of which . . ."

"What?"

Monica bites her lip. "Well, Mammy says she thinks . . ."

Aoife pulls away now, doing the old classic flounce. "I know what she thinks."

"And?"

"And what?"

"It it true? Are you . . ." Monica finds she is having trouble with the word "pregnant." The air around them is stirring in a most distracting way, rippling its fingers through the leaves, and she knows that they are both thinking the same thing, that their minds are picturing the same image of a hospital bed, of two people bent together in a cubicle.

"I am," Aoife says, not meeting her eye.

"Oh, Aoife."

"What does 'Oh, Aoife' mean?"

"I don't know. Just that . . . well . . ." Her voice is high and strained. She pulls her sister to her, surprised as always by how slight Aoife feels, how small her skeleton is, still, even though she's an adult, how it would be so easy for someone to hurt her. ". . . I . . . just that . . ."

"Just that what?"

Monica throws her hands up in the air. She is annoyed by the stinging of her eyes, by the compressed sensation in her throat. "There'll be another baby!" she exclaims.

Aoife nods. She opens the gate and heads up the path.

"What about the father?" Monica is asking, as she follows her up the path. "He's . . . involved, I take it? He's a lawyer, isn't he? Well, that's something. A steady job, a good income. But I think you should come back to London. You can't have it in New York, away from all of us. You could live at Gillerton Road for a while, have the baby there, and then—"

"Are you out of your mind?" Aoife hisses, as she opens the front door. "I would die. I would literally expire."

"Don't be silly."

"I'd rather have it in a ditch."

Monica giggles as they jostle about in the hall, removing Wellingtons and cardigans. "Aoife—"

"I would. I'd rather have it in a chicken coop, a cat box, anywhere."

Monica heaves at her left, recalcitrant Wellington, always her larger foot. "I can't get this one off," she whispers.

"A railway carriage," Aoife is muttering, "a toolshed, a coal scuttle. Give it to me." She tugs at the Wellington. "Come on, you fecker." She gives a great heave and the Wellington flies off with a sucking noise, sending Aoife reeling backwards, her head crashing into a lantern on a hook. "Bollocks," she says, rubbing her head.

Their mother's voice booms out of the darkness: "Will you two keep it down? Some of us are trying to sleep."

Monica and Aoife make their way along the passage and into the room they are sharing. Aoife collapses onto her side of the bed.

"Do you think it's possible to die from tiredness?" she says, her eyes already closed.

"I don't know," Monica says, and climbs between the sheets, "but I'm sure you must have given it a try."

· · ·

In the morning, Gretta and Monica make bread. They eat it in the front garden, spread with butter they bought yesterday from the place where they'd stopped to get petrol. They bring the kitchen chairs out into the sun and Claire spreads a blanket on the grass for the children. But they don't sit on it. Hughie balances himself like a bird on the wall and Vita rolls herself up in the blanket like, Gretta thinks, that kitten in the storybook.

"Are you not terribly hot in there?" Gretta asks her, from her perch on the chair.

Vita squints up at her, cheeks flushed pink. "Nope," she says.

Gretta shrugs and sips her second cup of tea of the day. She likes it scalding hot, properly steeped, black, without the slightest hint of milk. Always has.

The sun beats down on them all. When will this weather break? It can't last much longer.

Michael Francis and Claire sit together on the grass, his arm around her shoulders. Hughie, looking out towards the mainland, asks, Where are all the people, why is Ireland so empty?

And Michael Francis starts to tell him about the famine, about blighted potatoes, about the thousands and thousands of people who left, got on boats and sailed away and never came back. Hughie listens, a slice of bread in each hand. Vita chants the word "diaspora" to herself, over and over, as she rolls about in her blanket.

At about ten o'clock, Aoife staggers out of the front door and collapses onto the step. She groans, jams on a pair of sunglasses and sticks a cigarette into her mouth.

"What time is it?" she rasps, searching her pockets for a lighter.

In a flash, Monica is out of her seat and snatching the cigarette from her mouth. "Don't you dare," she says.

Aoife regards her, her face screwed up. Monica bends down and takes the packet away from her, and the lighter. Aoife groans again, buries her face in her arms.

"What's up with her?" Gretta hears Michael Francis ask.

Claire shushes him, says, "Never mind."

"Do you want a slice of bread?" Gretta asks her youngest daughter.

"No." Aoife raises her head and seems to rethink this reply. "Actually, yes."

"Good girl." Gretta gets up, pleased to have a task. She doesn't like sitting about, no matter what is wrong in life. It does you good to have something ahead of you, regardless how small.

She is in the kitchen, shaving curls off the top of the butter, when she hears Hughie burst out, "Look!"

Gretta lets the knife slide from her hand.

"What?" Michael Francis says.

"Look who's coming!"

Gretta is out of the door, into the sunlight and down the path. At the gate, she stops. She shades her eyes with her hands. A person is coming off the causeway, just setting foot on the sloping track of the island. A stooped walk, head bent. As they watch, one hand rises in greeting.

"Is it him?" Monica, who's always been shortsighted but would never admit it, says.

Gretta swings open the gate, stepping out of the garden. She raises her own hand to wave back.

"It is," she says.

ACKNOWLEDGMENTS

Thank you, Mary-Anne Harrington and Victoria Hobbs.

Thank you, Emily Griffin, Hazel Orme, Georgina Moore, Helena Towers and all at Headline.

Thank you, Jordan Pavlin.

Thank you, Ruthie.

Thank you, Bridget.

Thank you to my mother for, among other things, the loan of the Connemara map, and to my father for meteorological detail; any inaccuracies are, of course, my own . . .

Thank you, Wendy McMurdo, for filling me in on the life of a photographer's assistant.

Thank you, Carly Pattinson and Rebecca Tamas, for your patience and imagination.

Thank you, Juno. Thank you, Iris. Thank you, Saul.

And thank you, Will, for, well, everything.

A NOTE ON THE TYPE

This book was set in Fairfield, the first typeface from the hand of the distinguished American artist and engraver Rudolph Ruzicka (1883–1978). In its structure Fairfield displays the sober and sane qualities of the master craftsman whose talent has long been dedicated to clarity. It is this trait that accounts for the trim grace and vigor, the spirited design and sensitive balance, of this original typeface.

Typeset by Scribe, Inc., Philadelphia, Pennsylvania
Printed and bound by Berryville Graphics, Berryville, Virginia
Designed by Maria Carella

An
Unthymely
Death

China Bayles mysteries by Susan Wittig Albert

THYME OF DEATH
WITCHES' BANE
HANGMAN'S ROOT
ROSEMARY REMEMBERED
RUEFUL DEATH
LOVE LIES BLEEDING
CHILE DEATH
LAVENDER LIES
MISTLETOE MAN
BLOODROOT
INDIGO DYING
AN UNTHYMELY DEATH

With her husband, Bill Albert, writing as Robin Page

DEATH AT BISHOP'S KEEP
DEATH AT GALLOWS GREEN
DEATH AT DAISY'S FOLLY
DEATH AT DEVIL'S BRIDGE
DEATH AT ROTTINGDEAN
DEATH AT WHITECHAPEL
DEATH AT EPSOM DOWNS
DEATH AT DARTMOOR
DEATH AT GLAMIS CASTLE

Nonfiction books by Susan Wittig Albert

WRITING FROM LIFE
WORK OF HER OWN